The First Thing and the Last

The First Thing and the Last

a novel by

Allan G. Johnson

Plain View Press
P.O. 42255
Austin, TX 78704

plainviewpress.net
sb@plainviewpress.net
512-441-2452

.

ISBN: 978-1-935514-69-5

Library of Congress Number: 2009939985

Cover art: "Clouds Over Death Valley," pastel by Karen Jones.
Cover design by Susan Bright.

Acknowledgements

Recognition and thanks go to the following:

"With the Dog at Sunrise" by Jane Kenyon, in *Otherwise: New and Selected Poems* (St. Paul: Graywolf, 1996); excerpt from "Lullaby" by Cris Williamson and Shaina Noll; "The Thanksgiving Grace," a widely used song based on a poem attributed to Alice Corbin Hendersen, source unknown; the untitled poem that begins, "Do not stand at my grave and weep," by Joyce Fossen in *Earth Prayers*, Elizabeth Roberts and Elias Amidon (eds.), (San Francisco: HarperSanFrancisco, 1991).

For Nora, always

Also by Allan G. Johnson

The Forest and the Trees
The Gender Knot
Privilege, Power, and Difference

Searching for God is the first thing and the last,
but in between such trouble, and such pain.

Jane Kenyon
"With the Dog at Sunrise"

One

1

For an instant, Katherine forgets what is happening and feels as if she is flying. Like an object hurled into the air and weightless at the apogee of flight, she is aloft, unbound in the vast and timeless space between one heartbeat and another, before the gravity of being draws her back to who and where she is and what is what.

She has felt this way before, when she was younger, before Ethan was born, and she sometimes dreamt of flying in the yard outside her old elementary school. In the dream she is eight years old, her auburn hair shoulder length around the small rounded features of her face. She stands among the other children at recess, with them but apart. She is wearing a dusty rose nightgown with long billowing sleeves and embroidered with blue cornflowers, but no one seems to notice. And then she extends her arms to raise herself up on her toes, leaning her body forward as if to catch a lifting breeze, and leaves the earth to float and soar and dip above jungle gym and carrousel and earthbound children oblivious to the miracle above their busy, noisy play. She is never afraid and never falls. She lands when she chooses and where.

Then there were blanket tosses at summer camp, lying on her back and looking up at the sky as she ascends, laughing, never doubting being caught on the way down. Unlike her brother, Jack, who assumes that falling without the expectation of being caught is the natural order of things. As a boy, he would stand at the end of the diving board at the town pool, toes barely to the edge, a finger laid along his lips, and look down as if trying to figure the distance or calculate the odds. Then he stepped off, tentative, still clinging to the possibility of changing his mind, arms tucked close to his body, eyes shut, knees bent to absorb the blow.

But Katherine was acquainted with the end of the diving board only in passing as she flung herself into the air, each arm and leg seeming to have a direction and purpose of its own, eyes open as she hit the water, which she trusted like her father's arms when he threw her into the air, face upturned in a smile, her looking down at his big hands awaiting her return.

Once again she is thrown into the air, but this time it is not a dream and no one waits to catch her, which she realizes as her ears fill again with David's enraged grunt of exertion from throwing her across the kitchen, and she sees the wall by the sink just as her shoulder and the side of her head slam into it, breaking the glass on the Monet water lilies print they bought together at the Harvard Coop one rainy afternoon. Something pops in her neck and blood begins to run down the side of her face before she hits the floor. Even then he is upon her, kicking her as she tries to curl herself into a smaller and smaller target.

"You fuck," he says, sweat running down his face, "who the fuck do you think you are?" And she has no idea except that it has something to do with dinner, her whole life suddenly reduced to a narrow focus on the hope that he'll wear out or get distracted and move on to something else. And that his voice and the blows landing on the familiar terrain of her body won't be enough to wake Ethan.

The last thing anyone who knew Katherine growing up would have predicted would have been that she would find herself thrown through the air across her kitchen by her husband, the object of a rage that could only be called murderous. In fact, it would have been so far from their imagining that it wouldn't have been the last thing, but no thing at all, not even occurring to them to rank below the rest.

Constance DeSilva, her fifth grade teacher, would have raised her short body to its full height, stuck out her chin, and declared that Katherine Stuart would never marry such a man as would do a thing like that to her. And if even if she did, she wouldn't tolerate it long enough for it to come to this.

Katherine's memories of that time are vivid and fine. At recess she often hung upside down from the jungle gym bar, her dress clutched between her knees to keep it from falling over her head. There had been some controversy about that — the wearing of dresses to school — and a running battle with the principal, Miss Burdock. Katherine insisted on wearing jeans because dresses were too easily torn and soiled in the dusty yard where the children played. Dresses made no sense, she said, her faced pinched around the futility of trying to convince an adult who was clearly set against her.

Miss Burdock listened patiently, head bowed, heels together, hands folded just above her waist, and when she thought she had heard enough, looked past the long line of her broad and ample bosom to the child below.

"Jeans," she said, "are inappropriate," as if the authority inherent in such a lengthy word was more than a match for any child's argument. But still it made no sense, and Katherine believed everything was bound to make sense. Miss Burdock, however, was unmoved and said Katherine could not come to school in jeans and would be sent home if she did, and if she did not come to school, her education and therefore her life would surely be a ruin.

There was a long silence as Katherine stared down at her feet and felt the pulsing of her heart in her ears. Children ran in the hall outside until a sharp voice slowed them to a walk. The clock on the wall clicked as it reached 3:00 and the bell sounded and she looked at Miss Burdock just once and then turned and strode out into the hall, borne along by the tide of children seeking the freedom of the outside air.

No. No one would have guessed, including neighbors who watched her play cowboys with the boys next door, resplendent in the Dale Evans outfit she received one Christmas after a year of relentless begging. It had a chocolate brown western shirt with scalloped decoration running across the chest and fringe that hung down at the forearms and a matching skirt. And it came with not one toy gun, but two, and not like the ones the other children had that took rolls of caps and spat out streams of paper that had to be torn off. Hers had small cartridges that looked like real bullets and came apart to insert a single round cap between the casing and the slug. She had a poster of Roy Rogers and Dale Evans on the wall in her room and she practiced her draw before the long mirror that hung behind the bathroom door. Her mother shook her head and sighed whenever she saw Katherine run out the door, armed to the teeth and slapping her thigh to mimic the rhythmic clip and clop of the horse that galloped beneath her. She despaired over her daughter's future which she knew would hang on her ability to make herself attractive to men, but there was something in Katherine that she found irresistible and so she became practiced at knowing when to give in and when to gently steer her on a more promising path to womanhood.

In seventh grade, Katherine discovered literature on a rainy day at the public library. She had read *Little Women* but knew nothing of the Brontë sisters or Jane Austen. She devoured them, and began to wonder if a woman's fate always hinged on the anguish of a man's tormented soul. It seemed that way from what she could tell. Never did the authors portray a man waiting, his life on hold, for the outcome of some woman's dark, heroic struggle for herself. Always it was she who waited, patiently and not without some danger lurking nearby.

In high school it was Edith Wharton whenever she could find the time between assignments to read Hardy, Dickens, and Hawthorne. When her grandmother cleaned out her attic, she gave Katherine a small carton of books that included the poems of Robert Frost, Emily Dickinson, and e.e. cummings, and inspired by images of slanting light on winter afternoons, little lame balloon men, and woods silently filling up with snow, she began to write poems of her own. She wrote them in a small journal she found among the books in her grandmother's box, and for years kept them to herself.

Her grandmother would not only have been shocked by Katherine's fate, but incredulous and furious. In Katherine's memory she was the tallest in any company of women and her face had all the sharpness of feature that Katherine's lacked. She was strong enough to lift Katherine into her arms with ease even as they both grew older and other adults declared Katherine too old for such things. When Katherine visited her on hot summer afternoons, she often found her in the back yard, bent forward as she labored behind her push lawnmower, the whining pitch of the blades rising and falling as she quickened and slowed her pace. She would stop when she saw Katherine and smile beneath the sleeve of her blouse drawn across her brow.

They would go into the cool kitchen where there was always lemonade in the refrigerator and sit in the dining room and talk about what Katherine was reading and what was happening in school and whether that Robertson boy still followed her home and slipped little notes of affection through the mail slot in the door, folded so many times she barely knew what they were.

It was remarkable to Katherine how unalike her mother and grandmother seemed to be — her grandmother so bold and full of life, a reader and a thinker who thought the meaning of life a question worth pursuing, and her mother so carefully modulated, so disinterested in books and ideas, so concerned with the opinions others held of her. When her grandmother heard that Katherine had been forbidden to wear jeans to school, she volunteered to set Miss Burdock straight on the matter, but then thought better of it, fearing it might only make things worse. Her mother, on the other hand, although she had finally stopped ordering Katherine back upstairs each morning to change into a dress, seemed to greet the news of Miss Burdock's ultimatum with relief and pursed her lips and looked away in a gesture of 'I told you so.'

Her father stayed out of it, hiding behind the morning paper, until she lost the Battle of Burdock as he would later call it, and retreated in tears to her room, and he followed her there and stood in the doorway, hands thrust into the pockets of his baggy corduroys, and watched her lying on the bed and crying into the pillow.

"It's not fair," she said in a muffled, stricken voice. "It doesn't make any sense."

He sat down beside her and put his hand on her shoulder. "Maybe not," he said. "But you have to play by the rules. It's the only way to get along."

"Even when they're dumb."

"Well," he said, "sometimes, yes. Miss Burdock is in charge and she gets to make the rules. That's just the way it is." He rubbed her back and she looked up into his round face and the fine hair already thinning on top of his head. "Besides," he said, leaning forward as if confiding a secret, "you look so pretty in a dress, and you're such a pretty girl."

"I don't care," she said, turning her face back into the pillow.

"You will."

The blows from David's hands and feet come slow but unrelenting, blending to a continuing flow of pain that Katherine thinks she cannot stand, until she leaves her body for asylum in a small space just outside her mind where the pain feels once removed and she can bear the terror of knowing that in this moment he can do whatever he wants.

He grabs a fistful of hair and slams her head into the wall. Then he walks to the kitchen table and sits down, exhausted from the effort. He reaches behind him and takes a dishtowel hanging from a drawer pull and throws it at her, then rests his elbows on the table and lays his eyes against the fleshy heels of his hands. "Why do you make me do this?" he says, his voice slurred from rounds of drinks before coming home. "You make me crazy."

Katherine's body bloomed later than most. In seventh grade, all around her girls sprouted breasts and carried tampons to school while she remained flat and unstirred. She wrote about it in her diary, this wanting to feel stirred up inside. And then it came to her one night when she couldn't sleep and wound up in the bathroom, sitting in the dark on the toilet, waiting for the mystery to stop flowing from between her legs, her head resting on her hands that pressed into her eyes to make the black nothingness come alive with sparks that shimmered blue and red and silver. And then she wondered, and slowly lifted her head and passed a hand gently between her thighs and touched an outstretched finger to the soft lips and brought forth a tiny drop, dark red, almost black in the night, and she raised it to her face and turned her finger from side to side as she examined it, and then with a small murmur of surprise slipped it into her mouth and tasted of the mystery she had become.

It wasn't until her junior year at the University of Vermont that she allowed anyone to know of her poetry. She didn't see it coming, this sudden desire to make her secret known to another, and would never have guessed the recipient would be Leonard Phippen, an aging professor of creative writing. His eyes squinted almost shut when he smiled, which was a lot, and his hair reminded her of her father's, except that what remained of it didn't lie neatly across his scalp, but instead strained and arced upward in all directions in a pattern that reminded her of solar flares. From time to time, especially when he was reading aloud during class, he would run his hand through his hair as if to bring some order to it, but the effect was always to rearrange the chaos in a new form.

When she submitted her first poem to him, he wrote across the top in a pencilled scrawl, "Uncommonly good. I hope you'll do some more." And after she submitted the second, he asked to speak with her after class. He didn't smile, and at first she wondered if she'd done something wrong, until he beckoned her to sit down and leaned back in his chair as he fingered the page that contained the poem.

"Every once in awhile," he said, "a student writes something I would like to have written myself." He looked up at her and made a little smile. "This is one of those times."

She blushed and looked down and then up and by the look on his face, knew that what he said was exactly what he meant.

"There's more, isn't there?" he said.

And before she realized what she was doing, she nodded and said there was.

"May I see some of it?"

She only let him see the ones she liked the best, and when he read them he told her she could give him poems at any time, whether she was enrolled in one of his courses or not, and that he would read them and tell her what he thought and help her make them better if she liked.

"You have a certain turn of soul," he said after reading the first batch. She asked him what he meant and he sat without saying anything for a long time before he shrugged and said he didn't know how to put it into words, which was a rare condition for him. "Just keep writing," he said. "Keep writing."

And she did, and then she met David Weston and fell in love for the first time.

2

*K*atherine lifts up her head and holds the dishtowel to the side of her face where the blood flows to the edge of her jaw and drips onto the floor. A hot and searing pain shoots down her neck and into her shoulder and back. Like a hungry animal circling a fence around her pain, looking for a way in, his voice comes to her from the table, distant and edgy. "You make me crazy," he says, "you do this to me. This is all your fault. I don't want to hurt you. I never want to hurt you." His voice is low and directed at the table. "I am not a violent man."

They met at Stowe shortly after Christmas in her junior year. On a lark, since he'd never skied before, David hitched a ride with his roommate at Harvard. He broke his ankle the first day out and she came upon him sitting on a couch in front of the fire in the lodge, his leg ending in a cast propped on a chair in front of him. He was asleep with a copy of *Catch-22* open on his lap and on the small table beside him a volume of American poetry resting beneath *The Grapes of Wrath* and Galbraith's *Economics and the Public Purpose*. Years later she would remember the chill in the air that smelled of wet wool, and the sight of him in the glow cast by the fire. She sat down and pretended to look into the flames while she felt his sleeping presence just a few feet away. A man who reads, she thought. How interesting.

When she returned later on, he was still there, but awake and with the book propped on his lap. There was something about him that looked almost perfect to her — the smooth skin on his face, so fair and hairless he could go for days without shaving and hardly anyone would notice, the broad shoulders filling out the sweater, the blue eyes that looked up at her when she said hello, standing over him with a cup of hot cider in her hand. She thought she saw something deep in those eyes, in the way that he paused and looked right at her before saying hello back. A poet's eyes, she thought, serious and inward looking, always fixed on something others could or would not see, half-shaded in the darkness of a secret life that came out on the page in fits and starts.

"Are you reading them all at once?" she said.

"Actually, yes."

"For courses?"

"No."

"Oh."

"I just like to read."

She nodded.

"You look surprised," he said.

"No."

"Yes," he said. "Definitely surprised."

"I just don't meet many men who like to read."

"You think because I'm a swimmer I don't like to read?"

"I didn't know you were a swimmer."

"Right. Well. I am. And I do." He looked at the book and then up at her again. "I think, too."

She felt a hot flush rise from up from her neck. "I'm sorry," she said, and thought to ask him which poets he liked the best, but knew it was too late for that. She'd already blown it, she thought, managing to insult him at the top of their first conversation.

And then he startled her as she stood to leave. "Don't you want to know who my favorite poet is?" he said. And she couldn't help but smile and then laugh.

"Yes," she said.

And he met her smile with his own. "Robert Frost," he said. "And my favorite poem is 'Birches.' You know, 'One could do worse than be a swinger of birches.' You like Frost?"

"Yes," she said, her face hot now as she turned and walked toward the dining room. "I've gotta go."

"Did I pass?" he said, calling after.

"Yes," she said over her shoulder.

As she would come to realize, what she saw in his eyes was not a poet's soul, but a profound depth of want and need that would fix itself upon her and refuse to let go. She had never been wanted in this way before, entirely, as if she were a prize that he would have at any cost. For years, she had opposed as a matter of principle this business of being wanted like that, as would her grandmother, based on the belief that a woman could be independent or wanted, but not both. But that was only in theory and now she suddenly understood in her body what her mother had meant when she reacted to Katherine's blithe announcement at the age of fifteen that she would probably never marry.

"You'll be alone," her mother said.

"I'll have friends."

"It's not the same. No marriage is perfect, Katherine. But even a bad one is better than being alone. Trust me. A man can be a bachelor and be all right, but not us."

They argued, with Katherine playing at Devil's advocate, trying out the sharpness of her mind, and it startled her to see the depth of her mother's alarm at her simple proposition. For her own part, Katherine was simply trying on an idea that made sense to her, that being able to do what she wanted without having to answer to a man was a good thing. But her mother seemed to be looking at something entirely different. It unnerved Katherine to watch her become so agitated.

"It was just a thought, mom."

"Well," her mother said, "maybe so. But just remember what I said."

She did remember, but she didn't recall it until spring was turning into summer five years later and she discovered that she liked being a wanted woman, rescued from the imagined fate of women alone, the Miss DeSilvas and Miss Burdocks in their lonely apartments or sharing a small house with an aging sister. She decided it must be possible to have it all, that there was no reason to choose between being wanted and loved on the one hand and her own person on the other. And if she did have to compromise ("It's all about compromise," her mother said), it would only be for awhile until things settled down.

In the meantime she was in love and the sheer power of it so expanded into her life that it crowded out almost everything else and seemed all she'd ever need. He was charming and smart. He doted on her every whim, opened doors for her and bought her roses and forget-me-nots and wrote poetry that he somehow managed to place beneath her pillow in the dorm where men were not allowed. The poetry wasn't nearly as good as her own, but she thought the ineptness of his verse made him all the more endearing, and to protect his feelings, she did not show him her own poems or even reveal their existence until years later.

He called her 'KitKat,' after the candy bar, 'my sweet cookie,' and wanted nothing more than to be with her. When she had to study alone or cut short their time together to visit her parents, his face crumpled in a look of such vulnerability and hurt that it nearly broke her heart to deny him. After he called her 'stupid' in the heat of an argument over the phone (to which she responded by hanging up), he took a midnight bus to Burlington and stood outside her window until she noticed her name being stage whispered from below and looked out to see him shivering in the cold. She raised the window and leaned out.

"I'm sorry," he said, arms folded across this chest, shifting from foot to foot. "I really am." And she shook her head and smiled and forgave him and wondered what it was about such strong and independent men that so quickly turned them into little boys when they fell in love.

When they were together, he wanted to know everything she'd done while they were apart, who she was with, what they'd talked about, and how much she had missed him. At dances, he wouldn't let other men cut in, and when they walked around Harvard Square or along the Charles River he held her hand or put his arm around her waist or rested a hand on her shoulder to leave no doubt in anyone's mind that Katherine was his own. He had the body of a varsity swimmer in the habit of winning the 100-meter butterfly, and standing next to her or hovering above her when they made love, he was a powerful presence, which she liked, feeling held by him and increasingly secure in the knowledge that he would never leave.

And then there were the times when she didn't return his calls and lied that her roommate, Karla, had forgotten to give her the message, times when she lay awake at night with the sudden sensation of not being able to breathe, and times when she left his thick letters unopened for days. Occasionally she stayed in bed all day, missing classes, and when Karla asked if she was sick or maybe depressed, Katherine wondered aloud if this thing with David was too much, too fast, and Karla rolled her eyes and told her she was crazy and didn't she realize what a catch he was and if she didn't want him, she'd be glad to take him off her hands.

Her family was mad about him. "He's such a gentleman," her mother said. As for her father, David always called him 'Sir,' never Richard or Dick. He looked him in the eye when they shook hands and never turned down an invitation to play cribbage, even though he lost most of the time. And Jack acted like he'd found the brother he never had. They played tennis and video games and basketball and wove a steady stream of fast and witty banter. They went driving in David's blue mustang and drank beer at the beach and drove fast with the top down.

When her grandmother met David, she shaded her eyes from the sun with one hand as she shook his hand and looked at him long and, it seemed to Katherine, rather hard. She poured them lemonade and they sat beneath a large umbrella that stretched over the wrought iron table on the stone patio out back, from which they could look into her gardens that would stretch from spring to autumn in a shifting flow of texture and color.

David praised the garden and asked questions as he pointed to one section and then another. Her grandmother watched him carefully, as if noting every gesture and expression, which Katherine figured was the normal thing for a grandmother to do on meeting her granddaughter's beau. But there was something else, subtle and barely seen, the slightest narrowing of the eyes, like a squint, only smaller, that seemed to come over her face whenever David touched Katherine, his hand on her back just below her neck, or his fingers entwining into hers on the table, or gripping her upper arm to steer her among the flower beds. Katherine thought it might be the sun or the dryness in her eyes that her grandmother attributed to being, as she put it, "old, senile, and decrepit."

The two women lingered on the front porch to say goodbye and held each other longer than usual. Katherine stepped back and looked into her face and saw again that little squint.

"What?" said Katherine.

Her grandmother looked past her shoulder to David sitting in the car out in the driveway and then back at Katherine. "He holds you very close," she said.

Katherine smiled. "Yes, he does." Her grandmother said nothing. "What?" Katherine said.

"Another time, dear. It's nothing. Really. We'll talk about it another time. There's no hurry."

"Grandma," she said, an edge of protest in her voice.

"It's nothing *fatal*," her grandmother said, smiling. "He's a charming young man. Now go on."

It bothered Katherine for days, the look she'd seen on her grandmother's face and whatever it was she saw in David that was enough to give her pause. She made up her mind to ask her about it, but things kept getting in the way — her summer job, time with David, going back to school — and then just before Christmas break her mother called with the news that her grandmother's heart had failed while she shoveled snow off the front walk. At the wake Katherine lingered beside the open coffin, staring down into her grandmother's face, waiting for it to yield up an answer to her question. But she realized her grandmother no longer inhabited the dry husk of a body lying against white satin amidst the smell of flowers all around.

David never hit her when they were dating. He didn't like it when she stood her ground in an argument, and when she went alone to visit her parents, his little boy look could quickly give way to sulking, angry withdrawal. But he never hit her. He might tell her she was stupid or make fun of her opinions or correct the way she did things. Or he'd say she was too dependent on her family.

"When we're married," he said, "you'll have to get used to being away from them. It'll be you and me." And then he'd see the worry flicker across her face and put his hand gently against her cheek and fold her in his arms and the idea of a life as 'you and me' began to seem large and full and just enough.

He lifts his head and looks at her with pink rheumy eyes beneath the hair fallen down and wet with the sweat on his forehead. "Where the fuck were you?"

She doesn't move. The question cuts through the air like a spot of light trained on her face. A simple question if a question is all it is. But it's not a question at all, only a pretext, for no matter what she says, or if she says nothing at all, the answer will be some variation on 'in the wrong place with the wrong person doing the wrong thing.' Her mind clears enough to remember what triggered him this time, her getting home too late from school to put the roast in the oven and him not liking the reheated casserole and stopping himself midway through chewing his third bite and throwing the plate against the wall and giving her the back of his hand and sending her chair tipping over backwards. She reached out to break her fall, but it didn't matter because his first punch to the side of her head drove her hard to the floor.

"So?" he says.

She sighs, keeping it slow and shallow so he won't notice, for even that might set him off again. Nor does she look at him, although there are no guarantees in that either. If she looks at him, he sees defiance. If she looks away, she has something to hide. The only thing that matters is what he thinks and feels and whether his rage is enough to make him want to hit her, and she's known for years that nothing she does or doesn't do will make the difference. She might as well try to stop the rain. The only thing to do is get in out of the downpour and try to cover herself and keep the chill from getting to the bone.

"I stopped for coffee," she says. "With Susan." Her lips tremble and tears mix with the blood running down her face.

He snorts. "I don't like her. I told you that."

Katherine says nothing.

"I said I told you that, didn't I?" he says, looking at her.

"I know."

"How many times?"

"I don't know."

"Well, guess," he says. "How many?"

"I don't know. A lot."

"A lot. What do I have to do to get through to you?"

Katherine says nothing.

"So, what were you doing with her?"

"I told you." she says, her voice soft and trailing away, "we had coffee." She tightens around a sinking in her stomach. *Don't say so much. Not so fast. Not so sure.* She feels his voice rise higher in his throat and his body tense toward renewing the assault.

He only hurt her once before they were married, the day they moved in together and went out drinking with friends to celebrate the new apartment. Later, he wanted to make love, but Katherine only wanted to sleep. He rubbed her feet and kissed her ears and drew pictures on her back with his finger, all things he knew she liked but which now only frustrated her longing to sleep.

Finally he stopped and lay awake in the dark, his anger palpable in the air, like a wave of prickly heat washing over her as she lay next to him. Suddenly she was awake.

"You give me such a hard time," he said.

"Jesus, David," she said, "I just want to go to sleep." She turned her head to him. "Why is that such a problem?"

She couldn't see his face, but could feel him brooding, breathing shallow in the still night air. "You know I love you," she said at last. She reached out and gently squeezed his cheeks, holding his face with her hand over his chin and puckering his lips between her thumb on one side and her fingers on the other. "Say chubby baby," she said, playing their private little game, and the phrase percolated through his floppy lips, the words edged heavy and sullen but pulling a small snort of laughter behind. "Chubby baby," he said again and reached over and took her face in his hand.

"Chubby baby," he said, squeezing her cheeks, and she said the words and laughed and he squeezed a little harder. "Chubby baby," he directed again, his voice flatter, and she tried but couldn't because his grip was too hard for her to move her lips and then he squeezed harder still. "Chub — by — ba — by," he said, each syllable punching through the air between them and pulsing through his fingers into her face.

"David," she tried to say, but couldn't and grabbed his hand and pulled it from her face and moved away from him as she sat bolt upright. "That hurt!" she said. "What's the matter with you?"

"It wasn't that hard," he said, turning away.

They lay in a silence so still she could hear the numerals flip on the electric clock. "David," she said, and then realized from his slow and regular breathing that he was asleep.

The next morning she showed him the bruise on her cheek where his thumb had been.

"Oh, God," he said, his voice almost breaking, "I'm so sorry. I was only kidding. I didn't mean to hurt you. Really." And she knew somewhere inside her need to believe that her life had not gone all wrong, that it had to be true.

She felt moved by his remorse, the tender vulnerability of exposing himself without defense to the possibility of her anger and reproach. Far from fearing him, she felt sorry for him, and in her love for him, forgave. It seemed to her a paradox that he should be so strong and yet so weak, in such control and so easily undone. She always felt drawn to paradox, and so took it as a challenge to engage with this one now.

She would remind herself of this on her wedding day as she sat on the window seat in her room in her parents' house, dressed only in her underwear and a slip, staring into the middle distance as if contemplating a door that she was about to pass through that, like certain kinds of awareness, swings just one way and does not admit to the other side.

"Katherine," said her mother from the hall, "it's getting late," and then she was beside her, a hand on her shoulder, her face eclipsing Katherine's view of the yard. "Are you all right?"

"I guess."

"That doesn't sound very promising. Got the jitters?"

"Something like that."

"Keep thinking 'Oh God, what am I doing?'" said her mother. "It happens to everyone. You'll be fine."

Her mother helped her into her gown and called out to Richard to come and see and he stood in the doorway and Katherine thought she saw tears in her father's eyes, tears she had never seen before. Then she began to cry until her mother reminded her of her make-up and she held back the tears while her father took out a handkerchief and gently blotted her face. Later, she stood in the church vestibule and as she took her father's arm she saw, for an instant, in her mind's eye just inside the veil, her grandmother's face, and then the music filled the church and people rose from the pews and turned in her direction and the image disappeared as her father caught her eye.

"Ready?" he said, and he smiled at her and she nodded and as they stepped off together down the aisle she whispered to herself, "I'll be fine."

3

*T*he hard kitchen floor presses into Katherine's hip and she tries to shift away from the pain without looking as though she's going to stand. She doesn't dare move so long as he's watching her, the breath pumping out of him. Slowly, she lays the blood-soaked dish towel on the floor. She sees his eyes drop to the towel and then shift back to her face. The house is quiet. For a moment, she pictures Ethan asleep upstairs, the soft rise and fall of his covers with every breath. Stay asleep, baby, she thinks to herself.

The tether was there all the time, like a cord embedded in her solar plexus and wrapped around her heart, the place where fear and dread reside alongside hope. But the lead was so long and so loosely held that she barely knew it was there until he began to take up the slack. It first appeared as a tightness in his voice when she would tell him she was going out to spend some time with friends, or did something in a way he didn't like. It might be that she cooked the roast a bit past medium rare or let the house go too long between cleanings or felt too tired for making love. There was no particular pattern to it, no way to predict just when the tightness would appear, often accompanied by a fixed stare and some part of his body, often a hand, in nervous motion, rubbing his thigh or drumming fingers on the table. She began to notice that when she got off the phone, he would ask who it was and what did they want, questions she never thought of asking him. And when one day she called him, playfully, 'Mr. Nosey,' he didn't join in the play, but grew quiet and seemed to shrink into a hard, dense place inside himself.

The first time he hit her was in Mexico City, two years after they were married. David had been sent there by his company and they rented the third floor of a house in the Lomas district, an old upper-class neighborhood near the western end of Paseo de la Reforma. Katherine quickly befriended Bianca, the owner of the house, and they roamed the city while David was at work. They spent two days at the National Museum of Anthropology. They visited elegant shops in the Zona Rosa and one evening, when David was working late, Bianca took her to a square where mariachi bands played into the night and they sat at a table beneath a jacaranda heavy with purple blooms and drank Margaritas and laughed and talked about life and culture and when they began to get a little drunk, about poetry and sex, which Bianca said were hard to tell apart.

"Well," Katherine said, "at least good poetry and good sex."

"No," Bianca said, "Bad poetry and bad sex are the same, too. Sometimes I read a bad poem and I think to myself, 'I do not get it.' It is the same with bad sex, no?"

When Katherine walked through the door at just after 11:00, she was thinking that Bianca was right about sex and poetry, and remembering the first time she'd read *Lady Chatterley's Lover* and how surprised she was to see words like 'fuck' and 'cunt' and 'cock' used in such a loving way. David was sitting at the dining room table, a drink in front of him, and when he looked up at her standing in the hall, she saw in his face the narrow, hard look of a man who has just picked up an unfamiliar scent on his wife. She stood there, puzzled by his expression, wondering what he saw. It reminded her of one of the first times when they had made love and she was left unsatisfied and as he dropped off to sleep, she slid her hand between her legs and moved herself to a familiar touch and rhythm until she realized he was looking at her, lying on his side, head propped on one hand, with the same look on his face that she saw now, not mere disapproval or disgust, but a mixture of carefully contained outrage and disbelief.

"Where the fuck have you been?" he said.

"What?"

"I said, 'Where the fuck have you been?'"

"I know what you said, David. But why are you talking to me like that?"

He turned his head away, the sweat covering his forehead reflecting light from the lamp hanging over the table. It occurred to her that he'd been drinking for quite awhile, that he was probably sitting there as she and Bianca listened to the mariachis and talked about sex and poetry, and certainly while she ruminated on the gamekeeper and Lady Chatterley.

He drank from the glass and set it down hard on the table.

"Well," she said, "I'm tired. I'm going to bed." She hung up her coat and as she closed the closet door and turned, he was right in front of her, his face leaning into hers.

"I want to know where the fuck you've been."

"With Bianca."

"Doing what?"

For a moment Katherine didn't know what to say. "What is the matter?"

"Doing what?" he said, hitting the last consonant hard as it passed through his teeth.

She shook her head and started to walk by him, but he moved with her and wouldn't let her pass. She looked into his eyes, red and moist and, although trained on her, seeming to lack a proper focus, as if he were staring at something just in front of her face.

"We went to some square," she said, her hand dropping to the flutter of fear passing through her stomach.

"What square?"

"I don't remember."

"What did you do?"

"We listened to mariachis. We had a few drinks. We talked." Again she stepped forward and again he put his body in her path.

"What did you talk about?"

"I don't know. Lots of things. What does it matter?"

"Who else was there?"

"No one."

"Bullshit."

"Bullshit to you, too," she said as she stepped forward, but this time he pushed her back with his forearm across her chest and held her against the door.

"You're not going anywhere until I'm done," he said. In close she could smell the rum on his breath and felt the fear grow from a flutter to a wave.

"You're scaring me, David."

"You're always fucking someplace," he said.

"No, I'm not."

"Instead of with me."

"You were working."

"You're supposed to be here. Not off drinking with some bitch."

"She's not a bitch."

"I don't like her."

"Well, I do."

"But I don't," he said, pushing each word into her chest with his arm.

"Let go," she said, trying to free herself.

"Fuck you," he said, leaning his full weight into her.

She stopped moving and looked directly into this face. "Jesus, David, what is your problem?" And the last word was barely through her lips when his hand caught her on the side of her face and snapped her head back so hard it hit the closet door.

She flailed her arms to ward him off, but he hit her again, and before she could say anything, a third time, and when she began to cry he turned and walked back to the table. She ran past him down the hall and into the bathroom where she slammed and locked the door.

It was the first time that anyone had ever hit her in the face. For that matter, it was hard to remember when anyone had hit her anywhere, save for childhood fights with Jack or the rare spanking from her mother or father. But never in the face.

Sitting on the toilet, the side of her face already numb and swollen, Katherine could not stop crying. Suddenly, her life had come apart, filling her with confusion and disbelief. What had just happened could not have happened and she felt her mind slow around its muddled failure at making sense. And so she cried on into the night, rocking herself back and forth on the toilet as David began to knock on the door and call out apologies and regret. And then she could tell that he was crying, too, his body rubbing against the door as he sank to the floor, bewailing what he'd done, helpless to undo it, grieving already what he was sure he must have lost.

"Go away," she said, but he did not hear her above his own mournful wail, and then after awhile they both grew silent and the night thickened around them and she felt the drink and fatigue wash her into a restless, dreamless sleep.

When she woke, the sun slanted through the window, bright against the blue and yellow tiles that covered the walls. She was lying on the floor, a thin woven rug beneath her. Her head throbbed and her hips and back were stiff. She listened at the door and heard nothing. She thought for a moment that everything she remembered was just a dream, but the hope evaporated when she saw the bruise along the side of her face reflected in the mirror. Slowly, she opened the door and looked down the hall to their bedroom. The bed was made and she wondered if he had slept where he lay by the bathroom door.

He was not in the bedroom or the dining room or anywhere else that she could see. The kitchen clock read just past 9:00. She sat at the dining room table and looked out the window into the wooded ravine across the way and wondered what to do. Is this, she thought, how a marriage ends? Is one misstep enough? Or is this where faith and forgiveness deliver them both from the 'worse' they vowed to endure as they loved each other unto death? She remembered how pitiful he sounded on the other side of the door, as if he had done something so terrible that he would be cast out to live forever alone without love or hope. She felt torn by her fear and the pain in her head and the sound of his agony and remorse that wrapped itself around her heart and pulled her toward him.

She showered and washed her hair, lingering beneath the flowing water, her face upturned into the spray. She put on fresh clothes, made a cup of coffee, and sat on the couch, her legs drawn up beneath her and the steaming cup in her hands, and waited. Through the open window, birds called to one another from the ravine. Bianca descended the stairs, opened and closed the front door, her footsteps receding down the walk. Katherine wondered what her friend had heard and what she must now think of this American couple, and a wave of shame swept over her as she imagined the moment when they would look at each other with this awful knowledge between them.

She was about to make a second cup of coffee when she heard David hurry up the walk and slip his key into the downstairs door. He took the stairs two at a time and then stood on the landing outside the door for several minutes before coming in. The first thing she saw was the large bouquet of flowers in his hand, and then his face, puffy and red, the whites of his eyes unusually stark against his skin. Fear crept back into her belly, like a cat curling in her lap. She didn't move. He stood just inside the door, the room between them, dropping his hand so the flowers hung by his side.

Katherine felt drawn to the look of grief and desolation on David's face and the way his body sank toward the floor, small and vulnerable for all its manly bulk, bearing neither pride nor hope. He stood there, the agitation in his face growing as she said nothing, and then he was across the floor in a few steps, tears flowing down his cheeks even before he reached her.

In all her life, no one had ever truly begged her for anything, but he was begging her now, falling to his knees, the flowers rustling to the floor, burying his face in her lap as the words poured out of him, breathless and desperate, "Oh God how could I have done such a thing to you my sweet Kat I didn't know what I was doing I am so sorry I would rather die than hurt you oh please oh please forgive me please don't leave me I will never do anything like that again I swear never I swear never never never," and then he was crying like a boy in some inconsolable grief and she touched the crown of his head and spread her fingers down his neck to the tender place at the nape where the hair grew silky and fine, and she curled herself forward and held him as they cried together.

In the weeks that followed he was considerate and kind and doted on her every need. He rubbed her feet and made her coffee in the morning before she was up. He took her out to dinner at their favorite restaurant and kissed her in the back seat of cabs. He brought her flowers and presents and called her from work to see how she was and came home for lunch or met her at a sidewalk café. And when they made love, he was tender and slow, and one night she asked how he'd feel if she stopped using her diaphragm and he smiled and nodded and she left it in its little plastic box beside the bathroom sink.

Everything had the intensity of its first time and they were both so relieved to have stepped back from the abyss that they were giddy and even a little intoxicated with it, like men in war who come so close to dying they begin to imagine themselves impervious to death.

When Katherine missed her period she could barely contain herself as each day appended itself to the one before, and when she finally told him, he came home from work and they made love on the couch at just before noon.

But the tether was only loosened, not removed, and the lines began to blur between doting and control, eagerness and anxiety, love and possession. When he drank, which was more and more, he might wonder aloud where she really was that night, with whom, and with what result, and then he would cast a sideways glance at her swollen belly and she would feel again the fear curling in her lap.

The progress of the darkness and the rage that surrounded and enveloped him was like pollution in the air that comes on so gradually as to go unnoticed until one day someone remarks that they cannot see the mountains anymore.

He did not hit her again until midway through her sixth month. She felt once more the shock and disbelief followed swiftly by confusion and denial and then the intense euphoria when he brought flowers and apologized and cried and begged her not to leave and swore he loved her and would never do it again. They stepped back from the abyss a second time and things got better for awhile as the memory faded into something to be forgiven and put away.

When Ethan was born she was sure they had put their troubles behind them, that this sweet child would bring them together and soothe whatever it was that dragged David down into the angry darkness that spawned his violence. He attended the birth, his face by her ear as he coached each breath and push and whispered words of encouragement and love. And when Ethan's tiny head crowned and she pushed him into the air and into their lives, she heard David call out with a shout and felt herself sink into the relief that it was done and everything at last was good and fine.

But it was not. He soon complained that she was spending too much time with Ethan, spoiling the boy and neglecting the man. He found fault with everything she did, from feeding Ethan when he was hungry to using cloth diapers to getting up in the night when he cried.

"Let him cry," he said, lifting her nightgown over her head, and still he could feel her move toward the edge of the bed and caught her by the arm and held on tight. "He'll be all right," he said through his teeth.

Years before, she would have shaken him off, but in his fingers wrapped around her arm and pressing into her flesh, leaving a mark that would show the next morning, she sensed a danger she felt bound to respect, like walking out on an icy lake and hearing a deep crack from beneath her feet and knowing she could not walk blithely on as if nothing was wrong, as if she hadn't heard. But having traveled such a distance, so far from solid shore, and with a baby in her arms, she did not dare retrace her steps and so sought safety in not moving from the spot.

The first time he raped her she did not know that's what it was. He wanted sex and she did not, and when she offered to touch him he pushed her hand away and climbed on top of her, and when she said his name, her voice edged in protest, she felt his body stiffen as he held himself above her in the darkness and there was only the sound of their breathing until he spread her legs and pushed himself inside and complained that she was dry.

She was unhappy, but unable to make sense of her unhappiness. Her mother had warned her that once Ethan was born, nothing would ever be the same, that being a mother would take over her life and sweep her along and that for awhile, at least, it might be all that she could do to keep her head above the swirling water. And it was just so. She was up more than once during every night to nurse and change him. She slept during the day, often with the cradle beside the bed so she could reach out and touch him when he became restless. She became weary in a deep, enduring way and began to lose her sense of time as one day flowed seamlessly into the next.

But for every new and demanding thread that Ethan wove into the fabric of her life, David inserted two of his own. He did not just complain, but woke her in the middle of the night and kept her awake for hours, and when she nodded off he shoved her back to consciousness. When Ethan cried and she was slow to wake and go to him, a kick or pinch would shock her out of sleep. In the day when David was home, complaints and slaps and kicks and pinches came at her like a roomful of mosquitoes. Time began to shrink to the distance to the next feeding or the next sudden, capricious assault. She felt constantly off balance, lurching from moment to moment, unable to put one thought in front of another, except to know that something was deeply and terribly wrong.

David seemed enraged at everything, but especially at her, and she could not fathom why, no matter how carefully she attended to his moods and needs, like a sailor watching each ripple of wind advance across the water, looking for the one that might capsize her if she wasn't careful. It was as if he dipped his hand into a bowl and picked at random a card on which was written the next thing that would set him off. She might wake in the middle of the night with him pounding her with his fists. Or in midsentence, a darkening look would sweep across his face, like the long low line of cloud from which tornados drop suddenly to the ground. She knew then what was coming, but too late.

And always he came to her afterward, penitent and filled with remorse, begging for forgiveness, tormented by the fear of losing her, and through the dense inertia of her pain and fatigue, she could not find the strength or will to leave, to cast out not only the man who was her husband, but the father of her little boy, to break apart not only a marriage, but a family, and to go home to her parents' house and reveal her failure for all to see. She clung to what she thought had become the challenge of her life, to love well enough to save him and save them all. There could be, she thought in the dead of night, no greater gift.

But the first time he beat her, one blow following on another with no end in sight, blood dripping on her clothes, something gave way inside her, some restraint against self-preservation. She packed two suitcases and took Ethan to her parents' house.

"I'm sure he didn't mean it," said her mother. "Surely he loves you. I mean, what could have prompted him to do such a thing? Was it something you said? Did you provoke him?"

Katherine tried to answer, her mind grasping for some sense of what it was she'd done. But each thing by itself seemed so small that she felt foolish to speak of it. Should she tell them that he'd wake her in the middle of the night and drive her to the kitchen, smacking the back of her head as they went, and make her wash the dishes again because he'd found some tiny piece of food — a grain of rice, a speck of gravy — that she'd missed? Or that he might hit her if she was late in getting home or if dinner wasn't what he wanted or if she didn't want to have sex or if Ethan cried while they were making love and she went to him? So small the reasons were, so pathetically small, that she felt herself equally pathetic and small and could only shake her head, hot with shame, mumbling that she didn't know.

"Is he sorry?" her mother asked.

"Yes."

"And does he try to make it up to you?"

Katherine nodded but didn't tell her how he wept and begged and told her he couldn't live without her and would kill himself if she ever left, made her promise she'd stay with him forever.

"Well, then," her mother said, "it will pass. Surely. Just be patient."

Her father sat at the far end of the couch, eyes cast down. "You must work these things out," he said at last, slowly, "especially when you have a child. You have a family to think of." Still he didn't look at her. "Marriage is never easy. Sometimes you lose your way. But if you love each other, you can always find a way back."

Then, "Do you love him, Katherine?" and she shook her head as she said, "Yes," Ethan stirring in her arms.

"Perhaps he feels neglected," her mother said. "That often happens with a new baby. A man can feel left out, you know. Just talk to him. Find out what's troubling him."

She had already tried her mother's advice, but the more she asked him what was wrong, the more threatened he seemed to feel. "I don't want to talk about it," he'd say, huffy, turning away, or, "There's nothing wrong with me. You're the one with the problem." So, she'd leave him alone, but then he'd feel abandoned and suspicious and threatened. Either way, when he felt threatened, he hit her.

David pulled into the driveway of her parents' house and leapt from the car, leaving the door open as he took the front walk in long strides, his face red and contorted. "*My* wife," he said, looking directly at Eleanor and Richard, "and *my* son. How *dare* you break this family apart."

"We're concerned," said Richard.

"Don't be. We can handle this."

"But," said Richard, "you shouldn't. . .hit her, David."

"Did she tell you that? Did she tell you that I hit her?"

Richard looked at Katherine who glanced at David and then looked down at the floor.

"What goes on between a man and his wife," David said, "is nobody's business but theirs. If we've got problems, we'll work them out on our own."

Richard went to Katherine and stood in front of her. She lifted her head and looked into her father's face. He raised his eyebrows in a question and she nodded.

"I'll be all right," she said.

"You don't want me to call anyone?"

"No," she said. "No, daddy, that will only make it worse."

In her father's face she saw how much he wanted to believe her and for them to leave so that he could stop feeling so helpless and afraid.

As David backed the car out of the driveway, she looked at the house she grew up in, the safest place in the world, and knew there was no safety now for her, not here or anywhere.

"Don't you *ever* even *think* of pulling a stunt like that again," he said, pounding the steering wheel with the heel of his hand. It was almost midnight and Ethan was fast asleep. "Who the *fuck* do you think you are? You listen to me. I don't care where you go. I'll find you. Don't think you'll just disappear. So help me, I'll track you down and have you charged with kidnaping and you'll never see Ethan again. And if I have to, I'll kill you. Do you understand? I'll kill you both, and then I'll kill myself. Do you want that on your head? Is that what you want?"

Katherine sat in silence, eyes closed, her breath coming fast and shallow. And then he turned toward her and drove a punch into her shoulder, bringing tears to her eyes. "Do you understand me?" and she nodded and pushed a feeble "yes" through the pain. "I'll cut. . .your. . .fucking. . .heart out," he said, driving each word home with a blow that sent pain shooting down her arm.

She had read stories of the lengths to which a man might go in pursuit of a woman who'd left him, the distance he would travel and the years he would devote to the hunt. And she had read of the instant he caught up with her to deliver the load of death and hatred played out in a scene he'd rehearsed in his mind a thousand times. He would ring the bell and shoot her in the face when she answered the door and then he'd walk into the front yard and put the gun in his mouth. Or he'd show up where she worked and shoot her down along with any co-workers who got in the way. Or he'd break in during the night and rape her before he cut her throat. Or he'd go through the house and kill everyone he found, whoever had taken her in or become part of her life — children, parents, lovers, sisters. Kill them all, including his children, and then himself.

She had read the stories and knew in that moment that David had become just such a man.

He waited until she had put Ethan to bed before he dragged her into the bedroom and tore off her clothes and threw her on the floor. He dropped his pants and forced her legs apart as he got on top of her. When he felt her dryness, he slapped her across the face and then spit on his hand and rubbed the saliva along his cock and pushed himself inside her. And when she flinched against the pain, he slapped her again, even as he heaved himself against her.

When he was done, he left her on the floor and went into the living room and rifled through the secretary until he found the stationary box that contained her poetry. He spilled the contents into the fireplace and set a match to it. She did not discover what he had done until the next day when she noticed the pile of ashes, flat and leaf like, so unlike the powdered ashes left by wood, and off in the corner a small patch of verse that had escaped the flames. She was, at first, stunned incredulous by the image of him striking so directly at her soul and she ran to the secretary and pulled the drawer onto the floor. She felt a rush of relief when she saw the box right where she had left it, but as she went to lift it, she knew at once that it was empty, full of nothing where the pages of her life had been.

She sat in front of the fireplace and wept as she sank beneath the knowledge that he had taken them both across a line that separated one world from another. She was now a prisoner who no longer possessed the assumption that she could come and go as she pleased or decide what was done to her from one moment to the next. He had threatened to kill them all and when she looked into his eyes she knew he could and would and right here in the living room he had taken the first step toward killing her as no one else could do. And she knew that nothing would bring it on more quickly and with greater ferocity than the slightest move to leave. Until that day, she had believed she stayed with him by choice, as an expression of love and commitment to her family. You don't leave when things get hard, she believed, when your husband is in trouble, as he most surely was. That's when you hang on the hardest. That's what a woman is supposed to do. But on that day, something broke inside her and between them, and her neat rational model of a normal human life was swept away.

From that day on, each moment was an occasion that might provoke him and an opportunity to prevent it. Every word and gesture, everything remembered or forgotten or briefly overlooked, everything done with the slightest variance from the way she'd done it before had to be weighed against her strategy for survival, for keeping herself and Ethan alive for yet another day. She gave up trying to understand. She did as she was told. She made herself docile and submissive. She smiled, but not so much as to make him think she had something on her mind. She did not struggle against him. She let go of her body and let him do as he would with it. She became expert at keeping Ethan out of the path of his rage and deflecting the violence from him and onto herself.

She avoided long conversations with colleagues at school, lest they suspect something was wrong and force her secret into the open. David monitored her phone calls, demanding to know whom it was she spoke to and what it was about. When she went out, he went with her. He kept her up all through the night while he harangued and lectured, interrogated and grilled. And when he tired and fell asleep, she stayed awake for fear that when he woke he would attack the lapse in her attention.

Just as he controlled her misery, he also controlled her few moments of pleasure and comfort that came when he feared he might have gone too far — the flowers and compliments, the nights out at restaurants they couldn't afford, the little vacations at country inns, the interest in what she had to say, the look of caring in his eyes.

In every way, the small, dark world he inhabited came to define the limits of her own as the details of her life — what she ate, when she slept, when she went to the bathroom, the simple integrity of her mind and body from one moment to the next — were all reduced to an object of his rage for control. And the shame of being so reduced and degraded reached into the deepest center of her being and solidified the conviction that no one of any worth could bring such a fate upon herself.

Her sole refuge became a numb and frozen place inside herself where time and feeling stopped, suspended above her body while he beat or raped her, focused only on the simple goal of staying alive from one moment to the next, deflecting the blow, stanching the flow of blood, presenting the smallest possible target, saying nothing that might fuel what raged all about her, wondering if Ethan could hear and praying he would stay in his room just one more time.

4

Through the kitchen window she sees lights from the house across the way and wonders if the neighbors heard or if they saw her fly through the air and crash into the wall. Neighbors have heard and seen before. She remembers the humiliation of police at the door, invading her house with eyes that probed her darkest secret, stepping carefully through the debris of her ruined life littering the floor. She remembers the polished shoes, the sharp creases in uniforms standing out in pristine contrast to the mess and destruction, the neatly trimmed hair and the soft creak of leather straps and belts as they moved about the living room, their attention fixed on little notebooks in their hands. She hears again the questions and sees the furtive glances at her hunched and bruised body and the shame she cannot hide against the drone of David's careful if slurred replies to what they ask. And she remembers the mixture of relief and dread when they were gone.

She looks at her hand resting on the floor and realizes she has been leaning on broken glass from the picture, and only now feels the pain from the cuts and the dampness of the blood between her skin and the tile. She tries to shift her weight to ease the pressure without attracting David's attention. Her face hurts and in her mind she sees again the window racing by just before she struck the wall, hears the sound of breaking glass, feels the long slide down the wall and the weight of his presence towering over her and grunting as he kicked and punched.

And suddenly it dawns on her that tonight he has struck her in the face with abandon, and a depth of fear washes over her that she hasn't known before. Always he's avoided hitting her in the face, the face she turns to the world, what everyone sees first, where broken teeth, black eyes, and swollen, bloody lips are sure to be noticed. This savaging of her face is something new, as if it doesn't matter anymore who might see or know. Her mind struggles to raise into consciousness the puzzle of how he could be so out of control when he beats her, so frenzied in his rage, and yet, in the midst of it all, so very careful. But the contradiction is too heavy and she lets it go.

The clock ticks against the silence in the room as she wonders, marvels, at the lack of stirring upstairs where Ethan sleeps, or at least she hopes he does, not staring at the door to his room, alone and frightened, breathing quick and shallow through rosebud lips, straining to hear the sounds drifting up the stairs and through the floor.

From the moment of his birth, he was an easy child — 'easy Ethan' his grandmother called him. He woke to be fed or changed but rarely fussed about his food and when he woke from his afternoon nap he'd lie awake in his crib, eyes dancing across the brightly colored mobiles hanging overhead, and she would find him that way, softly cooing to himself. He showed little fear of strangers and would go to sleep in almost anyone's arms. And when his father tossed him high into the air, he squealed with laughter all the way down.

And so long as Ethan was nearby, David would not hit her, which fed the hope that Ethan might somehow be kept from knowing that his father beat his mother. She imagined a sleep so deep it carried him beyond the sounds from downstairs or the bedroom down the hall, and even if he heard, it would seem as if in a dream, without weight or meaning, he being a child who knew nothing of such things.

But midway through his second year, he began to wake in the middle of the night. She would go to his room and when she opened the door his cries would spill out into the house and the dim light from the hall would illuminate him standing in his crib, hands white knuckled on top of the rail, his face wet with tears streaming down toward a mouth open wide in a mournful wail. She would take him in her arms and carry him to the window looking out on the back yard and gently bounce him as she whispered shushing sounds in his ear. The sobs would subside into sighs that shuddered through his body, tremors and aftershocks of the quake that had shaken him from his sleep, his attention coming into focus on something in the world out the window, the moon hung low in the sky, a branch moving in a breeze, and he would lift his arm and point and she would talk to him in a soft and lilting voice as if together they were witnessing some magic going by and just for them. Then she would lay him down and draw the blankets over him as she rubbed his back, and stand next to the crib for awhile, the exhaustion from the endless stream of such nights turning her mind fuzzy and slow.

And then she would turn to leave and picture in her mind the bed where David lay, half asleep, his body tense with anger at being wakened yet again and her inability to keep it from happening night after night. She would tiptoe down the hall and slide into bed and lie as still as if she wasn't even there.

Already Ethan knew something, she was sure, but what it was or the form it took in a mind so young, she could not know and barely dared imagine. She watched him with David and thought at times she detected a hesitancy as he raised his arms to be lifted and carried about or thrown into the air. But whatever it was she saw, it was overwhelmed by the love he felt for his father who put him on his lap while they watched television, who brought him presents and tickled him, who read to him on rainy Saturday afternoons and showed him how to stretch a blanket between two beds to make a tent, who chased him squealing through the house.

In those moments, she glimpsed the David she had fallen in love with and who was being taken from her by a force she did not understand and whom by the power of sheer love she would save for her and Ethan both if only she knew how. But always nearby, just a breath away, was the David whose rage she was careful to keep tightly focused on herself.

She knew it was only a matter of time before Ethan began to feel that something was wrong, a feeling too strong for him to conceal. At first, when he would come into a room, drawn by the sound of a slap and a sudden cry, and see the color rise in his mother's face as she drew a finger across her eye to catch the tears before they fell, she told herself he didn't notice or was too young to realize what it was. But by the time he was four, she could deny no longer the knowing look in his eye, and seeing that David saw it, too, she knew that Ethan, now a witness, would be harder to protect. She watched as David's displays of attention and love intensified against a hardening edge of panic. He played with Ethan as before, but rougher. He held him, but tighter and longer. And when he grabbed Ethan by the arm to hold him back from where he wanted to go or to focus his attention on something he had done, she could see in the tightness of David's face the struggle to restrain his grip on such tender flesh, the muscles in his neck, shoulders, and arms drawn dense and short, like a spring coiling tightly unto itself, and she held her breath until the moment he let Ethan go.

Whatever doubt there was in Katherine's mind about what Ethan knew disappeared in the middle of a spring night just before his fifth birthday. At a little past 7:00, David walked in the front door, took a bottle of Johnny Walker Red from his briefcase, and came into the kitchen. She was standing at the sink washing carrots.

"Hello," she said, but he said nothing in reply. He took a glass from the cupboard and poured whiskey into it and disappeared into the living room where he stayed through dinner, eating nothing, drinking behind the evening paper. Later, Ethan, fresh from his bath, stood in his pajamas at the top of the stairs, a stuffed bear under one arm and a thumb in his mouth. He looked down the stairs for several minutes before calling out in a small voice, "Good night, daddy." He waited and then looked at his mother standing in the doorway to his room at the other end of the hall.

"Come on, sweetie," she said, "daddy's not feeling well."

David did not speak to her when she came downstairs, nor when he went up to bed hours after she'd gone to sleep and she woke to the sensation of him prying her legs apart. Drugged by sleep, not thinking, she called out in protest and stopped herself too late to avoid the slap across her face, and as he forced himself inside and she gave in to the tears and began to leave her body for a safer place, she turned her head to see Ethan standing beside the bed, his face bathed in moonlight through the window. In her horror she grabbed David by the shoulders and called out Ethan's name, begging David to stop, and as he raised himself up and leaned on one arm so that he could hit her with the other, he saw Ethan from the corner of his eye and a look of such rage swept across his face that Ethan stepped suddenly back as if he had been pushed.

"God dammit, Ethan, get back to bed!" his father roared, and Ethan fell backwards on his bottom and then scrambled to his feet and ran down the hall into his room and closed the door behind.

It was an hour before David was finished and sound asleep so that Katherine could slide from the bed without lifting the covers and make her way to Ethan's room. He was not in his bed. She looked in the closet, but he wasn't there. She found him under the bed with a blanket and his bear. Whispering his name, she reached in and gently shook him awake and without a word passing between them she guided him out and lifted him into her arms. She walked to the window and looked out into the moonlit yard as Ethan grew heavy with sleep. She was so tired and so filled with despair that when she tucked him into bed, she lay beside him on top of the covers and dozed until a dream suddenly woke her to the rising light of a predawn sky.

Like a dog told to stay while her master walks away, Katherine knows well this waiting game. From the corner of her eye she watches him as he sits at the table, his gaze fixed downward at the glass that he slides back and forth from one hand to the other. From upstairs she hears a sound, like a toilet seat being raised and gently tapping the porcelain tank behind, and she closes her eyes and tries to will Ethan back to his room and to sleep.

"So," he says, "you two get coffee klatsch and I get leftovers. Your priorities are fucked up, you know that?"

She looks down at the floor.

"Actually," he says, "it's not your priorities. It's you. You are completely fucked up. You know what I'm saying to you?"

She feels the room shrink with every word, each interrogation cutting the space in half and then in half again.

"Why is coffee so important that your husband should get leftovers? I want to know that. You tell me what's so important about coffee with some bitch?"

The room so small it squeezes out the air, rage displacing even light. She knows she must answer or he'll come at her again.

"My birthday," she says to the floor.

Silence.

"Your birthday?" he says. "What about your birthday?"

"It's today. Today's my birthday. Susan bought me coffee."

More silence.

"Oh, great," he says. "So now I'm made out to be some schmuck who doesn't remember his wife's birthday. Why didn't you remind me?"

The room is so small she can feel his breath on her ear as if his lips and hatred and rage are only an inch from her face. "I forgot."

"I forgot," he repeats in a singsong sneer. "Right. And while you were forgetting what were you two hatching up?" He is on his feet now. "Huh?" He leans toward her, his fists swinging at his sides. And then he straightens as if smacked on the forehead. "Oh, no," he says. "I don't think so." He steps toward her. "You think you're leaving me? You and Ethan bundle up some afternoon while I'm out working my ass off and then you make off with her?" He stands above her, fists tight, body rocking back and forth between whether to punch or kick.

Katherine looks up. "No," she says, but already he is on her, spreading his legs to steady himself as he punches downward to her head and shoulders. "You'll leave me dead," he says, breathing hard, "that's how you'll leave me." And then she feels him fall into a steady, familiar rhythm, like a long-distance swimmer whose secret is in the pacing, relentless but in no particular hurry. She knows this may go on for hours unless he tires of it sooner. Or unless he kills her this time. He uses his arms until they weaken and then switches to his feet and kicks her wherever he can without losing his balance, one hand resting on the wall above her. She crouches against the wall so that he can only kick her legs, but he reaches down and pulls her out over the floor and kicks her in the back and side. He is breathing hard through his mouth and spit falls onto the floor and onto her. After awhile he seems in a ritual trance, a litany of words falling from his mouth in accompaniment to each blow — bitch, cunt, whore, stupid fuck, who do you think you are — over and over, weaving a thick fabric of rage and hate that covers them both, driving out the air and the light.

Tomorrow he may be horrified at what he's done and beg her to forgive him one more time. But she knows tomorrow is a long way off.

5

*E*than opens his eyes. The sound of voices drifts into his room
from far away on the other side of the house where the kitchen
opens onto the back porch and the yard beyond, the grass crisp and
frosty grey in the February cold. He remembers a dream. There was
an animal, he thinks, a deer or maybe a small horse. Yes, he remembers
now, a deer, and he closes his eyes around the memory of his cheek
on the warm honey colored fur along the neck of the deer standing
over him, its head bowed low. The deer was whispering something in
Ethan's ear when he woke up.

He has to pee, which he thinks might have been what woke him
from his sleep. He throws back the covers and slides off his bed until
his toes reach the cool floor. It is a dark, cloudy night with light from
neither moon nor stars, his room so black he cannot see the wall. He
stands for a moment, not quite awake, trying to remember where the
door to the hall is. Around the voices coming from downstairs there
is a silence soft and deep, by which he knows the air outside is thick
with snow.

A loud noise from downstairs startles him. It sounds like a shout
and then a great thump and glass breaking and falling to the floor.
The urge to pee grows more urgent and he looks about for the door
but cannot see it in the dark. He presses against his penis with his
fingers to hold back the flow and frantically feels along the wall, his
hand passing over his little maple bureau and the white toy shelves
his father made last summer. Finally the smoothness of the wall is
interrupted by the molding around the door and he finds the knob
just to the other side, opens the door and steps into the hall.

He squints at the light coming up the stairs. The voices are louder
than before, especially his father's. His mother speaks so softly he can
barely tell it's her. He runs to the bathroom, lifts the toilet seat, pulls
down his pajama bottoms and leans forward. His thighs touch the

cold porcelain and he jiggles himself back from the shock of it but then holds himself steady as the warm stream flows into the bowl. Still sleepy, he drops his head forward, eyes closing as his chin rests on his chest and he listens to the pee meet the surface of the water, first strong and low in pitch and then soft and higher as he empties himself out to a trickle. He stands still, not yet aware that he's done. Then he starts to feel as if he's falling, as he sometimes does on the edge of sleep. He lifts his head with a start and opens his eyes.

For a moment the house is as quiet as deep new snow. He looks up at the bathroom window and sees the air outside swirling white in the glow from the streetlamp across the way, and then he hears his father's voice again. There is something wrong, as there has been something wrong so many times before, but he is never sure just what it is. Sometimes he goes downstairs only to be met halfway by his mother, her voice shaking, leaning against the wall or the bannister, looking up at him as he takes the stairs one at a time, holding the banister with two hands, bringing both feet to a stair before stepping down to the next.

"It's okay, honey," she'd say, "go back to bed."

"Why is daddy yelling?"

And she would tell him something — that daddy was excited or upset or just telling a story with angry parts in it. But whatever the reason that floated up from the gloom of the downstairs hall it always ended the same. "Everything's all right. Go back to bed now. We'll be up soon." And then his father's voice would call his mother's name, not calling, but commanding, impatient, the way his voice would get if he told Ethan to go to bed or come to him and Ethan dawdled or got distracted by something that kept him from doing what his father asked. And when he heard his father's voice change in that way, Ethan knew that he'd better do it because his father wouldn't ask again.

Even though he never thought it in his mind, he didn't believe what his mother told him and he lingered on the stair, his hands still holding the bannister, breathing shallow through his mouth, waiting for the truth. But the closest she came was to stiffen in her body, "Ethan," her voice low and tight, "go, now," even "please." And then he would climb back up the stairs and pad down the hall to his room. Though the sounds from downstairs frightened him, he left his door open because he felt even more afraid to close himself off from his parents, to be shut away alone in his room with the awful sounds that filled the house.

The next morning he would see how terrible his mother looked, how stooped she was, how slowly she walked, how she winced when he hugged her, the bruises on her legs and arms.

"What happened?" he would ask, and she would say that she'd fallen down and he tried to imagine what kind of fall that would be and could only think of tumbling head over heels all the way down the stairs. But he thought he'd hear a sound that big, even in his sleep.

Tonight, however, is different. He has never heard anything like that big thump or the breaking glass, and his father's voice has never sounded so angry and so loud. He sits on the top stair and grows heavy with a dread that pools and swirls inside him. He wraps his arms around his shins and rests his cheek on his knees and listens. His father is talking and Ethan straightens up when he hears his name jump out from the other words. There is silence and "No, David" in his mother's voice just as the air explodes with shouts and the dull sound of flesh and bone being kicked and punched. His mother calls out in grunts and cries muffled as if coming through a pillow over her face. The trembling in his stomach bubbles up in a sob of fear and he runs to his room and slams the door behind and crawls beneath his bed.

But the terrible sounds reach him even there, rumbling through beams and joists and walls and spilling through the crack beneath the door, a low dense fog rolling across the floor. There is no escape, and as the terror mounts inside him he can think only to be with his mother and not alone. Crying out, he scrambles from beneath the bed and gropes his way to the door. He runs down the hall, everything a blur to his eyes filling with tears, and takes the stairs as fast as he can, as if now some horrible thing is trying to catch him before he can reach the safety of the kitchen and his parents. Leaping off the bottom stair he runs toward the closed door at the end of the hall and pushes it open before him.

David is at the far end of the kitchen, bent over with his back to Ethan. He holds Katherine by the hair to lift her up as he punches her in the face. "I'll kill you first," he says. "Do you hear me?" He leans down closer to her ear. "No," he says, "I'll do better than that. I'll kill *both* of you before I'll ever let you go. *That's* how it ends. When *I* say, and *how* I say. But you will *never* be the one."

And then David hears a sound from behind, above his voice punctuated by the grunts of his own exertion, above the dull thump of his fist on Katherine's body. He turns his head, one hand still holding a handful of hair, the other poised for the next punch, and sees over his shoulder the small figure of Ethan standing just inside the kitchen door. His face is wet with tears, his mouth open as the shiny run from his nose spans the small distance between his lips. As David releases Katherine and stands, Ethan can see her face so swollen and covered with blood that he can barely make out her features, her white blouse spattered red and one shirttail pulled out from her skirt. Her legs are folded beneath her. She blinks as if trying to focus.

Ethan cannot move. He is crying so hard that he cannot stop to breathe and can only move his lips in a soundless 'mamma' at the end of a choking sob and then his chest reaches the limit of its collapse and shudders to inhale a gulp of air.

"You see what you've done?" says David. "You happy now?" He lumbers across the kitchen toward Ethan, leaning on the table as he goes.

"No, David," hauling herself up against the wall.

"Oh, yes," he says. "You've done it now and I'm gonna finish it."

"No," she says again, her voice rising.

"Daddy?" Ethan says, his eyes lifting to his father's full height above him.

"Think you're going to leave *me*," he says. "Dead is the only way. The only way. We all go or no one goes."

"I won't leave," she says, drawing a sleeve across her eyes to wipe away the blood. "David. I won't."

"Damn straight. You're not going anywhere. Ever."

"Don't," she says.

"Don't you *ever* tell me what to do!" he says, scooping Ethan in his arms and wheeling about to face her.

She struggles to get to her feet, grabbing the edge of the kitchen counter to pull herself off the floor. "Not Ethan," she says.

"Ever!" he screams.

"No."

"Yes, you cunt. When *I* say!"

"David, give him to me!" she cries, leaning her back against the wall, her arms wavering in the air in front of her.

"You want him?" he says, taking a step toward her. "Huh? *You* want him? Now? Is that what you want? *You* say?"

"David, *please*," pushing herself from the wall and getting to her feet.

"Well then *take* him!" and then David leans away like a bow being drawn to the limit of its pull and with a long deep bellow, he hurls Ethan across the room. Katherine opens her mouth but nothing comes out, so frozen is she by the sound of Ethan's scream. For an instant, everything slows in her mind as if to burn forever in her memory each detail of the horror before her eyes — David's forward momentum driving him to his knees, drops of sweat flying into the air from his face, head bowed toward the floor as he tries to break his fall with his hands and then his forearms, the light in the kitchen turning harsh and bright and cold, and Ethan, her tender Ethan, tumbling through the air, arms and legs flailing as if swept along by a river gone mad, hands grasping for purchase on anything that might hold him back, terror spilling from his mouth. And then, helpless to resist the rage that propels him through the air, he smashes head first into the wall and falls like a doll to the floor where he lies, his body limp and still.

From Katherine comes a scream that begins in her legs and pelvis and gathers force as it spirals upward through her body and bursts out into the room. It is a scream of utter terror and grief at what she knows against all her powers of denial has been done, after years of laboring to contain her husband's rage, giving over her own body to hold at bay the threats to kill her and Ethan if she ever dared to leave. But now that rage has spilled out over everyone like a nuclear reactor melting down when a freak accident, some pathetic little leak, drains away the cool surrounding waters of its container.

In a still, suspended moment, all that exists is the expanse of blue kitchen tile that separates her from Ethan. But as she crawls toward him, David lifts his head and sees what he has done, his eyes growing wide and frantic as he explodes in a rage beyond her worst imagining. Suddenly the air is filled with everything he can lay his hands on — pots, dishes, silverware, stove burner grates, knives, glasses, bowls, spice jars, vitamin bottles, cookbooks, a cutting board, the dish drainer, a coffee grinder, toaster, blender, tea kettle, food processor, drawers whose contents spill out a trail of utensils through the air. He rips the phone from the wall and throws it at her, then heaves the chairs. He is trying to bury them both, to make them disappear, but as he grabs the edge of the table, he sees that he has failed, that Ethan is still there, lying at the foot of the wall just as before, and that Katherine is still alive.

She looks at her right hand that has come to rest on the handle of a boning knife lying amidst the debris all around her. *This is when he kills me. He has killed Ethan. He has killed Ethan. And now he is going to kill me.*

Just as David's power ultimately lay in the promise, the hope that he might not do what he threatened to do, so now his power over Katherine drains away as she realizes there is nothing left to be saved by giving in. As she feels him step toward her, she finds the strength to rise to meet him, and in his hurry he does not see the knife that rises with her and that glides without effort against the momentum of his killing rage, through the soft cotton shirt she'd ironed just this morning and then the fleshy wall of his abdomen, beneath his lower rib, and up toward his heart. He gives out a gasp and slams his open hand onto her shoulder as if to hold himself up. She waits for him to grab her throat or smash his forehead into her face, but he just stands there, looking down at her. She looks into his eyes and sees the man she once loved, the father of her son, and the man whose murderous rage she hates and fears more than anything she has ever known. She feels her hand on the knife thrust upward beneath his ribs and as his legs begin to tremble and give way beneath him she realizes she is holding him up and feels the strength of her intention flow through her arm and shoulder and down the length of her aching body through her legs and feet and into the floor and the earth below. She looks into his face and feels the weight of his sinking life and knows that she is killing him, and yet still she waits for him to do something, to kill her in spite of all. His hand loosens its grip on her shoulder and he looks into her eyes and she sees the softness of a boy staring in wonder at something he doesn't understand. She feels a pang of sadness and even remorse, but it fades as her mind fills with the memory of Ethan flying across the kitchen and slamming into the wall. David begins a long slow slide to the floor, her hand still holding the knife in place as they come to rest on their knees. His breath is soft and shallow. His eyes lose their focus. His hand drops to his side. And then she lets go of the knife and he kneels for a moment as if balanced on a fine edge, and falls forward, his shoulder pushing past her and his face slapping the cold tile floor.

Katherine sits back on her heels, hands open on her thighs, her breath coming shallow and fast in the utter stillness of the room. A faint high buzz passes through her head, like the far-off song of a cicada warming up on a hot summer morning. She is a long blade of grass at the bottom of a pond, rocking slowly in the lazy timeless swirl of some deep and gentle current. She feels no pain. She looks at David lying next to her and knows that he is no longer there. His blood has pooled between them and runs along where her leg rests on the floor, but she makes no effort to move away.

Her gaze drifts down the long line of David's body and then from the corner of her eye she sees a small bare foot pale and still against the tile. Feeling rushes back into her as she fills with pain and sobs crowd into her throat, "Oh, no, oh, no. No," crawling to where Ethan lies by the wall and laying her fingers against his cheek that is already growing cool. She brushes the fine hair from his forehead and touches the cowlick that springs from the back of his head. She cannot see for the deluge of tears that flows from her now as she pulls him to her and lies down beside him, drawing him into her arms and rocking back and forth, feeling her heart come apart inside her, longing to ride this wave of grief and tears into some oblivion where none of this will ever have happened, where Ethan will still be alive or, if he must be dead, then unknown to her so that she will not have to feel the horror of such a loss. But her longing goes unanswered and when the police arrive they find her still lying along the kitchen wall, barely conscious, and yet they have to pry her arms away to retrieve the small dead body smeared with blood they will later determine not to be his own.

Two

1

*L*ike her parents before her, Lucy Dudley doesn't heat the upstairs even in the coldest Vermont winters and always sleeps with a window open. Waking to the familiar feel of something cold and wet against her cheek she reaches from beneath the covers to the grey muzzle of her black lab, Sophie, who stamps her feet and wags her entire rear end at the sight of Lucy waking, then adds low breathy grunts to the stamping and wagging. Lucy starts to move but thinks better of it when the arthritis in her hips announces itself as it has every morning since around the time she turned sixty, just over twenty years ago. She looks past Sophie and out the window. The fields and hills begin to glow as the sun shows through the trees along the white ridge line of mountains across the distant border in New Hampshire.

"Okay, girly," she says, throwing back the covers and swinging her skinny legs out over the floor. Sophie backs up to make room and does a little hop into the air. Lucy goes to close the window, kneading her hips while she takes in the view. Her house sits on a hilltop nearly cleared of trees, affording a view of layers of hills and mountains receding into the distance. She has lived her life here in what Vermonters call the Northeast Kingdom and has never seen reason to question the name. It is, she believes, something about the sharp clarity of light across the bowl of sky that gives the feeling of being in another world, or perhaps just the enhanced sensation of being in this one.

She reaches behind her head to check the condition of her hair and finds it still braided down her back. Again she forgot to take it down, the kind of lapse she notices more lately. She slips off her nightgown and dresses quickly, throwing on a t-shirt beneath an old denim shirt and stepping into bib-overalls that, when they faded from their original blue, she dyed purple in an old washtub set on the back porch. She pulls on two pairs of socks and then insulated boots. By the time she is done, Sophie is beside herself with enthusiasm.

"Are we ready? Time for breakfast? Get the goats up?" The old dog bolts for the door and takes the stairs with a clatter of toenails, then stands on the landing, eyes trained up the stairs. Lucy notices how much slower Sophie has become, how tentative she is about putting weight on her shoulders when she walks.

"Couple of wrecks."

The floor creaks in the cold as Lucy goes into the kitchen. She pulls on a pair of fingerless gloves and puts a kettle on the stove, then walks down the hall, pulling on her coat as she goes, and out the front door into the snow. Sophie hurries off to what Lucy calls her 'toilette' behind the rhododendron bushes around the west side of the house. The dry snow crunches beneath Lucy's feet as she shuffles cautiously down the walk to the box where her copy of the *Boston Globe* awaits. She looks across the fields where a cold platinum sun clears the distant mountain ridge against a pale blue sky. A small family graveyard surrounded by a low white fence sits across the hardpan road running by the house. The early sun casts long shadows from snow-capped tombstones, tilted at all angles, sometimes reminding her of a group of friends making their unsteady way home after a night on the town.

It's yesterday's paper, which she doesn't mind since the news rarely offers much that she considers new. It arrives in the afternoon, sometimes by snowmobile, but she leaves it for the next morning when she's refreshed and better equipped to digest what's happening in the world.

She crunches her way back to the house — Sophie limping behind, already stiff from the cold — and without removing her coat goes into the kitchen and puts down a bowl of food for Sophie and loads a small handful of Earl Grey into a white teapot that's missing the top half of its spout. She opens the paper on a long pine table that runs across the center of the room.

For many years she got both the *Globe* and the *New York Times*, but ran out of patience for what she saw as the *Times'* unfriendliness toward women and the apparent inability of its editorial staff to educate themselves about sexism. The *Globe*, she believed, was more progressive, so she cancelled the *Times*, accompanied by one of her many letters to the editor which never made it into print.

Had her father been alive to render an opinion, he would have disapproved of her choice, reminding her that the *New York Times* is a newspaper of record. But *whose* record, she'd want to know, making the point that it certainly wasn't the likes of her.

She wraps the thin wires of her glasses around her ears and immediately notices a headline just below the fold: "Banker and Son Killed in Gruesome Family Tragedy." The kettle whistles behind her, but she continues to read. Calls from alarmed neighbors in a Boston suburb brought police to a home where they found David Weston, investment manager for a major Boston banking firm, dead in the kitchen from a knife wound to the heart. His wife, Katherine, was alive but lay covered in blood on the floor. She was clutching the body of their five year-old son, Ethan, who apparently died of a broken neck. She refused to let go of him. She had suffered multiple injuries to her head and body and seemed in a state of hysterical paralysis. After being sedated by emergency medical technicians, she was taken to the hospital where she is being held for treatment under police guard until authorities can determine what happened. An officer on the scene remarked that, "It looks like they had quite a go at each other. And she won, although just barely. I don't know about the boy." As to whether charges would be filed against Mrs. Weston, the officer replied that it was too soon to tell.

She shakes her head and clicks her tongue. "For Pete's sake," she says, taking the kettle off the stove. "Too soon, my foot." She pours boiling water over the tea. "What's the matter with them? Don't they *read?* Where have they *been?*" She tosses the paper on the floor near the wood stove. Sophie stands by the back door and thumps the wall with her tail.

"I know." Sophie thumps faster and louder. "You're such a nag."

Out the back door and across the yard a red barn leans slightly to the southeast. It was full of Guernseys and Holsteins when Lucy was a girl but is now inhabited by goats. When her arthritis got so bad she had trouble getting around, Lucy heard about the healing properties of fresh goat milk and didn't hesitate to give it a try, supplied by her neighbor, Walter Finch, whose farm lies a half mile up the road.

The goats themselves came later. Lucy dropped by for milk one day and couldn't find Walter until she came upon him milking in the barn. They rushed over and surrounded her, noses reaching up to smell her face, younger ones taking inventory of her clothes, nibbling on cuffs and untying laces, heads tilted to get a better view as they ogled her with golden irises open wide around black oblong pupils. She bent down and touched her nose to a nose as they breathed each other in. She thought she saw a serene little smile and promptly fell in love.

Sophie follows Lucy into the sweet smell of the barn. The goats are lying down, clustered for warmth around the hay bin. Sophie roots through layers of hay on the floor, looking for scat like a pig after truffles.

Lucy is loading the bin with hay when the *Globe* story drifts into her mind. It doesn't say what happened, but she knows. She can feel it. This woman killed her husband as the only way to keep from being killed herself, but not before he got the little boy. "My God," she whispers, "how will she stand it?"

The goats are up and sniffing the air, a few at the door looking out at the day to gauge the cold. They step into the yard and fluff out their winter coats. Watching them, Lucy feels herself borne along by the constancy of their rhythms, their purity of attention. Life really is this simple, she thinks, but we make such a mess of it.

She walks back to the house and waits for Sophie who, judging from the little snorts of ecstasy coming from the back of the barn, has found something old and sweet to roll in. Lucy rattles the cow bells hanging on the back door and Sophie lumbers out from the gloom and into the sunlight, her shoulders dipping painfully with each step, but her face happy and alive. Lucy holds the door and they step together into the kitchen where Sophie heads immediately for her bed near the wood stove, circling three times and lying down with a groan. Lucy kneels in front of the stove and picks up the *Globe*, staring at it before crumpling the front section and tossing it in. She sighs at the sight of no kindling in the box and goes out to the woodpile on the porch, reminding herself that it's Thursday and her hired boy will come by after school to replenish the wood and muck out the barn.

She kneels before the stove and throws kindling on top of the crumpled newspaper and then suddenly begins to cry, sitting back on her heels and rubbing her fingers across her forehead as tears come freely and hot down the thin veined skin stretched across her face. Sophie looks up from licking her paws, her tail thumping the bed, pushing a moan from her throat.

Lucy shakes her head and wipes her eyes with the back of one hand as she puts lengths of split oak in the stove with the other.

"No," she says, striking a match and setting it to the paper. The flame takes immediately and begins to crawl beneath the kindling when suddenly she reaches in and pulls it out with a clatter onto the floor and beats out the flame with her hands. Sophie jumps up with a grunt of alarm and makes for the hallway. Lucy picks the charred newspaper from the pile and opens each crumpled page until she finds the one she's looking for and spreads it out on the floor, smoothing out the wrinkles. She reads the headline again.

"Shit," she says and hears the worried thump of Sophie's tail from the safety of the living room.

She rebuilds the fire, then lays the front page on the table and pours a cup of tea. She glances over at it sideways, then snatches the page from the table and slides it in the bottom drawer of a small pine bureau against the wall.

She takes her tea into the library, which used to be the dining room, but, living alone, she had little use for it and the house was filling up with books that lay about in whatever spot seemed handy when she was done. They were stacked against walls, piled on toilet tanks, scattered up and down the stairs, perched on newel posts, strewn across her bed. It was getting out of hand but she couldn't bring herself to get rid of them. The moment of truth arrived when she mislaid her copy of Howard Zinn's *People's History of the United States* and finally came across it in the refrigerator beneath a carton of eggs.

She turns her mother's old rocker toward the east window and drinks the tea as light changes over the fields and hills. A hawk wheels high against the sky. A pickup rattles by, the sound muffled by the packed snow on the road. Walter on his way to town. She feels old and tired. She thinks of Michael and wonders how he's been since she saw him last, just before Christmas. Even a mother, she thinks, can do just so much.

The day crawls past at a slower pace than most. After breakfast she backs the old red Subaru out of the barn and drives to town with Sophie looking over her shoulder from her place in the back seat, her panting breath billowing into the air and fogging the windshield. She runs into Walter at Dewalt's café and they sit over coffee and talk about the weather and aching joints and scandals in Washington. She notices a folded copy of the *Globe* tucked in his coat pocket and feels suddenly annoyed and cuts the conversation short.

She stops by the feed store to order a dozen bales of hay for the goats and then goes to the library to pick up a new collection of Jane Kenyon's poems. She stands outside and looks across the street where Sophie is making nose prints on the car window. Lucy doesn't know what to do with herself. She doesn't want to go home, plagued by a peculiar restlessness, a diffuse, itchy, ill-at-ease feeling she remembers from the early stages of menopause, as if something was shifting inside her and pulling her along against a deep reluctance to go.

She gets into the car and takes the long way home, reaching north and then looping east and south. The fields are smooth with snow, dotted with stands of trees and farmhouses visible at a distance from chimney smoke curling into the sky. By the time she gets home it's well past noon. She has a sandwich for lunch and then loads the stove and takes the Kenyon book upstairs where she climbs into bed and reads until sleep carries her away.

She wakes to a bark from Sophie and then the sound of Jason dumping wood onto the back porch and footsteps crunching down the driveway to the road. She goes downstairs and gives Sophie her supper, and the sun is already near to setting in the western sky when she pulls on her coat and goes out to put the goats in for the night.

After supper she sets the rocker before the stove, but the restlessness is with her still and she cannot get comfortable. She supposes if she reads long enough she'll make herself so tired that sleep will become irresistible, but at ten o'clock she is still wide awake. She drinks a glass of warm milk and lets Sophie out one last time before going upstairs to see if reading in the embrace of her bed will hasten the descent.

When finally she sleeps, she dreams an old and troubling dream that wakes her with a start. Moonlight streams through the window and across her bed. Sophie whimpers and trembles in a dream of her own. Lucy pulls a second pillow beneath her head and props herself up to gaze at the pale moonlit air outside her window. "Ghosts about," she says to herself. She puts on robe and slippers and scuffs downstairs with Sophie padding behind, yawning and curious. It is just past 2:00. She puts her hand on the stove. It is still warm.

She takes a bottle of Jack Daniels from high up in a cupboard and pours herself a short glass and then rummages in the bureau for the lone cigarette left over from the last time Michael was here. She breaks the filter off the end and tosses it on the bureau, then takes the whiskey and walks to the stove where she draws a wooden match across the stovepipe and holds the flame to the end of the cigarette in her mouth.

She sits in her mother's chair and rocks and drinks and smokes her way toward a certain peace that creeps gently in. But when she sips the last of the whiskey and flicks the glowing stub into the stove, the restlessness reawakens beneath the soft haze in her mind. It is hopeless, she knows, no escaping it now. She pushes herself out of the chair and crosses the kitchen, opens the bureau drawer and pulls out the page. She carries it to the phone, lifts the receiver, and dials zero. The operator is long in coming, but, then, it is very late.

When she finally hears a voice on the line she speaks in the hushed tone of someone trying not to wake a sleeping household. "Information for Boston, please."

2

*K*atherine cannot see. She tries to open her eyes, but they are held shut by pads and a bandage wrapped around her head. She cannot breathe through her nose and her mouth and lips are dry. She feels her body entombed, mummified, floating in a thick ether of pain. She struggles to form a thought but can't remember how.

Bruises crowd over much of her upper body and face as well as her arms and legs. There is a deep bruise on her left breast. Both eyes are swollen shut and her nose is broken. There are two stitches in her left ear. Several teeth are loose and two in the front are badly chipped. There are bald spots on her head where clumps of hair have been torn out.

But it's worse inside.

When they rolled her into surgery and opened her up, there were murmurs of surprise at the amount of blood pooling in her belly and disbelief that she was still alive and that anyone could inflict such damage with only their hands and feet. It was the image of such a rage as this must have been that haunted the young surgeon for days to come. While he bent over the sterile field in which he worked so feverishly, he could feel the rage that had so ravaged this body swirl through the blood and tissues and rise like a vapor above the table and fill the room. He stopped and looked up and then from side to side and even over his shoulder, his hand poised in the air at the end of a long strand of suture anchored in her liver. He listened and then shook his head and lowered his eyes to the bloody flesh beneath his fingers.

He removed her ruptured spleen, repaired the torn liver, and sewed her up. But within the hour it was clear that she was still bleeding inside and when he opened her again he found her kidneys as torn as her liver had been.

The chart hanging at the end of her bed doesn't speculate as to how she'd come to be in such a state. In this it resembles the record kept by her family physician who once noted she'd been "hit by a chair," as if she was unlucky enough to be in the path of a piece of furniture that had flung itself across the room. She sat on the examination table, her legs dangling in the air, like a child. The silence grew between them, broken only by the scratch of his pen as he took notes on her condition. She closed her eyes while he cleaned the wound over her eye, his head tilted back to get a better downward angle through his bifocals. Now and then he breathed out in a peculiar way that almost sounded to her like a little moan, as if responding to a particularly moving line in some internal dialogue that replaced the conversation he might have had with her. And then, when he was done, he stretched his lips in a weak little smile and asked her if she'd like him to call David to come and get her.

Into the deep blue sky comes the sound of shuffling feet and a chair scraping across the floor. Voices join in soft but earnest conversation. Farther off a cart wheels by in tune to the rhythmic squeak of rubber soles. A doctor's name is called through a loudspeaker. She feels the bed beneath her and the pain suddenly has weight that drops her from the sky and presses her downward through floor after floor and into the earth below.

The bed sags beneath someone sitting down. A warm moist hand settles on top of her own but she soon feels only the sensation of her arm floating in the air, detached and free. A familiar voice says her name, then again, and slowly, reluctantly, she rises from the earth and settles on the bed.

Whose hand is this? It feels too small to be David's and then she remembers with a start the look on his face as he sank to the floor, the feel of her hand pressing toward his heart. His face hovers before her eyes as if he were in the room. She starts to shake. The hands that grasp her legs must be his, she thinks, working their way up and up until he splits her apart.

But he is dead. He must be dead. And the grief that washes over her mingles with the dread of being found by him even here, even now.

To be found, no matter what — so delicious for one who waits to be discovered and carried off, prized in the having. "You'll never get rid of me," he said, smiling into her smile the night she agreed to marry, and she rose to the promise like a diver looking to the surface of the water far above her upturned head, lungs aching for the sudden gasp of air.

"Katherine," says a voice, a man's voice, "Katherine, can you hear me?" and she can but does not listen. "*Ninety-nine, one hundred! Ready or not, here I come!*" a child's voice echoing in her mind, crouching in the dark rear of the closet among long forgotten shoes and fallen hangers, the sound of footsteps drawing near, "*Katherine. Oh, Kaaatherine, where are you?*" the last words sung in a high and lilting tone. She pulls up her knees to make herself small and then listens to the steps recede, the seeker giving up, too young to keep at it long enough. Katherine left unfound, the sharp edge of triumph slowly rounds beneath the passing of a quiet little melancholic cloud. And then she sighs and tiptoes from the closet to seek the seeker. "*Here I am!*" she crows. Not hide-and-seek, but hide-and-be-found. She always knew that.

David once nearly tore the house apart looking for her and when he found her locked in the guestroom closet he broke in the door and dragged her into the hall where he warmed up by punching holes in the wall.

"Katherine," she hears again, "it's your dad, Katherine," the voice wavering, breaking around the words, "honey, can you hear me, please say something if you can," turning away, quieter now, "do you think she can hear. . .is she conscious?" other voices low and serious, drifting around her as she sinks beneath a weight of shame and sorrow.

Oh daddy go away, the words circling for a pathway into the air, *please go away,* only to fade unspoken in the rise and fall of breathing in and breathing out. She sees her parents' faces when they first found out that David hit her, lines of age deepening in shock and disbelief. And fear. There was fear. But of what and for whom?

The hand slides away and the bed rises and she moves her hand toward what was there but no one sees as voices drift to the far side of the room. She feels she has died and longs to leave her body and its broken life behind. Even the pain grows more distant as if not her own and she feels a pang of empathy for the woman lying here.

The morphine carries her back to sleep and dream, walking beneath a starlit sky in the cool of autumn, the air quiet except for leaves and small branches beneath her feet. She whistles a tune she cannot name, arms swinging as she walks, and begins to run through the alphabet, trying to jog her memory, when suddenly there are footsteps crashing through the underbrush and she looks over her shoulder as she begins to run, faster as she sees a figure move across a line of trees. Branches lash across her face as a voice behind grunts with rage in the effort of pursuit. She leaps across a stream and splashes through tall grass growing from the water's edge and as she disappears into the trees on the far side she glimpses in her second sight a figure sitting on a rock in the middle of the stream, a small form, a child's, and it is only as the forest closes in behind that she realizes it is Ethan who sits there watching her in flight. And did he reach out to her in passing? Was it a hand she saw lifted toward her? And did he say something or was it just a little cry?

But she pushes on before the narrowing pursuit, driven by the terror of what follows close behind. And then suddenly she swings herself high into a tree with a strength and grace she has never known. There she sits, breaths coming fast and deep as she looks at the dark ground below where a man paces back and forth, a familiar man, but like the familiar tune, she can't call up the name. And then he bellows out a roar that almost shakes her from the tree as he turns and lunges back through the woods. She closes her eyes with a sigh, feeling her breathing slow until the sudden gasp as she sees his path through the woods toward the stream.

She cries out and spreads her arms and steps from the branch and into the air. She drops into the night and takes flight through the woods, rising above the black leafless trees and beating her arms against the sky, a fury swelling her chest around the pounding of her heart. From far below she hears a cry, the high and piercing cry of an entire being swallowed whole by a terror so sudden, so complete, so incomprehensible, that it disappears like a speck of light in a great black hole.

Frantically she pulls herself toward the dark earth below but she keeps rising toward the stars like a swimmer diving deep, reaching to the drowning soul receding downward in the murky water but relentlessly carried upward and away toward the air, unable to hold herself down against her own buoyancy. Higher she rises, the stars clear and cold in the deep blue night. The earth grows small and silent beneath her. She stops the beating of her arms but even then she does not fall, suspended in the sky, drifting slowly upward, cold and alone.

When Katherine wakes, the first thing she notices is the light. The pads are gone from her eyes and sunlight through the window warms her face. Someone is sitting beside the bed, breathing in the slow even rhythm of settling in for a wait. A door opening, rubber soles padding briskly to the far side of the bed, someone leaning over to straighten a blanket, the smell of freshly laundered cotton, crisply pressed and rustling as it moves. She tries to pull her eyes open against the swelling, enough to see without being seen, and peeks into the face hovering over her, framed by dark hair tied in a bun beneath a stiff white cap, lips pursed and eyes drawn together in concentration. And then the face widens in a little smile at the subtle shift into consciousness that creeps across Katherine's face.

"Mrs. Weston."

She opens her eyes a little more, looking down.

"How are you feeling?"

Katherine repeats the question in her mind with no idea of what to say from the enormous absence inside herself, her body detached, unable to move beneath the numb inertia that envelops her. To say a single word would take a strength and will she cannot imagine.

How are you feeling? The words wander through her mind until they encounter David's face and she flinches as if from a blow and then the long desperate cry of Ethan hurtling through the air cracks her open in a scream that fills the room. Hands lay upon her and she tries to beat them away, but they are too many and too strong and every movement sends pain shooting through her body. She trembles in their grasp and cries and shrinks herself small, her eyes squeezing shut as something stings her arm and the voices and commotion grow watery and soft and she slides down and down into a thick and dreamless sleep.

She wakes to an empty room. The sky outside her window is hung with low grey clouds bathed in half-light. Dusk or dawn, she doesn't know, hung over, her mouth pasty and dry, stomach gnawing, empty and small and sour. Her mind is empty and still.

The door opens and a nurse appears before Katherine can close her eyes. "Ah, you're awake," says the nurse, walking to the bed and picking up Katherine's wrist while she stares down at her watch. She lays the hand on the bed and slides a blood pressure cuff around Katherine's arm.

"Are you hungry? You haven't eaten since you got here. I'm not sure what you're ready for, but I'll see if we can do better than that stuff dripping into your arm." She nods at the tube snaking from the bottle hanging beside the bed. "Although how much better, I couldn't say," she says with a little smile.

She must not know, Katherine thinks. She couldn't know and smile like that. But then it occurs to her that for all the cheerful friendliness, the nurse never looked at her, not into her face, always focused on what she was doing or on the pillow just above Katherine's ear.

She looks out the window. A thin line of pale blue sky shows where the clouds have lifted just above the horizon. The sun passes swiftly down, sudden and bright through the crack before it disappears. She licks her lips but her tongue is dry and does no good. She reaches for a glass that sits on the bedside table and winces from a spasm of pain in her chest. She maneuvers the straw into her mouth and tears leak from her eyes as the cool water skirts along the edge of the vast and arid place she feels herself to be.

A knock on the door so startles her that she cries out and nearly drops the glass as another spasm of pain grips her chest. She doesn't think to say anything but only waits, focused inward on the pain. The door opens and a man enters and sits in the chair beside her bed, and it is only then that she realizes she is holding her breath. He wears a grey suit and smells of the outside world, the faint and lingering odor of aftershave and fresh air mixed with the smoke of a cigarette. Smells of normal and everyday life, unbroken and as yet unruined. He props his elbows on the arms of the chair and knits his fingers together.

"Mrs. Weston," he says, "I'm Robert Shipley. With the police department." She turns her head toward the window and stares at the night coming on. "I hope we can talk," he says. "I need to ask you about what happened."

About what happened, she repeats to herself. What happened. What happened. Happened. The word becoming ridiculous and numb. Hap hap happened. Happenstance. Hapless. Happy. . .

"Can you tell me?" he says, then a pause, "Do you know what happened? Do you know about your husband? About your son?"

She turns to see his eyes, blue and unexpectedly soft, and nods. "You know they're both dead," he says, and she nods again.

"Who killed your son, Mrs. Weston? Ethan, that was his name, wasn't it?" And that little word closes her eyes like fingers passing over the eyelids of the newly dead. She cannot bear to look at Shipley and feels herself shrink into the bed. She can barely breathe, as though he were sitting on her chest.

"I know this is hard," he says, "but you're the only one who can tell us what happened. We have to know."

Her mind fills with the sound of dishes and rage crashing into the wall all about her and suddenly David's hand is pressing on her shoulder as he struggles to keep himself from sinking to the floor, and the hidden softness of his heart passes down the length of the knife and into her hand. She lets go a little moan. *I'm so sorry.*

Shipley says nothing as she floats high above the kitchen, looking down at the blood billowing out across the floor and the little body lying against the wall, barely visible beneath the woman who holds him to her chest. She floats above the kitchen, held aloft by the warmth of blood and life escaping that rises like a vapor to meet her on its way to the cold and starlit sky at her back. A door opens and a man walks into the room, hands in his pockets as he walks amidst the wreckage, his head shaking slowly back and forth. And then he looks up at her.

She breathes in a lung full of air and lets it go with a sigh and David's name. "I killed him."

"You killed your husband?"

"Yes."

"And Ethan?" he says, saying the name carefully as he drops his hands into his lap. He leans his head to one side to get a better view of her face.

"David," she says.

"Your husband killed Ethan."

"Yes."

"How did he do that?"

She is watching the words retrieved from someplace inside herself that she doesn't know. "He threw him," she says.

"He threw him?"

"Yes. At me."

"What happened then?"

"What do you mean?"

"Ethan. . . "

She shakes her head. "The wall. He hit the wall," a numbness creeping across her face and through her mind, borne on the sound of Ethan's neck against the wall, her body turning into lead cell by cell. She is far away and alone, her words drifting in the air like notes in tiny stoppered bottles thrown into the sea.

He walks to the window and looks out at the lights of the city, hands in his pockets. "Why did he do that?" he says.

A silence swells heavy and thick.

"Mrs. Weston?" he says, turning and leaning against the sill, arms over his chest. "What happened just before he threw Ethan?"

She tries to disengage her mind from the impossible question of why David would throw Ethan against a wall, but she is frozen before the inconceivability of it, the same hands that held her so tenderly, that lifted Ethan onto his lap, hurling Ethan through the air to his death.

"Did he say anything?"

Yes, she thinks, something, "Take him," she says aloud, "he said, 'Take him.'"

"Take him where?"

Katherine shakes her head. "Just take him." The numbness reaches her chest and starts down her arms.

"I don't understand," says Shipley.

"I asked him to give Ethan to me."

"You mean custody?"

"No. Just to give him to me then." She sees the puzzled look on his face. "He was holding him. I wanted him to give him to me."

"Why?"

"I was afraid."

"Of what?"

"That he was going to hurt him."

Shipley looks out the window. "So, you killed your husband to protect Ethan?"

"No."

"Your husband had already killed him by that point?"

"Yes."

He looks at her. "Then why?"

She closes her eyes and she is kneeling on the floor, the smooth tile beneath one hand and the knife handle in the other as David takes the first lunging step and she is suspended between crouching into a ball on the floor and bracing for the blows to come, and rising to meet him like she would a wave rolling toward a beach. She tries to focus on the instant when she rises instead of falls, when her fingers close upon the handle and they rise together as if the blade is an extension of her arm, her entire being drawn up and up toward the soft unguarded spot over the pathway to his heart.

"I didn't want to," she says.

He nods. "Why, then?"

A tear rolls down her cheek. "He was going to kill me," she says, not believing the words even as they pass her lips. How could any of this be true? Who would believe such a thing? Who could walk into that kitchen and find what was there and still believe their own senses? How could anyone who knew this family ever believe it could come to this?

He says something that she doesn't hear.

"What?" she says, the numbness encircling her hips and infusing her womb.

"Why did you think he was going to kill you?"

"The way he looked at me."

"How?"

"Crazy. Enraged."

"Did he have a weapon? A knife?"

"I don't think so," pausing, her eyes moving slowly back and forth, "just his hands. . .and feet. He would have found what he needed. It was time. I knew it was time."

"How did you know?"

"I just knew." And then she looks at him, her eyes searching his face. "And Ethan."

He walks across the room and sits beside the bed. "How did you come by these injuries?"

Katherine looks at him, the words 'come by' sitting in her mind like a roadblock she can't get past.

"Did he beat you up?" Shipley asks.

She shrugs and nods.

"Why?"

"Because I made him angry."

"What did you do that made him angry?"

She looks out the window, trying to focus on what they were talking about before he started in on her. Slowly, she reconstructs the day in her mind, seeing herself straighten up her classroom and look at her watch, figuring the time until she would meet Susan for coffee. It was her birthday. Her students had sung to her.

"I was late getting home from school," she says. "And I only had time to heat up a leftover casserole and I stopped for coffee with Susan because it was my birthday and he was mad that he'd forgot and he thought I was going to leave him," the words tumbling into silence as the pinched look comes across her face once again and then a hot flash of embarrassment and shame. Something happens when she speaks the reasons into the air and hears them with her own ears. Those can't be the reasons, she thinks to herself. They are too small to be the cause of this.

"He couldn't help it," she says. "He was so angry."

"Had he been drinking?"

She nods.

"Had he done this before?"

"Drink?"

"Yes, and beat you up."

She nods again.

"How long?"

Katherine tries to remember when it was that the threat of his violence took over her life, but it reaches back so far she cannot fix a point when it began.

"Years," she says.

"Did you ever call the police?"

"Yes. Once."

"And what happened then?"

"They came."

"And?"

"They took David into the kitchen and talked to him," she says. "I couldn't hear."

"What did they say to you?"

"Counseling," she says. "They suggested counseling."

"Why didn't you press charges?"

"They asked me if I wanted my husband in jail, but that would only make it worse, him in jail, coming home," her head shaking back and forth.

"Why didn't you leave?"

The numbness spreads to her legs and feet. She is disappearing, leaving only her voice and a small portion of her brain behind to manage while the rest of her is away.

"Mrs. Weston?" His voice sounds far off and watery. He is leaning forward, his eyes fixed on her face.

She slowly turns what remains of her attention to the soft blue eyes.

"I was wondering why you didn't leave your husband."

"I did," she says.

"What happened then?"

"He came and got me. He said he'd kill us."

"You could've gotten a protective order."

She shakes her head and looks out the window. He does not understand. He thinks the world is a rational place where protective orders protect. He assumes a woman can be beaten only if she stays and that once she leaves, safety is available if only she will ask.

She will not tell him about the counselor who urged patience, the minister who spoke of love, faith, and forgiveness, the divorce lawyer who looked at her as if she were a prostitute who'd come to complain about being raped. She will not tell him about the people who asked, earnestly, what was happening, and as soon as she found the courage to tell, turned away, averted their eyes, changed the subject, paid the check and hurried off. Nor will she tell him about the women in her life — her sister-in-law, her mother, her friends, even Susan — who would not accept the enormity of what was happening to her.

The clouds have moved away and she fixes her gaze on Venus shining just above the horizon. She hears the rustle of Shipley's suit as he stands and moves away from the chair. The silence is punctuated only by the sound of her own breathing against the background of movement beyond the door, a metal cart rolling by, voices passing in the hall, elevator doors. A siren wails from the street below, coming near and then receding in the distance. She is completely numb now and can feel even that small residual portion of her mind rising above the bed, her voice in tow not far behind like a dinghy drawn by a boat setting out on a dark and moonless sea.

"I'm very sorry," he says. She does not hear him leave.

3

*T*he sun has been up for hours, but Lucy is still asleep in the rocker, head slumped forward and hands resting in her lap. Her slow and steady breathing is occasionally broken by a lilting snore that prompts a thump from the tail of Sophie who lies in her bed by the stove. A goat blats from the barn to protest the lateness of the hour. And then heavy footsteps on the back porch and a knocking at the door bring Sophie stiffly to her feet with a cascade of barks that flow together in a soaring moan of alarm.

Lucy wakes and squints into the sunlight streaming through the window. She swings her head to see Walter's bulbous nose as he peers through the back door glass, one hand over his eyes to shade against the glare of the morning light slanting across the yard and over his shoulder.

She is annoyed to be caught in this way, uncomposed, dressed only in a nightgown, robe and slippers, hardly awake enough to form a thought. "Hell," she says, rocking forward and spilling her weight onto her feet. Her neck is stiff and for a moment she stoops and stares into Sophie's upturned, panting muzzle.

"Oh, go away," she says with a wave of her hand, to which Sophie only pants harder and stamps her feet. Lucy straightens herself and shuffles toward the door where Walter waits, his breath fogging the air. She opens the door and Sophie dashes out and around the side of the house.

"You okay?" He leans to one side as he looks up beneath her hands that shield her face from the sun. "I was driving by and saw the barn still closed up and wondered if everything was all right."

"I'm fine, Walter," she says. "Thank you."

"You sure?"

"Of course." She sighs. "You want a cup of coffee?" She'd rather not invite him in but can't think how not to without hurting his feelings or arousing his concern and curiosity even more.

"Oh, no," he says, "that's all right. I just wanted to make sure nothing had. . .happened."

She squints at him and is reminded of why she has always liked him, his large brown eyes nestled in a faceful of loose skin aged to a leathery wrinkle by years of outdoor work. Cow eyes, she thinks, big cow eyes with a coat of moisture that suggests a tender sadness.

"I had a long night is all," she says. "Nothing to worry about. Thank you, Walter."

He nods. "Well, good then," he says, straightening himself. "You take care of yourself, Lucy."

"And you," she says. "Say hello to Margaret." Her eyes follow him across the packed snow, lifting his hand in a wave as he rounds the corner of the house.

She feeds Sophie and then pulls on her coat and makes for the barn where she finds the goats waiting for her just inside the door. Gertrude, the eldest, stamps her feet and looks up into Lucy's face, her long bony head cocked to one side.

"Don't you start," says Lucy pushing past, "it's none of your business." And then she feels them encircle her to the rustle of hooves on hay, curious, heads upraised, coats fluffed out against the cold, and she stands among them, motionless, her hands resting on the warm fur along their backs, her eyes closed, breathing in the sweet familiar scent of the barn and the lingering sense of peace carried on the breath of creatures who sleep and dream together through each long winter night.

As she loads hay into the bin she thinks of Katherine Weston. She knows almost nothing about her and yet feels as though she knows a great deal. She imagines her in a hospital bed, alone and avoided by all those who feel ashamed or embarrassed or contemptuous or repulsed by the sight of her. Above all, alone. The blessing and the curse. Her husband is dead. Her little boy is dead. And there she lies, still alive to bear the enormity of what has happened, of what he has done, of what she has done, through the rest of her life.

She wonders if police and prosecutors have figured it out by now and are content to leave her be. And she wonders who will have her and where she will go, this woman with the battered body and ruined life.

Inside the house she puts the kettle on and drags the rocker into the library. Sophie lifts her head from her morning nap, watches Lucy load the stove, then yawns and lays her head back down to sleep.

It is just past 9:00 when the phone rings.

"It's Ruth."

"Yes."

"Are you all right?"

"Of course."

"Oh, good. I was worried. My service said you called at 3:00 in the morning, and I figured it was something bad."

"Well, yes, it is, but not about me."

"Is it — "

"No, dear, everyone's fine. I'm sorry to have startled you so. I must have lost track of the time and didn't realize what you might think. I'm sorry."

"That's okay. So, what is it then?"

She shifts the phone to her other ear. She doesn't quite know herself why she called and now waits for the answer to come to her. "Have you heard," she says at last, "about the woman near Boston who killed her husband? The one whose little boy was killed?"

"The Weston case?"

"Katherine."

"Yes."

"I read it in the *Globe*," says Lucy, "and was wondering how it's going. I know that must sound odd, calling you up in the middle of the night, but I wanted to know. I know she couldn't possibly be all right, but — "

"I don't know much, Lucy. Only what I've read in the papers. I think she's still in the hospital."

In the silence that follows, Ruth looks out the window of her law office to the busy street below lined with piles of dirty late-winter snow, and wonders about her friend living alone in the wilds of northern Vermont at the tail end of a long, cold winter. She isn't surprised by Lucy's interest in Katherine Weston, but she is unsettled by the sense of urgency that comes with it.

"Oh," says Lucy.

"Is there something you want me to do?"

"Well, I know you must be terribly busy — "

"Lucy," says Ruth, "don't worry about that. Just tell me what you want. If I can't do it, I'll say so."

Lucy is surprised at the difficulty she is having expressing herself. She is unused to that, especially in relation to this younger woman who was a child when she first knew her. She is about to feel foolish but pulls herself back just in time. "I was wondering if you'd look into it. I'm happy to pay you for your time. I know how annoying it is when friends call you up and — "

"Lucy. Stop."

"I know. All right."

"Tell me what can I do."

Lucy makes a sigh. "I'm not sure. I have a feeling. I can't get her out of my mind. And her little boy. I keep thinking I'm supposed to do something. The paper mentioned they might charge her with a crime of some sort."

"They might," says Ruth. "They probably shouldn't, but I've seen dumber things than that. It'll come down to what they think happened to the boy. If they decide he killed him then she's got a much better chance of claiming self-defense. But I'll tell you, Lucy, these days the courts are locking up a lot of women who kill men who beat them up. I know it doesn't make sense but there isn't much sympathy out there. You don't kill the king in his castle and get away with it."

"But there's a chance for her, isn't there?"

"Yes."

"And what then?" says Lucy. "What becomes of her? Where will she go?"

"She must have family."

"Yes, but will they want her? Now? And will she want them?"

"I don't know," says Ruth. "We don't know this woman, Lucy. We know nothing about her really."

"I know that."

"There's no way to know where this might go."

"I suppose I sound foolish."

"Not at all."

"And if I did, would you say so?"

"Of course."

Lucy nods. "So."

"I could try to find out what family she has," says Ruth. "That's the place to start."

"Yes."

"I'll let you know."

"Thank you."

"How are you, by the way? Has the winter been hard?"

"It's always hard," says Lucy. "You remember. No harder than usual."

"How's Sophie?"

"Stiff. But happy. Like me." The two women laugh. "And you? Are you well? Do you still like lawyering?"

"Mostly. But I don't know if I'm cut out to be a city girl. I miss you all."

"Well," says Lucy, "it would be good to see your face. Perhaps it won't be too long until I do."

"I'll be in touch."

"Yes. Thank you, Ruthie. Goodbye."

Lucy makes a second cup of tea and carries it to her mother's chair in the library. She thinks of Ruth, the girl who became a regular visitor all through high school, often stopping off to say hello on her way home. Ruth, who never came home from college or law school without making the trek to the top of the hill. Ruth, who always seemed to know more than Lucy expected, who saw but did not speak of what she made of it, leaving the knowledge to lie between them, like a sealed envelope they silently agreed to leave unopened.

She sits and drinks and rocks and wonders what she will do next and feels the expansive freedom of knowing it is entirely up to her. Whether she goes upstairs for a nap or takes a walk or sits among the goats or reads or drives to town. Whether she puts on underwear or simply throws overalls over her nightgown. Whether she eats and what and when. Who she talks to or visits or welcomes into her home or, for that matter, into her bed, even now. And for none of it is she accountable to anyone.

She lifts her knees and rests her heels on the lip of the chair, thinking of Katherine Weston and knowing she's lived for years without any of the freedom or safety that Lucy takes for granted now, always on the run inside herself, hunched over, afraid to raise herself up to her full height lest she draw attention or appear too proud, always braced in anticipation of the senseless blow that's yet to come. And above all, tormented by the incomprehensibility of such a life, set against a desperate need to understand what was happening to her.

A squirrel darts across the snow, sunlight silver through its fluffed out fur. Lucy rests the tea on the window sill, then stands and crosses the room to the stereo that Michael put in a few years ago. She roots through a small pile of tapes until she finds the Bach solo cello suites. Lucy remembers the sight of her mother and her cello in this same room when it was almost filled by the long table and chairs. She would turn a chair to the east window Lucy now favors for herself, and spread her knees and embrace the body of the beautiful instrument, its luster warmed by the soft light through the window. She would sit for a moment, the fingers of one hand poised above the strings, the bow in the other by her side, her head bent down and to the right as if attending to a small bird perched on her shoulder and whispering a secret. Lucy would stand in the kitchen and look through the doorway, still, not wanting to disturb what seemed a reverential moment. And then her mother would slowly lift her head to gaze out on the fields and hills beyond the window, her hand rising from her side and drawing the bow across the strings in a tone so vibrant, deep, and slow it never failed to close Lucy's eyes and make her sink just a little toward the floor around the softening that flowed downward through her spine and hips and into her knees.

Lucy sits as the sweet rolling sound fills the room. She tilts her head and looks into the kitchen where Sophie lies sleeping beside the stove. Even at a distance Sophie senses the attention and cocks an eye in her direction. They look at each other for a moment and then Sophie lifts her head and pulls herself to her feet. She gets up and hobbles into the library and lies down with a soft grunt on an old blanket folded beside the rocking chair. Lucy sits back, her arm hanging down, fingers gently playing in the fur along Sophie's back.

"So much violence," she says, "so much rage."

She looks at Sophie's upturned face.

"Come on," she says.

Sophie is on her feet almost at once with deep grunts of anticipation. Lucy goes into the kitchen and pulls on boots and coat, draws a purple hat down over her ears and thrusts her hands into wool mittens. Sophie is whimpering now, toenails clacking on the floor as she stamps her feet by the back door. Lucy adds a log to the stove and then they are out the door and into the sunlit snow beneath a big sky.

They walk together out behind the barn and then down the hill sloping toward a grove of sugar maples. Lucy bends and scoops a handful of snow, packs it into a ball, and throws it into the air with a whoop. Sophie dashes along the line of flight, looking up over her shoulder like an out-fielder shagging a long hit ball, and then stops, turns, and rises just a bit off her front paws to bite the snowball out of the air. Lucy throws another and then another until they reach the maples where the snow lies soft and deep. She stops to catch her breath and closes her eyes as she breathes the cold air deep into her lungs. "So," she says, opening her eyes to search the bright blue sky above, "what?"

4

*K*atherine hurts whenever she moves. She wishes she could just sleep and wake up in another place, another body, another life, but she keeps waking to the same view out the same window, the same sounds up and down the hall, the same body, the same visions of blood and ruin, the feel of Ethan's skin cooling beneath her fingers.

She has lost all sense of time, whether it's night or day or Tuesday or Saturday, and the more she struggles to pin it down the more weary she becomes until she realizes it doesn't matter. Because everything has come undone, including something deep inside that she can feel only as an all-consuming absence, an immense vacuum that collapses her entire being into a speck floating through the cosmos, invisible and unknown.

When her mother, Eleanor, enters the room, bent nearly to a crouch, tentative and afraid, Katherine imagines her approaching from a great distance, a form on the horizon, barely discernible as human. And so when her mother speaks, Katherine hears her from afar, a tiny voice probing for some response.

"It's your mother," she says, taking Katherine's hand and then starting to cry as she does on every visit, mascara streaming down her face. Katherine feels herself going numb once again, but this time something draws her back as a tear gathers in the corner of her eye, pausing like a diver at the edge of a high board before it falls, pulling Katherine into the room and the touch of her mother's hands and drawing a wail from deep inside her emptiness.

Eleanor stops crying and looks frantically toward the door. "Katherine," she says, patting her hand, "It's all right. Please. It's all right," but knowing it's not all right and that nothing she can do will make it so. She drops Katherine's hand and sits back as if pinned to the chair as Katherine covers her face with her hands. The door opens and Richard appears, his face stricken as he rushes to his wife and stands behind her, looking back and forth between Katherine and the neat grey curls on Eleanor's head.

Nothing in the lives of Katherine's parents has prepared them for this. Their daughter has entered another world, bound up in the murder of her own son and covered in her husband's blood spilled by her own hand. When they visit the house to fetch some of her clothes, they are horrified by what they see in the kitchen, a vision that thrusts them into a nightmare brought back from the depths of some tortured sleep and made visible and touchable in the light of day. It is no longer a kitchen. It is a slaughterhouse, a piece of hell, and they shrink from it with a gasp, fingers over their mouths, eyes cast down. They hurry upstairs and Eleanor gathers clothes from the closet and the cherry bureau they gave Katherine as a housewarming present. Richard sits on the bed and looks down at his feet rolled outward and sole against sole like a boy's. They say nothing about what they have seen — not then or anytime after, the violence and the blood and the horror unspeakable between them.

And so the grief erupting from Katherine drives them from the room, Richard helping Eleanor to her feet and gently pushing her toward the door as he looks back over his shoulder. He turns and walks toward the foot of the bed. "Katherine," he says, "we'll come back another time," but she doesn't hear through the sobs pouring out from behind her hands.

The memories come suddenly and without warning, exploding into consciousness like a clap of thunder from a cloudless sky and with such ferocity she hardly knows what to do in the face of them except to yell or cover her eyes. They never come as coherent memory, a story, a sequence of actions or images, but always as a fragment out of context, a disembodied fist emerging from the dark to smash into her face. She might suddenly be overcome by the smell of liquor on David's breath as he would labor on top of her and draw in close to sneer something in her ear. Or she might panic as if wakened in the middle of the night and dragged from bed onto the cold hard floor. Or she relives the instant when he put his hand on top of her head as she lay soaking in a hot bath and pushed her down and held her there.

And Ethan is everywhere. There is no place, no sunlit view, no dark corner of dreamless sleep where his face cannot suddenly appear, or the smell of his hair or the sound of his voice as she tucks him in and feels his arms around her neck.

This is how the phantoms come upon her — immediate, vivid, and real whether sleeping or awake. When she dreams of the bath she wakes each time clawing the air and breathing in gulps dissolving into sobs. And so she does not sleep, or sleeps, but badly, and wakes more weary than before, head pounding, breathing shallow and tight as though he still holds her by the throat.

The room is empty. Her parents have been here. She knows this but little else for sure, and even this lacks a clear or certain meaning she can grab hold of. Her life feels as unreal to her as if it never actually happened but only lingers in her mind like the vague, elusive memory, an odd lot of fragments, clips of conversation.

It seems she was never a girl or a young woman or a wife and mother. There never was a Katherine who read voraciously and all the time — on the bus going to school in the morning or after dinner instead of watching television, even in the pup tent out back on summer evenings. No Katherine who never traveled without a half-dozen books in her suitcase whose weight made David groan in protest when he lifted it into the trunk of the car.

Why couldn't she take just one? he wanted to know.

Because she never knew what she might want to read.

There was never a Katherine who sat in the window seat of her room while her parents slept down the hall, and gazed up at the moon and stars and wondered. No Katherine who loved so deeply it made her groan just to think of it, who carried a baby inside her and then pushed and bled him into the world and fed him from the miracle that pulsed through her own body.

There is no such Katherine. She is obliterated and gone and as she melts away inside herself so does her connection to anyone who might have thought they knew her. They come to see her. They open the door slowly and walk in quietly, heels never touching the floor, leaning in to look at her as if peering into the shadow of a hooded face. Often she is asleep or pretending so, and they stand for awhile looking from her to the window and sky and then back again. Sometimes they whisper her name. And then they leave, relieved to have done what they came to do and not obliged to come again.

Or a flicker of recognition passes between them before they look away, the one from the pain and Katherine from her own reflection in their eyes. "I'm so sorry," they say, or "How are you?" or even "Is there anything I can do?" but Katherine doesn't know what to say or cannot bear to say it. They look helpless and overwhelmed by the enormity of the horror that swirls around this woman they thought they knew, this neighbor, colleague, friend, this mother of the little boy who used to come over and join their children in play. Then comes the awkward silence, the shuffling feet, the anguished, furtive look, the apology born on a sigh and followed by a softly mumbled goodbye.

Even Susan cannot bear to stay for long in the presence of such loss and ruination. It is the same feeling she has when she encounters someone horribly disfigured or whose body has been ravaged by some terrible disease, their arms and legs and necks cocked at bizarre angles, fingers bent like claws, mouths contorted in tortured garbled speech. It is a feeling deeper than embarrassment or even shame and closer to fear than she allows herself to know.

Jack flies in from San Francisco a few days after Ethan's funeral. His mother makes tea and they sit in the living room facing into the gardens out back, now covered with crusty late-winter snow. Sun streams through the windows, illuminating particles of dust dancing on currents of air.

"So," he says, "how is she?"

"Terrible," she says, releasing the word as if she'd been carrying it around for days behind clenched teeth. Richard gently lays a hand on her arm.

"Is there permanent damage?"

"She lost her spleen," says Richard.

"Can she do without it?"

"I think so. From what I gather, it's not good for her immune system. But nothing critical."

"What else?"

"Well," says Richard, "she's pretty banged up inside. They had to repair her kidneys and liver. She was bleeding quite a lot. It was pretty close there for awhile." His voice trails to a hush. "And she cracked some ribs."

"Three," says Eleanor, not lifting her head.

"Yes. And her left eardrum was burst and her eyes pretty swollen. But her hearing and vision should be all right."

"Her nose," says Eleanor.

"Oh, yes. Her nose was broken. And a few teeth."

"And her hair," she says, setting down her cup and beginning to cry.

"Her hair?" says Jack.

"Some of it was. . .pulled out," says Richard, looking out the window.

"Good God," says Jack. "It's unbelievable."

Eleanor leans into Richard's arms and begins to sob. Jack goes to the window, puts his hands in his pockets and looks into the yard where he and Katherine used to play.

"Did they just go crazy or something?" he asks, turning back to the room.

"No one seems to know," says Richard.

"Had anything like this happened before?"

Eleanor stops crying and blows her nose. "Well," she says, "of course they had problems. After all, who doesn't? But certainly nothing like this." Her eyes seek out Richard who looks at her for a moment and then turns his head toward the window.

"And then there's Ethan," says Jack, shaking his head.

"Oh, God," says Eleanor, choking down sobs to make room for the words. "It is simply unforgivable. That little boy. So innocent."

Richard looks at her. "Surely you don't blame Katherine. Not for that."

She looks at Richard and at Jack and then away.

"Eleanor?" says Richard.

Eleanor stiffens her jaw. "She was his mother."

"And?" says Richard. "What are you getting at?"

"I'm not sure I know," Eleanor says. "Maybe it's that she might have protected him better. Or taken him away. Or done something about her marriage. I mean, it can't *all* have been David's fault. It takes two to make a marriage and two to make it wrong. And now two people are dead, and she *killed* one of them. My *daughter*, Jack's *sister*, killed her husband. She stabbed him in the heart with a kitchen knife for God's sake."

"And *he* killed Ethan," Richard says. "Have you forgotten that?"

"Of course not," she says, her voice rising, angry now, "but there she is, our Katherine, my little girl, in the middle of this awful bloody mess strewn across her kitchen floor and the front page of the *Globe*."

Richard looks at her, his eyes wide, then at Jack, who looks away.

Eleanor carries the tray into the kitchen. Richard's gaze follows her out of the room.

"How long will she be in the hospital?" says Jack. Richard says nothing, his eyes fixed on Eleanor in the kitchen. "Dad?"

"What?"

"I asked how long she'll be there."

"Another week or so," says Richard and then in a quiet voice, looking into his lap, "It's been very hard on your mother."

Jack nods and sighs. "I can hardly blame her."

When the door swings open and Katherine sees Jack step into the room, they are silent as he leans back against the wall, hands in his pockets, and looks at her. She imagines the sight of her barricaded behind a wall of pillows piled on either side and across her chest, her arms and face bruised purple and yellow, eyes swollen, her hair wild and strange.

"Hi," he says, and when it occurs to her that he came all the way from California to see her, she begins to cry. She hears him sit down on the chair by the bed, his hand touching her arm.

She reaches for a tissue to wipe her face and blow her nose. "How can you stand to look at me?"

He shrugs. "It's not easy." There is a pause and then, "I'm sorry," and he looks away, shaking his head, "It's unbelievable."

"I know." She looks at him, noticing the thick muscles around his neck and shoulders, and remembers the Jack who used to wrestle her to the ground when she defied him, and who sat on her, pinning her shoulders beneath his knees and riding her like a bucking horse as she reared her hips and belly beneath him and screamed at him to get off. But he was bigger and stronger and could wait her out and only when she quieted beneath him like a broken colt, sullen and resigned to the weight of his authority, would he agree to get off.

She crumples the tissue into a little ball in her hand.

"Is there anything I can do?" he says, not looking at her.

She looks at him and then away. "I don't know what to do," she says. "There are all these things that have to be sorted out." Her voice drifts toward him in disjointed bits and pieces, like faintly overheard conversation from a nearby table in a restaurant.

"I don't know if I have any money to live on. I can't remember anything about that or focus long enough to. . . " She shakes her head. "I can't imagine going back to school . . . There's the house, but I don't know how much of it we own. I don't even know how I'm going to pay for all this. . ."

Suddenly he stands and goes to the window, looking out, and she feels startled and then frightened by the sudden release of energy from his body, as if he had leapt away from her and thrown himself at her at the same time.

"What?" she says, shrinking into the pillows.

"Nothing. I just need to move around a little." He stands looking out the window. "I'll see what I can do," he says. "I can't stay long. I have to get back pretty soon. But I'll do what I can before I go."

"You don't have to," she says.

"Yes, I do."

Katherine dreams of Ethan and when she wakes and remembers she begins to cry as she feels the enormous empty space where he used to be.

She dreads the emptiness the most, something in her core gone missing beyond the reach even of memory, the sense of absence always there, appearing in the subconscious like the vague discomfort of something you were supposed to remember but whose only trace is the fading sense that you did not.

5

*O*nly a few hours before Lucy called, Ruth was staying up late watching a video of *Six Degrees of Separation*, a story based on the idea that any two people in the world are separated by no more than six degrees, one person knowing someone who knows someone who knows the other person with no more than six 'someones' or degrees between the first and the last. She finds it ironic that this idea should be fresh in her mind when Lucy asks her to find out about Katherine Weston's parents. As she hangs up the phone she wonders how many degrees stand between Lucy and who she's looking for.

It occurs to her that the principle doesn't quite apply in this case because Katherine is in the news and Ruth has a friend at the *Globe* whom she calls right away. He calls back within the hour to tell her that Katherine Weston's mother and father live near the shore north of Boston. A brother lives out of state. No sisters. The family name is Stuart.

She calls Lucy later in the morning.

As the day goes on, Lucy feels herself caught like a leaf in an eddy of a slow moving stream, pulled along and held back at the same time, all the while moving in circles, waiting for the subtle shift that will tip the balance and send her on her way.

Just past noon, the sun low in the southern sky, something waits to be born. Some intention, some act of will, some movement off of center, but in its own time, she knows, if at all. She eats her lunch in the library, looking out the east window, the plate balanced on her knees. She feels itchy and skittish and doesn't know what to do.

Clouds thicken in the west and it begins to snow. She stands with her face near the window and looks out at the heavy flakes falling in the yard. Sophie walks in from the kitchen and sits beside her and they look out the window together until Lucy turns and goes upstairs.

She walks down the hall toward the doorway to the attic and stops outside Michael's old room. It looks the same as when he went to Vietnam so many years ago and returned as a man who couldn't find his own way home. He visited but never stayed for more than a night or two and even then, inexplicably, always in the guestroom, never in the room he'd slept in as a boy.

The model he built of the *U.S.S. Constitution* is on top of the bureau in the far corner of the room. His small writing desk sits in the opposite corner next to a bookcase of remnants from the collection he amassed over the first two decades of his life. There is Oz and the Hardy Boys and Horatio Hornblower on the top shelf. Below lies what he might call more serious stuff — plane geometry, *Walden*, *Ten Days that Shook the World*, *One Flew Over the Cuckoo's Nest*, *The Complete Sherlock Holmes*, *Leaves of Grass*, the Raven edition of Edgar Allen Poe, and Bertrand Russell's thick tome on western philosophy, which Michael had borrowed from her on a whim (or so she thought). He never got past the first few pages but held onto it just the same and she never thought to take it back.

He took the rest of his books when he moved to Burlington several months after the North Vietnamese and then the Army let him go. He worked in a small bookstore near the university and when the owner decided to retire he arranged to continue on and eventually assume ownership himself with the help of a loan from her.

She walks into the room and sits on the iron bed that stands with its foot against the window, affording an expansive view of the western hills. She remembers the day the house suddenly filled with the sound of his bed scraping across the floor as he dragged it from its place against the wall.

"What are you doing?"

"I want to look out," was all he said with a shrug.

"Good idea. You'll have a fine view."

She remembers the boy's voice, pure and full of intent, "I want to look out."

Standing in the doorway she wonders if she might turn the room to some more useful purpose but cannot think of one.

She walks past the guest room and opens the attic door, cold air from above sinking down around her ankles. She turns on the light and climbs the stairs, closing the door behind. At the top she looks toward a gable end of the house where snow falls outside a half-moon window and only then does she wonder what has brought her here. She looks around. Along one side, stacked against a kneewall, is an assortment of trunks and boxes full of old clothes, games, children's toys, photographs, tax records, linens. A discarded floor lamp tilts precariously to one side, it's shade torn and cocked at an angle like a hat on a woman striking an attitude. A wooden kitchen chair sits nearby.

On the opposite wall are piles of books, the overflow from downstairs, the ones she's unlikely to read a second time and would give away were she not such a squirrel given to nesting among ideas and images and stories. She holds onto them to keep company with a great multitude who've been where she's going and it comforts her to think of so many, so near.

She pulls the chair over and sits and scans the faded titles barely visible in the light cast by the bulb hanging from the ceiling. She does this from time to time on the off chance she'll encounter an old friend and renew their acquaintance. Her eyes move rapidly across the rows of books, deep in a section of long forgotten biographies, when she is startled by two titles juxtaposed. She sits up and looks away to the window, the snow falling faster now, and then slides off the chair and comes to rest on her knees where she can get a closer view. Catherine de Médicis adjoins Mary Stuart, Queen of Scots in such a way that the given name of the one aligns with the surname of the other.

She sits back on her heels with a sigh and lays her hands on each other in her lap. She is still for several minutes, the quiet so deep she almost thinks she can hear the snow landing on the roof. Then she leans on the chair to bring herself to her feet, wincing from the pain in her hips and knees, and walks to the far side of the attic where she picks among the boxes until she finds an old leather suitcase which she carries downstairs, forgetting to turn the light off as she closes the door.

The last time Lucy was on a bus was in 1975 when she went over to Burlington to visit Michael in the hospital. Her car was in the shop getting a new radiator and Walter drove her into Montpelier where she caught the afternoon express. She sat in the front seat, her small leather suitcase beside her. The bus was crowded and she passed the time staring out the window and thinking about Michael.

In many ways his recovery had been remarkable and it was only to be expected that he'd have times like this when everything seemed to come apart. He had spent almost two years in a North Vietnamese prison and the harshness of the treatment he received was not softened by the fact that he was a medic and not a combat soldier. From what she could gather from the little he told her, he was beaten and tortured as part of an almost daily routine designed to punish the body and break the spirit so that he might say and do what they wanted. And they wanted more than anything that he admit that U.S. involvement in Vietnam was a fraud and a crime against humanity. And behind their wanting was a tightly controlled rage such as he had never encountered before, not even in his father.

It always seemed ironic to her that Michael, of all people, should have found himself in that position. More than most of his peers he let his ambivalence about the war show through his lack of enthusiasm for the romantic lure of proving his manhood through patriotic combat. She saw in him a gentle and thoughtful man and was surprised when he decided to go, even as a medic. She would have stood by him through almost any alternative, including refusing the draft and even prison if it came to that. They also had friends in Montreal who would gladly take him in and the Canadian border was just a short drive away. But something bound him to this nightmare in a way he couldn't shake loose.

It is Lucy's way to move quickly once she decides to go. She asks Walter to take Sophie for a few days and drive her to the bus station. He thinks for a moment on whether to ask what this is all about before he says, "Yes, of course," and she thanks him and he can hear in the little silence before she says it her gratitude for his not asking. She calls Jason who will tend the goats first thing each morning on his way to school and again on the way home. Walter will come by in the evening to put them in for the night. She calls Michael and leaves a message on his machine that she'll be in Boston for several days, then calls Ruth.

She packs her suitcase before going to bed. Sophie sits in the corner and watches, thumping her tail whenever Lucy looks her way, and pushing a groan from her throat.

"Don't you worry," says Lucy. "You like Walter. He'll probably treat you better than I do." But Sophie is not reassured and the more Lucy talks, the more she thumps and squeaks.

Getting to sleep is more drawn out than usual. She lies in the dark and listens to Sophie's breathing slow and deepen as she falls to sleep. She doesn't know why she is going to Boston and tries to push the question from her mind. She has no plan other than to get there, going almost completely on instinct, carried by the belief that once she puts herself in motion the next step will make itself known in time for her to take it.

Sophie whimpers and kicks her feet as if running while lying on her side. Chasing rabbits, Lucy thinks, unless she is herself the prey of some other, fleeing for her life.

When at last Lucy sleeps, aided by the darkness of the new moon and the steady beat of Sophie breathing in and out, she dreams of an autumn night, wind-blown leaves scuttling and scraping across the ground. Ferns and grasses, yellow and bent low, break beneath her feet as she walks down the hill toward the woods behind the barn. There is no light but she steps as though she can see every stone in her path, every root arching into the air. She nears the line of trees, their trunks drawn dark against a blue black sky, and her feet are drawn unerringly to a small square cobblestone set into the ground, luminous even in the dark, and she bends down and touches it with an outstretched finger and the earth begins to soften and move.

She wakes with a start to Sophie sitting by the bed, her muzzle a few inches from Lucy's nose, ears pulled back in alarm. The room is bathed in a still half light, too much for sleep, too little to pull her out of bed. She reaches from beneath the covers and scratches behind Sophie's ears and tries to remember the dream. She closes her eyes and allows her mind to float and wander, but it will not come.

The sun begins to glow behind the crest of the eastern hills and Lucy throws back the covers and swings her legs into the cold air. She walks to the window and looks out at the fresh layer of new snow and then she sees the stone in her mind and shakes her head with a sigh.

Walter arrives at half past nine and they drive to St. Johnsbury. They talk of weather and the possibility of an early spring. Sophie stands on the back seat, her head thrust forward between them.

He inquires about Michael. The bookstore is doing just fine, she says, and he seems happy, or at least enough.

Walter shakes his head. "That was a bad business."

"It was," she says, and they are silent the rest of the way until he opens the trunk and lifts her suitcase onto the curb. He looks at her, his restraint and her appreciation for it filling the space between them.

"You let me know when you're coming back," he says, "and we'll come get you."

"Thank you, Walter." He smiles and touches a finger to his brow in a little salute and she picks up her suitcase and walks into the station.

She sleeps a deep and dreamless sleep all the way to Boston where the driver gently shakes her awake and she looks out the window to see Ruth waving through the window.

Ruth takes Lucy in her arms and hugs her without letting go even when Lucy drops her arms, uncomfortable with such public displays of affection.

Ruth's apartment in Cambridge takes up the third floor of a white frame house that sits just off Mount Auburn Street and a ten minute walk from Harvard Square. It is Lucy's first visit and at first the talk is of Vermont and living in the city and the practice of law. There is no mention of Katherine Stuart until they are sitting at the table after dinner and Ruth asks her if she'd like a second cup of coffee and Lucy shakes her head and looks down while she plays idly with the spoon resting in her saucer. She looks up at Ruth, then away, suddenly embarrassed that her lack of a plan should be so apparent.

"So," says Lucy, "where is she?"

"A little hospital north of here. Do you want me to take you?"

"Yes," says Lucy. "Is it a bad idea?"

"I don't know. What exactly is the idea?"

"For some reason, I keep thinking I'm supposed to be here, as crazy as it sounds. At least it does to me sometimes." She looks at Ruth. "I don't know what I'm supposed to do now that I'm here. That poor woman doesn't know me from a hole in the wall."

"No idea at all?"

"None," says Lucy getting up to clear the table and then sitting back down. "Just before I fell asleep on the bus, I had a sense of being in her room. I was sitting in a chair by the door, looking at her lying in the bed. I don't think she knew I was there. There was so much pain, like a fog, but I felt all right, even peaceful if you can imagine. I just sat there. Didn't say a word."

"What happened then?"

"I fell asleep."

Their eyes meet and Ruth smiles. "I'm glad you're here," she says, remembering Lucy's way of doing things that brought them together years ago, drawing her to the Dudley farm and the solitary woman who spoke whatever came into her mind, surrounded by goats and books, sometimes forgetting to take off her boots when she came into the house, bits of hay stuck in wads of goat scat jutting out from beneath her feet. She couldn't resist the way Lucy thought about the world and lived in it at the same time, as if nothing separated one from the other. She might be talking about a poem or the meaning of death and Ruth would realize she was talking while holding a goat by the leg and clipping its hooves, her hip wedging the animal against the wall of the barn to keep it still, the words drifting up in bits and pieces over her shoulder between breaths.

They clear the table and stand at the sink doing dishes. "Where's Sophie?" says Ruth.

"Having a sleep-over at Walter's." Lucy rests her arms on the edge of the sink. "Do you think they'll let her go?"

Ruth nods. "They found some of the father's skin under the boy's fingernails. They're pretty sure he killed him. Which makes her lucky in a perverse sort of way."

"They'd have charged her with murder?"

"It happens all the time. The law says you can't kill someone in self-defense unless they're about to kill you, and since he didn't have a weapon the law says she can't use one either. It's all based on hypothetical encounters between men in barrooms. It has to be a fair fight. You can't use guns and knives to defend against feet and fists."

Lucy shakes her head. "A fair fight."

"Yes, I know," says Ruth. "They have no idea of women being tortured and terrorized in their own homes. The closest they get is seeing her as deranged — battered women's syndrome or some such thing. So even if they acquit her they want to put her away. They're more likely to convict her of a lesser charge like manslaughter."

"But it doesn't occur to them that she acted reasonably in defense of her life."

"No," says Ruth. "But the little boy changed all that."

"I don't want to make things worse," says Lucy. "I don't want to upset her."

"I know."

"I wish I knew what I was supposed to do."

"Maybe it's not about something you do," says Ruth. "Maybe it's just showing up."

"Answering the call."

"Yes."

Lucy sleeps poorly amid sounds of traffic and neighbors so close she can sometimes make out the details of their conversation. It is, she thinks, an unnatural way to live. At night the only things up and about should be skunks and loons and owls and the occasional deer or bear silhouetted against the snow. Toward dawn she sleeps for a few restless hours but then is awakened by the sound of Ruth making breakfast.

They drive north beneath a dingy white sky.

Katherine's mind is clearing beneath a lower dose of morphine. It is a mixed blessing, the dull haze gone but in its place an unrelenting flood of memory roaring through her mind and pelting her from every side with tastes and smells, a wound suddenly torn open, a cry in the middle of the night. She is like the woman in the Greek story, set upon and stoned by a vengeful mob.

She escapes by disappearing into a numb oblivion, but all the while her mind stretches thin across a raw sensitivity that can overwhelm her in an instant. The nurse comes in to take her vital signs and Katherine is so startled by the sight of her that she shouts a cry of shock and alarm that stuns them both. For a moment they are frozen in place, Katherine recoiling into her small fortress of pillows, the nurse backed against the wall, a hand laid on her chest.

"I'm sorry," says Katherine, shaking her head at the inadequacy of anything she might say, perpetually off balance, unable to assemble herself into a coherent whole. She cannot, as her father might say, get a grip on herself, but is instead a collection of mismatched parts that only vaguely resembles a self. She has not looked in a mirror since that night and dreads finding out if she will recognize the reflection.

The nurse works beside her with quiet efficiency and then leaves Katherine staring out the window at a flock of pigeons who busily come and go from the ledge on the building across the way. In her mind she hears them fuss and coo as pigeons do and remembers how she waded among them in the park when she was a girl, a fistful of breadcrumbs held high above the birds bustling about her feet.

She will wonder later why she does not notice the door open and the small figure of a woman enter the room and sit in the chair near the door. She will also wonder why it takes her so long to turn her head to see who is there, and even when she does, why so slowly and so lacking in suspicion or alarm.

She is an old woman, as old as Katherine's grandmother was the year she died. Her face is deeply lined, lips small and thin but not drawn tightly across her face as lips so often are in the old, settling into a kind of grim acceptance of something that goes unspoken and barely remembered. Her eyes look directly at Katherine who can see the softness even at a distance. Wispy strands of white hair stray across her forehead from beneath a purple woven hat. She holds a brown winter coat in her arms, her fingers long and thin against the fabric.

Lucy says nothing, only sits and looks upon Katherine as if standing vigil over an ailing child, lending her presence to a fevered state, asking nothing, not even a word of conversation to help pass the long hours, content and gathered within herself. Katherine looks back at her and wonders who she is. Not a social worker, who'd be full of questions or suggestions or expressions of concern and would move with a mindfulness of schedules and the next appointment. Not just sit there and look at her the way this woman does.

But Katherine does not ask, content to return the steady look from across the room. And in that strange contentment the storm of memory wrapped in numbness dissipates and she feels her body let down its full weight upon the bed. Minutes pass in silence. The old woman turns her head while keeping her gaze upon Katherine's face as if shifting the angle for a better view.

The door opens and startles them both and Lucy is on her feet before the nurse is fully in the room. She looks at the nurse, her face flustered beneath the purple hat, and looks back at Katherine and then back at the nurse.

"I should be going," says Lucy. "I'm sorry." She looks at Katherine. "Goodbye, dear," she says and walks out into the hall.

She hurries away to a place where the corridor widens into a small sitting area and settles herself into a chair by the window, dropping her coat to the floor. She can feel her heart beating and when she looks down her hands are trembling.

She had not prepared herself for the sight of so much damage, yellow bruises around her eyes, bandages on her head and nose, and above all the sense of a person utterly broken and undone. She knows all about the suffering that human beings can inflict on one another, but the details were buried deep in her memory until the moment she sat in the chair and looked at Katherine's face turned toward the window and catching the morning light. The pain Lucy had imagined as she dropped off to sleep on the bus was suddenly palpable, drifting on the air as the face turned away from the window.

For a moment it was all she could do to stay in the room, until she felt the presence of something else between them, an undercurrent beneath the pain and fear that held her there as she sank into the chair, her sense of time and place slipping away until the nurse came into the room.

When Lucy returns the next morning, she brings a book. For more than an hour she sits in the chair by the window of the waiting room and accustoms herself to the sounds of the place.

At a quarter past ten she closes the book, gathers up her hat and coat, and walks down the hall to Katherine's room. She considers knocking but then pushes the door open and goes inside.

She can tell from the stillness in the air that Katherine is asleep. She hangs her things on a hook inside the door and sits in the chair, opens the book on her lap and begins to read. Minutes pass, the silence creating an envelope within the steady stream of sound and movement coming from the hall beyond. Occasionally Lucy lifts her head and looks at her. She surveys the wall of pillows arranged like a fort built by a child. She wonders at the content of her dreams. Birds fly by the window and she pictures the goats in her mind and is speculating on what they're doing when she realizes that Katherine is looking at her.

"Hello," says Katherine.

"Hello."

Katherine's eyes drop to the book in Lucy's lap. "What's that?"

Lucy smiles, "Annie Dillard."

"Oh," says Katherine. She looks out the window and then back at Lucy. "I don't know you."

"No, you don't."

"Do you work here?"

"No."

"I didn't think so."

Lucy closes the book. "It's difficult to explain. I'm not sure I understand it myself."

"Understand what?"

"What I'm doing here."

"Oh."

"It's nothing like that," says Lucy, leaning forward in the chair. "I'm not some kind of kook or anything like that. Really."

"I didn't think you were."

"Well, I can see how you might," says Lucy. "Perhaps I should go."

"You don't have to. I mean, I don't mind you here."

"All right then."

"What's your name?"

"Lucy."

"I'm Katherine."

"Yes. I know."

Katherine looks at her, intent as if waiting for her to finish a sentence. "Which book is it?"

Lucy smiles. "*Pilgrim at Tinker Creek*. Would you like me to read to you?"

"Would you?"

"Of course," says Lucy, opening the book. "Anything in particular?"

"I like the part about seeing. It's near the beginning, I think."

Lucy begins to read and can sense that Katherine is looking right at her. She reads on and after awhile is immersed in a familiar world of frogs and flowing water, light and dark, flying insects and a sky full of stars. She pauses and lifts her head and sees Katherine looking out the window and returns her eyes to the page and reads on. An hour passes and she reaches the end of a chapter and looks up to see that Katherine is asleep. Lucy closes the book. She feels the need to pee and goes into the hall in search of a restroom. When she returns Katherine is sitting up straight in the bed.

"You forgot your coat," she says.

"No, I just stepped out for a moment."

"You know about me," says Katherine.

Lucy pauses to collect herself. "Yes," she says, standing by the chair.

"And what I did."

"And why — "

"Who are you?"

Lucy takes in a slow deep breath. "My name is Lucy. Lucy Dudley. I live in Vermont, up north."

Katherine's face has a puzzled look. She shakes her head. "I don't understand."

"I read about you in the *Globe*."

"But why are you here?"

Lucy sits in the chair. "I've been asking myself that for days. I thought it would be clear once I got here."

"And is it?"

Lucy shrugs. "So far all I've managed is to read to you from a borrowed book. I don't imagine I came all this way for that."

"No. But I liked it, though. Thank you."

On the third day Katherine again asks Lucy to read from *Pilgrim at Tinker Creek* and again she falls asleep, but when she wakes, Lucy is also asleep, snoring lightly, the book open in her lap. Katherine wonders what sort of life she left behind in Vermont, what sort of old woman would come all this way to see her without knowing

113

why. She rearranges the pillows, fluffing up the one on her chest and folding her arms over it. There is something about their falling asleep in each other's presence that both puzzles and comforts her. And frightens her by reminding her that she doesn't know this woman and has no more reason to trust her than she does anyone else, which is no reason at all.

The nurse comes in, takes Katherine's pulse and temperature, and by the time she leaves, Lucy is awake.

"Do you live in the woods?"

"No," says Lucy, "I live on a farm, or what used to be. In my parents' time.

Katherine tries to picture it in her mind. "You have fields. . ."

"Yes."

"And a barn. . ."

"Yes."

"And what else?"

Lucy stretches her arms over her head and yawns. "Some woods and a pond," she looks out the window, "a toolshed, a family plot. And the house, of course."

"What color is the barn?"

"Red."

"What kind of trees are there?"

"All kinds. Sugar, red, striped maple, birch, cedar, white pine, poplar, hemlock, oak — "

"Do you have animals?"

"A few. Goats. And my dog."

"What kind?"

"She's a lab."

"And who takes care of the animals?"

"You mean now?"

Katherine nods.

"My neighbor, Walter Finch, and a boy I hire to do things around the place."

"You'll need to get back to them."

"Yes. Pretty soon."

Katherine wakes up screaming three times during the night. When she wakes just before dawn, she feels herself at the bottom of a deep hole, looking up at a small and distant patch of blue. She has been running all night long and each time her flight ends where it began, locked with David's rage in a small, dark, and airless room, his fists pounding the walls in search of her, and just before she screams herself awake the air before her face parts and gives way, like water against the bow of a ship, as the blow rushes in.

She does not look at Lucy stepping through the door, but keeps staring out the window.

"Good morning," says Lucy, but Katherine says nothing in reply, buried too deep to hope anything she might say will be heard at such a distance. Lucy stands near the door, her coat over one arm, a book in her hand. There is a long silence and then she turns and hangs her coat on the hook behind the door and sits in the chair. Katherine feels Lucy's eyes against the far-off patch of blue, her steady gaze a thread between them, too weak to pull her up and into the light. She waits for her to give up, for the rustled movement as she gathers up her things to leave, for the sounds from the hall to grow louder as the door opens wide and then fade as it closes in behind. But the silence goes on, Lucy's presence unwavering against the blackness around them both.

"Shall I go?" Lucy says at last and sees Katherine's head shake slowly back and forth.

"Then I'll stay," she says, settling back in the chair and opening the book in her lap.

She follows the lines of print but each time she reaches the end of the first paragraph she has no idea of what she has read and so begins again. After the fourth attempt she closes the book and looks up. The room is completely still. Even the steady stream of noise from the hall fades beneath the weight of Lucy's effort to sense what Katherine sees beyond the window. She moves to the chair beside the bed and looks across the pillows and rumpled bedclothes arrayed like a range of rounded hills, her gaze now paralleling Katherine's. She leans forward and rests her arms on the edge of the bed and as it takes her weight she feels something shift in Katherine, some small and subtle movement of energy toward her, like the single leaf on a tree moving in response to an unseen force while everything else remains still.

Lucy draws a breath and holds it as she gathers herself behind it. "I know how terrible the dreams can be," she says in a voice just above a whisper. "I have them still."

2

The last and only time Katherine has ever been in a hospital was thirty years ago when she had her tonsils removed. They kept her overnight and she barely slept, lying awake in the middle of the night feeling frightened and alone, small in the huge bed. It is the fearful loneliness she remembers most, not the pain in her throat or the nurses who brought her pillows to pile up around her. She left with a dread of hospitals that has stayed with her ever since but pales against what she feels now on the day before she must leave for a world that no longer feels like home.

"Of course you'll come and stay with us," her mother says.

Katherine imagines her mentally calculating a reasonable period of time — weeks but not months — and wonders what figure she'll arrive at and whether her father will argue for more or less. She doesn't blame them. They love her, after all. But children aren't supposed to come back to you, their lives broken and with no place to go, no future, dragging some unspeakable horror into your home. It isn't fair.

Her father stands at the foot of the bed, his hands resting on the rail. "We fixed up your old room," he says. "We put a television and a phone in, too." He shifts his weight back and forth from one foot to the other.

"Thank you, daddy," she says and her eyes fill with tears as her mother sits down beside her.

"Now don't worry," says her mother, glancing at Richard. "Everything will be all right."

"I know, mom. I know," she says, looking out the window.

When Lucy opens the door, Richard is helping Eleanor into her coat, and Eleanor stands for a moment, awkward with one arm in its sleeve and her other hand poised above the armhole.

"Hello," says Lucy. "You must be Katherine's parents."

"Yes," says Eleanor, her hand sliding into the sleeve, "This is Richard and I'm Eleanor."

Lucy extends her hand to Katherine's mother. "I'm Lucy Dudley." Richard nods from behind his wife and says, "Hello." They stand for a moment looking at Lucy, then at the floor or each other and then at Katherine.

"Lucy's been visiting," says Katherine.

Lucy makes a little smile.

"Well," says Richard, "we were just going. We'll leave you two to visit."

As the door closes behind them Lucy walks to the chair by the bed and sits.

"No book today," says Katherine.

"No. I can't stay long. I'm going home today." Katherine looks away. "What will you do now?"

Katherine holds the pillow tighter to her chest. "Stay with them for awhile. Until I'm over the surgery. I don't know about after."

"Perhaps when the time comes."

Katherine looks at her. "You said you still have bad dreams."

"Yes."

"What did you mean?"

"That I have nightmares like the ones I think you're having."

"How do you know I have nightmares?"

"How could you not?"

"Did what happened to me happen to you?"

It is only the second time anyone has asked Lucy to speak the truth of this and it stuns her for a moment, the simplicity of it.

"Yes, it did. Not all of it. But enough to know something of what you're going through without having to imagine."

"Was it your husband?"

"Yes."

"He beat you?"

"Yes."

"What happened?"

Lucy thinks for a moment. "He went away."

"You were lucky."

"I suppose I was."

They sit in silence and then Lucy looks at her watch. "I have to go," she says. "My friend is waiting to take me to the bus."

"I know."

Lucy begins to stand but something pulls her back into the chair, like a goat tugging at her sleeve, and she realizes she is not yet done, that she has still to do the thing she came to do and now, for the first time, sees clearly what it is.

"I don't know what you'll make of what I'm going to say. For all I know, you'll think I'm a kook after all." Lucy leans in closer. "You may come to a time when you need a place to go. I have plenty of room." Already Katherine is shaking her head. "It's a lovely and peaceful place to be."

"No," says Katherine, "thank you. But, no, I couldn't do that."

"I know. But you may feel differently later on. And if you do, I want you to remember what I'm saying to you now. I would welcome you there. You can trust in that. I'm too old not to know my own mind."

"But what would I do?"

"I don't know exactly. Cook, eat, sleep. Read. Become acquainted with goats. Walk in the woods. Drive into town." She shrugs with a little smile. "Live, I suppose. For awhile at least, until you feel ready to move on. Sort yourself out. Grieve."

It is at the mention of that word that Lucy feels Katherine begin to shrink into herself in the closest she can come to leaving the room. Suddenly Lucy's heart sinks, feeling she's gone too far and spoiled everything.

She sits back in the chair and looks out the window where Katherine's gaze has now returned. The sun is high in a bright sky. She feels far from home and the rhythm of animals and the coming and going of the moon and sun over the hills.

Lucy retrieves her wallet from the pocket of her coat and opens it to take out a pen and notepad. She sits by the bed and writes her name, address, and phone number and lays the piece of paper on the bedside table.

"This is where you can find me," she says. "I don't have an answering machine, so if I'm not home you'll have to call again. But keep trying. You can also write to me. I will write back. I promise." She watches Katherine stare out the window and wonders if she's bitten off more than she can chew.

She leans over to look into Katherine's face and then sits down on the bed. "Whether I see you again or not," she says, her voice soft and clear, "I wish you well. I will think of you often. Goodbye."

The words drift through the dark thick air toward the bottom of the hole where Katherine has sought refuge, and by the time they reach her she can barely make them out as they land softly all around, like leaves on water.

They ride halfway to Boston in silence.

"So, did you find out what you were supposed to do?"

"I think so," says Lucy. "I told her she could come and stay with me. I doubt she will. But I had to offer just the same."

"She will if she's got any sense."

"But that's just the point. She's so badly hurt. So frightened and alone. She's in a burning house full of smoke and she can't see the way out and may just sit down to die."

Walter loads Sophie in the back seat and drives up the road to Lucy's house. He checks the water in the barn and then goes into the house and lays a fire in the stove, which he leaves unlit. He's looking about the kitchen when he realizes he is having a rare moment alone in Lucy Dudley's house.

He walks into the hall and looks up the stairwell. Her bedroom is up there, he thinks, where she sleeps and dreams each night while her clothes hang silently in the closet and rest easily on one another in the oak bureau she bought from him years ago. He would climb the stairs and sit in her room for just a little while, on the edge of the bed, perhaps, to see the view from where she lies. But he is sure she would sense his presence when she returned, and so does not.

She looks tired coming off the bus but smiles at the sight of him and Sophie who grunts and pants to the beat of her tail thumping against the back seat. They say little on the drive home. She asks about the goats and the house and he tells her everything is fine.

"Did things go well in Boston?"

"Well enough," she says and they are silent the rest of the way.

He carries her suitcase into the kitchen. "There's a fire laid if you care to light it."

Her eyes fill but she does not let him see. "Thank you, Walter," she says, looking away to hang up her coat. "I appreciate everything. Very much. I am indebted to you. As always — "

"No," he says, "no such thing. Good night."

Toward midnight she lies in bed as a quarter moon rises over the eastern hills and Sophie snores in the corner. She thinks of Katherine lying awake through her last night in the hospital, peering from behind her pillows at the world beyond the window, watching the same moon lift itself into the sky. The house is quiet and still. She closes her eyes and goes to sleep.

7

They come for her first thing in the morning. The nurse has already been in to help her dress. Her hair is washed and circled with a scarf to hide the bare patches. Slacks cover the bruises on her legs. She asked her mother to bring a pair of dark glasses. She knows they are coming and focuses on the door so she won't be startled by them coming through.

"Well, then," her mother says, "all ready?" and Katherine nods. Her father appears with a nurse behind a wheelchair and as they push her through the open doorway into the hall she feels as though she is emerging from a dark underworld into a light that stuns and blinds and all but throws her back. Her skin is tender and unused to contact with the rough textures and surfaces of everyday existence. She is disoriented and slow, her senses overwhelmed. Everything seems off center, nothing the way it's supposed to be inside or out or where the one meets the other.

And in every eye that turns to note her going by she sees suspicion and reproach and the slightest hint of fear in the care they take not to get too close.

Jack waits in the car. As the wheelchair glides down the hall, the automatic doors swing open and the cold air shocks her cheeks and lungs. Suddenly, like a newborn having second thoughts, she wants to be back in her room on the fifth floor. But it is too late, for someone is already changing the bed for the next patient and now her father is pulling the seat belt across her hips and locking it into place.

The silence spreads through the air in the small closed space, wraps around her shoulders, sits upon her chest, stares into her eyes, and then she realizes they're all struck dumb by the utter shame and ruination of her life, unable to say so much as a single word.

"Would you like to go up to your room and settle in?" says her mother.

Katherine looks about the hall into the kitchen and living room then up the stairs. She feels unsafe and wants to be alone, but is tired of beds and bedrooms and the phantoms and nightmares that hatch out from her solitude. She wants to sit in a proper chair and breathe in a real room with newspapers on the coffee table and carpet and upholstery and plants and a view of the yard.

She is afraid to go up and afraid to stay down. Suddenly she realizes they are all standing around watching her.

My God I'm almost forty years old and I can't decide whether to go up or down.

"I'll sit in the living room for awhile," she says, her voice sounding hollow inside her head. Her father steers her to the stuffed chair opposite the couch and she is sitting down when she realizes she doesn't want her back to the dining room. "No, over there," she says pointing to the couch, and he pulls her upright and sits her facing the large windows overlooking the yard.

"Can I get you something?" he says. "Are you hungry? A cup of tea?"

"No," she says, then, "yes, tea would be nice."

"What kind?"

"I don't know. Whatever you've got is fine. Thank you."

"Are you okay?" he says and she looks at him and then away, her mouth slightly open as if trying to remember, her eyes settling on a point in the air in front of her as she forgets that he is there.

okay

"I'll get your tea," he says.

She feels the silence give way to a careful tentativeness filling up the house. No one lets their full weight down when they walk. No one speaks in a normal voice, as if she were sleeping in the next room. Or dying. Everything they do and say is tethered to an awareness of her presence that mutes and modulates, rounds and dulls, every conversation taking on the hushed tone of an awful secret.

She gets to her feet and goes into the hall, her body hurting with every step. She takes hold of the railing and mounts the stairs like a small child, one at a time, both feet coming to rest on each tread before rising to the next.

okay

At the top of the stairs she pauses to breathe and as her lungs expand a spasm of pain paralyzes her chest. She closes her eyes, her hand bearing down on the newel post, and focuses on keeping herself still until it goes away. Voices drift up from below. She looks down the hall at the open doorway to her room. She can see the corner of her old white bureau in the sunlight coming through the window. She walks down the hall and through the door and closes it behind. She looks about the room, the small bed, the window seat, the stars and moons on the ceiling, and a dull weight settles upon her as she realizes how much easier it would be if only he had killed her as well.

A television sits on a cart near the closet door. It is one of her visions of hell to be locked in a small dark space with a television that won't turn off. She wonders why they put it here.

Someone pads softly down the hall, then Jack appears in the doorway bearing her suitcase in one hand and a mug of tea in the other.

"You should have asked for help getting up those stairs."

"I'm okay."

"We didn't know what you took in it," he says. "I can get you milk or sugar if you want."

"No, it's fine." She takes the mug and sits on the bed. "Thanks."

"For what?" he says.

"Everything you've done."

"It isn't much."

She nods. "I guess you'll be going home soon."

"I suppose," he says, looking at the floor. "We should talk, though."

"I know."

"When you're up to it."

"I wouldn't wait for that if I were you."

"You let me know then. It won't take long."

"That bad."

"No. Well, not good." He takes a half step backward toward the door. "Look, let's not do it now. You just got here."

He is standing in the doorway.

"Take it easy for awhile and then we'll talk."

He is in the hall.

She nods.

"I'll be downstairs."

easy

She turns on the television but without the sound. People play a game for prizes, stand behind little podiums, answer questions, jump up and down when they've got it right. She changes the channel. A chef swirls chopped vegetables in a hot oily pan. She changes the channel. Two heads fill the screen. A man and woman move their lips in silent conversation as they look deeply into each other's eyes. She changes the channel. Bill Cosby encourages a little boy to eat some chocolate pudding. She changes the channel.

She sleeps through lunch and wakes, chilly, curled on her side, still dressed in shoes and street clothes on top of a white chenille bedspread just like the one she slept beneath as a girl. It has left a pattern where her cheek lay against it. Small white clouds dot the blue sky out her window. The darkened television sulks in the corner.

Dusk settles on the house as her father helps her downstairs and into the dining room. Her mother is in the kitchen cutting green beans, standing at the sink and glancing toward Katherine with a smile when she catches her eye.

"Did you have a good nap?"

Katherine nods. Her father settles on the couch and opens the newspaper.

Her chair faces the windows overlooking the yard. She stares at the bare trees and snow as Jack sits beside her and shuffles through a thin sheaf of papers on the table.

"So," he says, clearing his throat, "I checked into things. It looks okay, at least for awhile." He looks at her. "Do you want all the details?"

She doesn't answer for a moment, then, still looking out, says, "Yes."

Carefully, his voice crisp and even, he goes through each item, beginning with assets and ending with liabilities. He leans toward her with his elbows resting on the table, pointing to each addition and subtraction even though she's staring out the window. Richard looks over the top of the paper at her back and, to her right, Jack looking at the papers, then at her, then down again. Eleanor stops cutting beans and looks out the kitchen window, her hands resting on the counter, still holding the paring knife and an uncut bean.

Katherine will break even on the sale of the house and one of the cars, leaving her with some furniture, the other car, and just under $20,000. "That assumes, of course," he says, "the house doesn't take long to sell. Because you still have to make the mortgage payments. That'll cut into what's left by almost $1,000 a month. I figure five months, given that spring is coming. It's a good time to sell." He sits back in the chair and looks at the papers on the table. "It should be enough to last you for awhile."

She can feel him waiting for some movement, some change of expression, a shift in the pattern of her breathing, a tear down her cheek, but she barely moves, her face impassive, fingers loosely knit in her lap.

"Thank you," she says, glancing at him from the corner of her eye. "Really," the word catching in her throat and he looks at her as if expecting her to cry but it doesn't come.

"That's all right." He glances at the polished surface of the table and into the kitchen where his mother stares out the window. "Look," he says, "I could lend you some money for awhile," and the words barely clear his lips when he sees the color rise from her neck and over her face to her eyes that brim with tears that do not fall.

The shout wakes Eleanor first, who thinks she must be dreaming. She looks at the clock which reads just after 3:00 a.m. and she is trying to recollect the dream when it begins again, the sound that comes from being snuck up on from behind and startled in the worst way, producing a fright that's deep and bony and goes on and on. She nudges Richard awake.

"It's Katherine," she whispers. "She must be having a nightmare." If it were 30 years ago she'd already be making her way down the hall to comfort her, but she doesn't move, afraid of whatever has such a grip on her daughter.

"Do you think we should go?" he says.

"I don't know. It's stopped. Maybe she's okay."

Richard gets out of bed and walks softly to her room and listens outside the door. A sound of agitation from the other side, like an animal trapped in a small confining space and racing back and forth. A knot grows in the pit of his stomach as he stares at the doorknob, his hand suspended in the air only inches away. Then the door behind him opens and Jack is looking at him through the milky gloom. The sounds from Katherine's room subside and the house is still once again. Jack closes the door and Richard walks back down the hall.

"What?" says Eleanor, lying on her side facing Richard's back.

"What do you mean?"

"I can tell you're thinking." He rolls over and looks up at the ceiling, silent, his eyes wet with tears she cannot see.

"Are you going back to sleep?" she says.

"No. Just wondering." He sighs. "If we should have done something." He feels her stiffen beside him.

"She told us it'd be all right."

"I know, but why did we believe her? We could have done something anyway."

"But what, exactly?"

"I don't know," he says. "Call the police."

"And tell them what? Besides, she said it would only make it worse."

"Maybe she was wrong."

"But how could we possibly know?"

"I don't *know*," he says, his voice rising. "I just know she was alone and good reasons or not we didn't help her. And now she's lost everything."

"That's not our fault."

"Jesus," he says sitting up and looking at her, "that's not the point."

"Keep your voice down. And yes, that is the point."

"All right, then, Eleanor. I absolve you. Will that do it?"

"Richard — "

"It wasn't your fault. It was her fault. It was his fault. It was God's fault. But none of it ours." Tears crest the rims of his eyes and roll down his cheeks.

"Stop it," she says.

"And now you can absolve me and we can go back to sleep and let her stew in her own juice."

"Why are you taking this out on me? Do you think you're the only one who's been hurt by this?"

"No."

"Well, you could have fooled me."

There is a long silence.

"I'm sorry," he says, his voice thick and soft. "I just don't know what to do."

"I know. But blaming ourselves won't help."

"But I don't want to blame her, either. I wish I understood how this could happen. I never saw this in him."

"None of us did."

"But why not?"

"I don't know."

"And why didn't she leave? Why did she go back with him that day? She must have known what was going to happen. And still she went back."

"I don't know. Maybe we don't know her as well as we think we do."

He lies back on the bed and lays his hand on the pillow next to her cheek. She raises herself up and moves close to him and rests her head on his shoulder as he wraps his arm around her.

"You know," she says, "I always thought the worst thing would be to have one of my children die before me. Sometimes this feels like that. Only slower."

Katherine cannot look at the moons and stars pasted on the ceiling without thinking of Ethan lying in his bed, a bear wrapped in one arm ending in a thumb wedged in his mouth. He points a bent finger upward and asks her to name this one and that, sometimes interrupting to suggest an alternative he likes better.

"Archie?" he says, screwing up his face. "What kind of name is that?"

"You don't think that's a good name?"

"No," he says, "not for a *star*, mom."

"Well, what then?"

"How about," he says, his voice trailing off in thought, his wrinkled thumb hovering in front of his mouth, "Ethan."

"Excellent choice," she says, "Ethan it is."

They name them all and then forget which is which and have spirited disagreements that end in him being tickled and laughing so hard he has to remove the thumb from his mouth.

She stares upward in the early morning light, then suddenly scrambles to her feet and scratches at the ceiling until the bedcovers are strewn with bits of plaster and mangled moons and stars and then she climbs beneath the covers and pulls them over her head and rocks herself to sleep.

She does not come down for breakfast. The three of them sit quietly around the table. Richard folds the morning paper by his plate and glances at it sideways while he chews. Jack stares out the window. Eleanor rests her cheek against her fist and uses a fork to rearrange the food on her plate. Then, with a sigh, she pushes back her chair and carries her plate to the kitchen where she scrapes her breakfast into the sink. She feels Richard come in beside her, wrapping an arm around her as she leans her head on his shoulder.

"I don't know if I can do this," she says.

"I know."

"She frightens me. My own daughter, and she frightens me."

He goes upstairs and stands outside Katherine's room. He knocks softly and, hearing no answer, knocks again and then slowly opens the door. The room is dark, the shades drawn against the morning light. The air is close and slightly sour. She is curled almost into a ball beneath the covers. He cannot see her head.

"Katherine?" he says in a low voice. She doesn't stir.

"Are you awake?" In the stillness he remembers coming into her room before dawn in the middle of winter to get her up for school. He remembers her small face, puffy with sleep, buried in the covers and reluctant to come out. Suddenly he feels awkward watching her while she sleeps and he slowly backs out of the room and closes the door.

Katherine studies the inside surface of the sheet, its texture barely visible in the light coming through from the room beyond. She waits until the footsteps grow softer and then slowly pulls the covers from her face.

"I don't see how she can avoid it," says Jack.

"Perhaps we could go," says Richard.

"But we don't know what she wants to keep," says Eleanor.

Jack shakes his head and looks down at the remains of his lunch. It's just past one o'clock and Katherine still hasn't come down or, as far as they can tell, left her room more than once to go to the bathroom.

"She has to go back there," says Jack. "Unless she just wants to chuck it all, which I doubt. And someone has to go with her. She can't do it alone."

"Well it won't be anytime soon," says Eleanor. "She's not well enough for that."

"No," says Richard.

"I'll go with her," says Jack, "if I'm still here." They both look at him, then away. "I'll look for a realtor today."

As he pushes his plate away, his eyes meet his father's.

Richard clears his throat. "I want you to stay until she goes through the house."

"I don't know if I can."

"Please."

"I have a job, dad. And a family."

"I know that," says Richard, his voice tight and low as he glances toward the kitchen. "But surely you can manage just a few days more."

Jack plays his fork against the tablecloth, the tines pressing a dotted line in front of his plate.

Richard leans toward him. "She's your sister, Jack."

"I know that. And she was also David's wife. And Ethan's mother."

Richard studies his son's face for a moment, wondering whether to ask the question, decides against it, and then is surprised to hear himself say, "What is that supposed to mean?"

"Nothing. I'm just saying what's true."

"No you're not."

"No," says Jack, putting down his fork. "You're right. I'm also saying this may not be as simple as it's made out to be."

"And how is that?"

Jack straightens in his chair. "Katherine the poor victim to big bad David."

"But look at what he did to her."

"Yes. And look at what she did to him. The man's dead. Have you forgotten that? He's dead for Christ's sake. Just who got the worst of it here?"

"He was going to kill her — "

"Maybe. But I don't know that and neither do you. Maybe he was just really pissed at her and maybe he hit her sometimes and maybe she had it coming and maybe she didn't, and regardless, maybe she took it as an excuse to shove a knife in him."

"I can't believe I'm hearing this from you." Richard leans forward and tries to meet his eye but Jack keeps his gaze fixed on the table.

"What about Ethan? Are you blaming her for that, too? Did she make David throw that poor boy against a wall?"

"Of course not," says Jack, "but she might have done something to prevent it. Do you honestly believe there was nothing she could do? Did he have her chained up in the cellar so she couldn't get away? Did he drug her up so she couldn't think? She had two legs. She could've walked and taken Ethan with her and none of this would have happened."

Richard sits back in his chair and then turns and looks out the window.

"Tell me I'm wrong, dad."

Richard looks to the kitchen door where Eleanor stands with a dishtowel in her hands. Their eyes meet for a moment before she turns back into the kitchen.

"She tried," Richard says.

"Tried what?"

"To leave."

"Really? And what happened?"

"She came here."

"And?"

Richard sighs. "He came after her. He was very angry. He made quite a scene. And then she went home with him."

"And why did she do that?"

"I don't know, Jack. Maybe she was afraid not to."

"If she was so afraid, why didn't she call the cops? Isn't that what they're for?"

"I don't know. I suppose. She said it wouldn't do any good. It would only make it worse."

"Well," says Jack, rising from his chair, "I don't see how. I mean, things got a lot worse anyway, didn't they."

A flush of red flows up Richard's face as he stares down at the table. "Don't you love her?"

"Jesus Christ, dad, of course I do. But this isn't about love."

Jack takes his plate into the kitchen and puts it in the sink.

"I'll tell you what," he says, standing in the doorway, "I'll take care of the realtor today. And then I'm going home."

"I think," says Richard, still looking at the table, "that might be a good idea."

Katherine wakes, wild with terror, the remnant of a dream. She feels a presence outside the door, a quality of stillness that tells her someone is there. She pictures his hand poised above the knob, his lips set thin and hard. She throws back the covers, working against the pain to pull herself out of bed, and is halfway to the closet when she remembers and stops in the middle of the room, holding her breath and listening until she hears footsteps pad down the hall toward her parents' room.

She draws a breath and trembles as she lets it go. The furnace faintly rumbles into life two floors below. A car drives by, its headlights playing across the walls and ceiling. She slides her feet into her slippers and pulls on her robe, then settles on the window seat, her knees beneath her chin, and looks into the back yard emerging in the predawn light. The snow is beginning to thin with grass showing through. A light goes on in a kitchen across the way and a woman stands before the sink and fills a kettle as she looks out the window. Katherine wonders if the woman is happy, is she safe. A man crosses behind her, buttoning his shirt, and at the sight of him Katherine pulls her head away from the window. She goes back to bed.

There is no place for her to hide, save here in her own bed, asleep or feigning sleep. But she knows this can't go on forever even though the oblivion of forever is what she wants more than anything. The dreams come every night, often more than once, in shattering, incoherent fragments of terror. She is afraid to sleep. She has given up changing nightgowns every time she wakes in a cold sweat. She grows accustomed to feeling chilly and damp, her hair matted against her head. She smells, even to herself, as if she were decaying while still alive, the essence of her being slipping away, gangrenous and fetid. When someone comes into her room she braces herself for the look on their face, the eyes drawn close in disbelief, nostrils flaring as the nose rebels. She doesn't know how they can stand to be in the same house with her. The more hopeless and disgusting she becomes, the more she feels herself disappear.

A visiting nurse stops by to check her incisions. "Honey, when was the last time you took a bath?" she says screwing up her nose.

"I don't know."

"Well," she says, "you're asking for an infection if you go on like this. Are you eating?"

"Some."

"Not enough by the look of you." She sits back in her chair. "Look," she says, "this won't do." She pulls back the covers and gently lifts and swings Katherine into a sitting position, her legs hanging off the side of the bed. "Come on," she says, pulling her to her feet, "where's the bathroom?"

She steers Katherine across the hall and sits her on the toilet while she turns the shower on and adjusts the flow. "You want some help or can you do it yourself?"

"I'll be all right," she says.

The nurse nods. "Okay then. I'll leave you to it." She closes the door, then opens it enough to admit her head. "No coming out 'til you're clean enough to squeak."

It is a mother's voice, one that Katherine vaguely recognizes. She remembers sitting on the toilet in just this way to watch Ethan take his bath, surrounded by bubbles, a small clump on top of his head where he'd reached up to scratch.

She shakes the memory from her mind and stands. She steps out of her slippers, lets her bathrobe slide to the floor, and pulls her nightgown over her head. The air feels thick, almost tropical against her skin. As she turns toward the shower, she sees the cloudy image of a woman reflected through the mist settling on the long mirror behind the door. The sight reminds her of a dog she once saw on a back country road in New Hampshire, crouched low, tail between his legs as he walked toward her. He peed in the dust as she drew near, a sign, she later learned, of submission, and as he passed she saw an open sore on his haunch and patches of fur missing along his back. He glanced up at her without lifting his head, and when he was safely past he disappeared into the tall grass beside the road.

Pale yellow bruises range all the way from her ankles to her face. One eye is hooded by a puffy lid that droops heavily toward her cheek. A long closely stitched wound splits her in two from just beneath her breasts down past her navel, and another runs around her left side. The top of her head looks as though patches of hair were glued there by a clumsy child.

There is nothing she can see that is untouched and unharmed. It is as though her body were taken from her, pounded and torn to pieces, and then hastily reassembled before being handed back. She recognizes nothing.

The image blurs and fades as fog thickens against the glass. She turns away and steps into the shower.

8

The day Jack leaves for California, Katherine stays in bed. He comes in after breakfast to say goodbye.

In the afternoon her father drives her to the house. He unlocks the front door and swings it open, but she shakes her head and motions for him to go in first. She watches him remove his coat and walk into the living room.

"I'm sorry," she says, trembling, her eyes large and wet. "I just can't do this."

He thinks for a moment. "I'll tell you what," he says, "I'll get my pad and pencil and we'll sit out on the porch and see how much we can get done. And if we have to go inside, we will. How's that sound?"

She shakes her head. "I know I should be able to, but I can't. I'm sorry. Give it all away. I don't want it."

And then she turns and walks out to the car.

Each morning she watches the woman across the way. Unable to sleep, she gets out of bed before dawn and drags her blanket to the window where she wraps herself into a cocoon on the seat. She waits for the light to go on in the kitchen and for her to stand over the sink and fill the kettle. She watches and searches for clues to the woman's life. She sees no children. On most mornings the man passes back and forth a few times and then settles at the table to eat a bowl of cereal and drink a cup of coffee. Sometimes he comes up behind her and circles his arms around her waist. She smiles and tucks her chin toward his face over her shoulder. She says a few words and he lingers before letting go and stepping away and out of sight.

When the woman leaves the window, Katherine tries to imagine what she cannot see and wonders if someone ever looked at her own house in this way and asked themselves what went on inside. All these houses, she thinks, looking just the same and no one having any idea what happens to the people who live in them. We assume everything is fine, that smiles and waves actually mean they're happy and safe, that homes are a refuge and not a prison where privacy is a trap. She remembers a line from a poem by Stevie Smith, drifting in the ocean and seeing someone on the shore — *you thought I was waving, but I was drowning.*

Days go by before she is aware of how her stomach tightens whenever the man appears or disappears from the panel of light framed by the window, and how she leans forward when he stops and looks at his wife while she stands with her back to him, vulnerable, unable to see the expression on his face or what he might do next. She waits, but each day goes by like the one before, unremarkable and ordinary, all she ever wanted for herself.

She stops watching.

She begins to lock her bedroom door at night, leaving the key half turned so it cannot be displaced by one inserted from the other side. During the day she goes downstairs for meals and occasionally to search through the assortment of boxes in the basement that her father retrieved from the house, unable to do as she asked. She takes an armful of photo albums and carries them to her room, and when her parents are out shopping one afternoon she comes downstairs and finds a roll of tape and a box of thumbtacks which she takes to her room. She rolls the television into the back of the closet and buries it beneath dirty clothes. She covers one wall with photographs of Ethan and of herself growing up. And just as buds begin to show on the maple outside her window, she begins to lock the door during the day.

She will not leave the house. Her mother invites her to go to the movies or shopping, but always she says she doesn't feel well or isn't strong enough, though both of them know that none of it is true. The bruises are gone, the incisions fading to smooth lines of pink and white. Her ribs and nose are mended and her chest no longer seizes up in pain when she coughs or turns the wrong way. Her hair is growing back and she hears again through both ears.

She goes to the bathroom and sits on the toilet. She is unrolling a few sheets of tissue when she remembers the day Ethan took hold of one end of the roll and walked all the way downstairs with it. And then it occurs to her that she's heard no one speak his name since she left the hospital. Nor David's. As if they never existed and this enormous portion of her life never happened, or must now be forgotten, cut loose and left behind without a trace

except for me

She stands and turns toward the door and is stopped by her reflection in the mirror, her gaze settling on the curls covering her head.

Ethan's hair

She locks the door and opens the medicine cabinet, scanning the shelves, noting labels on little bottles of pills, most of them bearing her mother's name. How easy it would be, she thinks, like going to sleep. And then no more of this, nothing to endure, no more going on for the lack of anything else. Then she sees the scissors she was looking for. Head bowed, she looks up enough to see her face in the mirror and then through a blur of tears she begins to cut the hair. She watches it fill the sink. When the top and sides are bare she does the back by the feel of the scissors as she lays them against her scalp before drawing the blades together.

There is a knock at the door. "Katherine," says her mother, "are you all right?"

She leans on the edge of the sink. "Yes."

In the silence she can feel her mother on the far side of the door. "Are you sure?"

"Go downstairs, mom."

Movement in the hall and then silence as she gathers the hair from the sink and floor and flushes it down the toilet. She replaces the scissors in the cabinet. She listens at the door and, hearing nothing, unlocks and opens it. She stiffens at the sight of her mother's face.

"Oh my God," her mother says, raising her hands to her mouth. "What have you done?"

She pushes past her mother and goes into her room, closing and locking the door behind.

When she sees him sitting on the end of the bed, leaning forward with his forearms resting casually across his thighs, his head cocked to one side but his eyes looking directly up at her, she gasps and shrinks back against the door with such force it cracks one of the panels. The sound so startles her mother that she stumbles backward from where she stands outside the door and nearly falls.

For weeks she has felt his presence on the other side of the thin veil between them, and for weeks she has anticipated and dreaded the moment the veil would finally fall away.

"Katherine," says her mother, "what was that? What happened? Are you all right?"

The voice comes to her as from a distance. She can barely make out the words. She is frozen to the spot, her eyes on his face as she feels the energy coalesce inside him like a snake about to hurl itself through the air.

She hears her name spoken urgently through the door and glances toward the voice and when she looks back into the room he is gone.

Her mother is knocking on the door, asking to be let in. Katherine hears her father mount the stairs two at a time. Suddenly it is David in the hall, pounding out his rage that she'd dare to lock a door against him. She covers her ears and closes her eyes and steps away until she feels her back against the wall, sliding to the floor, shaking her head, bracing against what she knows is about to come through the door and fling itself across the room.

"Katherine?" Her father's voice, stripped of any pretense to authority, rising on the word, full of worry. "Please. Open the door and let us in."

Her breaths come in soft descending pants, like an animal almost run to ground who listens from a secret refuge to the sounds of pursuit fading in the distance. She opens her eyes and looks around the room. There is no one there. She feels a dampness between her thighs and realizes she has wet herself.

A stillness comes over her. She takes in a long deep breath and lets it out on a sigh. And then she is aware of her parents on the other side of the door, their voices hushed and anxious. They will stay there, she knows, until she finds words to make them go away, words that soothe and reassure. She doesn't want to speak at all, as if the sound might break the container that holds her safely where he cannot find her, at least for now.

She looks at the door. "Katherine," her mother says.

"I'm all right."

"Will you let us in?"

Katherine shakes her head. "I need to be alone."

"We're worried about you," says her father.

"I know. I'll be all right. Really."

As weeks go by there is a blurring of the boundary between sleep and nonsleep, dream and nondream, night and day. Rhythms go awry, slipping sideways like a rudderless boat, drifting from thought to thought, memory to memory, knitting them together in a fabric she wraps about her as she wanders through the house. And always punctuated by specters of terror and loss that come crashing in upon her without warning, only to be gone as suddenly as they appear.

She goes downstairs in the middle of the night, foraging for things to eat, sitting in the dark of the living room and smoking one of the cigarettes she persuaded her father to bring her from the world outside. The house is still and quiet although sometimes she thinks she can feel her mother lying awake above the ceiling, sniffing the air and staring into the gloom as she listens for sounds from below.

There is a vase on a table in the corner of the dining room, that reflects a small red light in the kitchen, the clock, perhaps, on the microwave. She focuses on the point of light in the smooth outward curve of the vase and as she stares it becomes the glow of a cigarette and then around the cigarette she sees the dim outline of his fingers and then his hand and arm and shoulder and head. He is leaning back with knees splayed outward and hands resting loosely on his thighs.

He looks at her, but she cannot see his face. She imagines if she keeps her gaze fixed upon him, he will not move, and so she is absolutely still, each breath coming slow and shallow.

She lights another cigarette and watches the red point of light from the dining room fade and reappear. She yawns and her vision blurs behind tears that would pull her into sleep, laying the cigarette in the ashtray and closing her eyes to ease down toward some quiet place between this world and somewhere else. Her mind drifts, slipping in and out of sleep and dreaming, letting go her sense of time and place.

And then she sees, through the half-sight of nearly closed eyes, a movement of the light, a small but unmistakable sideways shift that snaps her eyes wide open, staring hard until she sees it move again, upward now, as if being raised to the lips and pausing to finish a thought, but before the movement is done she is on her feet and running toward the hall.

Where the fuck you think you're going?

She is halfway up the stairs when she sees him on the landing and turns and stumbles back down to the hall and throws open the front door and is out and crossing the yard. She runs down the middle of the street, through the alternating light and shadow cast by the lamps, her feet slapping softly against the pavement, breathing hard and settling into a steady rhythm of flight. At the end of the street she turns and goes on toward the small park where she played as a child. She remembers the incisions from her surgery and touches a hand to the scar that split her in two, but feels no pain and does not slow her pace.

The park is not where she remembers it. She stops and looks down the line of houses on each side of the street, her breath deep and foggy in the cold air. Nothing is familiar, until she realizes she is looking at the front porch of her own house and that is him sitting on the stoop, lifting his head to smile a brief and glassy smile and she is running by the time she hears his first step on the walk.

At the end of the street she turns onto a road that winds toward the center of town. She passes the pharmacy where she used to sit on a stool and drink cherry Cokes from a tall glass and she sees just behind her reflection in the window a shadow matching her step for step. She cries out and stumbles against the curb as she rounds the corner and watches the twin reflections race past the long line of storefronts. And then suddenly the shadow disappears as she crosses the empty street and turns toward the high school.

Long before she reaches the broad granite steps she can see his pale, hard face, his fist slapping his palm in a slow and steady cadence as he stands and waits. She stops in the middle of the street and looks at him, her lungs burning, groaning as she watches him descend the stairs.

She runs down streets she has never seen before, one after another, each corner like the last, every turn leading back to the house where he sits on the step and waits, a cigarette glowing in his fist. She runs to a neighbor's house and pounds on the door but no light shows and no one answers. She runs to the next and the next but there is no one who will let her in. And then suddenly he is behind her, his breathing heavy and desperate in her ear, but when she screams and turns, he is gone.

She stands in the middle of the moonlit street with sobs pouring out of her as if she were turning inside out. She walks slowly on cut and bleeding feet until she sees her parents' house. She stops at the front walk and looks at the door that still stands open, revealing nothing in the darkness within. A breeze cools her head and she reaches up a hand and is surprised to feel the thickness of hair between her fingers. Her nightgown moves about her legs in the wind. She looks across the line of bushes that front the house to the maple at the corner and she draws a sharp breath at the sight of a small red dot glowing in the shadows, that moves as suddenly as she, and he almost catches her by the arm as she leaps through the door and takes the stairs two at a time, running to her room, her feet slipping on the polished floor, slamming the door and turning the key and pulling it out and leaping into the closet, frantically searching for the hole to insert the key and then driving it home to lock herself inside.

Allan G. Johnson

She sits among shoes and old clothes in the utter darkness of the small closed space. There is no sound from beyond the door, only the high, hoarse pant of her lungs gasping for air. She closes her eyes and wraps her arms around her knees to draw them close to her chest. Her breathing begins to slow in the silence. And then suddenly she is not alone and there is the soft pop of a match flaring before her face.

Don't you move. Not one fucking move.

Three

1

*L*ucy wrote to Katherine several weeks after returning from Boston.

Dear Katherine,

I thought about you all the way home and you've been in my thoughts ever since. I know that telling the difference between what's real and what's not is anything but certain when your world comes apart. I imagine you may wonder if I was ever there or was something you dreamt. I want you to have this letter to remind you I was there and the offer I made was something I don't expect to regret.

In case they've been mislaid, here are my address and telephone number. Use them when you think the time has come for it. You are always welcome here.

Yours, Lucy Dudley

She received no reply. She had not expected one, at least not right away. But now, in the middle of April, she wonders if she should dare to write again and what to say. Three times she begins and three times crumples the page and throws it toward the fire. Sophie thumps her tail and pulls herself to her feet to retrieve the paper into her bed by the stove and chew it into a soggy little wad.

Lucy looks at the three white lumps arrayed before Sophie's muzzle. "If I have to work at it this hard," she says, screwing the fountain pen into its cap, "it probably isn't what I ought to be doing."

They drive into town to the local bookstore that occupies what used to be a bank. The children's section is located in the vault, with poetry where the safe deposit boxes used to be. Lucy scans the shelf and gives a little whoop of surprise at finding what she's looking for, *Otherwise*, a collection of Jane Kenyon's poems. She writes inside, "For Katherine, from Lucy," and takes it next door to the post office. Standing in the back seat of the car, Sophie pants and follows her progress, and by the time Lucy returns, the windows are well fogged.

"Now that's more like it," she says, pulling away from the curb and wiping the back of her hand across the windshield. "Why send her Dudley when she could have the likes of Kenyon?"

Weeks go by and she calculates the time for it to arrive and how long for Katherine to feel moved to write something in reply. She realizes she has cast a soft hook into the water and, as her father taught her to do, now sits and waits for a gentle tug on the line to signal some interest in the bait.

She waits as spring edges on toward summer. The mud dries and the hills turn green as trees come fully into leaf, the rhododendrons along the side of the house bloom and fade, perennials reappear in her gardens, beginning with bluebells, primrose, forget-me-nots, violets, and bright yellow wallflowers.

Memorial Day comes and goes and still there is no reply as the gardens give way to a cascade of purple columbine, bellflower, delphinium, and iris.

And then on a rainy afternoon in the middle of June there is a letter in the box, addressed in an uneven scrawl with just the letter 'K' for the return. Lucy sits in the library and holds up the envelope to the late afternoon light coming through the window, her hands beginning to tremble just enough for her to notice and wonder why. She lets the letter fall into her lap as she rocks and listens to the comforting sound of wicker creaking beneath her. She looks down at the handwriting, almost like a child's, a collection of unformed bits and pieces set down with effort, and tears come into her eyes.

She opens the letter and unfolds the small sheet of paper.

Dear Lucy,

Please forgive me for taking so long to write. I haven't been well. Your letter sat on the table beside my bed for months and when the book arrived I used the letter to mark my place. I tried many times to write but it kept

*coming out wrong. I love the poems. How did you know? It says she lived
on a farm in New Hampshire and I wonder if your place is like hers. She
had a dog and she writes about him a lot and I remember you saying you
have a dog but I don't remember her name or if you told me. I can see this
letter is already no good but I'm going to send it anyway. Because I must
at least thank you for sending me the book and thinking about me. I don't
know why you do.*

Katherine

She reads the letter a second time and looks out at the rain slanting
by the window. Sophie stirs on the floor beside her and Lucy drops a
hand to gently play her fingers through the hair behind Sophie's ears.
Lucy looks at the wrinkled page and it occurs to her what a small
miracle this is, words smuggled out from one of the darkest places a
soul can imagine. 'Lucy' and 'Katherine' on the same page and in her
own hand, a connection, slender, new, and fragile but unmistakably
there. She hears her father's voice from three steps down the river bank
— Don't let the line go slack, bring it in so you feel the tug at the other
end — and she rocks forward and out of the chair and goes into the
kitchen. Sophie watches her for a moment and then lifts herself off
the floor and follows, settling with a soft grunt by the stove.

Lucy takes out pen and paper and sits at the long pine table in the
kitchen. *Dear Katherine*, she writes and lifts her head to look out the
window where goats have gathered just inside the barn to stare out at
the rain and chew their cud.

*I'm glad you like the book. If I'd thought of it I'd have brought her when
I came to visit, but I didn't and my friend only had the Dillard.*

*My dog's name is Sophie, after my great aunt whom I'll always remember
for liking me and never hesitating to tell me so. She also loved to hunt, which
seemed strange to me alongside such a capacity for affection. Sophie reminds
me of her in both ways although she doesn't really hunt. She chases, which
isn't the same, and she's gotten too old to do even that anymore. She does like
to pretend, though, especially with chipmunks whose squeaky cries inflame*

her passions something awful and set her lumbering off in their direction. They run like hell every which way and then up trees or into tiny holes in the ground. They put on a good show, which Sophie seems to enjoy. And it's good for her joints, which are the worse for wear, not unlike my own.

She lifts the pen and reads over what she's written and then shakes her head as she looks out the window. The rain has stopped and it's just after 4:00. She puts a kettle on, spoons tea into the pot, and pulls a box of crackers from the cupboard. While the tea steeps she leans back against the counter and looks out the window and eats crackers from the box.

She sits down again and takes the pen in hand.

You wonder why I think of you. I don't know how I could not. The horror that was done to you is something I know about and not from books. When I found you in the hospital I felt something kindred pass between us and now each day I wonder how you are and what will become of you. I expect I will keep wondering until I know one way or the other.

The guest room is in a corner of the second floor that looks out to the north and east. The view includes the hills of New Hampshire and, closer in, the barn and fields that run down to the woods. The bath is right across the hall. The walls are white with a hint of peach. There is a closet and a single bed that I'm told is quite comfortable. There is also a small bureau and a bookcase with some room in it and a table for writing in front of the window.

Yours, Lucy

She puts her glasses on the table and rubs her eyes with her knuckles. The late afternoon sun cuts through the scattering clouds and slants across the barnyard. She reads over what she's written and corrects two misspellings and adds a comma before she folds it and seals it in an envelope and then rummages in the bureau for a stamp. Sophie follows her into the hall and out the front door. The walk is bathed in light from a mostly blue western sky and the air is fresh and clear from the rain and blown by a cool breeze. She slides the envelope into the mailbox and raises the flag, then closes her eyes to stand for a moment with her hand resting on the box. Sophie stamps her feet and grunts from the porch. It is long past time for supper. She goes into the house with Sophie at her heels.

Katherine tries to remember what Lucy looks like. She remembers a purple hat and the voice reading to her, soft and even, but the face is elusive. She does not open the letter on the day it arrives or on the next, but tucks it in the book of poetry with the other. On the third day she opens it, and when she reads 'the horror that was done to you,' she puts the letter down, for no one has spoken so directly of it to her before. She has lived in the middle of a great and awful silence, which everyone assumes is necessary for her to heal. But unknown even to her is that the silence has an edge that cuts the wound afresh and deeper still by isolating her in a small windowless room lined with mirrors reflecting her shame no matter where she looks.

But even as she recoils from Lucy's words, she feels drawn to them in a way she does not understand. She picks up the letter and wonders what it is that Lucy knows 'and not from books' and what it has to do with her. There was no shame in the woman she remembers from the hospital nor in this letter or the one before. But Katherine is so full of shame she cannot imagine how Lucy could look at her and see anything that might remind her of herself. And yet that is exactly what she seems to do.

Perhaps, she thinks, it is Lucy who doesn't understand and therefore doesn't see the shame, but how could that be, for it permeates every cell and seeps from every pore. When her mother coaxed her into a trip to the market it seemed that everyone looked at her and she couldn't help but look away. She knew they saw the shaved head beneath the floppy woven hat pulled over her ears and when she saw their faces she wanted to disappear, to shrink into a tiny space amongst the produce, to become anonymous and small like a dull brown potato in the bin. And then a young man pushed a long line of carts through the automatic door, crashing across the threshold just behind her, and she let out a cry and grabbed her mother's arm and everyone looked their way and she saw her mother's face stricken as if she'd dug her hand in the pile of beans and come up with excrement.

"I have to go," Katherine said, her voice low and desperate in her mother's ear, "please, I can't stay here, I have to go, please," and her mother mumbled that of course it was all right and left the cart in the middle of the aisle and hurried past the young man's startled face and out into the parking lot. Strangely, she thought, it was her mother and not herself who cried all the way home, for Katherine had receded to a numb and silent place, unable to speak, eyes wide and dry and fixed on the road ahead.

"Your mother says you got pretty upset today," her father said that evening, sitting on the edge of her bed. "Can you tell me what it was?" and she felt overwhelmed by the flood of images and sounds that drove her toward a corner of her mind like beaters flushing game.

"Did something frighten you?" he said, and she looked away. How could she tell him that everything frightens her? How could he understand what it is like for her, when the world is still something that makes sense to him, the earth still solid beneath his feet? She watched him through the window when he went out to the car and waved to a neighbor and stopped to chat across the hedge. She watched him smile and gesture and heard his voice rise and fall in the telling of a story, the pause before the laughter at the end. She saw a man at ease, safe in the assumption that his neighbors would not kill him, nor his wife turn on him in the middle of the night. She saw a man who slept well except when he lay awake and worried about his daughter. For him the fundamental order of being was still intact and he could not understand how reality itself and its cradling web of assumptions of safety and reason and the simple assurance of each moment flowing into the next could disintegrate into a million fragments so small and light they could scatter on a breeze.

He could not understand how much his sense of who and what he was as he stood talking across the hedge or reading the paper or touching his wife depended on keeping that web of relations whole and intact or how quickly its undoing could be his own.

Nor could he understand that fear and shame are no longer just feelings that come and go, but rather something she has become.

"We want to understand," he said.

She nodded as he searched her face for something more.

"I know this has been terrible for you," he said, "but you know that sooner or later you'll have to find a way to get on with your life."

She wondered what he meant by her life and getting on. She had been waiting for this moment. She had expected it much sooner than this, when they stood outside the closet door and threatened to take it off its hinges if she wouldn't come out on her own. She had thought that would be the moment when they'd have had enough of her sad craziness and crazy sadness, when their own fear would be too much and they would send her away. But that wasn't it. She told them she'd unlock the door and slide out the key if only they would leave and let her come out to an empty room. And then she listened to her heart beating as they decided and her father cleared his throat and agreed and she turned the key in the latch and slid it through the crack of light beneath the door.

She could not look at her father. She focused on the cover of the book in her lap, the book that Lucy Dudley gave to her, the title, *Otherwise*, running her fingers over the word. "Do you want me to go?"

"No," he said, "not at all," the words stumbling out. "It's just that it's been several months now. And you seem. . . well. . .to dwell on things, and that can't be good for you. I know it must be terribly hard, but you need to put this behind you, don't you think?"

There was a long silence in which she tried to imagine how to leave herself behind.

"What if I can't?"

He looked startled by the idea and the edge of anger in her voice.

"I don't know."

She felt hot and her vision went out of focus. "I think it's time for me to go."

"No. That isn't what I mean."

"Maybe it should be."

He shook his head. "You can stay as long as you want."

"No, dad," she said, looking at him, her voice flat and hard, "I can't," and she both saw the pain in his face and felt the relief in his body letting down beside her. She didn't blame him or her mother. There was a monster in their house and they were too frightened to ask it to leave, like the summer evening when a bat got in and fluttered from room to room and the only thing they could think to do was open a door and hope it would find its own way out.

She saw his eyes fill with tears for the second time in her life as he gathered her in his arms. Her father could not save her and they both knew it now. Not from this, perhaps not from anything. And perhaps it had always been so.

2

*K*atherine finds herself moving toward a vision of Lucy Dudley's spare room, facing north and east, curtains gently billowing from the window like sails before a breeze. She begins by taking down the photographs of her and Ethan from the wall. Then she gathers her clothes, folding the clean ones on the bed and piling dirty laundry by the door. She wonders what to take and what to leave. It can be cool up there, she knows, even in July, so she may get by without shorts or short-sleeved shirts, which is just as well since she stopped wearing them years ago. It was the only way she knew to leave the house without people noticing the bruises on her arms and legs.

She pauses in the middle of folding a sweater as it occurs to her that she has no idea how long she will stay, and however long that might be, she will inevitably have to leave. She tries to imagine what might come after but cannot get past an awful sense of dread and emptiness. She sits on the bed, the sweater in her lap, and looks out the window toward the house across the way. She has survived David. She is alive and safe from his violence. As far as anyone can tell, her wounds have healed and she is free to come and go. But she has won her freedom and her safety at horrendous cost. She has become a woman without a home or friends or neighborhood where people know her name and smile at her approach. Her husband and boy are dead and with them all her dreams of family. And the family of her birth seems to barely know her anymore.

And deep inside where people cannot see, she carries the greatest wound of all, the shattered self wrapped in shame and a gnawing terror that will not go away. It inhabits her dreams and leaps upon her without warning, in supermarket aisles or looking into the bathroom mirror as she brushes her teeth and sees the shower curtain stir behind her, or walking down a street and listening to birds call out to one another and hearing the snap of a twig. She has become the cage that once imprisoned her.

She feels the darkness close in around her mind and shakes her head to focus on the sweater in her hands. "I can't stay," she whispers. She wants to fling herself headlong into some forward movement, anything to escape this room and this house, but she moves in slow and fruitless motion, a prisoner to inertia, like the childhood dreams where she tries to run away and her muscles and the air take on the consistency of mud.

She puts the sweater on the bed and stops wondering what to take. She will take it all and use what she needs and hope that Lucy Dudley understands the rest.

She reads the letters several times before she begins to write. She can find inside herself no compelling reason to trust anyone, but she must at least pretend to trust this, like running out across thin ice when you must get to the other side and there is no other way.

Dear Lucy,

Are you sure? I don't want you to wish someday that you changed your mind. Please don't say yes unless you are sure. I am not. But I don't know what else to do.

Katherine

She seals the letter in an envelope, but cannot bring herself to put it in the mail. She slips it into the book of poetry. The next day she takes it out and reads what she has written. It seems to her pathetic and small and she crumples it up and throws it away. She stares at the basket, then retrieves the letter, smoothing out the wrinkles against the cover of the book. She reads it again and then lays a fresh piece of paper on the book and copies the words.

After lunch she goes to the corner and slides the letter into the mailbox, walking quickly away, sure that someone must be watching.

For days she struggles to keep her mind off waiting for Lucy's reply. She tries to busy herself doing laundry and cleaning her room and reading, even retrieving the television from the back of the closet but then putting it back without turning it on.

She sits in the back yard and closes her eyes as she turns her face toward the sun.

She makes small forays into the world, walking first to the end of the block beyond the mailbox and then back, and once as far as the park.

She collects the mail each day when it comes through the slot in the front door at just past noon, but there is nothing for her and she begins to sink beneath the dread that she has ruined even this, that Lucy Dudley saved herself just in time.

One afternoon she comes upon her mother standing in the hall, sorting through the mail, and sees in her face a tenderness that she remembers from no particular time or place but rather as a sense memory lodged in her cells that now shows itself as an invitation to confide what she is longing for and fears she cannot have.

"I wrote to Lucy Dudley," she says.

"Oh," her mothers says, the word coming out with a slight tremble in her voice. "And?"

"Nothing yet."

"How long has it been?"

"A week or so."

"That's not too long. After all, who knows how mail gets delivered way up there." She smiles and Katherine nods and looks away. "It's hard to want things," her mother says. "I try to avoid it when I can." And before she knows it Katherine is in her arms and Eleanor feels her daughter's heart begin to break against her and looks past her shoulder with a curious, startled look, her hands full of mail, suspended for a moment just above her back and then alighting like two leaves, almost weightless, drifting gently down.

"Don't worry," she says, "It always seems longest when you're waiting for something. Try not to wait."

Katherine steps back and reaches into the pocket of her mother's blouse for the tissue that is always there and wipes her nose and eyes. Eleanor looks at her daughter, the stubble where her hair used to be, the puffy skin around her eyes, dark from lack of sleep, and allows herself to hope that Lucy Dudley will take her in. I should be better at this, she thinks, more giving. I should have a big lap like mother had, big enough to hold her even now. But I've never had much of a lap. This will have to do.

Katherine begins to wonder if something has happened to Lucy. She is an old woman. Perhaps she is ill or has died. Katherine wheels the television into her room and turns it on.

In her dream she drives along a country road, dense forest on either side. The view in the mirror is all dust billowing out from beneath the tires. Light from the late afternoon sun flickers through breaks in the trees. And then rounding a bend she is startled by a large bird flying low across the road in front of her, turning to show the underside of its belly and wings, like a bobsled banking a long slow turn as it disappears among the trees. She cannot take her eyes off it and realizes she has stopped the car and stalled the engine because she didn't think to put in the clutch. She turns the key but it will not start.

Her eyes still fixed on the opening in the trees, she gets out of the car and walks in the direction of the bird's line of flight. The forest floor is spongy and soft beneath her feet, thick with needles and leaves. She hears a high and piercing cry from far away and she turns and runs toward the sound until she crests a small hill and stops to watch and listen, but there is only the wind and the sun dipping below the line of hills, darkness coming on. She looks around and cannot remember where she left the car. She begins to run, branches lashing her face as she plunges through the woods, blind to everything but her fear as every direction looks the same in the darkness coming on.

When a letter bearing a Vermont postmark finally arrives, Katherine takes it to her room and closes the door. She sits on the bed, the envelope in her lap, closing her eyes as she feels the paper in her hand. She goes to tear the flap and then pauses, her hands trembling, holding her breath.

Dear Katherine,

I am so sorry for the delay in writing to you, but I went to Burlington to help my son and when I returned there was a stack of mail and newspapers and somehow your letter made its way into a copy of the Globe and it wasn't until days later — just now — that it fell out when I opened the paper. I almost threw them out when I got home, but it's raining today and I felt restless and decided to see what had happened while I was away.

At any rate, of course of course I am sure. No, I shouldn't say 'of course' because it isn't that to you, but it is to me. I am as sure of this as I am of anything. I cannot be sure for you. Only you can be that and if you must decide to come without it then that is where you'll have to begin. But I can be sure for myself and I have no doubt that making a place for you is what I mean to do.

If you want to come by car I'll send directions. Or you can take a bus from Boston to St. Johnsbury and Sophie and I will meet you at the station. You need only tell me when.

Lucy

She reads the letter again and then again, searching for the slightest hint of doubt or pity, but finding none.

She goes into the basement and brings up her suitcases and packs her clothes that have been neatly stacked on the floor along the wall for more than a week. She roots in the drawer of the bedside table and retrieves the small piece of paper Lucy gave her in the hospital. She lifts the receiver off the phone, the first time she has touched it since arriving four months ago, and dials the number. It rings without an answer and she waits for a machine to pick up but then remembers that Lucy has none and so lets it ring on. She imagines her with goats in the barn, hearing the phone off in the distance through the screen door to the kitchen and waiting for the ringing to stop and when it does not, putting down whatever she is doing and hurrying to the house. But the phone keeps ringing and Katherine begins to weaken beneath the weight of her need to hear a voice at the other end, to be reminded of the woman behind the words she feels compelled to believe in spite of all.

She hangs up the phone. "Keep moving," she says to herself. Her eye falls on the television in the corner. She wheels it into the back of the closet and closes the door.

At dinner she waits until they have finished eating. "I've decided to go to Vermont," she says. "To spend some time with Lucy Dudley."

"Then you heard from her," her mother says.

"Yes," she says and looks up to see tears in her mother's eyes. Eleanor shakes her head as if to regain her composure but it doesn't work and she begins to cry. Richard watches her from the other end of the table and begins to stand but she holds up a hand and he sits back down.

"I'm all right," she says, her forehead resting on her hands making a visor over her eyes. Then she gathers her silverware and lays it on her plate as if about to clear the table.

"I just want you to be happy," she says, looking at Katherine and then down. "I don't know what you need. I don't understand any of this." She looks at Richard and shrugs, then looks back at Katherine. "And I can't stand seeing you so miserable and not being able to do anything about it." She pushes her plate away and folds her napkin on the table.

"I know," says Katherine. "I'd feel the same way." And she looks at her mother and as their eyes meet there passes between them the shared recognition that Katherine is no longer anyone's mother and will probably never be in a position to find out if she would feel the same. And her mother cannot restrain herself from lifting her eyebrows for an instant in a slight but unmistakable expression of reproach.

As Eleanor sees the color rise across Katherine's face, she hurriedly takes her plate and carries it to the kitchen. Richard follows her with his eyes and then looks at Katherine, his face pale.

Beneath the silence between them is the sound of running water and dishes laid in the sink.

"How will you get there?" he says at last.

The color deepens in her face as from somewhere in the back of her mind a disgusted presence lies in the dark and looks out at her, incredulous at the sight of an adult woman unable to decide how to get from one place to another.

She cannot move. She cannot clear her plate, for that would bring her to her mother's side at the sink. She cannot flee the room, because then she'd leave her plate for someone else to clear, like a self-absorbed teenager or a thoughtless guest. And she cannot stay in her father's gaze and the silence of his waiting for an answer to the simple question he offered up to deliver them all from her mother's reproach.

"I don't know," she says, but the words are lost in the ringing of the phone.

Her father goes to answer it and his voice drifts through the living room, low and restrained, until, "Oh," he says, "Yes. Fine, thank you. Yes. Yes, she is. I'll get her," and already she is on her feet, her stomach light and airy beneath the rapid beating of her heart. "It's Lucy Dudley," he says but can see in her face that she already knows.

"I'll go upstairs," she says and he follows her to the hall and watches her run up the stairs and listens for the sound of her coming on the line. He hangs up the phone and stands there for a moment remembering when she was younger and they enacted this scene so many times, except that it was always some young man on the other end. He senses something of that in this, some strong attraction held close and private that always holds the promise of taking her away from him. He walks into the dining room and clears their plates from the table.

"Hello," she says. "Lucy?"

"Yes, it's me." Katherine closes her eyes and feels herself drawn to the sound of the Dillard voice. "How are you?" it says.

"All right, I guess. I got your letter."

"Well, I'm glad of that," says Lucy, "but you know I should have called. It's so stupid of me, but I use the phone so rarely that I forget the damn thing is there. I suppose I could have saved you the trouble of waiting for the mail if I'd thought of it."

"No," says Katherine, "it's all right."

"Anyway, I thought we should talk. If we stick to the mail we'll be at it forever. Have you decided what you'd like to do?"

For a moment Katherine's mind is fixed on 'like to do,' holding it out as if turning a strange object in her hand to see all sides of it in the light.

"Yes," she says, letting go the words and feeling the weight of her own, "I would like to come. For awhile."

"Good."

"I expect to pay my way, I have money," Katherine's voice becoming tight and airless.

"Of course."

"I'll hold up my end. I'll help do things around the place. I won't be a burden."

"That's fine. Have you decided when?"

"I haven't got that far."

"Anytime is fine by me," says Lucy, "but it's up to you."

A pause. "What day is it?"

"Tuesday."

Another pause as Katherine feels her mind awash in possibilities.

"Would you like to wait until next week?" says Lucy.

"No. That'd be too long. I'm all packed."

"Then sooner."

"Yes."

"That would make it Thursday, Friday, Saturday, or Sunday. Like any of those better than the rest?"

"Saturday and Sunday seem a long way away."

"Right. Well, then, it's Thursday or Friday. Shall we flip a coin?"

"Okay."

"You got one?"

"No."

"How about a pen and paper?"

"Yes."

"Good. Write down a number. Any number you like."

Katherine writes the number 16.

"Got it down?"

"Yes."

"Okay. I'll tell you what. If the number's odd, it's Thursday. If it's even, it's Friday. What have you got?"

Katherine looks at the pad and feels her heart sink.

"Thursday," she says, scratching the pen back and forth across the number.

"Good — "

"No, actually it came out Friday. But I want to come on Thursday."

"I think if Thursday's what you want, then Thursday's what you get," says Lucy.

Tears crowd the edges of Katherine's eyes. "You know what I really want?"

"What?"

"Tomorrow."

3

The Vermont Transit daily express to St. Johnsbury leaves Boston at noon and makes only one stop in White River Junction. Eleanor packs a lunch and hands it to Katherine at the front door as her father takes the suitcases to the car. Katherine stands before her mother and marvels that no matter how old she becomes, whenever she returns to her parents' house her adult self is joined by Eleanor and Richard's little girl and, somewhere inside her, she is feeling about eleven years old.

"I love you," her mother says. "Come back whenever you need to."

"Thank you," she says, knowing her mother means it even though it isn't true. "I love you, too." She had thought the night before that she would cry at this moment and not be able to get out the door, but her eyes are dry as she hugs her mother and then turns to join her father in the car.

Last night she couldn't sleep, lying in bed and looking out the window at the sliver of moon in the sky and trying to imagine where she was going. She dozed for awhile until waking from a dream. She remembered none of it except a pack of dogs chasing her, their eyes red in the dark. She drifted in and out of sleep until she finally gave up just before dawn and rose to dress. Then she sat on the window seat and read poetry and occasionally glanced at the window across the yard. When at last she heard her parents stir she closed her book, gathered up her things, unlocked the door to her room, and went quietly downstairs.

"Do you have everything?" her father says. They are standing by the bus as the driver puts her suitcases down below.

"Probably not," she says, adjusting the cap she wears to cover what's left of her hair.

"You'll be fine," he says and tries to smile.

She looks at him. "I wish I could believe that, dad."

As his arms circle around her she wishes something as simple as this could make her feel safe again. They say good-bye and she turns and looks up the stairs into the bus. Once inside, she thinks, the door will close and she won't be able to get out. She looks at people already in their seats, a young couple turned inward toward each other and at the back a man with a beard. He looks at her looking at him, blinks, then looks away.

She sits three rows back from the driver on the opposite side where she can see what he's doing. She puts her lunch and handbag on the seat beside her to discourage anyone from sitting there. She holds the book of poetry as if it were a talisman with the power to protect her from anything that might spring at her without warning. People board the bus and as they walk past her seat she tightens her grip on the book and stares at the back of the seat in front of her. A little girl holding her mother's hand passes down the aisle. Katherine looks straight ahead.

A man throwing a suitcase into the overhead bin gives her such a start that she almost cries out. She can feel the man sitting behind her, his hands pulling on the back of her seat as he wedges himself in next to the window. Through the crack between her seat and the window she can feel his presence, sniffing his runny nose and clearing his throat before noisily leafing through a magazine.

She gathers up her things and moves to the seat in front. The driver looks at her over his shoulder and smiles. Her skin feels wet and clammy, the air warm and close. She pulls open the window and puts her nose to the opening.

A car alarm sounds from across the parking lot and she thinks that is just the way she feels, like those wailing sirens that go off when a woman struggles by with two sacks of groceries in her arms and bumps a fender or momentarily leans against the door to rest herself. Or they go off for no reason at all. She feels like an entire city full of alarms going off at random, their sensors gone haywire, seeing danger in every movement and every sound.

She might worry that she was paranoid if the man throwing his suitcase overhead only reminded her of David. But somehow in that instant he *was* David and the crashing overhead was everything in the kitchen being thrown at her at once and she was only moments from the knife and the blood and the dying and the loss. In that instant there was no 'as if,' no metaphor, simile, or even memory. She was there and it was happening all over again. And then, just as suddenly, it was gone and she was wherever she was before, in the second row of the express to St. Johnsbury, watching the driver count tickets before closing the door.

The bus swings out into traffic and Katherine watches people rush along the sidewalk and wonders how they do it, the women in particular, how they move about with so little awareness of the razor thin line that separates the illusion of safety from the suddenness of violence and death and oblivion. They have no idea how quickly everything can be snatched away and how little sense there is in the choice of who is taken and who is not. She watches a woman walk alongside the bus, tall and standing to her full height, her chin slightly raised, a briefcase in her hand, carrying herself forward on strong, confident strides. Katherine longs to join her, to lie once again in the embrace of illusion and denial. But she can't and feels she never will, the weak member of the herd, left behind by the rest in their hurry to escape the predators who wait patiently at the margins, and she runs until the rumbling of hooves recedes in the distance and she is alone with the sound of her own labored breath against the eager pants of those behind who gain and gain in their desire to pull her down.

The last time Katherine passed through White River Junction was a few months before graduation when she took the bus from Boston back to Burlington after spring break. What was then a small town on the edge of the Connecticut River now seems crisscrossed with highways and the once sleepy depot is surrounded by 24-hour gas stations and restaurants.

She remembers that David traveled this route the night they fought on the phone, when he called her stupid and then appeared outside her window to beg her to forgive him and she did.

The bus pulls into the station and the woman and her daughter get off. They are met by a man who lifts the girl with one arm while he hugs the woman with the other. He wears a green baseball cap that the girl promptly seizes and turns around backwards on his head. He crosses his eyes and looks at her with a goofy smile and then kisses her on the cheek and she laughs and reaches back to grab the hat and pull the bill around to the side, a game they seem to have played before. There is animated talk as they walk to the car and then drive off together. Katherine stares out the window, feeling nothing but the numb inertia of her body on the seat.

A young man climbs into the bus, carrying a guitar case covered with decals, peace signs, flowers, and words she cannot make out as he passes by. An elderly woman is just behind him, wearing a blue cotton dress and holding her handbag close to her body. She sits in the seat across from Katherine and opens her bag and takes out a candy bar, noisily peeling back the wrapper and sinking her teeth into the chocolate as her eyes close around a look of pleasure that makes Katherine turn away.

She tries to remember the taste of chocolate but her body has no memory of pleasure or beauty or rest or peace of mind, of feeling moved by an image or a metaphor, of collapsing beneath a tickle, touched by something funny, carried off on a shuddering orgasm or a good laugh. In some portion of her mind she knows about such things as she knows the mechanics of boiling an egg. But the delicious buttery smoothness of spooning it into her mouth is all theoretical and dry, strangely removed and without feeling.

The bus swings north onto the highway and she tries again to remember what Lucy looks like and suddenly feels a fear that has lingered just beneath the surface for days, that she doesn't know where she's going or what she's doing and this is simply one more mistake in a long line of fatal mistakes. She is lost somewhere between the living and the dead, riding a silver bus into the wilderness because she could not stand any longer to stay with the last two people in the world who might still have reason to love her.

When the bus arrives in St. Johnsbury Katherine looks out the window at an old woman walking briskly across the lot, thin legs jutting out from a long cotton skirt of many colors, blue sneakers on her feet. Her hair is white and pulled back behind her head. Her face is long and thin and as she scans the windows of the bus, Katherine knows she is looking for her.

The driver is the first one off and then the young man wrestling his guitar through the narrow opening and a young woman who runs down the stairs, calling out a greeting to her boyfriend who opens his arms to receive her.

And then Katherine turns the corner and stands on the top stair looking down.

Lucy has never seen her standing up before, only lying in the middle of a fortress of bedclothes and pillows. She is no taller than Lucy, just over five feet, and the features of her face, free of the bruising and the swelling, are small and round and pleasing to look at. She is wearing jeans and a long sleeved white blouse and a floppy hat that cannot quite conceal a general absence of hair. It reminds Lucy of women undergoing chemotherapy who make a futile gesture to soften and hide their loss beneath a bit of color. And as Lucy has seen them do, Katherine reaches up to touch the hat as if making sure it's still there.

They smile and then look away in the strange awkwardness of knowing so little of each other while drawn together in such intimacy, like a couple meeting for the first time to enact an arranged marriage.

"Katherine," says Lucy and they hug briefly and without ease, as if holding an egg between them. Katherine breathes in earth and sun and what she will identify later as hay and goats. The skin along the old woman's neck is creased and fine and her nose is lined with thin blue veins and her eyes are so moist that Katherine wonders if she is about to cry.

Even at a distance Katherine can see Sophie standing in the back seat of the car, mouth open and the entire rear end of her body wagging back and forth at the same time that she makes little hops into the air that make the car move up and down. Katherine opens the door and Sophie's grunting and panting spills out into the air.

"Is this all for me?"

"Oh, yes."

Lucy pulls the car up behind the bus and Katherine gets out and fetches her bags and piles them into the trunk. It's not an easy fit and the sounds of struggle and frustration are unmistakable to Lucy's ear.

"Need some help?"

"No," says Katherine, raising her hands in front of her as if to push her away. "I can do it. I probably shouldn't have brought so much stuff." Lucy gets back in the car and a moment later the trunk lid slams and Katherine slips into the seat beside her. "All set," she says, clicking her seat belt into place. "Sorry."

"Nothing to be sorry about."

In a matter of minutes they are out of town and driving west through endless shades of green, from the almost yellow green of pastures and fields in full sun to the dark green of pine and cedar covering hills ranging into the distance. Katherine had thought Sophie would settle down, but the commotion in the back seat only intensifies and the more she tries to ignore it the more agitated it becomes. Lucy reaches out a hand and makes shushing sounds, but to no avail.

"This isn't like her," Lucy says. "Is it too much?"

"I'm all right," says Katherine, but she is not, her body clammy with sweat and feeling unable to breathe. She rolls down the window and sticks her nose to the opening but it doesn't help. Suddenly Sophie's muzzle appears between the seats and she whimpers as she sniffs Katherine's clothes and then pants and groans. Katherine shrinks against the door with a small shout and Lucy promptly pulls the car to the side of the road and shoos Sophie back into the seat, wagging her finger as she orders the dog to lie down and stay. Sophie sinks into the seat and lowers her eyes.

"I am sorry," says Lucy.

Katherine runs a finger across her brow to press out the sweat that has collected there. She is breathing fast and shallow and her mouth is dry.

"It's okay," she says, gripping the door handle so hard that veins swell out against the back of her hand. "We can go. It's okay."

Lucy pulls the car onto the road and they travel on in silence. Sophie goes to sleep. Katherine wonders what just happened and wishes she were someplace else but cannot imagine where that might be. Lucy scolds herself for not thinking to leave Sophie at home, but then considers that if it weren't one thing it would be another.

They drive for half an hour and then leave the paved road to turn onto the network of gravel and hardpan roads that crisscross much of rural Vermont. They climb into the hills past widely separated farms. A stream runs beside the road and Katherine lowers her window and listens for the sound of water coursing over rocks, the air cool against her face. She looks into the back seat where Sophie lifts her eyes without moving her head, and worries that things have gotten off to a bad start.

They are rounding a gentle curve in the road when suddenly she sees a man walking beside the road and she knows it is David, not wondering or suspecting or guessing but knowing as surely as she knows anything at all, and stifles a gasp and is about to cry out when it comes to her that he is dead. It cannot be him, and yet, in that instant, the simple fact has no purchase on her mind and that is exactly who it is. She is breathing hard and can feel Lucy looking back and forth from the road ahead to her until the man turns and Katherine catches her breath at the sight of a face she's never seen before.

"Are you all right?" says Lucy, her voice sounding far away. Katherine fumbles to force words from her mouth, anything to keep from telling what she's seen, how real it was and yet impossible. She nods and they drive on in silence.

She is gazing out the windshield, wanting to disappear, when a red-tailed hawk flies directly in front of them and then turns and follows the road ahead. Its flight seems effortless, its wings barely moving as it powers itself forward and then, as suddenly as it appeared, lifts itself into the sky above the trees arching over the road and is gone.

The road winds upward through forest until it emerges onto an open hilltop dotted with small stands of oak and birch and ribbed with low stone walls. The sky is a bowl of clear blue light held by the hills all around. And at the highest elevation, just before them now, is Lucy's house with its broad porch beneath an old maple tall enough to shade the second floor at noon on a summer day. Across the road behind a low fence sits a graveyard, the white markers bright in the sun.

Sophie is pacing back and forth as Lucy turns into the driveway and parks in the yard near the back door. The goats, resting in the cool recesses of the barn, appear in the doorway, eyes fixed on the car, jaws working cud.

Katherine steps out and looks at Lucy over the roof of the car. "I had no idea it was so beautiful."

Lucy smiles and nods.

The kitchen is cool and the wide pine boards creak beneath her feet as Katherine follows Lucy and Sophie into the hall and up the stairs. The house has a smell both strange and familiar, strange in that she cannot remember another house like it and yet familiar in its power to touch an elemental earthbound place in her she'd forgotten was even there. Her mother's house and her own always smelled clean, but this house smells fecund and alive as if rooted like a tree in the ground. She stops halfway up the stairs and touches her nose to the wallpaper.

At the top of the stairs is a large bright room with a four-poster bed, which she assumes to be Lucy's. Just down the hall is a room where Lucy is raising a window and pulling back the curtains as Katherine steps inside.

"This is it. I cleared some space in the closet and the bureau. The bathroom is just across the hall. There are towels in the hall closet."

Katherine sets her suitcase down and walks to the window that looks to the north and the barn. "Thank you," she says.

Lucy nods, her hands holding each other in front of her waist. "Take your time. There's no hurry, no schedule. Rest yourself. Take a bath. Go for a walk. Do nothing at all. Whatever you like. If you're hungry, help yourself to whatever's in the kitchen." She walks to the hall and turns back into the doorway. "I'll be downstairs or out back. Just give me a shout if there's anything you need."

"Okay."

"I'm glad you're here, Katherine."

"Me, too." She walks toward the sound of Lucy's footsteps down the stairs and then closes the door and sits on the edge of the bed and holds and rocks herself as she begins to cry, unable to keep at bay the feeling that she has done it all wrong once again.

4

As evening comes the midsummer air softens and cools, first in shadows cast by trees and the barn, its red boards cut in angled swaths of light and dark, and then in the broad expanse of open fields suddenly alive with the song of crickets and peepers. Katherine hasn't left her room above the kitchen since she arrived. She follows Lucy's progress downstairs — a kettle set on the stove, a chair scraping back from the table and the creak of wicker beneath a body sitting down, a spoon against the side of a cup and then silence punctuated by cup against saucer, a throat softly cleared.

Katherine lies on the bed and stares up at the ceiling, its plaster cracked and water-stained from a hundred years of ice dams and weathered shingles. The walls are luminous in the fading light. She begins to worry what Lucy must think of her, hiding herself away, self-centered and neurotic, but there is something in the silence drifting up from down below that is contented, and for just a moment Katherine lets down into a kind of peace that almost passes into sleep.

She hears the screen door open, the spring straining outward and then rapping shut against the frame. The sound of footsteps down the back porch steps and across the yard draws her to the window where she sees Lucy standing at the edge of the shadows inside the barn, surrounded by goats who lift their faces to meet her hands floating through the air from goat to goat. Lucy's eyes are closed as she turns in a slow circle and touches them, caressing a nose or scratching just above the eyes or running her hand through the hair along the back. And then the goats are still and Lucy smiles and opens her eyes and says something. A goat cocks its head and looks up at her moving lips and she leans in and their noses seem to touch and all the while she talks and smiles like a teacher gathering a yard full of children to tell them a story.

There is a clatter of paws on the stairs as Sophie labors to the second floor, pads down the hall, and sniffs along the crack beneath the door to Katherine's room, then softly moans as she lies down against it.

Katherine stares at the door, wondering if she's being barricaded in or besieged by the hope of coming out.

Unable to think of what else to do she unpacks her clothes and sits on the bed and scans the titles in the small bookcase — several poetry anthologies, novels including one by Edith Wharton, a half dozen short story collections, and biographies of Queen Elizabeth I, Eleanor and Franklin Roosevelt.

She sits before the small writing table that looks out the east window. The single drawer holds a small stack of writing paper and an assortment of pencils and pens.

Below the window runs the driveway and beyond that a field of grass and wildflowers sloping down to a low stone wall. The distant hills are layered one upon another to the horizon, above which hangs the dusty presence of a freshly risen moon.

Sophie stirs against the door, pulls herself to her feet, and then walks back down the stairs, leaving Katherine not the relief she had expected but an edge of disappointment. She opens the door and looks down the length of the darkened hall. The house is quiet.

"Sophie," she whispers, and then again, but this time drifting into the air on a two-note melody, followed by the swift response, paws on bare floor, the long black nose rounding the post at the top of the stairs, tail wagging as she clambers down the hall, and before Katherine knows it she is on her knees, her fingers in Sophie's fur, the grey muzzle before her eyes, the sound of sniffing in her ear.

The screen door slams and Sophie turns and bolts toward the sound and Katherine cannot help but follow her down.

The kitchen is lit by a single lamp on the bureau, a deep red shade casting a warm glow across the room. Katherine stands in the doorway and looks at Lucy standing before the sink and scrubbing a carrot while Sophie sits beside her, watching every move. And then suddenly, like a clap of thunder inside Katherine's mind, as if a switch had been thrown to go from one reality to another, there is blood everywhere she looks and the air is thick, almost unbreathable around a small and lifeless shape lying in the shadows against the wall. She is breathing hard above the pounding of her heart, frozen to the spot, unable to move in or away as Lucy turns and sees Katherine staring past her from a dark and faraway place that she knows from her own reflection in a mirror many years ago.

"Katherine — "

She does not move or speak.

And then as suddenly as it appeared it is gone and Katherine looks about the room, unable, for a moment, to figure out where she is.

"Katherine," says Lucy, gently touching her arm.

They stand stock still in the doorway to the kitchen and then Lucy takes Katherine by the hand and guides her to a chair beside the table and then Katherine begins to tremble and even the calm and reassuring tones of Lucy's voice cannot make it stop.

Katherine does not know how much time has passed, slowly becoming aware of sitting in a chair and surveying Lucy's small frame at the kitchen sink, the white hair tied up with an occasional wisp trailing out into the air, the sweater not quite on one shoulder and the line of the cotton skirt hanging from what is left of her hips and flowing down to end at blue sneakers on her feet turned slightly out.

Lucy sets down the dish with Sophie's supper and then looks up and studies Katherine's face.

"Is the room all right?" says Lucy, trying to draw Katherine out.

There is a pause as Katherine tries to think what room she might be speaking of, and then, "Oh, yes. It's fine. Thank you."

"Are you hungry?"

"No."

Lucy scrambles eggs and makes toast and asks again and Katherine nods and takes the small plate held out to her.

They eat in silence and then Lucy takes a deep breath and releases it on a sigh as she starts in on building some semblance of a conversation. "There's no dining room anymore," she says. "It's all books now. You can help yourself. The attic's full of them, too." She leans in closer. "I get carried away when it comes to books. How about you?"

"Sometimes."

"Ever do any writing?"

Katherine looks down at her plate. "Not really."

"I try a little verse now and then," says Lucy. "I don't *work* at it, of course, but sometimes a line or two will come and I write it down. I love when that happens." She looks at Katherine pushing the last of her eggs into a neat little pile at the edge of her plate. "I'm going to have some tea. You want some?"

Katherine nods. She clears the table and washes dishes while Lucy puts a kettle on and spoons tea into the pot.

Lucy stands next to her and looks sideways into her face. "You don't quite know what's what."

Katherine shakes her head and lays the plate she is washing in the sink. Her eyes are wet and she looks down at the water flowing into the drain.

"It's an awful thing," says Lucy. "Just awful. The worst kind of lost there is."

Katherine begins to tremble as her eyes brim with tears and Lucy takes her into her arms. The kettle whistles and Katherine stiffens against her and pulls away, "I'm sorry," turning back to the sink.

"Whatever for?"

Katherine puts the last dish in the drainer. "Do you have a towel?"

Lucy takes Katherine's hands in her own and looks into her eyes. "Listen to me," she says. "It is very important that you not apologize. I'm sorry to be so direct, but I'm old and I can't help it."

Katherine looks into Lucy's eyes, shining and wide, and feels herself start to spin and fall into a dark opening in the sky, but Lucy does not let go and slowly Katherine returns to the stillness in the center of the old woman's eyes. She dips her head and sees Sophie beside them looking from one to the other with her ears pulled back against her head. Lucy bends down and takes Sophie's head in her hands, cooing "Don't you worry" and "everything's okay."

"She must think we're an odd species," she says, grabbing the edge of the counter and pulling herself up. "The awful things we do to one another. She'd have no idea about that. Dogs are very forgiving. It is their saving grace and sometimes their fatal flaw."

In the evening Lucy shows her through the house, beginning with the library and the living room across the hall, a large and airy space with a fireplace in the corner and landscapes and small family portraits on the walls. There is a couch in front of the fireplace and a writing desk against the wall between two windows facing west.

"I hesitate to call it a living room," Lucy says, "because I do so little of that in here. Make it yours if you like."

"Do you ever have a fire?"

"Rarely. I run the wood stove all winter and a fireplace isn't much help. By September, though, it can get cool enough for a fire to feel good in the evening. You might like that." They look at each other and Katherine wonders how long she will be welcome here, how soon it will be before Lucy grows tired of her and asks her to leave.

"You'll notice there is no television," says Lucy, stepping into the hall. "I used to have one but I got rid of it when I realized I was using it to keep me company. I think it was depressing me. Do you watch television?"

"Not much. My parents put one in my room and I put it in the closet."

"Exactly. It's so frantic. Always selling something. It wears me out. I'd rather read or go to sleep or take a bath or masturbate for pity sake." She waves her hand in the air on these last words and then brings it over her mouth. "Oh," she says, "pardon me. I forget myself sometimes. Too much living alone!" She strides into the kitchen. "Come on, Sophie, time to go out. Poop! Pee! To bed!"

Katherine stands in the hall and watches Lucy go out the door and then turn and lift her hands in a shrug.

Katherine sits on her bed and listens to the house grow quiet around her. She waits for Lucy to finish in the bathroom, then crosses the hall and quietly closes and locks the door. She brushes her teeth and only then realizes there is no shower, just a claw foot tub positioned to afford a view out a westward facing window. A narrow board is laid across it like a desktop and on it rests a book. She pictures Lucy in the tub, steam rising all around, reading and occasionally looking up at the sun dipping behind the hills. She sits on the toilet and stares at the tub and remembers the last bath she ever took, more than three years ago, and the sensation of drowning.

Lucy softly clucks into the darkness and pats the bed beside her. Sophie jumps up and curls into a ball next to her hip as Lucy strokes the fur behind her ears and gazes out the window.

She thinks of Katherine at the sink, so present in one moment and so utterly gone the next. She thinks she knows where she goes, having been there many times, transported to a timeless interior space where the world drops away. She saw it in her eyes, the blankness of isolation in the presence of another, the elevator going down and the face disappearing in the glass.

It is apparent to Lucy that the damage to Katherine's body has healed, or mostly so. But standing beside the sink she felt herself staring into an open wound, a wound in Katherine's very being, a wound to the soul, the terms of her existence forever altered, leaving her unable to live in the world as she did before.

Lucy feels an aching in her heart, a longing to save and to be saved. She longs for a mother she never had, some great Demeter, beside herself with grief, raging from one end of the earth to the other in pursuit of her lost Persephone, willing to lay waste to everything to force the gods to reach into hell itself and bring her back. Or some father who would take her in his arms and carry her to safety before the horror had time to envelop her and close her off from view, who would have seen it for what it was.

Sophie stirs and whimpers inside a dream. Lucy closes her eyes but does not sleep.

Katherine startles herself awake, her mouth dry, a stinging in her eyes, her body covered with sweat, sheets and nightgown sticking to her skin. She cannot remember the dream except for the blood and the sound of an animal screaming in terror as if being flayed alive.

There is a soft knock against the door and for a moment she is lost, unable to grasp the meaning of the sound in the aftermath of the dream. She holds her breath and listens and when it comes again she remembers where she is, but still doesn't know what to make of the soft rapping on the door, until a voice gently says her name and the door opens and Lucy's small frame crosses the room and sits beside her on the bed, the only sound their breathing in the darkness.

"I was dreaming," says Katherine.

"Yes."

"I'm sorry if I woke you."

Lucy nods. "I have an idea. Let's go downstairs and sit on the porch. Have some tea."

"All right."

Lucy pauses by the door. "It's cool outside, so you'll want to wear something over that. I'll go put the water on."

Katherine gets a towel from the bathroom and dries herself before putting on fresh clothes and going downstairs.

They sit on a wide swing that hangs from the front porch ceiling. The sky is full of stars and from the fields across the road drifts a steady chorus of peepers and crickets. They sit in silence, sipping the tea.

"No mosquitoes," Katherine says.

"They don't like the cold."

More silence. Katherine looks at the cemetery across the road. "Do you mind living so close to that?"

"Oh, no."

"It's not depressing?"

"Not at all. My family's over there. My grandparents on my mother's side are just by the gate. Those two stones that lean into each other are theirs, which is a lot like they were when they were alive. My parents are right behind them. I can visit anytime."

Katherine grows quiet.

"What was the dream?" says Lucy.

"I don't remember."

Lucy lifts the cup to her lips as she pushes her foot against the floor to set the swing in motion.

"I remember you said in the hospital that you still have bad dreams," says Katherine.

"Yes. Not so often, but, yes, I do."

"What happens?"

"In the dreams?"

"Yes."

"I'm running away mostly, from something after me. No matter what I do it's always there in front of me. No escape, except waking up, and sometimes even that doesn't work right away."

"I have those."

"Sometimes Philip is in the dream, but not always. He doesn't need to be for me to feel afraid."

"Was he your husband?"

"Yes."

"What happened to him?"

Lucy is silent amidst the slow creak of the swing.

"Tell me more about your dream," says Lucy, looking straight ahead, then turning to Katherine, "what?"

"I was wondering what happened to him."

"Who?"

"Your husband."

Lucy looks across the road.

"He went away."

"He just left?"

Lucy says nothing.

Katherine shakes her head. "I can't imagine that."

Lucy sighs. "Tell me about your dream."

Katherine is quiet for a moment. "I don't know. I don't remember it very well."

"Tell me what you do."

Katherine is silent for a long time, feeling her jaw setting in her face like cement.

"You killed him with a knife," says Lucy.

Katherine stiffens on the seat. Lucy keeps the swing in motion and sips her tea.

"Yes."

"That must have been horrible."

Katherine says nothing. Lucy leans over and looks into her face until Katherine nods.

Lucy sits back against the swing. "So what do you remember from the dream?"

Katherine focuses on a crack in the floor just in front of her feet. "Blood," she says, "and some kind of animal."

"What was it doing?"

"Screaming," says Katherine. "It was screaming."

Lucy allows the silence to settle in around them, the rocking of the swing, the peepers and crickets in the fields, and they drift together through the minutes passing by and seem content to let it be until suddenly Katherine speaks as if continuing a conversation that Lucy knows nothing about.

"You know," she says, "I think I dreamt once about a hawk that I saw from the car."

"Really."

"I've never believed in things like that," says Katherine, "dreaming about what happens later."

"Maybe it's not exactly that," says Lucy.

"What do you mean?"

"Maybe the lines between the present and past and future aren't as clear as we think." She looks at Katherine and shrugs off a little smile. "It's hard to get old and not become a bit of a mystic. Your life slows down. It's hard not to notice."

Too tired to talk, Katherine and Lucy go back to bed and sleep until Sophie agitates for breakfast and going out and goats get restless and play games of tag and kick and leap against the inside walls of the barn.

They sit at the kitchen table and drink tea and eat cereal from a box. "We should go shopping," says Lucy. "I can show you around town and we can get what you like to eat."

"This is fine."

"This is what you usually have?"

"It's fine. Really."

Lucy sits back in her chair. "What's your favorite thing for breakfast?"

Katherine sighs and looks down at the table, her eyes moving back and forth, but Lucy waits her out, not moving, her face calm beneath a steady gaze. Katherine looks up at her, then down again, "I used to make my own granola, but that was years ago."

"What was in it?"

"Oats. Honey. Nuts. I don't know."

"We can get that," Lucy says. "We have a food co-op in town. Big bins full of stuff. Are you a tea drinker?"

"Sure."

"For breakfast?"

"Not usually."

"What, then?"

"Coffee."

"Regular or decaf?"

"Regular."

"Okay."

"Well, no. Half and half. I like to mix them together."

"We'll get both. What else?"

"It doesn't matter."

"Yes, it does."

"Fruit, then."

"What kind?"

"Bananas, I guess."

"Sounds good," says Lucy, "what else? Peaches? Strawberries? Blueberries?" and then detects in Katherine's face the smallest traces of a smile.

"What's so funny?" says Lucy, smiling back, until she sees something happen in Katherine's face as she shrugs and says, "Nothing" and then whatever was there is gone as Katherine stares down at the table and shrinks into the chair.

Lucy leans quickly in and says, "No, dear, I meant that as a question. It wasn't a trick. I really want to know what you were smiling at." In the silence Lucy remembers the dreadful sense of danger that followed every act of self-assertion, no matter how small and insignificant, every gesture that made her own life visible as something not under his control, separate from what he wanted or felt one moment to the next.

Katherine seems to be disappearing in front of her, as if Lucy could wave her hand and watch her dissipate like a vapor. Lucy bends low over the table to look up into her face but cannot get her eye. Suddenly she pushes the dishes out of the way and climbs up onto the table, using her chair as a step, and slowly lies down on her back with her head beneath Katherine's face.

Katherine blinks and lets out a little gasp as if suddenly pulled back from the edge of falling asleep.

"It's just me," says Lucy.

Katherine looks from one end of Lucy to the other and frowns. "What are you doing?"

"Trying to get your attention. You went away just as we were on the verge of having a good laugh."

Katherine looks into Lucy's face and wonders if this is oddest person she has ever known and what will be coming next. And then suddenly she is embarrassed and looks away. "I'm sorry," she says.

"Don't be," says Lucy, "nothing to be sorry about. Not to me." There is a pause and then she bears down upon the words. "I really do know how it feels, Katherine."

"What?"

"Never feeling safe, like you're always this close to getting hit for something you never see coming until it's too late. I know about that. And so do you."

Katherine's eyes grow wet and large.

"Tell me I'm wrong," says Lucy.

Katherine looks away, "You're not wrong," she says.

Lucy looks at her face, noticing a fine scar beneath her lower lip. "Katherine," she says, "how about you look at me and say that."

Katherine sniffs, pauses, then turns her head and looks into Lucy's eyes. "You're not wrong."

Lucy nods. "Right," she says. "You know about that."

Katherine nods.

"We both do," says Lucy, pulling a tissue from her pocket and handing to Katherine. "So. We were talking about pleasure. And fruit. And having what you want. And how funny I am."

Later in the morning Lucy introduces her to goats. Katherine steps up to the fence that forms a yard around the barn door and the goats come to her en masse, jockeying for position.

"Do they bite?"

"Not really." Lucy leans against the barn. "They're nibblers mostly, especially cuffs and back pockets."

A small goat, her coloring a mixture of white and honey, sticks her nose through the fence and Katherine leans over and brings her face in close. They sniff each other and she remembers the story of the Alaskan Inuit who kiss not so much by rubbing noses as by drawing near enough to mingle their breath. She looks into the goat's eyes and when their noses accidentally touch, Katherine starts backward, but the goat stands her ground, cocking her head to one side until Katherine returns and breathes in the sweet smell of hay.

"Can I go in?"

"Of course," says Lucy stepping toward the gate. "The thing to remember is their heads are hard as rocks and they may take a swing at you." She unlocks the gate. "They're not trying to hurt you. They're just wanting a scratch."

"So what do I do?"

"Keep an eye on where they are."

Katherine steps through the open gate and is immediately surrounded by goats, faces upturned, eyes wide and fixed upon her. At first she holds her hands up high and close to her body like a girl wading into cold water, but the animals are warm and soft and solid against her and soon she brings her hands to rest on their backs, seeking out the small one she met at the fence.

"They're beautiful," she says.

Lucy smiles and turns toward the barn.

"Where are you going?" says Katherine.

"To change their water." She turns and looks at her. "You'll be fine. Just remember what I said." She disappears into the barn.

Katherine feels a wave of panic and her arms suddenly hang awkward and stiff from her shoulders. Every movement of the goats gives her a start as if they might knock her down. Something hard rubs against her hip and she looks into the face of the honey white who seems suddenly more wild and unpredictable than cute and much larger and heavier than when she stood on the other side of the fence.

Nervously, Katherine lifts her hand and scratches the goat's head and to her surprise the rubbing against her hip stops and she finds herself looking into a face gone soft and dreamy-eyed beneath her touch.

"A bunch of pushovers," says Lucy, coming out from the barn.

At that moment something hard hits Katherine on her elbow and she cries out and jerks her body away, scattering goats in all directions as she makes for the gate.

"Gertrude wanted equal time," says Lucy, laying a hand on Katherine's arm, but Katherine pulls away and backs against the fence.

"You didn't see it coming," says Lucy.

Katherine sets her jaw and shakes her head.

"When you get the hang of it you'll have an eye out without even knowing it. Your hands will know where to be long before your brain. Like your feet know where to go when you dance." Katherine still shakes her head, her arms crossed over her chest. "This isn't like before," says Lucy. "You're bigger and smarter than they are and they haven't a mean bone in their bodies. Cranky at times and certainly wild in their way, especially in the spring. But we're in charge and they know it."

"You, maybe."

"Yes. And you, except you don't know it yet, and they're a little confused by that."

The goats reassemble by the gate and stand around in a half moon, attentive to the conversation between the two women.

"I have an idea," says Lucy, holding out her hand. "Come on."

Katherine looks at the goats and then at Lucy's hand.

"Trust me," says Lucy.

Katherine takes Lucy's hand and they walk to the middle of the yard.

"Stand with your back against mine," says Lucy. "Lean in a little, so you know I'm there."

Katherine leans back. The goats come around and she puts out her hands to ward them off. "This feels silly."

"Good," says Lucy. "Now. . . take a step forward." Katherine steps forward as Lucy takes a step back. "Now to your left," and they step together, "and your right," their spines still against each other, "how does that feel?"

"Funny."

"Well, we could sure use some of that. Okay. I've got you covered and you've got me. So imagine we're just floating in the ocean and these goats are little swells and waves. Keep your hands out there since there might be a piece of driftwood that could whack you if you're not careful. But mostly just float and enjoy the ride."

Katherine stands still, her arms stretched out straight toward the goats drawing in close.

"And don't forget to breathe," says Lucy.

Katherine lets go the breath she's been holding, feeling Lucy's back against her own, bony but solid and going with her every movement. The honey white goat is next to her again, looking up, and Katherine begins to sway back and forth as if held and carried along. From the corner of her eye she sees a head swing in toward her and she reaches out to intercept it with a scratch. Her other hand roams through the air, settling on this goat and that, patrolling, sensing the living movement all around them. They drift together, all of them, and for a moment she closes her eyes and feels the sun on her face and her feet on the ground.

"How you doing back there?" says Lucy.

"Okay."

"Good. Let's take a walk. You decide where and I'll follow."

Katherine steps forward and stops as she loses touch with Lucy's back.

"Keep going," says Lucy, "I'm right here," and they walk together about the yard, surrounded by the soft bustle of hooves on dry packed ground. Katherine stops and the herd draws in close.

"Do they all have names?"

"Oh, yes."

"What's this one?" says Katherine, pointing to the honey white.

"That's Elsie. I named her after an old friend of mine."

Katherine looks past the fence and the house to the hills in the distance and the blue sky along the horizon. The goats start to wander away, except for the honey white.

"What now?"

"Whatever you like."

"Do you know what time it is?"

"Why?"

"I'm hungry."

"Then it's time to eat."

"How do we get out of here?"

"Just pick a direction and go."

In the kitchen Lucy notices that almost everything Katherine does is preceded by the slightest hesitation, a single beat inserted between the impulse and the act. The simplest thing, like setting the table and choosing where to put a plate, becomes an occasion for doubt and then worry and a kind of paralysis, her body tense and braced in anticipation of something she cannot see. A certain fluidity is missing, a taken-for-granted ease of being and motion through time and space has been broken and now strains and rattles and lurches to get anywhere at all. She is like a driver with one foot on the gas and the other on the brake, her fingers white-knuckled against the wheel.

"Is this all right?" says Katherine, pointing to the table.

"It's fine."

They eat lunch and then drive into town. The road winds down the hillside into thick woods where it skirts the end of a long narrow pond. The water close in looks dark and cool in the shade and is dotted with lily pads topped with yellow flowers.

Katherine turns and follows the line of water out of the shadows into the sunlit middle where a bird floats on the surface and then suddenly disappears.

"Do you like to swim?" says Lucy.

"I used to."

"We have the pond pretty much to ourselves. All the land on this side is mine and a big chunk on the other side belongs to Walter Finch. The rest is state forest and I've never seen anyone there."

"Who's he?"

"Walter?" Lucy smiles. "A man I've known most of my life. He and his wife have the next farm over. They took care of Sophie when I came to see you."

They drive on through the woods, the tires noisy against the road, a cloud of dust trailing out behind, the road ahead dappled with sunlight coming through the trees. Katherine leans forward and looks up through the windshield and Lucy wonders if she's looking for another hawk.

"How is it. . .being out in the world?"

"Is that what I am?" Katherine sits back and looks straight ahead. "Okay, I guess."

"I wouldn't leave the house after he was gone," says Lucy. "Not for weeks. The idea of going into town scared the daylights out of me. I didn't feel safe at home, either. I had the general store deliver food. They left it on the porch. They must have thought I was crazy, which I suppose I was. I kept thinking he was coming back. I'd go around the house at night and check the locks on all the windows and doors and then I'd get in bed and start to worry and go check them again."

"I get that way sometimes," says Katherine, "even though I know he can't."

"Because he's dead."

"Yes."

"It doesn't matter, does it."

"No," says Katherine, looking at her.

"What?" says Lucy.

"I was wondering how you knew that."

A look comes over Lucy's face that Katherine hasn't seen before. A certain hesitation, a loss of composure, as if taken by surprise, a slight darkening around her eyes.

"It just makes sense," says Lucy.

The ride smooths out as they turn onto the blacktop.

"Anyway, my friend Elsie figured out something wasn't right and came to stay for the summer. I don't know what I'd've done without her."

"Does she live around here?"

"Not anymore. She died some years ago." She looks at Katherine. "That was something, you getting on that bus. I don't know that I could've done it."

"I didn't know what else to do."

They go to the grocery store where the clerks greet Lucy by name and are chatty in the checkout line. Katherine hangs back, her hands resting on the cart until Lucy takes her by the arm and gently pulls her forward to introduce her. She smiles, but only a little, like a girl with a new set of braces.

At the bookstore Lucy shows Katherine the poetry and children's books in the vault, and introduces her to the owner, Annie Harris, a large, tall woman with a big-boned face, her hair tied back behind her head beneath a dark blue scarf covered with silver moons and stars.

"Annie keeps our brains alive around here," says Lucy.

Annie laughs. "And Lucy keeps me alive."

"Katherine is a book lover herself," says Lucy.

"Come in whenever you want," Annie says, pointing to a stuffed chair in the corner by the front window.

They stop at Dewalt's for coffee and a donut shared between them and then take the long way home as large white clouds drift in from the west. Katherine lays her head against the seat and closes her eyes, suddenly exhausted, and Sophie, lulled by the rhythm of the wheels against the road and inspired by her example, circles twice, lies down, and goes to sleep.

Each night, the commotion of Katherine's dreaming draws Lucy to her room. On some nights Katherine makes no noise or Lucy has sunk so deep in sleep that she doesn't hear. On the first such night Katherine lies awake until morning. But on the second she pads down the hall to Lucy's room and stands in the doorway, looking at her asleep.

When Lucy begins to snore softly, Katherine goes back to her room but is stopped by the sight of rumpled bed clothes, chilly and without color or warmth in the pale light. She turns and goes back and as she crosses the threshold Sophie rises from her bed with a grunt and wagging tail, stirring Lucy toward the sound.

"It's me," says Katherine.

"Come and sit."

Katherine sits on the bed and Lucy yawns and lays a hand on her arm. The air smells faintly of cold cream and hay.

"Shall we go down?" says Lucy.

As on so many nights, Katherine hesitates, wanting not to go and yet feeling unable to resist the pull of a need she cannot name that she sees reflected in the old woman's eyes as she waits for Katherine's reply. And so, once again, they go downstairs to sit and rock and talk.

Lucy offers tea, then sensing hesitation, retrieves the bottle of Jack Daniels from the cupboard.

They sit on the porch, sipping the whiskey neat. "I wouldn't mind a cigarette," says Katherine.

"Neither would I. But I smoked the last one in the house months ago."

"I have some," says Katherine, like a girl at camp revealing a cache of cookies sent from home. She goes upstairs and gets a crumpled pack from the bureau in her room. She watches Lucy break off the filter and put the other end in her mouth.

"You don't fool around."

"Too old for that," says Lucy. She lights a match and draws on the cigarette and leans back to blow the smoke into the cool night air. "I don't eat sugar-free, fat-free ice cream, either. I don't see the point."

They sit and rock and sip and smoke and Katherine begins to feel a certain ease until she hears Lucy clearing her throat. "Tell me about David."

There is a long silence.

"I don't want to talk about him."

"Why not?"

"I don't know."

"Sure you do," says Lucy. "It feels terrible."

Katherine nods.

"Well, honey, seems to me it's already pretty bad."

"It could be worse."

"I don't see how."

Katherine gets up and walks to the end of the porch where she leans against the rail.

"I know how bad it can feel to say it out loud," says Lucy, "but believe me, silence is a whole lot worse." She rocks forward and stubs the cigarette on the sole of her slipper. "I remember that awful truth sitting in my mouth, like excrement. I didn't think I could stand the sound of it." She finishes her whiskey and sets the glass on the floor. "But it's the silence that kills you."

Katherine flicks her cigarette into the air and watches the glow spinning end over end onto the lawn.

And then Lucy is beside her. "Katherine," she says, her voice low, "you do what you want. You don't want to talk, then don't. But I'd be a poor friend if I didn't tell you it'll stay a nightmare that's sunk so deep inside it'll feel like something you are. And you'll be alone with it because there's no way I or anyone else can get in there on our own."

Katherine stares into the darkness, her jaw set hard.

"It took me months to realize what happened to me wasn't a nightmare or something *about* me or who I was. It was something he did to me, out in the world, which is where I have to deal with it."

"But you married him."

"Yes," says Lucy, "I did. But I didn't marry *that.*"

"Why then?"

"Why did you?"

"Why does anyone?" she says, her voice tight in her throat. "I loved him."

"Right. And what exactly was so lovable?"

Katherine sighs and brings a hand to her face.

"Charm?" says Lucy, "Intelligence? Good looks? Wanted you so bad he couldn't let you go? Just nod or something when I'm getting warm."

"He used to write poems and sneak them into my dorm room. On my pillow."

Lucy is just beginning to say something when the sensation hits Katherine along the entire length of her body like a shock wave from an explosion. Suddenly he is on top of her, humping, slamming himself into her, the taste of blood in her mouth, cries frozen in her throat. She bolts across the porch and catches her leg on the swing and falls to the floor. Tears pour down her face as she gulps for air. Lucy goes to her and tries to help her up but Katherine pushes her away and crawls across the floor toward the wall of the house. Lucy watches her curl herself into as small a target as possible, knees pulled up to her chest, forearms blocking her face. She is, Lucy knows, no longer here, but back in that house with him and as long as she is there Lucy can only sit and wait for her to find her way back again.

Minutes go by and Katherine slowly quiets down and begins to rock herself back and forth as if comforting a child. And then she is still as she looks across the porch to where Lucy sits and watches from a distance. Katherine's face is red and puffy, streaked with tears. She wipes the back of her hand across her nose. They sit and look at each other for a long time.

"Do you know what that was?" says Lucy. "Where you were?"

Katherine shakes her head.

"Was he here?"

Katherine's eyes grow wide, unable at first to make the words come out of her mouth.

"He's dead."

"I know. But was he *here?*"

Katherine looks into her lap where the fingers of one hand are worrying the fingers of the other, and then, without looking up, she nods.

"Was he hurting you?"

Katherine looks up and stares into Lucy eyes, saying nothing.

"What was he doing, Katherine?"

Katherine's face reddens in the light coming through the library window. She looks away and then back again. She sees no judgement in Lucy's face, nor even anticipation, looking as though she has just asked the most mundane question in the world — where you were born or are you left or right-handed or what's your favorite color — and now waits for an answer with an ease beyond patience. But Katherine cannot give herself over to this deep pull to speak, to hear her own voice fill the air around them, unable to trust that this is real, that there is no danger waiting to reveal itself when she least expects it.

"Come here," says Lucy, sitting on the swing. Katherine sits beside her, looking out over the road to the pale tombstones on the other side. A breeze rises from beyond the trees and rustles through the leaves before washing over the porch. Lucy pushes off with her foot to set the swing in motion.

"What was he doing?" says Lucy. "Don't say it to me. Tell it to the trees. Or them," she says, pointing her chin toward the cemetery.

"It's important that you say the words," says Lucy. "I can't do it for you."

An owl hoots far off in the distance. "All right," Katherine whispers, looking across the road. "He was raping me."

Lucy nods and follows Katherine's gaze across the road above the tombstones to the fields and dark woods beyond.

"It doesn't make any sense, does it," says Lucy. "This man who loved you, raping you."

"No."

"This charming man." Lucy hands her a tissue.

Katherine wipes her eyes and blows her nose and suddenly sees her grandmother's face in her mind, *he holds you very close.*

"You gave yourself to him — " says Lucy.

Katherine begins to cry.

" — and now you think it was a stupid thing to do."

Katherine squeezes her eyes shut around the tears and shakes her head.

"Well," says Lucy, "I don't think it was stupid. Unfortunate. Awful. Terrible. But not stupid."

Katherine shakes her head faster as if to keep the words away, until a single thought inserts itself into her racing mind to crowd out all the rest. "You don't understand."

"Tell me what I don't understand."

But Katherine is on her feet now, pacing away across the length of the porch, muttering to herself what Lucy cannot hear, repeating it like a mantra as if to keep some awful specter at bay, while Lucy keeps saying her name, "Katherine, Katherine," until suddenly Katherine stops in the middle of the floor and screams, "I. . .should. . . have. . .KNOWN!" the words coming out of her with a force that stuns them both into silence.

Lucy feels the swing come to rest beneath her. There is no sound but the peepers and Katherine breathing hard as she stands motionless at the far end of the porch. Lucy is afraid, of what, she doesn't know, except that it comes not only from Katherine standing in the shadows but from inside herself as well. Lucy closes her eyes to gather her courage around her.

"So," she says at last, "it was all your fault then."

"I should have known," says Katherine, slowly beginning to pound her head with the heel of her hand.

"You should have known," says Lucy, coming to her and gently taking her wrist in her hand. They stand in stillness beside each other, Katherine looking down at the floor.

"You were supposed to know what he was really like."

Katherine nods, the tears rolling down her face.

"That he would try to control you. That he would hurt you."

There is a long silence.

"Tell me, Katherine, after he beat you, did he apologize?"

Katherine nods.

"And was he contrite? Did he tell you he loved you? Did he swear it would never happen again?"

She looks at Lucy, wondering how she knows. "Yes."

"And you believed him."

"Yes."

"Because you loved him and you wanted to keep your family together."

Katherine nods.

"That was your job."

"Yes."

"And so you forgave him."

Katherine turns away, a stricken look on her face, shaking her head, "What was I supposed to do?"

"I think," says Lucy, sitting down on the swing, "you believed you were supposed to give him the benefit of the doubt because that's what every good wife who wants to make her marriage work is supposed to do. And you believed your love could heal his wounded self and get through to the loving man beneath the violence and the rage. All you had to do was hold on long enough. Endure enough."

Katherine looks at her for a long time, her lips barely moving as if in response to some voice deep within herself, and then turns away.

"Of course you didn't see it coming," says Lucy. "Or saw bits of it but doubted yourself enough to keep on going."

Katherine sits down beside her and lights a cigarette and holds up her empty glass.

"Maybe I should just get the bottle," says Lucy.

"All right."

Katherine hears the screen door slam softly against the jamb and in the silence notices the chorus of crickets and peepers for the first time since she came outside. She goes to the steps and sits down and looks up into the sky, dark blue, almost black, and full of stars. Beneath the aching in her body she feels a vague sense of release in knowing that for all of Lucy's probing, the awful dread she carries in the pit of her stomach still remains unspoken and thus unreal, and that keeping it so is what will save her and allow her to continue the semblance of a life that is now all that is left to her.

Lucy sits beside her and puts the bottle on the step between them. A car emerges from the woods at the bottom of the hill and its headlights play across the trees as it climbs towards them, the dull clatter of tires on gravel and dirt muted by the heavy night air, and then the light washes over the house and the porch and the tombstones across the road and illuminates a small frog hopping its way to the other side, and without a word the two women lift their glasses toward the car in the gesture of a toast as it rumbles by and disappears down the hill, its red lights obscured by the dust kicked up behind that settles slowly to the ground into something like sleep.

5

Mommy. Middle of the night, a single word enough to announce his coming on padded feet down the hall for reassurance that a dream is just a dream or for the comfort of knowing he's not alone, that she's still there if only to take him by the hand and guide him back to bed and tuck the covers in, whisper that she loves him and say good night. It comes to her not as in a dream or a memory but as real, spoken in the air, *mommy,* rousing herself toward the sound of footsteps in the hall that fade as if going the other way, gone by the time that she remembers.

She thinks she cannot bear these endless visitations, to feel him still alive and wanting only to be with her, only to realize that he is not, to suffer the loss of him not once, but over and over again. She curls into a ball and tries to hold herself against the sensation of him cradled within her. She remembers the months of playing with him through the thinning wall of her belly, talking to him, fingers spread out across the taut hard skin, waiting for the next kick or turning, the next hiccup, the next stillness when they seemed to be as one. And she remembers when she knew he was on his way at last, as if she'd become the earth itself and every living thing was about to erupt into life from within her. But her belly now is flat and covered with scars from where he was ripped away. She rocks back and forth and thinks she cannot stand it one more time and then the small strong hands are upon her and she smells the familiar scent of cold cream and hay and they rock together until she quiets and Lucy touches the tender spot behind her head and wonders at the depth of the terrible wound she feels through her hands and how if ever it might be healed.

Some days are better and some are worse. They spend an afternoon in the garden and Katherine is full of questions about flowers and laughs once or twice as she works the moist earth, sweat running down her face. And when they go into the kitchen for lemonade she drinks it with a kind of open-throated gusto Lucy normally associates with working men.

But when they go back into the garden Katherine has less and less to say, drifting in the silence to a place where Lucy cannot go, a numb depression she can feel in the body next to her filling with despair. Katherine begins to use her trowel as a weapon, stabbing at the earth, annoyed by the reluctance of a deep-rooted weed to yield. Finally she sits back on her heels and throws the trowel into a dense thicket of flowers and almost runs into the house, feet pounding the steps, the back door slamming hard.

She does not emerge from her room until after dark when Lucy finds her sitting at the kitchen table and staring down into a half-eaten bowl of cereal, her face pale and sunk low. Lucy makes a cup of tea and sits across from her. Katherine doesn't move. Lucy stirs and drinks her tea. Sophie lies down by the stove. The ticking of the clock is the only sound in the room.

"I'm sorry," says Katherine.

"I know."

Katherine goes to bed but doesn't close her eyes, afraid of what will come from the darkness inside herself. Just before dawn she falls into a short and restless sleep and wakes to the sound of Lucy in the barnyard with the goats. Her body feels dense and stiff. The sun through the east window has already heated the room, leaving her eyes puffy and dry, an ache in her head, her stomach gnawing but with no desire to eat.

She climbs out of bed and watches Lucy through the window, leaning against a large wooden spool the goats use for climbing. Two goats stand on top and behind her, one of them the honey white, heads bent low as if to whisper in her ear. Three others are grouped around her on the ground as she talks to them and rubs their heads. Elsie suddenly leaps to the ground, turning in the air like a dancer and giving a little outward kick.

How Katherine longs for such easy tenderness. She goes into the bathroom and locks the door, pulls the nightgown over her head and climbs into the tub to wash herself from the spigot, dousing her face with cold water until her mind begins to clear and the ache subside.

She dresses quickly and hurries downstairs, glancing self-consciously into Lucy's room as she passes, the bedclothes neatly laid and even Sophie's empty bed bearing witness to Katherine being the last one up. The rooms downstairs have been spared the morning sun and the floors are cool beneath her feet.

Lucy comes through the back door with Sophie who begins to grunt and wag her tail at the sight of Katherine.

"Good morning," says Lucy.

"Morning."

"Rough night."

Katherine looks away.

Lucy washes her hands and then turns and leans against the sink, working a towel between her fingers. "I have an idea," she says. "Today we take a walk to someplace you haven't been."

Katherine stands in front of the open refrigerator. "I'm okay here."

"I know that and I'm going out on a limb here, but I think you'll be glad you came."

Katherine does not think before she speaks and is surprised to hear the words coming out of her, "I really don't need you to take care of me," surprised at the edge in her voice, caught between wanting to be taken care of in just this way and wanting to be left utterly alone.

Lucy stops drying her hands, her face alert, eyes narrowed. "Right," she says, "of course." She studies her fingers as she works the towel. "Are we going to have our first fight?"

Katherine looks at her, startled, "No," looking back into the refrigerator, "why do you say that?"

Lucy lays the towel on the counter and crosses her arms over her chest. "Because you're angry enough for two."

"I am not."

"You're not angry."

"No. I'm depressed." She closes the door hard. "There's a difference."

"I have to say it's hard to tell from here."

"How do you know how I feel?" says Katherine, no longer surprised, her voice edgy and brittle, "what?"

Lucy looks away for what seems a long time and Katherine doesn't move. A whimper comes out of Sophie as she looks from one to the other.

"Of course I don't know how you feel," Lucy says at last. "And I apologize if I acted as though I did." She turns and hangs the towel on a hook inside the door beneath the sink. "Sophie and I are going for a walk around 11:00. I'm going to pack a lunch and I'll make enough for you in case you feel differently by then. I hope you will, but it's okay if you don't."

She steps to the back door and holds it open for Sophie. "I'm going to wear a bathing suit under my clothes and you might want to do the same. Walking shoes would be a good idea, too."

Lucy begins to step through the doorway and then stops and looks at her. "I know I can seem terribly sure of myself, like I think I know everything. It probably comes from living alone with my own thoughts for too long. I can be as full of hot air as anyone. But I am on your side, Katherine, enough to fight with you. But not over taking a walk or what to call the things you're feeling."

Lucy spreads her lips in a joyless little smile and then goes out the door and Katherine stands still as she listens to footsteps across the yard.

Katherine takes the stairs two at a time and closes the door behind her and drops to her knees by the bed and pulls a suitcase from underneath. She opens it and turns first toward the closet and then the bureau and then the closet again before sinking to the floor and beginning to cry. She cannot stop the trembling and begins to hit herself on the head with the heel of her hand in a steady rhythmic counterpoint to the word 'stupid' said over and over again. She has, she thinks, let loose the monster and now Lucy, for all her kind and gentle patience, will soon realize her mistake and get rid of her.

Through her window Katherine hears the delicate tone of a trowel striking small stones as it digs into the dirt. She listens, then goes to the window. Lucy is in the garden on her hands and knees, weeding and loosening the soil. Katherine waits for her to turn and show on her face some sign of what has happened between them. Sophie comes up behind Lucy, sniffing among the flowers, and then her nose wanders to Lucy's rear end and with a whoop Lucy clamps a hand behind and straightens up.

"You freshy," she says. "I am *not* a dog." Sophie wags her tail and sits as Lucy continues talking, the words drifting in bits and pieces on the air. Lucy scratches Sophie behind the ears and Katherine can tell she's talking about the walk they will soon take, her voice rising in the animated way adults are with small children being prepared for an adventure, and then, amidst the stream of words her heart leaps at the sound of her own name and she holds her breath to listen for it again until it comes, clear and unmistakable.

She wipes her eyes and blows her nose and rummages in the top bureau drawer until she finds her bathing suit, puts it on and then dresses again. She sits on the bed and closes her eyes and concentrates on breathing slowly and deeply. The screen door slams beneath her window and she opens her eyes and hurries downstairs.

Lucy is at the sink, washing her hands, and turns toward the sound of her entering the room. They look at each other for a moment, saying nothing, and then Lucy nods and Katherine nods in return.

They pack sandwiches and carrots and apples and pears and lemonade in a purple knapsack. In a second bag Lucy puts two flashlights — saying it might be dark when they return — and then bath towels, suntan lotion, a plastic pouch of dog food, reading glasses, and a book. Katherine gets the Edith Wharton from the bookcase in her room.

Sophie is turning in circles by the door, gathering momentum for the instant when it opens and she bolts through and out past the barn and into the field that slopes toward the woods. The grass is tall and she bounds as if running in shallow water, the women following behind.

"Where are we going?"

"You'll see."

Sophie reaches the woods and takes a few steps into the trees and seems to disappear. Katherine cranes her neck to see where she has gone, but cannot find her. At the line of trees she follows Lucy along a small path on a downward slope into cool shadows. She stops and looks back but cannot see the fields, only slivers of sky through the trees. She continues on, following the spot of purple on Lucy's back. A crashing of twigs draws her eye to Sophie who lumbers after a chipmunk squeaking as it runs away.

And then a breeze rises up the hillside and washes over her and she looks up to see blue sunlit water sparkling through the trees. Lucy stops and looks over her shoulder and smiles and then forges on down the hill, her sneakers slapping against the hard packed trail.

At the edge of the pond is a clearing and a small cabin at the water's edge. On the uphill side of the clearing is an out-house, reached by a small stairwell carved into the hillside and braced with stone. A chimney rises through the cabin's red metal roof and the clapboard siding is a light grey. On either side are stands of cedar and white birch, some arching out over the water.

They step onto a deck that wraps around two sides of the cabin and Lucy leans against the rail to look out over the pond, and when Katherine draws abreast of her, she sees her eyes closed, the breeze off the water stirring the strands of hair that escaped being tied back with the rest. She looks at Lucy's face, soft and full of peace, and feels a pang of envy and desire.

Katherine looks at the water, so clear she can see pebbles on the bottom several feet from shore. A narrow dock extends outward, a ladder at the end and a green canoe upside down on a wooden rack. It is perhaps a quarter mile to the far shore and half that far to a pair of small islands, a larger one closer in and a smaller one just beyond. All around is a bowl of green hills extending back as far as she can see.

"Not bad, is it?" says Lucy.

"It's beautiful. How do you manage?"

"My son Michael takes care of it," says Lucy, looking out over the water.

A sound draws their eyes to the sky and a pair of loons fly over, white bellied with great black backs, their wings beating with a pulsing, labored rhythm.

"I never heard a bird work so hard to fly," says Lucy, laying her pack on a table by the door.

"I'm sorry about before," says Katherine.

Lucy looks at her. "There's no need," she says, making a little smile. "You didn't break anything."

"But I was rude."

"I don't expect impeccable manners from someone who's recently been to hell. Sometimes it just grabs you by the throat and pulls you in. I'd wonder if you didn't feel angry."

"You shouldn't have to put up with it."

"I can take care of myself," says Lucy. "Besides, I invited you here, remember?"

Katherine nods, then her head becomes still. "But why?"

"Destiny," says Lucy, smiling with a wave of her hand, "Come on, let's eat. This place always makes me hungry."

They go inside. The floor is laid in wide boards of yellow pine and the ceiling is tongue-and-groove fir between rough-sawn beams. A small wood stove sits in a corner with a portable radio on top. Along the rear wall are cabinets and a counter with an old wooden dry sink lined with tin. On the counter are a two-burner camp stove, plastic jugs filled with water, and a dish drainer with a plate and a bowl, a few pieces of silverware, and a brass tea kettle. A cast iron frying pan hangs from a nail driven into a beam.

The cabin is furnished with a hand-made pine table surrounded by an assortment of kitchen chairs, a lantern hanging from a beam overhead. A brightly colored woven blanket is draped over an old couch that sits in the middle of the room and faces one of two large picture windows that look out on the pond. To its left is a rocking chair, its frame deep maroon against flowered print cushions. A twin bed lies along one of the windows with folded blankets, sheets, and a pillow at one end.

"You can see why we call it a camp," says Lucy, unzipping her knapsack on the counter. "But it's clean. And dry when it rains. And so quiet you can hear a mouse fart, which you might if you pay attention."

Katherine smiles and walks around the room. The whitewashed walls hold paintings of loons, a clock set in a polished cross-section of maple, and a topographical map in a frame. A second door exits to the deck on the left side of the cabin, and on the wall beside it, wooden pegs hold a bright red slicker, a Panama hat, and a pair of binoculars hanging by a leather strap. In the corner, three canoe paddles, the varnish worn thin on the grips, stand with a broom among an assortment of life jackets piled on the floor.

Lucy turns from the counter with two plates and motions them outside.

Katherine gathers up glasses of lemonade and napkins and pushes the door open for Lucy. They sit at the table, on benches built into the outer wall, shaded by trees along the water's edge. Sunlight reflecting off the rough surface of the water plays on the bark and leaves of a large white birch that arches out over the dock, creating a pattern of soft pulsating light.

"Have you always lived here?" says Katherine.

"Oh, yes."

"Never went away? Not to college?"

"No."

"Really."

"You're surprised."

Katherine shrugs. "All those books, I just assumed — "

Lucy sticks out her tongue and retrieves a bit of sandwich hanging on her lip. "I have great respect for formal education," she says, "but it does encourage the notion that the only way to learn is to have someone teach you." She swallows. "And that's after they decide what's worth knowing. I have no problem with children learning to read and write and which side of the globe they're on." She lifts a carrot from her plate and bites off the end. "But then there's what happens when we get old enough to start thinking for ourselves."

"You don't ever wish you'd gone."

"Sometimes I do." Lucy pops the rest of the carrot into her mouth. "Every once in awhile I'm around people with fancy degrees and I feel a little lack in myself. But at my age there isn't much they know that I don't that matters to me. And there's always my library card and Annie."

They finish lunch and go out on the deck and stand at the rail. "What's over there?" says Katherine, pointing to a cluster of small white shapes in the water on the far side.

"A little cove. Those white things are the tops of boulders. The pond's full of em." Lucy watches Katherine scan the shore. "How about a walk around? There's a trail."

"All right," says Katherine. "I have to pee first."

"Ever used an outhouse before?"

"No."

"Well, there's an adventure for you."

Katherine mounts the steps to the skinny little shack nestled into the hillside, made of weathered barnboard with a small window set up high and a yellow moon above the door. The floor is covered by a scrap of linoleum and a toilet seat is bolted to a wooden platform. She looks out the window and sees blue water through the trees. When she lifts the seat she sees a small dark pile and waits for an awful smell to reach her, but there is none. She pulls down her pants and sits on the seat and imagines some creature about to nibble her behind. Slowly, she opens her legs and peers into the gloom. Nothing stirs. Then she looks out the window to the sky and trees and feels herself let down.

Sophie leads the way along a narrow trail beside the water. The forest is old growth, the trees thick and tall. They walk single-file until the path widens near a stream, fed by overflow from the pond, that winds away through the woods. Sophie wades in and drinks while they step from stone to stone to the other side, and Lucy reaches back a hand to stop Katherine and then swings her arm around to point toward the larger island. At first, Katherine sees only the shore, but then something moves and a great blue heron lifts a long skinny leg and steps forward. Sophie leaps from the stream and the startled bird spreads its broad wings as it lifts itself into the air and disappears behind the trees.

They walk on through the woods, the trail hugging the shore lined with driftwood bleached white by the sun. They are past the islands and can see the length of the pond where sunlight reflects on something bright which Katherine realizes is a car passing by on the road going into town.

They come round to the cove where boulders rise from the water, white and dry in the sun. Across the pond they can see the cabin and the dock. The two women sit down on a log while Sophie snuffles her way off into the woods.

Lucy points her chin toward the boulders. "Those are the old ones," she says. "Been here thousands of years. Maybe longer. Sometimes when I get worried about my little life, I just go sit with them for awhile."

They look out over the water and in the silence Katherine feels her body grow heavy against the log.

"What," says Lucy.

"It's so beautiful. And I feel so sad."

"I know," says Lucy leaning in closer, "and the worst part is thinking no one understands, that no one can possibly know what you've been through. I suppose it's true. But I also know there are millions of women in the world who have a pretty good idea of it. And they came by it the hard way, just like you."

"I don't know if I can stand this."

"Yes, you can," says Lucy. "You've come this far. You're here. You're alive."

Sophie rustles in behind and Lucy moves to make a space as she comes in between them, tongue lolling in the heat. Katherine smiles and shakes her head away as Sophie sniffs her hair.

"Where you been, girl?" says Lucy. "You find something good back there? Besides ticks and fleas?"

Sophie wags and pants.

"Apparently not," says Lucy, pushing herself off the log. "Let's go. I could use some cooling off."

At the cabin Lucy strips down to her bathing suit and claps her hands for Sophie to join her out the door and down to the water. Katherine hears a clatter of paws on the dock, a quickening step, and then a splash followed by a whoop from Lucy and another splash. She pulls out a chair and sits and listens to Lucy's voice drifting up from down below, soft and small like a girl talking to a doll, and then for an instant it is Ethan and she shuts her eyes and shakes her head as if clearing out a thought, waiting it out, like a pain that comes and goes, minutes going by, sounds coming up from the water, Lucy's voice more and more distinct, slowly drawing Katherine out, opening her eyes, getting to her feet, opening the door.

She leans on the rail and looks at them in the water. Lucy lifts a hand and waves. "Come on."

Katherine goes inside and removes her clothes. She looks down the length of her body to make sure no scars show past the confines of her bathing suit. She lays a hand against her belly and closes her eyes and listens to the sound of water splashing and Sophie clambering onto shore and shaking water from her fur.

She walks out the door and down the path and notices that the large birch angled over the water has wrapped around its trunk a thick rope with a large knot in the end. She follows the line of the rope to where it attaches to a limb, recognizing a swinging rope of the kind she knew well at summer camp — the long moment poised high on the bank, the rope in her hands, waiting for the will to gather inside and then the instant of commitment when the muscles tightened in her arms and her feet left the ground, seeking out the knot, fear turning to joy as her body followed the arc of the rope's journey downward and then up into the air to that weightless point between going up and coming down where she let go, sky above and water below, and let herself fall. But all she feels now is a tightness in her chest, no more of that for her, too afraid and done with falling.

Katherine joins Sophie at the edge of the dock, water dripping from the tip of the dog's wagging tail as she looks out at Lucy. Lucy smiles and waves and ducks below the surface and Sophie's tail droops low as she leans forward, her head going back and forth to see where Lucy has gone. When Lucy reappears, the tail begins to wag again and Sophie looks up at Katherine and startles her with what appears to be a little smile.

"Sophie," says Lucy, the word coming out in a seductive little tune. Sophie pulls back her ears and stamps her feet and then launches herself into the air as Lucy lets out a whoop.

Katherine sits to dangle her feet in the water, cool against her skin and then braces her hands on the edge of the dock to slide herself forward and down, making sure to keep her head above the surface.

"What do you think?" says Lucy, watching her.

"It's great," says Katherine, watching Sophie paddle past, breathing heavily with an occasional snort. She reaches out to let her hand pass lightly along Sophie's fur as she goes by and then dips beneath the surface just enough to cool her head. She begins a slow breaststroke past the end of the dock while Lucy turns onto her back and floats with her arms drifting out as she looks up at the sky.

Sophie climbs the bank, shakes herself, and lies down in the dappled sunlight at the end of the dock, her nose just over the edge. Katherine looks at Lucy and wonders what she thinks as she bobs on the water and stares into the sky, if it could possibly be as peaceful and free of care as it seems. And then she remembers Ethan at the town pool, his skin smooth and new, and a wave of sadness comes over her, convinced there is no end to this horrible weight of dread and loss and guilt, except perhaps, if she only had the courage, to surrender herself to the vast emptiness of water closing over her one last time, breathing out a final breath into a dark and dreamless sleep.

Late in the afternoon the sun swings around above the western hills and finds the deck where they sit and read, their feet resting on the rail. The sun is warm on Katherine's face and she closes her eyes to the sound of water lapping on the shore, pages turning, Sophie rolling over, and for a moment imagines herself floating in the light as if it were a liquid bearing her weight away.

The sun dips below the trees, softening the sky and reflecting dusty purple on the underside of long thin clouds over the hills across the pond. They light a candle on the deck and watch the moon rise into a deep cobalt sky dotted with stars. They pack their knapsacks and Sophie leads the way home. The woods are cool and close and Katherine does not look back as she keeps Lucy's sneakers within the small pale of light cast before her. The path winds uphill for what seems to Katherine a long time until suddenly the sound of crickets and peepers announces the open field and beyond, the dark form of the house and barn outlined against the bowl of stars.

The goats are waiting in the yard, standing about like statues. "They're very still when it gets dark," says Lucy.

The goats fall in behind as Katherine follows Lucy into the barn.

"You can fill those buckets at the spigot,"says Lucy. Katherine is watching water flow through the beam of the flashlight when Elsie's nose appears beside her face.

Katherine watches Lucy by the bin mounted on a low wall dividing the goats from the back of the barn where hay is stored. "This way," says Lucy, pulling open a door in the wall.

Katherine contemplates the crowd of goats between her and the door.

"Just come on through," says Lucy, and the goats part like water, turning up faces as she passes by, sniffing, hooves rustling in the carpet of hay on the hard dirt floor.

Through the door she sees a great stack of bales. Lucy roots her hand in one and then pulls it to the floor and takes a knife from a nail on the wall and cuts the twine that holds the bale together. She pushes flakes of hay through an opening near the top of the low wall and there is a rush of goats toward the sound of it falling into the bin on the other side.

They go out into the yard and Lucy closes the barn door and then they go into the house where they scramble eggs and sit at the long pine table and talk about the moon and goats and Kenyon's poetry, and when they finally go up to bed Katherine is so full of sleep it is all she can do to brush her teeth and drop her clothes to the floor and slide between the sheets as she lays herself down.

6

Observing Katherine, Lucy sometimes feels as though she's watching a time lapse film of the sky played at double speed, a rapid flow of weather — light and dark, grey, white, blue, purple, and pink, clear and then full of clouds and rain or snow, calm and then swept by winds that hurl clouds from one horizon to the other, and all of it passing by so quickly she can see it change in front of her in no time at all.

At first she tries to notice what brings on one state or another. She is careful not to startle her by closing doors too hard or coming up behind too softly and speaking her name too close. But she soon discovers that what happened to Katherine tore the web that anchors her in the world and now draws her without warning into another plane of existence that Lucy can only imagine, a place of sudden horror and violence and loss and full of guilt that places her beyond even the comforting reach of grief.

Most apparent are the nightmares and waking moments when Katherine seems to jump inside her skin and cry out as if a monster had leapt at her from the shadows. It happens once when they are sitting across from each other in the library, reading, and Lucy draws in close and sees her eyes move rapidly back and forth as if there is a screen between them and Katherine is watching a film projected onto it that is no film at all, but absolutely real. Softly, carefully Lucy says her name again and again as if pulling on a lifeline that might break at any moment, and slowly the focus in Katherine's mind shifts outward to encompass Lucy's face. And then Lucy watches her sink beneath the realization of what has happened yet again and where she has been, drawn low by sadness and despair, eyes closing as she slowly shakes her head.

And there is the time in the middle of the night when Lucy hears a noise and comes downstairs to find Katherine going around the house testing locks on windows and doors and at the sound of Lucy speaking her name, does not respond, as if she is asleep.

Less obvious is a certain posture, a quality of tension through which Katherine holds herself in a perpetual cringe, as if anticipating a blow.

Katherine sleeps often during the day because she sleeps so little at night, and even so is tired most of the time, her vitality drained away. And close by fatigue is the vacuous numbness of depression that Lucy can sense the moment Katherine walks into a room. Beneath it all, like a fire burning underground, is a heartbroken rage that Lucy knows is there but shows itself only in depression or the occasional flash of irritation.

To someone who has never traveled between the worlds that Katherine now inhabits she would seem neurotic or even crazy. But Lucy knows it is not so simple, that the trauma of her loss is registered not simply in her mind or her psyche but in the cells of her being, and she is no more crazy than a woman whose damaged brain sees everything upside down and who lives in chronic fear of falling to the ceiling from the floor.

She notices that Katherine hasn't drawn a bath since she arrived and wonders how she manages to wash and why she would deny herself the luxury of soaking in a tub with such a magnificent view.

"Do you not enjoy a bath?" she says one evening as they sit on the front porch sharing yesterday's *Globe*.

Katherine stares down at the paper.

"I was thinking," says Lucy, "that if you prefer a shower, we could get one of those things you hitch to the spigot, with a little rubber hose and a spray head at the end." She is looking at Katherine's face as she talks and without knowing it, bending in for a closer view. Suddenly their eyes meet and Katherine looks away.

"I used to take baths."

"Oh," says Lucy, "and what happened?"

Lucy recognizes the look on Katherine's face, as if she isn't there. "Where'd you go?"

"Nowhere."

Lucy looks at her, deciding what to say, noting the beads of sweat standing out on her forehead. "Tell me what happened."

Katherine looks away into the middle distance and is silent for a moment. "I was in the tub," she says, "and he came in and said something about my taking a bath when the house wasn't clean."

Katherine folds the paper in half while she talks and then in half again.

"What happened then?"

"He put his hand on top of my head and pushed me down." She begins to tremble and Lucy pulls her chair in close and lifts the newspaper from her lap and takes her hands.

"I thought I was going to drown."

"One more thing that was taken from you."

Katherine looks out across the road.

"I have an idea," says Lucy, taking Katherine by the hand.

Katherine follows Lucy up the stairs with Sophie close behind. In the bathroom Lucy puts the stopper in the tub and turns the water on full. She looks back over her shoulder at Katherine standing in the doorway.

"You want bubbles?"

Katherine says nothing.

"You get to choose. Bubbles. No bubbles."

"Okay."

"Bubbles?"

Katherine nods.

Lucy goes to her room and returns with a book under her arm and a chair she sets by the bathroom door.

"Here's the plan," she says. "You leave the door open or closed or anywhere in between. It's up to you. I'll sit out here while you take your bath, or, if you'd rather, I'll go somewhere else. Wherever you like. If you want, I'll read to you." She holds up *Pilgrim at Tinker Creek*. "I'll keep you company and stand guard." She smiles. "I'll be your crone at the door. And you can stay in there as long as you like."

Katherine looks from Lucy to the tub and back again. "Okay."

"Good,"says Lucy. "Check the water to make sure it's right."

Katherine adjusts the flow and then goes to her room and returns wearing just her robe. At the door Lucy takes her by the arm and looks into her face.

"You have a right to take a bath, Katherine."

Katherine nods but without conviction as she steps inside. Sophie lies down on the rug in front of the tub and Katherine closes the door all but a crack.

"What would you like me to do?" says Lucy.

"You can read to me if you want."

"That's just what I'll do," says Lucy, opening the book in her lap. "'Heaven and Earth in Jest,'" she begins. "'I used to have a cat, an old fighting tom, who would jump through the open window by my bed in the middle of the night and land on my chest . . . .'"

Katherine sits on the toilet and looks at the mound of bubbles in the tub. Outside the window a thrush sings in the evening air and blends with the sound of Lucy's voice coming through the opening in the door. Katherine closes her eyes and listens for awhile and then stands with a sigh to let her robe fall to the floor as she steps toward the tub, careful not to look at her body. The water is hot against her legs as she lowers herself down, up and over her thighs and belly and breasts and shoulders until she is lying back and looking past her knees to the window and the pale light fading over the distant hills.

"'On a dark day'," Lucy reads, "'or a hazy one, everything's washed-out and lackluster but the water . . . '"

Katherine focuses on the sound of Lucy's voice, barely noticing the words, just the steady rise and fall of one image and another, the turning of a page, the clearing of Lucy's throat, in soft counterpoint to the thrush's song that is at once both thick and light, quicksilver in the air. Katherine sinks down, closing her eyes and for just a moment feels safe in the arms of the old woman sitting by the door.

She drifts into half-sleep and then opens her eyes to the sound of Lucy's voice and bubbles breaking in the cool air above the tub.

"Lucy," she says, in a sleepy voice.

"Yes, dear."

"Would you open the door a little?"

"Of course. How are you doing in there?"

"Fine."

There is a long silence and then, "Lucy," her eyes beginning to fill.

"What?"

"How did you get to be the way you are?"

"One bath at a time, honey. One bath at a time."

In the morning after breakfast Katherine stands on the back porch and looks out past the barn to the field running down to the woods. Lucy emerges from the barn, followed by a retinue of goats. She passes through the gate and walks slowly toward the house.

"I was thinking we could take a walk," says Katherine.

"You go ahead. I'm not feeling so well."

"Are you all right?"

"Just tired," says Lucy. "Why don't you take the dog?"

"Sophie? She wouldn't mind?"

"She'd love it. She's right there," says Lucy, pointing to where Sophie stands beside Katherine. "She came over the moment you said her name."

Katherine looks at Sophie and then at Lucy. "I'm afraid she won't stay with me."

"Just give her a shout and she'll come."

There is a lightness in Katherine's stomach as she walks across the yard with Sophie padding along beside her through the cool shade of the barn and then out into the open field yellow and green in the sun. Sophie stays close until she stops to sniff a breeze passing over the tall grass like a great hand bending it low, and then, with a little hop to get her started, she gallops off the path and disappears from view.

Katherine scans the field for signs of her but cannot tell the movement of the dog from the wind. She feels suddenly alone and Lucy far away and turns toward the house only to stop herself, unable to think of what she would say walking into the kitchen all alone. She goes a few feet down the path and then turns to retrace her steps, muttering, berating herself for thinking the dog would stay with her, it being, after all, not hers but someone else's, and for being afraid, for not being able to come or go, to decide a thing as simple as that. And then she turns again and there she is, sitting in the middle of the path and looking up at her, tail wagging, an old tennis ball in her mouth.

Katherine is breathing hard, her hands balled into fists, and she wonders at the anger and what Lucy said about her having enough of it for two. She kneels down, tears coming into her eyes as she strokes Sophie across the top of her head.

"Come on," she says, "let's go," and then Sophie drops the ball on her foot and it bounces and rolls between them and she snaps it up and gives it two quick chews before laying it on the ground to let it roll against the toe of Katherine's shoe. Katherine smiles and picks it up. "Okay," she says and cocks her arm and throws the ball as Sophie turns and lumbers in the direction of its flight before Katherine has even let it go. They go on this way toward the line of trees, falling into the rhythm of a game, Katherine calling out encouragement and praise, laughing when Sophie gets up on her hind legs and snatches the ball from the air on a high bounce.

When Katherine notices the limp, the favored shoulder, she takes the ball from Sophie's mouth and tucks it in her pocket and leans down and kisses her on the smooth broad space between her ears, lingering there to close her eyes and draw in the sweet smell of earth and dog. She stands and looks up the hill where only the weather vane atop the barn shows above the slope of grass.

She turns and cannot find Sophie until she looks to where the path disappears into the woods and sees her looking up at her, black against the shadows, waiting to go on, and Katherine feels herself unable to follow, held in place by a sudden weight of longing and fear. She steps to the edge of the woods and looks down the path, the air rising up from the pond cool on her face.

"Come on, girl," she says, "not today," turning along the line of trees edging the field, but Sophie follows on a parallel path through the woods just below. Katherine plucks a long blade of grass and sticks the end in her mouth, glancing into the woods to see Sophie still there.

They come to a narrow dirt road, overgrown and deeply rutted, barely wide enough for a small tractor or truck. She stands on the grassy crown of the road and looks up the hill where fields continue to the left, bounded by more woods, while above her and to the right are the house and barn and a stand of trees against the sky and a large bird wheeling high above on currents of air.

They follow the road up the hill and then turn on the road leading by the house. She stops at the driveway and looks across to the cemetery and its stones, bone white against the grass, and suddenly feels small and exposed and then full of shame as she hurries into the house.

Katherine is sitting in the kitchen when Lucy comes in from the hall, "You have a letter," in a quiet, church-like voice, placing the envelope in front of her. Katherine stares at her father's careful script, not wanting this reminder of who she is, how easily her life can seek her out, sliding through a slot in the door in the middle of the afternoon.

She leaves it unopened on the table and goes outside and sits on the back porch to watch the goats watching her.

The screen door opens and Lucy sits down beside her. She says nothing, except to call out to a goat to leave another goat alone. "I think I'll take a walk," she says, standing and going down the stairs. "Be back in a bit," and she is gone around the side of the house.

Katherine lingers awhile longer before going into the kitchen to read her father's letter.

My dear Katherine,

I have agonized over this but I am sure it is nothing compared with what you are going through. Your mother and I cannot escape the burden of guilt we feel over what has happened. In my mind I try to explain it away but always I come back to the simple fact that we knew that something was wrong and failed to give you the help you so desperately needed. We had no idea it was as bad as it turned out to be, but that is beside the point. There is no excuse that I can offer. We were blinded by our wish that it not be true.

We will do anything in our power to help you through this difficult time. I must leave it to you to decide if there is something that you want from us.

I hope that you are well. With all my heart. From what you have told us of Lucy Dudley and from our brief encounter in the hospital, I am sure you are in good hands.

I hope you will find it in you to forgive us.

Love, Dad

When Lucy returns, Katherine is sitting at the kitchen table.

"Bad news?"

Katherine shakes her head and moves the letter across the table. Lucy looks down to read.

"I don't know what to say to him."

"He wants to know if you're okay. Are you okay?"

"As much as I can be right now."

"Then you could tell him that."

"What about the rest?" says Katherine.

"Whatever is true."

In the evening Katherine sits in her room, a piece of notepaper on a book resting in her lap.

It must have been hard for you to write to me. I really don't know what to say. Maybe I will someday. I hope so. There are so many things I do not know. I don't know what it means to forgive, whether it's me or someone else.

I never needed to know before.

I am okay, considering. Please don't worry if you don't hear from me. I'm where I need to be.

Katherine

As before, Lucy brings a chair into the hall and sets it beside the bathroom door while Katherine adjusts the flow of water into the tub, then opens the book on her lap, finds the place, and is about to read when Katherine says her name.

"There's something on me. I think it's a tick."

"Can you reach it?"

"No."

"Do you want me to get it for you?"

There is a silence as Katherine tries to think how to cover herself. She puts on her robe over her bra and underpants and then drops it back over her shoulders to reveal her upper back. But the tick is farther down than she thought, so close to the scar that runs around her left side that Lucy will surely see it.

"Will it drop off by itself?"

"Eventually, but first it'll fill up with blood and deer ticks carry Lyme's disease and you don't want that."

Katherine's legs go weak beneath her.

"Shall I come in?" says Lucy.

"All right." Katherine turns toward the window as the door swings open and she feels Lucy's fingers on her skin.

"There," says Lucy, snapping the tick loose in a single sure motion and flicking it into the toilet. And then she is silent as Katherine feels her standing behind her, not moving, then a sinking murmur of surprise, "Oh, my."

Katherine closes her eyes. "Is there another one?"

"No, dear."

Lucy lifts the robe back over Katherine's shoulders and then lays her hand over the scar along the small of her back. The hand seems hot even through the thickness of the robe. They do not move. Sophie comes down the hall and sits outside the door. Beyond the window the thrush begins to sing. The trees are black against the sky, dusty blue in the fading light. The silence grows around them as Katherine waits for Lucy to turn and leave, but the hand remains.

"Katherine," says Lucy, her voice soft and even, "you don't have to carry this all by yourself. It's too much for anyone to bear alone." Lucy feels a tremor move through Katherine's body, beginning at her waist and ending in a sob held close in her throat.

"Let me see, dear."

Katherine stiffens and then feels something slowly give way inside her, a yearning she cannot resist as she takes a small step forward and turns and looks down at the floor and lets her robe fall open.

There are tears in Lucy's eyes as they follow the dull lines that mark the enormous wound. She does not move away, but her shoulders fall as she stands her ground, and then rise, lifted by a lungful of air as she nods and looks up into Katherine's face. And then, without a sound, Katherine slowly draws the robe around her and Lucy crosses the small distance between them and takes her in her arms and they stand there for a long while, saying nothing, listening to the thrush and feeling the night coming on.

Katherine stares into the open grave to where Ethan lies face down in the dirt. She can hear them coming, shovels dragging on the ground, come to fill in the hole, and all she can think is to cover his body with her own, in the desperate hope that she will be enough to protect them both. The pit is damp, the earth cool against her skin as she feels his lifeless body beneath her and tries to hold back the tears, focusing her mind on willing the men away, but there is only the sound of shovels digging deep and then, just before she wakes, the dull weight of dirt finding them at the bottom of the hole.

Lucy wakes to the sound of Katherine entering the room and standing beside the bed, her jaw rattling so hard she can barely speak.

Lucy sits up in the bed. "What is it?"

"I'm so scared," says Katherine, "I'm so scared," closing her eyes around the words coming out again and again until Lucy reaches up and takes her hands that feel cold to the bone.

"Come on," she says, pulling down the covers, "get in."

Katherine slides beneath the covers that Lucy draws over her, pulling her knees up to her chest to curl herself into a ball.

Lucy looks at Sophie and pats the bed on the far side of Katherine, "come on, girl," and Sophie struggles to her feet and climbs up beside Katherine's trembling body and lies down against her back to hold her in the space between them. "It's all right," says Lucy looking down at Katherine's face.

"No," says Katherine, "it's not."

Lucy pulls a stool from the corner of the kitchen and climbs up to reach the highest shelf in the cupboard for a fresh bottle of Jack Daniels. She sets it on the table and fetches two short glasses from the cupboard, pouring whiskey into each.

"I think it's time," says Lucy.

Katherine does not drink the whiskey but holds the glass between her hands resting on the table, her face puffy from crying. "For what?"

Lucy takes a long slow sip and sets the glass down. "To talk about what happened."

Katherine grows heavy against the chair, staring down at the amber liquid until her vision goes out of focus.

"Don't go away," says Lucy.

Katherine shakes her head and drinks the whiskey. "That's all I want to do."

"I know. But don't."

"Why not?"

Lucy leans back in the chair. "Do you remember asking me how I got to be the way I am now? What did you mean by that?"

Katherine is quiet for a long time. "That you're okay."

"You mean I'm okay about having lived with a man I loved who raped me and beat me up?"

Katherine looks at her and then away.

"And you think I'm over that," says Lucy.

"You seem to be."

"Well, I'm not. And I never will be."

Katherine tries to look at her but every time their eyes meet she looks away as if from a bright light. "You seem happy enough."

"I have moments."

"Well I don't," says Katherine.

"Is that what you want, then? Moments of happiness?"

Katherine pours another drink. "I want to sleep at night and not be scared," taking a sip, "the nightmares to go away, the phantoms," putting the glass down, "not feel so low all the time, to breathe all the way down." She takes a long drink. "I want to remember Ethan. Do you know how hard I try not to think about him? Is that possible? Can you be someone's mother and actually forget? I don't even know where he is, where he's buried." She looks up with eyes wide and dry. "I don't know where David is either. I don't know where anything is anymore."

"You weren't at the funeral."

"I was in the hospital."

"And you never saw the grave."

"I couldn't stand it."

Lucy sits in silence, imagining Michael not coming home alive from Vietnam, picturing a small white stone somewhere and wondering if she could bring herself to see the patch of ground knowing that all that remained of her boy lay beneath her feet. And then she wonders if she could stand it not to go, what it would cost her to cauterize the wound as Katherine is trying to do right now, this open wound to the soul she doesn't know how to heal.

"You remember Elsie," says Lucy, "my friend who came and stayed with me."

Katherine nods.

"I don't know what I would have done if it hadn't been for her, the two of us getting through each day, cooking, shopping, going for walks, her holding me when I couldn't stop crying and never asking why I stayed or letting me think for a second that what Philip did was anyone's fault but his own. And then one day she started asking me what I'm asking you — to talk about what really happened. The things he did. But I was having none of that. Just like you."

Katherine looks at her.

"And then," says Lucy, "there came a day when I just gave in, and the first thing I saw was how I kept it inside like some terrible knowledge that I couldn't let other people know. It was like I'd been visited by beings from outer space and if I told people my secret they'd think I was crazy and lock me up. And the more I kept it to myself, the more it got like it'd never happened at all and I just thought it had and was losing my mind."

Katherine drains the glass and pours another.

"But of course I knew what had happened. So on top of it all I had to deal with feeling locked away in a tiny room with a crazy woman who looked just like me.

"So, whatever you see in me that looks like something you want for yourself, it began with my talking my way out of that tight little room."

The two women sit quietly and smoke. Lucy pours another whiskey and sets the bottle down.

"So. Tell me — "

"It won't do any good."

Watching Katherine take a long swallow gives Lucy pause, but still she plunges on. "Tell me anyway."

"He's dead."

"No, he's not."

Katherine narrows her eyes.

"He's here right now. He's in your bed at night." Katherine shakes her head and looks away. "And when you come into my room, he stands out in the hall and waits." Lucy leans forward. "He isn't dead if you can't say the things he did."

"Stop it," says Katherine, her chair scraping against the floor as she stands.

"No," says Lucy, "I won't. You don't have to listen. You can go back to your room with him and I won't follow you there, but I won't be quiet, because I know what I'm saying."

"I won't do this," says Katherine, stepping toward the hall. "There's no point."

"Don't you see, Katherine? What's unspeakable — and unspoken — has ten times the power when it stays just between the two of you."

Katherine is halfway down the hall.

"Your little secret. It binds you to him."

Katherine turns at the bottom of the stairs and begins to climb.

"But it also keeps you from your life," says Lucy, her voice louder to carry the distance, "because part of you is always off with him."

Footsteps receding up the stairs.

"You can't breathe all the way down," Lucy calls out after her, "because you breathe the same air he does. Full of those awful words you will not say."

"Fuck!" says Katherine as she turns and goes back down, her feet pounding the stairs. "What fucking words? What the fuck am I supposed to say?"

Lucy is in the hall and looking up at her on the stairs, "Have you told *anyone* what he did?"

"No one wants to *know* what he did!"

"I want to know."

"No, you don't."

"Yes. I do."

Katherine glares down at Lucy, trying to stop from shaking by holding on to the bannister. "You want to know," she says, breathing hard.

"Yes."

"You want the words."

"Yes."

"You don't know how hard this is."

"Yes, I do — "

"No, you don't. You haven't been through what I've been through."

"I have — "

"No, you haven't. You said so yourself. Not all of it. You didn't lose Michael."

"No — "

"And you don't kill someone and get away with it."

"No," says Lucy, "you don't, but you must tell me what he did."

Katherine doesn't move, her face darkening as her body seems to grow smaller, shoulders sloping down. She looks at Lucy through eyes welling with tears, "I don't have to," she says, coming down the stairs and almost pushing Lucy aside as she goes down the hall and through the kitchen and out the door, slamming it behind.

Lucy stands in the hallway, feeling the rapid beating of her heart and the dryness in her mouth. She doesn't know what to do, how to bring her back, or what to do even if she does. She is stepping toward the kitchen when suddenly the back door slams open and Katherine bursts into the room, wild-eyed and her arms beating the air.

"Everyone talks about how I survived this," she says, spitting out the words, "but I don't know what they're talking about. I don't have a body anymore. There isn't a square inch of me he didn't ruin —"

"Tell me everything," says Lucy, afraid of the wildness in Katherine's eyes, some combination of whiskey and fear and grim determination.

"Everything," says Katherine, "everything. . ." muttering to herself, turning inward to the images in her mind racing ahead of her ability to form the words, "everything you can imagine, not a place on me that he didn't punch, my arms, my belly, my back, my face, he broke my nose and broke my ears, and then, of course, his favorite place, my breasts," Katherine pacing about the kitchen, not looking at Lucy anymore, not hearing the gasp coming out of her, gathering momentum behind the words, "his fist so hard his knuckles got white and when his arms were tired he used his feet to kick and stomp and he broke my foot, my hand, and he took me by the hair and dragged me across the room and slammed my face into the wall."

Katherine is by the sink, panting, so full of whatever has possessed her that Lucy imagines her lunging across the room. "You don't believe me. Well of course not, why should you, it is unbelievable, after all, I wouldn't believe my own life if someone told it to me, Katherine Stuart and her banker husband from Harvard in their nice little house in the suburbs, of course not, how ridiculous, it never happened, how could it?"

"I believe every word."

"You do."

"Keep going. Tell me the rest."

"The rest?" says Katherine, her voice rising to a pitch that cracks in the air, "you want more?"

"Yes."

"You want me to say that he raped me."

"If that's what he did — "

"All right, then, HE RAPED ME. He reached inside and tore me out by the roots and what he couldn't rip out he burned, my letters, my poems, all of it — "

"He burned your poetry."

Katherine looks away and nods.

"You're a poet."

"I was," says Katherine through her teeth.

Lucy leans against the jamb of the kitchen door to quiet the trembling in her body, afraid to go on but unwilling to let it go. "You left something out."

Beneath the stillness that settles over the kitchen Lucy can feel such turmoil in Katherine that she fears for what she'll see when she turns around. Her hands are gripping the edge of the sink as if holding on for dear life when all at once her shoulders rise up and then fall as slowly she slides down first inside herself and then to the floor and turns, eyes closed tight against the images racing through her mind, helpless to resist, everything coming undone all at once, defenses falling away, sobs pouring out of her, trying to speak but choking on the words, "I would have done anything. I didn't care what he did to me."

Lucy steps into the room to close the distance between them.

"All I wanted was for him not to hurt Ethan," says Katherine, the words broken by sobs of a despair so deep that it stills Lucy's progress across the floor, "and I couldn't even do that. I might as well have killed him myself."

Lucy goes to where Katherine sits on the floor, pressing the heels of her hands into her eyes as if to obliterate the images in her mind. "Oh, God, Ethan," and then Lucy is taking her in her arms to rock her back and forth, feeling her own heart break apart inside of her.

In the days that follow, Lucy will berate herself for failing to appreciate the magnitude of the guilt that Katherine has carried ever since that horrible night. But not now in this night that stretches on toward dawn, suspended in the eternity between one heartbeat and another. Lucy watches Katherine being swept along in a flood of tears and grief, a river that long ago crested its banks and yet somehow still she managed to hold it in until now, this pain deeper than pain, a suffering wrapped around her heart and refusing to let her go. Once or twice, Katherine rises above the churning and the turmoil and tries to speak, only to be dragged back down again. Lucy holds on, bending in close to whisper in her ear the way a mother might talk to a child who has disappeared inside a coma, needing to say the words as much as to be heard, holding out against worry and fear, hanging on to the only thread that she can see.

As each hour passes into the next, Katherine becomes still and silent, closing her eyes as if in sleep before opening them again to something in the middle distance. Lucy struggles to her feet, the stiffness in her hips so bad that she wonders if she can stand at all. She goes to the sink and wets a towel and lays it across Katherine's forehead, a simple act of tenderness that releases another wave of tears.

Lucy sets a chair near Katherine and settles in to wait.

Around 3:00 in the morning it is so quiet that Lucy notices the ticking of the clock on the wall. She looks at Katherine leaning back against the cupboard door beneath the sink, eyes closed, hands resting in her lap, her face puffy and raw, her upper lip crusted with the dried running of her nose. Katherine opens her eyes and looks up at her, the silence held between, fragile and new.

They are sitting on the front porch swing when the sky begins to lighten in the east.

"Why did you shave your head?" says Lucy.

Katherine is silent for a long time, the only sound the soft squeak of the chain as the swing moves back and forth, and then she speaks in a small hushed voice, "He had his mother's hair."

"Ethan."

Katherine nods, staring straight ahead across the road.

7

*K*atherine wakes late in the afternoon to the sound of Lucy chopping on the cutting board in the kitchen. She looks up at the ceiling and draws her hand through her hair as she remembers Lucy's question and her reply, and then a weight of sorrow settles in around her bones making her wish she had never stirred from sleep, but instead found some oblivion beyond the stars she gazed at when she and Lucy went out onto the porch and sat on the swing in silence, there being nothing more to say. Safe inside a deep and endless sleep, a dreamless sleep, where every breath draws in a forgiveness she knows to be impossible.

I might as well have killed him myself.

There is a pause from down below and she imagines Lucy in the kitchen, looking up at the ceiling. She wishes she could disappear into some strange and alien land without mirrors and anyone whose face might reflect back to her what has happened and what was done.

She closes her eyes around the pounding in her head. Her mouth is dry and sour and her belly aches from the work of crying. She doesn't want to get out of bed because then she will lose the cover of sleep and will have to go downstairs and face Lucy with no idea of what to say or how to be.

And then the clatter of Sophie up the stairs brings the sound of sniffing along the crack beneath the door and, then, just behind, Lucy footsteps, and Katherine imagines them standing in the hall and listening together for signs of Katherine come to life.

A faint knock on the door and instinctively Katherine pulls the covers over her head like a child feigning sleep or trying to hide in the illusion of being invisible to anyone she cannot see. The soft padding of shoeless feet across the floor, the gentle weight upon the mattress, and then she waits for Lucy's voice, the beginning of whatever happens now, but there is only silence in the late afternoon air. Katherine thinks how much she wants only to be left alone until suddenly she feels Lucy stir as if to rise and without thinking extends her hand from beneath the covers, like a probe, and quickly lays it down, as if pretending it had been there all along. A held breath inside a pause and then Lucy's hand is on her own, the skin cool from the well-water coming through the kitchen tap, an old hand and yet still strong enough to take hold and not let go. Katherine begins to cry softly to herself, not moving except for the tears against her face. And yet, even this, Lucy seems to know, her other hand coming to rest on Katherine's shoulder, gently milking a small sound, but enough for both of them to know that Katherine is here.

"Come down when you're ready," says Lucy through the covers. "The day's not over yet."

They sit in the kitchen, a pot of tea between them, scraps of food remaining on their plates. They have not spoken since Katherine walked into the room, avoiding Lucy's eyes. Katherine stares into the cup of tea in front of her, watching it cool.

"A hard night," says Lucy.

Katherine looks up at her, then down, "I don't know what good it does."

"Talking."

"It doesn't change what happened."

"No."

"Or bring him back." Katherine wipes her eyes.

They sit in silence.

"It's so much easier," says Lucy, "to forgive someone else."

Katherine looks up at her. "And have you?"

Lucy shrugs, "I think so. But not for a long time." She sips the last of her tea and then stands and gathers dishes from the table. "One day Elsie said to me, I don't remember how it came up, but she said, 'what a. . . ,'" Lucy pauses to remember the exact words, ". . . 'what a sorry, pathetic son of a bitch he was.'" She carries dishes to the sink and looks at Katherine. "And I knew, all of a sudden, that's exactly what he was, and something about it brought him down to human size. And then I remembered how afraid I was of him but also, in a way, not afraid, not at first, because I thought I was the strong one and he was the one in trouble, how sorry he could be, feeling so bad about what he'd done, so worried I was going to leave him all alone."

She begins washing dishes. "There was a boy lived up the road a long time ago. I knew his mother. He was autistic and sometimes he got so frustrated he punched her or gave her a kick. She'd try to calm him down and I'd watch her and think how strong she was in her love for him, her faith, her hope. Something. Whatever it was, I think I felt like that with Philip. For awhile at least."

She turns and leans back against the sink, folding her arms across her chest and looking at the floor. "And I think," she says, "for me, forgiveness is accepting that he was in the grips of something so horrible that hurting me was the best that he could do."

"But what he did — "

"Was inexcusable, yes, I know. And I can hate him for it. Sometimes I think if it hadn't been for him, Michael never would have gone to Vietnam. But mostly I just count myself lucky if I don't think of him at all." She turns back to the sink and then sighs and turns around again. "But he was not a monster, Katherine. He was a human being, and so am I. And all I know about forgiveness is that if I don't know that, I can't forgive him or anyone else. Including me."

They look at each other.

"You seem surprised," says Lucy. "You don't think I need forgiving. We all do." She sits down at the table. "You're not stupid, Katherine. And you're no coward. And for all that, you didn't see it coming. Neither did I. Or anyone else. This isn't just about you."

In her dream, Katherine is standing in the moonlight in a grassy field. She hears the wind through the trees and closes her eyes and turns her face toward the sky, enjoying the night air. And then the smell of freshly excavated earth rises up to meet her and she looks down into a deep hole. She is puzzled to see it there, not noticing it before, until she makes out in the gloom the small crumpled figure lying at the bottom and she is paralyzed by the horror that fills her body, desperate to run away but unable to move, when, from a distance, a remote portion of her mind slowly takes hold, that it is only a dream and she can wake herself, which she does with a gasp resounding through the darkened house.

She lies in bed, her eyes filling with tears, her body bathed in sweat. She waits for sounds of Lucy coming down the hall, but there is only the sound of her own breathing. She gets out of bed and goes downstairs and takes the bottle of whiskey to the porch where she sits in the swing and drinks, hoping to still her mind. But it does no good, drunk and still unable to dull the steady stream of memory, and so she goes back upstairs and lies in bed until the sun shows itself above the hills.

It is the same night after night. During the day she tries to work herself into exhaustion, mucking out the barn, weeding the garden with such a frenzy that Lucy comes out to stop her from pulling up perennials. Lucy comments on how poorly she looks, asks what she can do, but Katherine only shakes her head and Lucy knows she is in a place where she cannot reach her and Katherine will have to find her own way out and home.

Even through her own weariness, Katherine can tell that something has changed with Lucy, increasingly slow to get out of bed, as if a weight of fatigue stays with her even when she is up and about. Katherine wonders if her own condition is somehow contagious, if she is bringing Lucy down to her own miserable level of existence, but beneath that worry is a deeper fear that something else is wrong.

On a morning near the end of August, Katherine dresses and goes down the hall, shoes in hand, laying her feet softly against the floor as she stops at the doorway to Lucy's room. Sophie raises her head, looks back and forth between Katherine and Lucy still asleep, and then lifts herself to her feet and follows Katherine downstairs.

Katherine stands just inside the door of the barn, animals milling around, and closes her eyes to breathe in the smell. She draws water and replenishes the hay and then steps out into the sunlight angling across the yard.

She takes a cup of coffee to the front porch and sits looking out across the road to the cemetery and fields beyond. She hears footsteps on the stairs and then Lucy is through the door and beside her on the swing.

"I'm turning into a regular slugabed."

"Maybe you should see a doctor."

"I'm just getting old," says Lucy, waving her hand. "It'll happen to you, too, if you're lucky. How are the animals?"

"Okay."

"And you?"

A shrug is Katherine's only reply.

Lucy slaps her hand on Katherine's knee and pushes off to stand herself up.

"Well," she says, "I don't know about you, but I'm hungry," which Katherine takes as a reassuring sign.

They are sitting at the kitchen table when Lucy drops her spoon in her half-eaten bowl of cereal and sits back to look at Katherine. "Why don't you take Sophie to the pond," she says, "get away from here for awhile."

"Will you be all right?"

"Go on. I'll be fine."

Katherine follows Sophie's lead to the path out past the barn where Sophie wanders off into the tall grass. A hawk circles slowly in the sky and Katherine shades her eyes to see it going round and round, closing her eyes and feeling the breeze on her face, the ground beneath her feet, until the hawk calls out and Katherine looks to see it gliding down over the trees in the direction of the pond.

She looks about for Sophie, but there is no sign of where she's gone. She calls her name but still the dog is nowhere to be seen, and as she stands by herself in the middle of the field she feels a sudden urge to run to the safety of Lucy and the house, stopped only by the image of Sophie's upturned face and its look of wondering at where she went, how she could abandon her and leave her all alone.

Katherine closes her eyes and waits for the beating of her heart to slow and then takes a deep breath and moves a few steps down the path, calling out her name, a few steps more, and the name halfway out when the tears quicken in her eyes at the sound of the barking in reply, calling from the cool shadows of the path at the edge of woods where she has been all along, staking out the direction of her desire. At the sight of Katherine coming toward her, shaking her head, Sophie spins and dashes down the hill and into the woods with Katherine not far behind.

Cool air surrounds her descent to the water. She looks through the window of the cabin at the small bed and imagines waking to the view of the pond as the sun is coming up. She looks out over the water where birds dart in and out of a low hanging tree, its leaves trembling as scarlet fruits are plucked and carried off. She watches the rhythm of their flight, two pumps of their wings followed by a long and easy glide, and imagines a kind of exultation, reaching out to meet the wind, unbound, beyond gravity or history, and free.

Katherine sees the first sign when she walks into the kitchen, an ordinary piece of stationary tacked to the frame of the back door, with large, hand-printed letters — DAVID WESTON BEAT AND RAPED KATHERINE STUART. HE HAD NO RIGHT. THERE WAS NO EXCUSE. IT WAS NOBODY'S FAULT BUT HIS OWN.

She stares at it and begins to sweat, pulling it down only to see another on the doorway to the hall — DAVID WESTON MURDERED ETHAN STUART.

She lifts a hand but feels restrained, as if the words possess an authority beyond her own, but still she tears it down as she sees a third on the front door, which she can read from where she stands — KATHERINE STUART HAS A RIGHT TO BE ALIVE.

She walks down the hall, tears down the sign, and looks up the stairs where another is taped to the newel post at the top. She cannot read it in the dim light and climbs up to it. KATHERINE STUART IS A POET. She sits on the landing, the pages in her hand, as footsteps come up behind.

238

"I didn't do it to upset you. It's something Elsie did for me."

Katherine leans against the wall.

"I don't want to get up every day and look at this. I want to forget it," she says, throwing the sheets of paper into the air over the stairs.

"I don't think you can," says Lucy. "With some things, the best you do is remember in a different way."

"Like this?"

Lucy leans down and looks into her face. "If Ethan were having a nightmare, what would you do?"

Katherine looks away.

"Tell me what you'd do."

"I'd go to him."

"And then what?"

"I'd wake him up."

"Yes."

Lucy is making tea when Katherine comes into the kitchen, the pages in one hand and a few tacks in the other.

"I'll try to use the same holes."

As in the middle of almost every night, Katherine goes down the hall to where Lucy sleeps, but tonight she quietly descends the stairs. The signs on the walls stand out against the darkness. She goes out to the front porch and sits in the swing and sets it rocking as she lights a cigarette.

There is no moon and the sky is full of clouds that hide the stars. After awhile it begins to rain and Katherine wishes she'd put on more than a robe and slippers but stays where she is, rocking and smoking. Her eyes pass across the lawn to the road and the low picket fence and the cemetery on the other side, the stones barely visible through the rain and the dark. From deep in her mind, the memory of the dream struggles toward the surface. She blinks it away, but it has a buoyancy and soon it is before her, the hole cut into the ground and now a matching box beside it and men lifting at the handles, effortless, the weight being so small, and lowering it down. She blows the smoke into the air but the image is still in front of her, and when she closes her eyes she can feel him in her arms, rocking back and forth, his hair soft and fine, cheeks warm with sleep, small fingers opening and closing, grasping at something in a dream.

All the next day she is focused inward on the open hole and the little box, waiting for someone to fill it in, the sound of dirt falling on wood. In the afternoon she goes across the road and swings open the gate and walks across the ground, soft and spongy from the rain, wandering among the stones clustered beneath the sprawling maple with a few scattered along the fence like shy people at a gathering.

Lucy comes out to get the newspaper and for a moment the two women look at each other before Katherine shrugs and Lucy nods and crosses the road and walks to where Katherine stands in a far corner, arms across her chest, looking down, pressing the toe of her shoe against a small patch of ground.

"I keep seeing this hole," says Katherine, her voice catching in her throat, "I know what it is, and who it's for."

A warm breeze comes across the field and Lucy lifts her head to look up at the sky and sniff the air. "Maybe," she says, "it's time to fill it in."

In the evening Lucy finds Katherine on the living room couch, staring into a box of photographs on her lap, fingers gripping the corners of the box as if holding it together. She does not look up as Lucy enters the room and sits beside her and notices the one on top of the pile, a small boy standing beside a swimming pool, the sun behind him casting a shadow over his face, but not so much as to conceal the smile directed at whoever is taking the picture. "It's not enough," says Katherine, wiping her eyes with the back of her hand.

"No," says Lucy, "it's not. Nothing will ever be."

"Then why?"

"Because it's next. You do it because it's the next thing to do. You think he took everything from you, but he didn't. This is how you find what's left. One thing at a time."

"What if I can't."

"You can."

"What makes you so sure?"

"Because you got this far."

There is a long silence and then Katherine takes her finger and slowly fishes among the photographs. "I can choose a picture," she says, "but I can't decide what else."

"Well," says Lucy, sitting back to look up at the ceiling, "how about things he liked?"

"I threw them all away."

"Oh," says Lucy, the word catching in her throat as she puts her hand on Katherine's shoulder. They sit for awhile in silence, the clock ticking on the mantel. "There must have been books that he liked," says Lucy, "and toys. We'll find something in town." She looks into Katherine's face. "You're still not sleeping."

"No."

The next day they find a copy of *Horton Hears a Who* at the bookstore and at the general store Katherine picks out a box of crayons and pad of colored paper, a purple squirt gun and a set of brightly colored wooden blocks in a little mesh bag. "I'll take these," she says to the clerk, a young girl who smiles and looks at her, a passing glance but enough to turn Katherine's face away, as if every shameful thing about her is plain for anyone to see.

It all fits in a paper bag that she holds on her lap on the way home. She is watching the woods go by when suddenly she remembers the girl's smile and a hot wave of shame passes through her, feeling foolish and exposed, this gesture, this little paper bag resting in her lap, as pathetic and small as she, and wants to roll down the window and throw it into the woods beside the road. But then Lucy's hand is resting on her own, her voice drifting through the air between them above the rattle of tires on the hardscrabble road, "It takes all the courage in the world to do the next thing. You must remember that."

They are home shortly before noon and Katherine goes into the barn and finds the shovel where Lucy said it would be — beside an old toboggan — and takes it across the road. She stands looking out across the field for a long time before she takes the shovel in her hands and lays the sharp tip against the ground and with her foot on top of the blade pushes down with all her weight.

She outlines a hole roughly two feet by four and cuts the sod out in sections that she lays to one side. The earth below is dark and moist but she is barely half a foot down when she begins to hit roots and then stones and rocks, some so large she has to scrape away the dirt to see their true dimensions. She hacks at the roots but they are too thick and the rocks too large to pry loose. She lays down the shovel and sits by the hole, catching her breath before going back into the house.

"I need something heavier. There are roots and rocks."

Lucy sends her to the barn for a crowbar, clippers, and assorted pruning and keyhole saws. Katherine assembles the tools beside the hole, gets down on her hands and knees, and sets to work. Whenever she feels tears coming on or a heaviness around her heart, she bears down and works harder, clipping away smaller roots and digging around larger ones to make room for the blade of a saw. The white roots stand out against the dirt and she tries to cut them back beyond the line of soil so they don't show and the walls of the hole will be even and dark.

She has never used a crowbar. It's five feet long and heavy in her hands. She holds it over the hole and lets it fall and hears it sound against the rock. She raises it into the air, shifts a few inches to one side, and lets it fall. Again it strikes solid rock and again she lifts and shifts and lets it fall until there is only the soft chunk of iron into soil. She pushes the bar to one side to pry against the stone but the bar isn't deep enough and soon gives way. So she lifts it higher and lets it fall at the same spot over and over, as deep as she thinks it will go, and then leans against the bar, but still the rock refuses to move. Sweat is pouring down her face, her arms aching, blisters showing on her hands unused to shoveling, and struggling to push from her mind the fear that she won't be able to do this thing, the simple digging of a hole. She looks at the rock and the bar resting in the dirt and tries to see what is needed, then finally plants her feet at the edge of the hole and commits her full weight to the end of the bar, holding her breath and bearing down until she thinks she will have to lift herself into the air, suspended like a counterweight, when suddenly the rock begins to move with a spring of the bar that sends her thudding to the ground, a shock of pain through her hip and the wind knocked out of her lungs. She lies back on the grass to catch her breath, opening her eyes to look up at the sky. Sophie's nose appears above her face and Katherine reaches up and touches her behind the ears and then rolls onto her side to stand beside the unfinished hole.

Using the edge of the hole for leverage against the bar she manages to shift the rock to the center where it reveals itself to be enormous. But from there she can move it no further, for the edge of the hole is now too far away and there is nothing to push off from except dirt softened by her digging. She draws her hand across her forehead to wipe the sweat away and then turns and goes into the house.

"How's it going?"

"I've unearthed the mother of all rocks," says Katherine.

"Try not to take it personally. It's why we have such beautiful stone walls."

Katherine washes her hands at the kitchen sink and takes a glass of water out on the porch where she sits on the swing and looks across the road to the little pile of dirt beside the neatly stacked sections of sod. The rock is just visible above the hole. She sips the water and pictures the distance between the rock and the edge of the hole and ponders the lack of something solid to lean the bar against. The whole point is to move the rock away from whatever edge she uses, which seems to her, by definition, self-defeating. She finishes the water and turns her head to the sound of a pickup truck rumbling up the road and past the house, a small pile of two-by-fours sticking out the back end.

She hurries into the house and is about to say, "I need some lumber," when she turns and goes out to the barn.

She takes a length of two-by-four across the road and lays it across the hole just behind the rock and then drops the heavy tip of the bar into the soil between the two and leans into it. But the board is too thin and almost cracks beneath the weight. Katherine takes a pruning saw and cuts the board in two and lays one piece on top of the other. Again she plants the bar and leans her weight against it, holding her breath from the effort until she lets it out with a shout when the rock finally begins to move. She does it again, shifting the boards to cut the distance and then inserting the bar until the rock is up against the low dirt wall on the far side of the hole. Then she takes the shovel and digs into the edge to create a gradual slope on which to roll the rock until it is high enough for her to get down on her hands and knees inside the hole and push it the rest of the way out.

She sits on the grass and looks at its pleasing lines, rounded on one side and roughly carved on the other with little peaks and valleys like a range of hills. She can see its light color through the thin layer of dirt that clings to it, a creamy white, with streaks of tan and specks of black among bits of mica reflecting the sun. She lays her hands on the rock and closes her eyes, feeling its weight and permanence and decides it will mark the spot if Lucy doesn't mind.

She takes the shovel and begins to dig again.

When she thinks the hole is deep enough, she rolls the stone to the far end where the grass is undisturbed beneath. She takes the two-by-fours and all the tools but the shovel back to the barn and returns with a bucket of water to wash the stone. And only then, as she sits by the hole and leans over to lay a hand on the cool dark soil at the bottom, does she allow the tears to come.

In the evening after supper Katherine gathers everything together on the writing desk in the living room. There is the photograph of Ethan by the pool and another she picked out of the two of them together sitting on a couch with him asleep, his head on her lap, his round belly — 'little Buddha belly' she called it — showing beneath the t-shirt he has already outgrown. Arranged around the photographs are the box of crayons, the coloring pad, the book, and toys.

Lucy walks in and holds out a white linen tablecloth. "I thought you could use this to line the grave."

Katherine starts at the sound of the word unspoken until now. "Thank you," she says.

Before they go to bed, Katherine will cut a length of her hair and hold it out while Lucy ties it in a ribbon and adds it to the rest.

The sun rises over large white clouds moving slowly from one edge of the sky to the other, the air cool as autumn begins its early arrival so far north. After breakfast the two women carry a wooden bench from the porch and set it beside the grave. Katherine arranges the photographs and the rest in a basket and lays the linen cloth over the top.

"Would you like some music?" says Lucy, standing in the hall, holding an armful of ferns and a basket of asters in late summer colors of maroon and rust.

"The cello from the other day would be nice."

"That would be Bach," says Lucy, turning to the library. She returns, the music swelling behind her, a small book under her arm. "An offering," she says, and then holds the door while Katherine passes through, the basket in her arms, and they walk across the road to the far corner where Sophie promptly finds a place to lie down. The deep tones of the cello drift through the open door as they spread the cloth over the mouth of the grave and tuck it down inside. Katherine stands for a moment, unsure of what to do, and then gets down on her hands and knees and takes the little bag of blocks from the basket and tries to stay the trembling in her fingers as she lays it gently in the center of the hole. Lucy kneels beside her while she takes each thing and lays it with the others — the crayons and paper, the squirt gun, the lock of hair, *Horton Hears a Who*. The photographs are last.

They sit on the bench.

"Tell me about him," says Lucy. "I'd like to feel what he was like."

Katherine sighs and shakes her head and looks down into her lap.

"Just one," says Lucy, "one thing you remember."

They stare out across the field, and then Katherine closes her eyes, "Sometimes I think that I can smell him, as if he was right here."

"Yes," says Lucy, moving closer.

"When he came in from playing, or after a bath, or the top of his head when he was just a baby." She wipes her eyes with the heel of her hand. "The look on his face when he was all done nursing."

"Tell me about that."

"There was this little shudder at the corners of his mouth just before he fell asleep."

She leans toward Lucy, their shoulders touching.

"He was such an easy boy, you know, even when he knew something was wrong. So alive, everything new." She looks at Lucy. "Isn't that how it's supposed to be. What it's all about?"

"I think so."

"Then I don't get it," says Katherine, looking into the hole. "I don't get it at all."

Lucy puts an arm around her, feeling her begin to shake, "Just remember him now, his voice when he said good night. He was your little boy, and now he's gone," and they are crying together beneath the clouds drifting by, Lucy hanging on tight as Katherine seems to crack open in her arms, her body turning inside out with grief.

They grow quiet and sit. A cool breeze moves across the fields. And then Katherine stands and goes to the far side of the grave, bending down to pick up the edge of the cloth. She looks at Lucy who takes the other edge and they move together to fold it over the opening in the ground. Then Katherine arranges the ferns on top and the flowers over those while Lucy takes out the little book she carried from the house.

"It's a poem I'd like to read."

Katherine sits on the grass beside the grave as Lucy settles on the bench and clears her throat.

Do not stand at my grave and weep.
I am not here. I do not sleep.

I am a thousand winds that blow.
I am the diamond glint on snow.

I am the sunlight on ripened grain.
I am the gentle autumn rain.

When you wake in the morning hush
I am the swift uplifting rush
of quiet birds in circling flight.
I am the soft starlight at night.

Do not stand at my grave
and weep.
I am not here. I do not sleep.

Katherine moves a flower to a different place and then leans over and takes a handful of dirt and spreads it on the flowers and ferns. Then she takes another and another and when she sees Lucy with the shovel in her hands she shakes her head and pulls herself to her feet and takes the shovel that Lucy holds out to her and digs deep into the pile. Lucy steps back and sits on the bench with Sophie beside her on the grass and together they watch the grave filling in until the dark earth is piled in a gentle mound, while far above their heads a red-tailed hawk rides the currents of air rising up from below and wheels a great circle in the sky.

8

*I*n the days that follow, a strange and unsettling quiet comes over the house. Summer is turning into fall, the fields lying down, the night air crisp and cold. Katherine sleeps and wakes full of energy, a semblance of normality that Lucy welcomes until it comes to her that it is merely the eye of the storm and will not last. In the morning Katherine walks as far as Walter Finch's farm and is back in time for breakfast. She works in the barn and garden, helps to cook and clean. To one who didn't know, she might seem content or even happy, but not to Lucy who realizes one day over lunch as she watches Katherine fidget with her silverware while they sit and talk that she is deep inside a quiet desperation to keep herself ahead of the slow pace of life in the country that follows her like an enveloping fog slowing gaining from behind. No television, no nightly news, no bright lights or noisy traffic, no place to go, nothing to distract from the simple truth of what she sees when she looks into a mirror or hears in the silence of her mind. After years on a runaway train Katherine's life has come to a screeching halt and now she can't sit still. She paces during conversations or works her fingers in rhythmic patterns or balances her leg on the ball of her foot and jiggles it up and down. When she speaks the words may come out as if picked at random from a hat, leaving Lucy to reassemble them in her mind.

And then comes a week of rain and a chill that settles on the house and animals. Goats stand in the doorway to the barn and chew their cud and wait. Lucy lights a fire in the stove and Sophie takes up her cold weather station on the bed beside it. Katherine doesn't know what to do with herself. She can't sit still long enough to read and a game of Scrabble on the kitchen table is over all too quickly. She tries to nap in the afternoon only to be left awake at night. She goes back to getting out of bed and sitting on the front porch with no company but the bottle of whiskey. One night she is making her way back to bed when she opens the attic door, mistaking it for her room, and stands confused before the darkened stairs until she realizes what she's looking at and makes a drunken little snort and starts to wonder what it might be like to sit in the quiet at the peak of Lucy's house.

She runs her hand up the wall to find the switch and then peers into the gloom barely lit by a solitary bulb hanging from the ceiling. She climbs the stairs and pauses at the top, amazed by the sight of long walls of books stretching to the far ends of the house.

She walks along the shelves, fingers lightly scanning rows of cloth and paper spines, noticing through the dulling buzz of whiskey how they are divided by subject — biography, fiction, poetry, psychology, religion and philosophy, Marxism, history, feminism and women's studies, and, in a small section near the far window looking out on the barn, war, violence, and Vietnam. She closes her eyes to listen to the rain beating on the roof until a soft creak turns her with a start to Lucy's sleepy face showing above the opening in the floor.

"Can't sleep?"

Katherine shakes her head.

"Me neither," says Lucy sitting on the top stair. "You found my hoard."

"You've read them all?"

"Mostly." She rests her elbows on her thighs and cups her face in her hands, closing her eyes. Katherine begins to wonder if she's nodded off when she thinks again of the change that she's been noticing for several weeks, less interested in food and the way she holds her stomach as if something isn't right and she's trying to divine what it is.

"I started with psychologists," says Lucy, opening her eyes, "because I figured they'd have the answer. I went through the whole bunch — Freud, James, Adler, Fromm, Bettelheim, Horney, Rollo May — but they weren't much help."

"What were you looking for?"

"Some idea of why a man who said he loved me would make such a project out of beating me up. And why I felt so crazy." She looks at Katherine. "I couldn't get a *grip*, you know."

"And did you?"

"Get a grip — "

"Find what you were looking for."

Lucy looks away for a moment, then back again. "I think so."

They sit and listen to the rain and Katherine wants only to sleep and yet cannot set herself in motion toward the stairs, her mind focused on Lucy's face staring at the window at the far end of the attic.

"Would you tell me?"

Lucy sits up straight and rubs her neck. "I suppose," she says, "although I don't know if it'll do much good."

"I'd like to hear it anyway."

Lucy shakes her head. "It's only words after all. There's only so much that someone else's words can do." They look at each other, Lucy noting the weariness in Katherine's face.

She takes a chair from against the wall and drags it next to Katherine. "No one's ever asked me this before," she says, sitting down, "so I don't know how it'll come out." She is quiet for a moment, then looks about and gets up and turns the chair to face the window. "That's better," she says, then sits and thinks, her face smooth as she stares out at the rain, and then Katherine notices a letting down in the muscles of her cheeks as if she had been trying to make something out at a great distance only to have it come into view as a source of great sadness. Lucy takes in a deep breath and lets it out. "Love was the hardest part. I couldn't wrap my mind around the fact that either he didn't love me or love wasn't what I thought it was." She takes a tissue from her sleeve and wipes her nose. "I eventually decided it was a bit of both. He didn't love me and I didn't know enough to see it for what it was. I was very young and I didn't know the difference between being wanted and being loved. He wanted me or some idea of me. And he had moments of such need that it looked like love. At least it did to me. But that isn't what it was."

Her face is motionless, looking out at the rain.

"I don't know why he took such an interest in me. I knew him from school, starting in sixth grade, and he never noticed me at all. Not that I blame him. I was no great beauty, not by a long shot, although maybe pretty in a way, at the right angle if the light was good. But not enough to get worked up about. And then senior year of high school, suddenly he discovers me. I will never know why, not to this day. Maybe he was lonely or just wanted a wife all his own and was afraid no one else would have him and thought I might be easy." She looks at Katherine. "He was right about that last part," and then whispers to herself as she turns her head away, "up to a point."

"Isn't it peculiar," she says, her voice quickening, "how everyone gets married when they're too young to know any better. My father told me not to do it — I have to give him credit — but he said it was my life and I could do as I wanted, which doesn't mean much when you consider what else there was for me to do, be an old maid schoolteacher or some such. So, I went ahead."

She stops talking and looks out the window as if watching something, following it with her eyes. "It's all backwards," she says, not taking her gaze from the window, "young people, barely grown, no idea of what they're doing, getting married, having babies," her voice trailing away, "going off to war."

The rain pours down outside, pounding on the roof. Lucy shakes her head and lifts her sleeve to wipe her eyes, her hand trembling, the other hand rising to steady it. "Anyway," she says, her voice just above a whisper, "where was I?"

"I'm not sure."

"Hm," says Lucy, shifting as if to center herself in the chair.

"Your husband."

Lucy nods, closing her eyes to still herself. "Yes. You know, at the start I thought I could always get out if I needed to. My first mistake. Well, not the first. But it didn't occur to me where I was going. Into this little room that kept getting smaller, and the windows and doors, too, so that after awhile there was no way out that I could see.

"And then I started to be afraid of him. Because I realized I wasn't in control of my life anymore. I couldn't decide anything. Every morning I looked at him sleeping next to me and the first thing I felt was where he'd hit me the day before. And then I'd wonder where he'd hit me today or what would set him off or whether he'd hit the same spot again before it had time to heal. Whether anyone would notice. How I was going to get through it. Even when he was asleep or away from the house I felt like I couldn't move. I couldn't get my balance. I couldn't clear my mind long enough to think."

Lucy looks at Katherine for a long time, her face without expression, as if gazing in a mirror.

"And then it got inside of me and took me over." She looks away to the window and the rain. "What I came to realize years later was an awful wounding in my soul. I think most people have no idea of this, how a person can disappear." She looks at Katherine, her eyes growing wide, "How God can disappear. How the world can go mad and stop making any sense at all. I had no rights. I did not exist. Like I was dead or had never lived."

Lucy holds up a hand and looks at it, turning it back and forth as it trembles in the air. "My," she says, "I do surprise myself." She looks at Katherine. "I didn't think I'd feel so much after all these years." She lays the hand on her chest and closes her eyes. Katherine watches the rise and fall of her breathing in the dim light.

"For years after he was gone I kept asking myself where such rage could come from, and for the smallest thing, you can't imagine," she looks at Katherine, "but, of course, you can," and then looks away, "not annoyed or even vexed, but enraged as if what I'd done or failed to do was so terrible that he had to do something even more terrible to keep me from doing it again. And I remembered Elsie saying how pathetic he was and suddenly it dawned on me that he was afraid. But this made no sense. Afraid of what? Here he was a big strong man and me a little slip of a thing. So afraid he had to do such things to me?"

The wind is blowing the rain and Lucy gets up and closes the window, leaning back against the sill.

"It took me quite awhile to see why he was so afraid. Which is strange when you consider how simple it really is." She lifts her head and looks at Katherine. "I was married to a man who needed me to be smaller than I was so he could see himself as larger. Smarter, stronger, better, in control." She shrugs. "A real man, I guess you'd say. And then he could feel safe. Until I did something he didn't like or that made him think he was losing his hold on me, and to him that was a challenge, some kind of mockery or defiance of his control, his *right* to me. And then came the violence, like a tonic to restore his precious manhood. You could see it in his face, a calm that came over him when he was done."

A stillness settles over the attic, the two women looking at each other through tears faintly visible in the dim light. Lucy looks down at the floor and closes her eyes and feels suddenly a terrible fatigue.

"And no one knew?" says Katherine.

Lucy shakes her head. "I find," she says, walking back across the floor and sitting in the chair, "that people have a way of not knowing what they'd rather not. And I was too ashamed and humiliated to call attention to myself." She stares into the middle distance, remembering the knocking on the door, the men coming into the house, how she tried to hide her face behind a dishtowel. "The police came once. I think Walter had something to do with that. I knew them of course. It's a small town. They were embarrassed, awkward, not knowing what to do. But the thing I remember most is how unhorrified they were by what he'd done to me. How they didn't pounce on him and take him away. They were not on my side. And yet the strangest thing is, in a way, they weren't on his side either. And so I asked myself — years later — whose side they were on, and I thought, well, it must be the law, but then wouldn't the law have been on my side, the one who was beaten up? If a stranger jumped me on the street they'd be on my side, wouldn't they? And this is where it gets tricky," she says, the words coming slow and measured, "because he wasn't a stranger and they weren't on his side. But they were on the *husband's* side, the man's side." Lucy looks away toward the window. "They didn't want to interfere with how another man managed his wife. *His* wife."

The rain beats out a steady rhythm against the roof.

Lucy looks at Katherine. "What are you thinking?"

"About my father," she says. "And my brother."

"Yes."

Just before dawn they are sitting in the swing on the front porch watching the rain still coming down. "You have so many books on war," says Katherine. "Why is that?" There is a silence long enough to make her wonder if it was a mistake to ask.

"Michael was in Vietnam," says Lucy.

"Then they're his."

"No. They're mine."

9

$\mathcal{K}$atherine and Sophie set off beneath the early morning sun. At the tree line Katherine goes into the woods, arms swinging at her sides, Sophie crashing through underbrush on a parallel path. Katherine quickens her pace when she sees among the trees the first patch of blue that isn't sky.

She stands on the deck and looks out over the water, closing her eyes to listen to the wind in the trees and for just a moment feels her mind growing still, unaware of where and who she is.

It comes to her now, the memory that appeared to her suddenly and for the first time late last night, on the edge of sleep, his face as he sank to his knees, already dying, astonishment and surprise mingling with the rage that had conspired with her rising up off the floor to sink the knife as deep as it would go.

She goes down to the water and sits on the end of the dock and pulls off her shoes and socks and rolls up her pants, *a sorry, pathetic son of a bitch,* swings her feet out over the water and holds them in the air before lowering them down, eyes closed, anticipating the cold against her skin.

High overhead an osprey makes its way across the sky. She has never seen one before and thinks it must be a hawk until she notices the belly all white. It surveys the water below and then rises before swooping down to rise again, circling, holding itself in still intent, and then hurtling down to crash into the surface of the pond. She wonders for a moment if it has fallen, but then watches it spread its wings, beat the water and then the air to rise, a silver fish in its claws, higher and higher until it disappears beyond the trees.

Katherine moves her feet in slow circles in the water, one way and then another, together and then in counterpoint, her eyelids sinking down as she feels the dock beneath her thighs, the sun warm against

257

her face. Birds call out to one another and Sophie breathes a sigh and Katherine wonders what is this simple feeling that comes over her before quickly moving on, familiar and yet strange and far away.

She lays a hand on Sophie and holds it there above the rise and fall of every breath.

They take the long way home and at the house she swings open the gate and goes over to the grave, the mound of earth sunk down and rutted by the rain. She reminds herself to rake it over and recalls Lucy saying to plant bulbs in the fall.

Lucy is at the kitchen table, writing out a list for town. There are deep circles around her eyes, a half eaten plate of food beside her elbow.

"Are you okay?"

"Not really."

"Shouldn't you see a doctor?"

"No, thank you."

"But if you're not feeling well — "

"They just have to wait," says Lucy. "I've been on that runaway train before. Besides, at the moment I'm more interested in you. How was it at the pond?"

"Fine."

"Good," she nods with a weak little smile, "go whenever you want."

"But you're not well."

"Katherine," she says, shaking her head, "I didn't invite you here to keep me company. Or take care of me. Besides which, there's nothing wrong with me that won't work itself out to wherever it needs to go."

Katherine looks down at her hands holding each other in her lap.

"Make no mistake," says Lucy, "it matters a great deal to me that you're here. I had a very strong feeling about that, and trusting it is one of the best things I ever did. And now that you're here you must go wherever you need to go. That's the point of it all." She leans over and looks into Katherine's eyes. "And you have to let me do the same."

Katherine packs a knapsack and walks down through the woods to the cabin, the sun high in the southern sky as she sets a folding chair near the canoe and reads while Sophie sleeps in the shade where the dock meets the shore.

She is so intent on the book that it isn't until she looks up to swat away a deer fly that she sees the loons, two adults with a pair of fledglings in tow, just a few feet off the dock. She is startled by the look of them, red eyes set in a smooth round head, coal black and goose-like, the breast pure white, the sides and back checkered in white and black. She follows their progress along the shore and then lays down the book and looks out over the water. She feels the weight of trying to understand what seems beyond comprehension, a world where fathers would beat and rape the mothers of their children and kill their sons and daughters, and where wives would kill the men they love as the only way to make it stop.

She thinks of Lucy and wonders about her husband, his leaving which seems to her a miracle. She gazes out over the water and sees a deer emerge from the woods across the pond and walk down to the water's edge, abruptly looking to one side and then the other before slowly dipping its head to drink.

It occurs to her that loons and deer occupy the same world she is at a loss to understand. But as the deer turns and walks away into the woods, she feels the distance they keep between themselves and human beings, a distance she feels a sudden longing to cross.

She rouses Sophie and they hike to the far side of the pond where she can look back across the water to the cabin and the dock, the sun behind them now over the western hills. She sits on the shore, the round humps of boulders showing just above the surface of the water. Sophie appears beside her and sits close to her hip, and Katherine thinks about her grandmother and wishes for another kind of miracle, that she had somehow known of Lucy and this place and been able to seek refuge here, carrying Ethan sleepy from the car into the house brightly lit against the night, sitting in the kitchen while he sleeps upstairs, looking across the table at Lucy and an Elsie she can only imagine, feeling the presence of these women as their voices fill the room with the sure and certain knowledge that they would face together whatever might happen next, that she and Ethan were safe and not alone.

She wipes her eyes as she gets to her feet and starts back down the trail.

The sun is low in the sky, the light soft against the water as Katherine gives Sophie her supper and lies down on the small bed by the window, propping her head on a pillow and looking out. A breeze stirs the leaves on the birch, shadows playing across Katherine's face as she draws up a blanket, closes her eyes and falls asleep.

She wakes to an indigo sky with blue grey clouds broken by a long thin line of dusty orange cast upward by the sun below the hills. She watches the colors change, softening and growing pale until there is only the night, the trees outside the window black against the sky.

And only then does she realize what has happened. "Oh, shit," she says throwing off the blanket and looking around the room as Sophie thumps her tail against the floor. She puts on her shoes and goes outside but she can barely see where the path begins. She hadn't thought to bring a flashlight. She calls Sophie and they go back inside.

"I guess it's you and me," she says, laying a hand on Sophie's head.

She considers the lantern hanging over the table but has no idea how to work it. She lights a candle and looks about the room. What had before felt modest, even small, now seems large and full of dark corners where something might hide that she cannot see. *He's dead*, she reminds herself, *he's dead*, but it gives her little comfort, knowing how easily he can appear in her dreams and waking visions that are as real as if he were alive.

She takes the candle to the outhouse and stands looking down into the hole, reluctant to suspend herself naked over it. She sits quickly but lightly and waits, but cannot let go. Then with a sigh she gets up and hobbles outside, a wad of toilet paper in her hand, stepping off the path to squat and pee on the ground.

Neither door has a lock save for flimsy hooks and eyes which she sets in place, then wedges chairs beneath the knobs. By the light of the candle she makes the bed and pulls a cushion from the couch to lay on the floor for Sophie. She sets the candle on the window sill and undresses to her underwear before climbing into bed, the sheets cool against her skin. Sophie stands over the cushion on the floor, sniffing at it but not lying down, looking up at her, ears laid back against her head.

Katherine pats the bed and then Sophie is beside her, curling into a ball in the space behind her knees, letting out a sigh.

Katherine closes her eyes but does not sleep. She listens to the steady in and out of Sophie's breath. Something scurries overhead and she thinks of mice. She looks out the window at the sky full of stars and from behind the cabin the moon's pale illumination plays out across the water. Leaves are black and still against the sky in this, her first full night of solitude — with no one else nearby — since the night seven months ago, the last night in her house, the last night she saw them alive.

She moves her fingers through the bedclothes and wonders who is this woman lying here beside an old dog who belongs to someone else, looking up at stars near the end of her fortieth year, all that once defined her swept away, not wife or mother, no easy assumptions about family, being a daughter or a sister. The woman remains, but with no idea what that might amount to, living inside a body as if in someone else's house. She struggles to remember when her body and her life were her own, before the invasion reduced them both to ruin, as in the aftermath of a war where she is neither combatant nor civilian, but the ground on which the battle was fought, one piece of ground looking much like any other.

She wonders where there is a place for her, for any woman who knows what she knows, how Lucy manages to carry this terrible knowledge of what human beings can do to one another, how she lives some semblance of a life when she knows what is happening, where she finds such strength as that. And then she thinks again of Lucy's fatigue and refusing food and feels a chill of being alone in a world so huge, boundless, and dark, her only hope disappearing before her eyes, to be buried in a little plot across the road.

Lucy wakes in the middle of the night to a quiet and empty house. She was dreaming of Philip. She stares up at the ceiling and thinks his face will always be the way it was the last time she saw it more than thirty years ago. In the dream he was weeping from somewhere in the house and though she followed the sound from room to room, she could find no trace of him.

She goes down the hall to Katherine's room and by the light of the moon stands in the doorway and looks in at the empty bed, neatly made, a book beside the pillow. She goes back to her room, pausing to look at where Sophie would lie sleeping in the corner if she were here. She goes downstairs and finds a cigarette and pulls on her coat and goes outside to sit on the back porch step. The moon is high above the barn. She lights the cigarette and listens for the goats, but everyone is asleep but her. By the light through the kitchen window she sees a ring of smoke rise from the tip of her cigarette and watches it float into the air, rotating, undulating as it slowly comes apart, unable to keep its form, and then is gone. Her eyes stay fixed on the last place she saw it whole and she thinks life is not much different than that, except for taking longer in the rising.

Katherine props herself on an elbow to look out the window at a fog so thick she cannot see the water. Sophie lifts her head and thumps her tail against the bed.

"Okay," she says, shooing Sophie to the floor. She dresses quickly and goes outside into the cool, damp air where above her head a streak of blue appears in the ceiling of grey and the fog begins to thin and move as sunlight catches the hilltops across the water.

Sophie is drinking from the lake when Katherine calls her and they climb the hill and cross the field to the barn where she goes inside to feed and water the goats. There is no sign of Lucy when she goes into the house and puts down food for Sophie. On the upstairs landing she looks into Lucy's room and sees her sitting up in bed.

"I'm sorry," says Katherine.

"Whatever for?"

"Staying away all night."

"I knew where you were," says Lucy. The sound of Sophie's paws on bare wood comes up the stairs and when the old dog rounds the corner at the top, Lucy's face brightens and she slaps the bed with her hands, "Come here, you!" and then Sophie is upon her, tail wagging as her tongue works over Lucy's face, Lucy laughing, ducking her head to escape, but Sophie undeterred, sniffing Lucy's hair until Lucy takes hold of her and gently guides her to a sit.

"I'm happy for you to spend nights at the lake, but I need you to leave her here with me." She sees tears in Katherine's eyes. "What, dear."

Katherine shakes her head and looks away and then back at her. "I'm afraid something is happening to you."

"Something is."

"What?"

"I don't know."

"Then why aren't you doing something?"

Lucy lies back against her pillow. "Because there's nothing to be done."

"But how can you say that if you don't know what it is?"

"Not an unreasonable question."

"You can say no to them anytime you want," says Katherine.

"Yes," says Lucy, "I can. Thank you for reminding me."

Each morning Katherine listens for sounds from the kitchen or outside her window that might tell her if Lucy is still in bed. On days when Lucy is slow in getting up Katherine feeds Sophie and takes care of the goats before brewing a pot of tea to take upstairs on a tray.

"Don't get me used to this," says Lucy, not returning Katherine's smile. "I mean it. You have better things to do."

"I want to do this."

Lucy shakes her head. "You're hovering."

Katherine says nothing.

"It won't make any difference," says Lucy. "I told you. It's not why I asked you here."

"But why can't I help?"

"You can. And you do. I just don't want your taking care of me to become some kind of project."

"Project?"

Lucy shakes her head as she rubs her forehead, "That's not what I mean."

"Do you want me to leave?"

Lucy looks at her. "I'd sooner you left," she says, "than stay with the idea of taking care of me. I can't allow that."

"But why not?"

"Because I have others who can do that if there comes a time for it." She looks out the window. "I'm not saying you can't be loving and kind. Of course you can. But you have things to get on with."

They close the distance between them in a long embrace and Katherine is surprised by how thin boned and spare she is, like a bird.

Lucy watches her disappear down the stairs and thinks to herself what she would not say — that the affection she feels from Katherine means as much to her as it ever has from anyone, made all the more powerful because she never saw it coming. And she doesn't want her to become more attached than she already is, because she's lost too much already and as far as Lucy can tell is about to lose something more.

10

Autumn comes as early to northern Vermont as spring comes late. Walter Finch has already come to take the second cut of hay from the fields behind the barn. Katherine sat by her window and watched the machinery pass back and forth through dust dancing in the sunlit air, Walter high up on the seat, a broad-brimmed hat slouched over his face. She met him later when he came into the kitchen for something cold to drink and to pass the time with Lucy. She studied him for clues of what it was that Lucy loved and found them soon enough. Something in his gentle manner and the directness of his speech, and she could tell from the soft eyes that looked at Lucy that he loved her, too, although something in the way he held himself back made Katherine believe he'd never told her so.

Katherine walks alone through the field behind the barn. She has left Sophie behind — her nose against the screen door — and carries a knapsack filled with books and food and a flashlight. She stops to look around at the hills, the brilliant red and orange of the maples having come and gone and leaving in their place a carpet of yellow and gold birch and oak dotted with the green of pine, cedar, and fir. Wave upon wave of color recedes into the distance bounded by a hazy white horizon defining the great bowl of sky.

She plunges into the woods, a breeze blowing up through the trees and her hair, grown longer now, and she runs her hand through it as she walks amidst leaves that clatter through the air like rain.

She has done this almost every day for weeks, going down to the water to read and walk and sleep and sometimes to remember a dream. Today she will take the canoe out for the first time. It came to her the night before, to drift across the water reflecting sky and clouds, and she resolved to do it.

She feels the weight of the books along her back. She is slowly reading her way through the attic, but for all her growing knowledge keeps returning to Lucy's words that either he didn't love her or love wasn't what she thought it was. How could I have been so wrong? And how can I be sure of anything again?

She goes down to the dock where she unties the canoe from the rack and rolls it into the water, surprised by how light it is in her hands. She imagines Lucy on the woven seat, a paddle across her lap, inviting Sophie in. She takes a deep breath to lift the heaviness around her heart and then steps into the canoe and pushes off on a course along the shore toward the island, perpendicular to the breeze coming across the water from the west. She paddles on one side and then the other to keep the canoe from turning, then remembers the stroke she learned at summer camp, that keeps the canoe in a straight line, and settles into a steady rhythm as her body recalls the soft slap of the blade entering the water, the pull against the muscles in her shoulders and arms, the drops falling from the paddle as she swings it forward for the next stroke.

Along the shore are fallen limbs bleached white by the sun and the trunks of toppled trees lie beneath the water like ribs and bones. She stops and drifts among them, looking down into the water as if floating above a boneyard full of memory. She passes above the stump of a large tree that grew here before this depression of land was flooded to make a pond, its roots fanning out in all directions like braids of hair. A small fish swims in and out of holes rotted in the trunk, exploring the carcass of some long dead creature, in one eye and out the other.

The air grows calm as she puts the island between her and the wind. She wonders if she knows what loving is, if she's ever known, how she could possibly have known and let her life come to this.

She paddles to the island and drifts in near the shore, her gaze settled on the water passing by, and she is startled by a huge, dark form looming just below the surface, silent and brooding as if about to rise beneath her, and she doesn't move, the wet paddle across her lap cold against her thighs. It seems to move from the motion of the water and then the light shifts and suddenly the boulder appears for what it is, a small whale of stone, the dark gray top smooth and curving to where it disappears in the darkness of the water, a slumbering presence, heavy with something more ancient than old. Her mind drifts around a being so powerful it can bear the knowledge of everything that has ever been, and tucked away in some small crevice is the story of her life. And then another and another, one almost breaking the surface of the water with its high arching back, the angle of light and reflected sky on the water making them invisible until she is all but upon them, emerging suddenly from the gloom only to disappear as she passes by. She looks across the water and realizes she is in a great resting ground, a repository, sepulcher, holy place, but more, some nascent sense of possibility, of new life waiting for the right moment to emerge, a nursery, hatchery, as if a giant bird had laid her eggs in this place a millions years ago. And she wonders when that moment will be, when the world might be safe enough.

She closes her eyes and feels the tears rolling down her face.

The soft jolt of the canoe bumping into something opens her eyes on a boulder rising several feet above the pond. A colony of bright green moss fills a depression on the shady side and a hemlock has somehow taken root in a crevice. She looks at it, amazed, and then sees past it to the shore of the island where a tall, slender white birch seems to grow up from nothing more than a rock beneath it. She guides the canoe to shore and sees the exposed roots gripping a large stone, like a reptilian foot. Her eyes follow the line of bark curving toward the sky and she thinks what a bad choice this birch has made and the hemlock and yet there is something beautiful in the choice and in the choosing.

She paddles along the shore. The island is small, no more than 50 yards across, but just large enough for a little cabin where she imagines herself asleep each night beneath this sky with water all around.

She closes her eyes and tries to remember David's face but cannot and just when she has given up, suddenly he is right there in front of her, her leaning forward with the paddle across the gunwales to steady the canoe that rocks beneath her, willing herself now to close her eyes and look at him, to make his face like it was at the very first, tender and strong and full of need. But no matter what expression she gives to him it dissolves into the face she saw as he sank to the floor, his heart in her hand, and she has to grip the paddle to keep from trembling, unsteady and afraid in the narrow canoe, holding on as the minutes go by until she feels him slowly drift away and it comes into her mind, that moment, that night, perhaps the truest that ever was between them, when every ounce of illusion, of rage and fear, of all that bound them to each other in the small, confining space of their life together, drained away in one shattering instant, flowing down the length of the blade, warm across her fingers and down her arm. And then she turns but cannot bring herself to look at the small space where the wall meets the floor.

"Ethan," whispered to herself, it seeming impossible that he be dead and gone forever, no growing up into a life. Impossible that a child should be the first to die, unreal to be here and sitting in the silence of such beauty while his small body fades away to nothing somewhere to the south at the bottom of a hole in a place she has never seen.

Late in the day the sky turns a dusty rose above the water greying in the fading light. Katherine has come prepared for the dark, choosing to test herself by coming home alone through the woods behind the slender beam of light emanating from her hand, the trees thick and dark around her. Halfway up the trail she stops and turns out the light and waits for him, the wind through the crowns of trees far above her head as she breathes deep to slow the beating of her heart, sounds coming from the darkness, leaves falling to the ground, small animals scurrying through the underbrush. Fear drains the moisture from her mouth and sweat drips down her spine but she stands her ground, closing her eyes and feeling the earth beneath her feet.

She looks up at the moon through the trees and then turns on the light and goes up the trail into the field behind the barn, its roof etched softly against the sky. She climbs the hill, watching for the lights from the house to appear, and through the kitchen window can see Lucy standing at the sink. She passes by the barn and pauses for the sound of goats settling in but all is quiet as she steps across the yard and up the stairs and reaches for the door.

The scream is loud enough to wake Lucy from a dream so wrapped in sleep she doesn't know it is a dream even when she awakens to the sound. In the dream she is on her hands and knees, the moon over her shoulder illuminating her hands digging in the earth, her fingers white against the soil. She is breathing hard, grunting, frantic in the digging, fingernails tearing, tears and the running from her nose falling in the hole. And then from the darkened woods comes a scream that sits her bolt upright, opening her eyes and not knowing where she is until the ceiling comes into focus and she hears Sophie's tail beating against the floor.

The screaming softens to the sound of weeping and a thrashing about in bedclothes. Pushing against the dull ache in her belly and the weight of her fatigue, Lucy throws back the covers and slides out of bed, her toes seeking out the slippers on the floor. The hall glows dimly in the moonlight and through the open door she can see Katherine sitting on the edge of the bed, her head in her hands, the trembling visible even from across the room. Lucy sits beside her, laying a hand on the tender spot at the back of Katherine's head. "A few weeks of peace," she says, looking into her face, "and now it all comes roaring back." Katherine nods, gulping air through the sobs.

As they sit and rock together Lucy tries to think how to tell her what to expect in the years to come, how to brace herself for a lifetime of stolen sleep and ravaged dreams and the terrifying sense of being randomly abducted in the middle of the night to be tormented and savaged before being dumped back into the silence of her own mind. Gone is the simple pleasure of closing her eyes to give in to the oblivion of sleep. She may go for weeks or months or even years without being wakened in the night or having something wet and full of hate whispered in her ear on a darkened flight of stairs. And then, when life seems almost normal, the horror rising up to sweep her into another world.

But Lucy doesn't try to tell her now, just holds her as best she can in arms already weary from the holding. She feels in Katherine a longing to be saved and thinks how much we all need to be saved and the grief of failing to save one another. She thinks of Michael as she has so many times and feels the futility of trying to imagine what she might have done differently, how she might have kept him from the horror or how she could have freed herself sooner from the illusion of thinking he was saved when he was not.

Katherine sets down the wheelbarrow beside the grave and is looking at the mounded earth when she feels a sudden emptiness that not even his bones are there but somewhere else, like a young soldier buried in a distant land where his mother does not speak the language and lacks the means to go. She knows she will have to travel there someday, a pilgrimage to the spot of ground that holds what's left of him, but not now or anytime soon, not until she is farther removed from the longing to bring him back.

She and Lucy were in the garden for several hours selecting perennials for transplant — iris, bleeding heart, and columbine for the spring, phlox and bellflower for midsummer, chrysanthemums for the fall. Katherine dug while Lucy watched and directed, identifying what was what and which was all right to take. Then they went into the house and Katherine opened her journal and used a page to lay out the plot, figuring how to arrange the plants in so small a space.

Bending over the grave, Katherine digs a hole and sprinkles a bit of bone meal across the bottom, lowers an iris into the hole and then fills in all around, pressing the soil to firmly seat the plant in its new home before taking up the trowel again. She works steadily and quietly and does not cry.

Lucy is sitting in the library, a book of poetry in her lap, looking out to the hills ablaze with color in the late morning sun. There is a muffled cough from Katherine in the kitchen. Lucy has been aware of her for some time, the chair scraping on the floor, the spoon in the cup and then the soft tap of it laid against the table and just now a sigh.

Lucy closes the book and says her name. The kitchen chair creaks. A throat clearing.

"What?" says Katherine.

"Would you come here."

There is a pause and then the chair scrapes back and she comes into the room, fingers in the pockets of her jeans, and for a moment in the light slanting through the window she looks young, her face open and smooth.

"What is it?" She says, her voice tentative and small.

"I was going to ask you that. There's something on your mind. I can feel it all the way from here."

"Oh," says Katherine, looking at the floor and Lucy thinks of Michael at fourteen wanting something he imagined to be too much, unable to think of how to ask, bracing himself to be refused. Katherine looks out the window, then at Lucy, "I've been thinking of going into town," a pause, "on my own."

"Of course." Lucy raises her eyebrows and smiles, then pulls herself out of the chair and goes into the kitchen. Katherine hears rummaging in a drawer and then Lucy is back with the key. "It may need some gas. There's Atkinson's where the pavement begins."

Katherine is suddenly embarrassed by the anxiety backed up behind the asking and which she realizes now must have been plain to see.

Lucy goes back to her chair.

"I'll take the grocery list. Do we need anything else?"

Lucy thinks for a moment, looking out the window, shakes her head.

It's been a long time since Katherine sat behind the wheel of a car and there is an exhilarating sense of freedom as she turns the key and hears the engine come to life. She shifts into gear and lets out the clutch too fast and the engine stalls and she looks around, expecting to see Lucy at the window bearing witness. But she is alone except for the goats arranged along the fence like visitors at a zoo. She starts the engine and orchestrates her feet to set the car in motion down the driveway and out past the cemetery to where the road disappears into the trees. She rolls down the window and rests her arm on the frame, looks up to see herself in the rear view mirror, her eyes serious and dark from too many nights of troubled sleep. She looks back to the road just in time to miss a dead possum. She stops the car and backs up to the spot where the animal lies in dappled sunlight. She gets out of the car and kneels beside it. There is no wound that she can see except for a small patch of dried blood beside an ear. She opens the back of the car and takes out the shovel Lucy keeps there and gently moves the possum into the woods beside the road.

In town she parks in the shade of a tall frame building on Main Street a half dozen storefronts up from the bookstore and Dewalt's. She walks slowly along the sidewalk, hands in her pockets, looking into each window to see what is there — stationery, restaurant, realtor, the food co-op, a clothing store with shoes and winter coats on display above autumn leaves scattered across the floor. Between the realtor and the restaurant is an open doorway before a narrow flight of stairs, a small sign at the bottom, "Hannah Rose Parmalee, RMT, Therapeutic Massage." She wonders what it would be like to spend an hour beneath the hands of a woman with a name like Hannah Rose Parmalee. She has never had a massage and tries to recall the last time she was touched in any way that might be called therapeutic, but gives it up when an old bearded man glides past her with a smile and a softly spoken "Excuse me" on his way up the stairs, a hand on the railing to pull him up with every step.

Farther down the street she stops before the window of Dewalt's. Walter Finch is sitting in a booth, a cup of coffee between his hands resting on the table. He looks up and smiles and lifts his hand in a wave and she smiles and waves as she steps away, startled to be seen.

The bookstore is filled with sun but Annie Harris is nowhere in sight, for which Katherine is both disappointed and relieved. She browses among the shelves, pulling out a novel and settling in a chair by the window.

Annie whistles her way through the basement door with a stack of books from her chin to her hands below her waist. A pencil is wedged behind her ear and her glasses have slipped most of the way down her nose. She doesn't see Katherine as she rounds the corner and disappears into the vault. Katherine looks up and listens to the whistling, a tune from *My Fair Lady*.

There is the sound of books being shoved along a shelf to make room for more and then Annie is walking across the room toward the counter by the register when she sees Katherine and stops, her lips still puckered for the whistle but the sound suspended in the middle of a phrase.

"I didn't hear you come in," she says, "how long you been here?"

"Not long."

"Well. Okay. Where's Lucy?"

"She's home."

Annie nods, looking away and then back, "She okay?"

They look at each other across a silence long enough for both to notice.

"I don't know. I don't think so. It's hard to get much out of her."

Annie works her lips, "Sounds about right."

Annie goes to the counter and opens a ledger as she pulls the pencil from behind her ear. Katherine goes back to the book but by the bottom of the page has no idea what she's read. She looks up at Annie looking at her then back down at the ledger only to close it and stare into the air in front of her face, her fingers drumming softly on the cover.

She stops drumming and looks at Katherine. "You want a cup of coffee?"

"All right."

"Let's go, then." On the sidewalk, Annie closes the door and turns over a sign with a little clock face and sets the hands to half an hour.

They settle in a booth at Dewalt's and Katherine imagines Walter Finch taking in the sight of her surprised and awkward little smile and her scurrying away. She shakes her head.

"What?" says Annie.

"Nothing. Sorry."

Annie notes to herself another instance of what she sees as the strange tendency of people to say they're sorry at the drop of a hat.

"How do you know Lucy?" says Annie as she pours maple syrup into her coffee and watches the color show in Katherine's face.

"It's a long story."

Annie nods and looks out the window and Katherine stares into her coffee and plays with her spoon, wondering what Lucy may have said.

"You want to know why I'm here," says Katherine, not looking up.

"I run a bookstore. I always want to know the story. But it's none of my business."

"Have you always lived here?"

"Born and raised. Only went away once, to college — to Daaahtmuth, no less," she says, sticking out her chin, "back in the good old days when they'd just gone co-ed and they'd drive by our dorms and tell us cunts to go home."

"They called you that."

"Sure did."

"Why did you stay?"

"I liked that they couldn't make me leave. I say, fuck 'em." She leans her arms on the table. "Well," she says, her voice low and confidential, "actually, not. I went elsewhere for that." She drinks the last of her coffee.

The bell above the door sounds and Annie looks up and says hello to a tall woman with auburn hair and sad blue eyes.

"Hannah," says Annie, "meet Katherine. A friend of Lucy's."

Hannah Rose Parmalee smiles and says hello and reaches out to shake her hand and Katherine feels amazed at how normal she feels, for just a moment, an ordinary woman going through the ritual of meeting another ordinary woman and everything just as it seems and perfectly all right and unremarkable. She observes the flow of friendly talk as Annie invites Hannah to sit for awhile but she says no, she

274

can't, a client on the way, turning to Katherine with a smile to say goodbye and it's been a pleasure, the words ringing true as Katherine smiles in return to say me, too, all of it utterly familiar and natural and strange.

"She's the massage therapist?" says Katherine watching Hannah go up the street.

"Is she ever," says Annie, "that woman can move your tides." She looks at Katherine. "So, Lucy's not doing so hot."

Katherine shakes her head.

"She's always been one to go her own way," says Annie.

"She seems awfully alone."

"She's a bit of an odd duck, our Lucy. Alone but never lonely. Enjoys her solitude. Which is a good thing given who she is and where she lives. Most people her age don't know what the hell she's talking about. She'd find better company in Boston or San Francisco. All those women who read and think. But not up here. Even I get lonely sometimes and I've got a lot of people coming in and out," a sigh, "you want another cup?"

"I think the half hour is up."

Annie looks at her watch and wrinkles up the corner of her mouth. "Oh, geez, you're right."

On the way out Katherine buys a small sack of scones to take home to Lucy. They say goodbye in front of Dewalt's, Annie lingering for a moment to look at her through a little squint of her eyes, as if making sure of what she saw. In the lengthening silence it is unnerving for Katherine to feel seen in this way by someone other than Lucy and she looks away across the street, wanting to say something but no idea of what and afraid of what might happen if she does. And so she stands there not knowing what to do until a little murmur of surprise catches in her throat and she drops the bag of scones as Annie leans in and gently kisses her on the cheek and then bends down to pick up the bag and smiles as she hands it over and turns and walks away.

Katherine watches her disappear into the bookstore and then goes up the sidewalk toward the car, past the doorway leading to the stairs with the name of Hannah Rose Parmalee, and thinks of her ruined body and shifting tides and a wave of sadness and loss comes over her as she stops and looks back down the street. Suddenly her heart is beating hard as she is down the sidewalk and across the street and up the steps and through the door where Annie looks up from where she stands behind the counter, her face curious as Katherine crosses the distance between them.

For a long moment there is only the sound of Katherine trying to catch her breath and then, "My husband," her mouth dry, stunned into silence as she realizes what she is about to do, is doing.

Annie, leaning forward, says nothing.

Katherine blinks to keep the tears away, "He. . . " but she cannot say the words, so monstrous a thing once said out loud, in a public place where people come and go in their normal lives, to this woman she barely knows. And of course she must know, the look on her face, no need to ask the question, but that she knows or even how Katherine no longer cares because there is something about the knowing in her face, her eyes drawing Katherine forward in spite of the fear as she leans into the counter to still the trembling in her legs, ". . . he beat me. . ." the sad letting go in the muscles of Annie's face, the sorrow coming into her eyes, and then Katherine thinks she doesn't know after all but now there is no going back, ". . .and my boy. . . Ethan. . ." her voice catching in her throat but pushing the words through the thickness gathering there, willing them into the air, ". . .he killed him," the words tumbling out, gulping for air, ". . .and I killed him," looking into Annie's eyes, ". . . and Lucy came and found me," the ground slowly steadying beneath her feet, "and asked me here and that's how I know her."

It seems a long, long time, the two women standing across the counter from each other, collecting themselves, holding the gaze between them. Annie nods, lifts a hand to wipe her eyes.

"That's why I'm here. . ." says Katherine, stepping back with a shrug, "you asked."

"I'm so sorry."

Katherine nods and looks away, "Okay," her voice quiet, "I have to go. . ." turning, lifting her hand as if to wave, letting it drop to open the door.

She doesn't begin to cry until she's nearly at the grocery store, pounding the wheel as it erupts from deep inside her, unleashed by the simple uttering of Ethan's name. She turns into the lot and drives around behind and parks beside a long green dumpster. She waits to feel the humiliation of Annie knowing, but can see only the sorrow in the eyes across the counter, large and full and never looking away.

Just inside the kitchen door she can feel something wrong from the stillness in the house and Sophie not coming in to greet her. She calls out Lucy's name but there is only silence and then a muffled voice from above. She takes the stairs two at a time and finds Lucy in her room, sitting by the window, her head resting in her hands.

"What's the matter?" Katherine kneels down beside her.

Lucy sighs and straightens in the chair. Her eyes are dark and wet and she looks away. "I need you to drive me into town tomorrow, if you don't mind. I have an appointment."

Katherine lays a hand on her arm and Lucy covers it with her own. "What else do you need?"

"You could take care of the goats for the next few days, and Sophie. It's time to find out what's going on."

Lucy's doctor, Paul Howard, wastes no time in sending her to Montpelier for a CAT scan.

"You think it's cancer."

"Yes," he says, "I do. But what do I know? It was only a scare the last time and that's all it may be now."

They look at each other across the old wooden desk littered with papers.

"But you think it's different now."

"Go to Montpelier," he says. "Get the scan. Then we'll see."

They are quiet for a long time in the car.

"Remember what I said about taking care of me," says Lucy.

"I remember."

"Good. That's important."

"I know."

"Thank you for driving me down."

"You're welcome."

It is two days later when Paul Howard calls to tell her the cancer is throughout her abdomen, especially in her liver, and there isn't much to be done.

"Thank God," she says. "The last thing I need is to spend the last months of my life throwing up and watching my hair fall out." She thanks him and hangs up the phone and breathes a sigh. She nods at Katherine as their eyes meet and Lucy wonders what she will do and is pleased to see her holding her ground, eyes full of tears, but holding her ground just the same.

"I have to call Michael," says Lucy turning toward the phone. "I'm going to need him now."

Four

1

*O*n the first morning that *River's Edge Books — Used and Rare* belongs to Michael Dudley, he dresses in jeans and a sweater pulled over a t-shirt and drives his faded green pickup through the streets of Burlington as the light begins to come up in the east. He parks in the alley and lets himself in through the back door. He stands among the rows of darkened shelves and closes his eyes to breathe in the smell of old books and dust and oiled pine floors. And then he begins to cry, soundlessly, as he learned to do years before.

He walks over floorboards that creak beneath his feet, running his fingers along each shelf of books as he passes by, feeling the texture of the cloth spines, pausing to look at one that seems especially fine. At the front window he looks out into the street. It is so quiet he can hear the clock ticking on the far wall, and when he turns to the sound he sees that it's just after six. A car drives by and it is then that he gets the idea of opening early and offering coffee and rolls to commuters. Over the next few days he builds a table to hold a coffee urn and clears a space for two small tables and chairs near the door.

He is mistaken about the commuter trade. No one comes. But he rediscovers the peaceful condition of the world at that hour and looks forward to solitude among his books each morning, making the occasional early morning customer seem almost an intrusion.

He is no stranger to early morning hours. Vietnam taught him more than he ever wanted to know about the stillness just before dawn, edged with sounds from men he never saw as they waited for the footsteps, relentless and purposeful but in no particular hurry.

He buys a second-hand radio and tunes it to classical music on National Public Radio. In the windows he hangs plants and tends them as he does his books, arranging, pruning, noticing where they need filling out or turning toward the light.

Lucy waits a month before coming to visit, giving him time to settle in. He pours her a cup of coffee, heats a raisin scone in the microwave, and sits with her at a table near the window.

"I like it," she says. "It has a nice feel about it."

He smiles and looks at the spoon he plays with in his fingers.

She watches him at the register where a customer pays for a small pile of paperback novels, and she notes how odd it is to watch her own child approaching middle age, thicker in the middle with a heaviness in his step, although she reminds herself that he's been that way ever since Vietnam. His beard is flecked with grey and the hair is thinning on top of his head. It's hard to imagine he was once small enough to sit cross-legged in the bathroom sink, all belly and baby fat below a self-contented grin. She keeps seeing the boy beneath the man who saw too much too soon and can never go back and undo what was done.

When he closes the register he sees her in the poetry section pulling a slim volume from the shelf and feeling the cover and raising it to her nose to smell the condition of the cloth. Then she opens it and begins to read. As long as he can remember she has been this way with books, a quality passed on to him.

Within a year of purchasing the store he repays his mother's loan and provides himself a modest living. He turns a storage loft into a sitting room with an oriental rug, a couch, and a wing-backed chair, calling it "Owl's Nest" after the character in *Pooh*. It soon becomes a place for students to do homework or write letters and drink coffee and argue philosophy and politics into the night.

He learns the tricks of finding the best buys at used book sales and prides himself on a collection that is broad and deep and just cheap enough to attract a steady flow of customers who love the feel and heft of a book in their hands and will go out of their way for the right title at a reasonable price. The store becomes a second home to him, and there are nights when he works so late shelving acquisitions that he sleeps on the couch rather than bother going home.

And there are times when customers find the store dark and locked against them, a hand-printed sign in the window — 'Closed because of illness' — placed there by a friend, another veteran of the war who spends the night sitting up with him when the dreams become too much to bear alone and sleep impossible and he drinks and smokes and shuts himself away from the world until he is able, sometimes days later, once an entire week, to find his way back again.

He lives on the third floor of an old Victorian on the outskirts of town, an apartment ringed with dormer windows with alcoves he has made into reading places with a chair or a window seat or just a cushion on the floor. On clear days he can look through the southwest window and see the sun reflecting off the water of Lake Champlain.

It is a quiet private space but not too much of either, for although he shied away from human contact in the years after his return, he also took seriously the advice of veterans to avoid drifting into isolation and made a point of putting himself where other people were bound to be, where he could not avoid the sounds of their coming and going. On the floor below him lives a young family with two small children and the first floor is inhabited by an elderly couple, the man a veteran of World War II. The two men have never spoken to each other of their experiences and Michael expects they never will.

Anyone walking into his apartment would be surprised to learn it belongs to a man living alone. It is orderly and clean with everything in its place. The living room has a couch and a rocking chair, a small table and bookshelves along an entire wall from floor to ceiling that sag a bit in the middle from the weight. On the remaining walls are hung inexpensive prints, all French Impressionists except for the Mary Cassatt of a woman bathing a child, his favorite of them all being a study of light on snow by Alfred Sisley. There are only two photographs. In his bedroom on a narrow bookcase beneath a window is a small framed portrait of his mother at age twenty-six, an old fashioned rendering with a white background and a sepia toned halo around the edges. Her face is serious and beautiful, leaning slightly forward as if to hear better something said, the eyes clear and looking directly at the camera. Michael came across it one afternoon while rummaging in the attic and asked if he could have it. She said of course, but only after looking at it for a long time before handing it back to him.

The other is on the bookshelf in the living room at the end nearest the window in a cubbyhole where several books might otherwise be. It is a picture of Michael and another man, young and dressed in fatigues and standing in an open space, each with an arm laid loosely on the shoulder of the other. The man is smiling at the camera and Michael is turning his head toward him and laughing as if at something he's just said. The man is tall and lean and Michael looks short and squat by comparison. In basic training they measured his height at 5'8", but he lost an inch or so somewhere in Vietnam, now drawn closer to the earth in part by a slight stoop in his shoulders. But mostly it's that his entire being is lower down, each cell less able to resist the pull of gravity and hold, if not lift, him higher.

The photograph is the only evidence he was ever in the army. There are no mementos, no unit plaques or insignias, no uniform hidden away in a closet or olive drab socks or underwear in a drawer. A few months after his discharge from the VA hospital he gathered his military clothes and folded them into a bundle with his dog tags at the center. He tied it with heavy twine and put it in a black plastic bag that he lowered carefully into the trash can by the street that ran in front of the rooming house that was his first home in Burlington.

He had stayed with his mother during the first few weeks after coming home but soon felt a restlessness he could not contain. His old room was too small to hold him and he couldn't stand to have her hear the screams and shouts and thrashing about in the middle of the night. Often it was the cries of other men and not his own that snapped him out of sleep, their calls for help, sometimes loud and piercing, but also soft and piteous or low and mournful, beseeching, lifted from dry lips into the air by the hope of being saved from the death that had attached itself to them. And always his name. Everyone in the unit made a point of knowing his name. When they were wounded and writhing on the ground, it was never "medic!" they screamed, but always Dudley or when they felt themselves falling away, Michael or Mike.

Of all his dreams only a few keep coming back. In one the air is hot, humid, thick as he walks across a pockmarked landscape devoid of vegetation, moonlike, surrounded by silence, no living sounds, not a breath of wind, only his lungs working in the heat. And then the air begins to move around him and a pattern of rotating light and shadow cuts across the ground. He looks up at the helicopter hovering high above and waves it down but it only goes higher into the sky. He looks down and all around him men are lying in the dirt soaked in blood. He walks among them, his medical kit hanging at his side. He looks up at the chopper and waves again but it does not move and when he looks down again the men are gone except for one. He kneels beside him and finds the wound in his chest which he covers with a dressing and is holding it in place when he notices the blood, the femoral pulsing between the legs. He finds the hole and tries to stem the flow knowing it will not work, and then he looks at him and says, "You'll be okay, hang on, I've got you now," as he always does. He watches the lips move around words he cannot hear and then the blood is coming out the ears and mouth and nose and the sockets of the eyes and Michael screams himself awake.

Even when his neighbors sympathized, it didn't last for long as he broke their sleep night after night during those first few years. He asked doctors to give him sedatives that would put him beyond the reach of dreams and often it was enough. But there were also nights when the dreams followed him down to pull him back. One summer he went home and lived in the cabin and his mother said she couldn't hear a thing, though he still wondered if she could, and he would have stayed had it not been for winter coming on.

Slowly the space between the dreams increased to weeks and then months. He joined a group of veterans trying to deal with the war they'd brought home inside, then phantoms, anger, guilt, and grief. Still he played the medic taking care of them before himself until they saw what he was doing and pushed and pulled to draw him out.

In the other dream he is running through the night, his footsteps soft against the ground, his feet light in the cloth slippers they gave him when they took away his combat boots and threw him in the cell.

He runs from danger all around but never seen or heard, runs toward the sound of a chopper idling somewhere in a distant clearing, waiting to lift him up and out toward home. But the sound never comes closer and his flight always ends in the long low corridor leading to the tiny room with its slit of a window high up on the wall, the bars casting shadows on the floor. And always they are waiting for him, patient, not bothering to pursue, knowing he belongs to them and will return, waiting with a rage that is measured and contained, waiting for him with truncheons and buckets of cold water and ropes and all the ways they know to hurt him, to beat his flesh and break his bones or slowly pull them from their sockets.

When the phone rings he is sitting at the kitchen table watching the setting sun. He has just spread that morning's *Globe* in front of him, having slept late after a restless night and rushing to open the store on time, leaving the paper on the porch. He tucks his wire rim glasses behind his ears and rests his heel on the edge of the chair as from the living room comes Bill Evans on the stereo, playing a long solo improv on *Danny Boy* that always makes Michael lift his head and look toward the sound.

He looks at the ringing phone for a moment, on the wall beside the stove, then drops his heel from the chair and reaches for the phone.

His mother has some news and he knows from the sound of her voice what it is. It is the voice he heard when she told him his father was gone and wouldn't be coming back, a voice measured, serious, and final.

It takes her only a minute to tell him what has happened and he listens and stares at the patterns in the linoleum that covers the floor.

"When should I come?"

"You mean to visit?"

"No. I'll do that right away. I need to close up the cabin at least. I meant when should I come to take care of you."

In the silence he can feel her holding back the tears, determined not to cry, not just yet, not on the phone.

286

"Where else would I be, mom?" he says, his voice soft.

She doesn't say thank you and he doesn't expect her to. He's expected a call like this for years, either from her or from someone like Walter Finch after finding her dead. He's rehearsed it in his mind — how he'd feel and what he'd say — and so it comes easily to him, this clear sense that to be with her now is simply in the nature of things, a reason to be alive.

He hangs up the phone and takes a bottle of vodka and a pack of cigarettes from the freezer. It is one of his rituals, the daily cigarette. He fetches a small ceramic dish and a box of matches from the cupboard and carries it all to an alcove with a western view.

He props his feet on a bookshelf beneath the window and sips the vodka and lights the cigarette as he looks at the fading light and notes the color of the sky, thick and grey. As he holds the smoke inside he feels the familiar rush and sinks into the chair, closing his eyes and floating inside himself and only then do the tears let down.

On Sunday morning he sets out in the truck. His mother mentioned a guest and he wonders who she is and what she's doing there and when she'll go. He tries to remember her name, going slowly through the alphabet, but he has forgotten.

He listens to the radio until the countryside becomes familiar in the way it lives in a child's memory, and as a heavy silence grows inside of him he turns off the radio. He stops for gas at Atkinson's garage, sitting in the cab and looking down the road leading into town. He hasn't been there since returning from Vietnam almost thirty years ago, always choosing the direct route to his mother's house when he reached this juncture in the road. But he knows that now he'll have to go back, to see her doctor and probably her lawyer and endless trips to the pharmacy and, for awhile at least, to the grocery store, until she stops eating and he has only to fend for himself.

The boy who pumps gas appears beside him and Michael hands him the money and shifts the truck into gear and eases onto the road toward town.

He passes what was the regional school when he was a boy, amazed they haven't torn it down, four square stories of red brick so old in places it's almost turned to black. The walls are lined with tall sash windows that remind him of working the long wooden pole to maneuver the hook into the brass dimple at the top of the window. He coveted the assignment, as most children did, the hefting of the pole with the others looking on, getting to decide just how far open was enough.

He slows the truck and pulls onto the grass at the side of the road, staring at the windows and seeing the faces of other boys as they were back then, what seems another life ago, when everything was simpler and sleep was mostly undisturbed. It is the boys he remembers, not the young men at graduation, full of themselves and what they were going to do, especially the ones who'd enlisted to beat the draft. The boys he misses now, who saw none of it coming, had no idea.

He was always among the smallest in his class. His mother kept telling him his time would come and she was partly right but not as he would have liked. He shot up a bit in the ninth grade and practiced standing up straight by leaning his back against a wall. He even hung by his hands from a chinning bar mounted in the doorway to his closet. But none of it added more than two inches by the time he resigned himself to being fully grown.

She told him there was nothing wrong with such a height, but still he wanted more, something closer to his father who was well over six feet. There was a way that taller boys looked down at him — especially the bullies — that he didn't like and figured he'd be safer if he could look them in the eye. But none of that mattered once they got to Vietnam where the army bulked him up to carry other men across his shoulders and even a bully knew enough to stay on a medic's better side. More than that, the men looked out for him, knowing medics to be a favorite target of enemy gunners.

He eases the truck back onto the road and is passing the small green in the center of town when a sadness wraps around the simple realization of what has kept him away. Nothing terrible happened here, no bad memories of these streets and the people who were here when he was growing up, many of whom still are. No, he thinks, that is just the point — to be reminded of what was lost, what was taken from him after he left, something he has not recovered and may never know again. And to be reminded of the ones who went with him and never came back, who could not be saved.

The buildings are as he remembers them but the storefronts are unfamiliar except Dewalt's. The hardware store is gone and the pharmacy and the diner across the street. The food co-op is new and the realtor and what used to be the bank is now a bookstore. He wonders what they did with the vault.

He doesn't think to stop to walk around or get a cup of coffee at Dewalt's, but instead feels carried out of town on the road heading north past a small shopping mall. He tries to remember what that patch of land had looked like before, whether it was woods or pasture or if corn had grown there in the summer. He opens the window and leans his face into the cool wind. He will take the long way to the farm, turning east at Nichols Dairy, the ice cream window closed for the season, and then a ways further on go south along the river.

Slowing in front of the house he notices the small rise of freshly mounded dirt in the cemetery.

He parks by the back porch and climbs the steps to see a woman not his mother standing at the sink, who looks up at him as her arms work above the sound of running water and dishes, then looks down, the pace a little faster than before.

He knocks on the door and wonders for a moment why, before pushing it slowly open to give Sophie time to step away.

"Hi," he says above the grunts and yips from Sophie wagging her tail and making little hops.

"You must be Michael."

"I must be," he says, wishing he could remember her name. He sits on the floor, extending his legs in front of him and leaning against the stove so that Sophie can stand between his legs and sniff his face while he rubs behind her ears.

"I'm Katherine."

He nods and smiles and says hello again.

"Your mom's in there," she says, tilting her head toward the library, "taking a nap. Are you hungry?"

"No," he says, gently moving Sophie away as he gets up. "Excuse me," he says and takes a chair across the kitchen, standing for a moment in the doorway to look to where his mother sleeps, her head leaning on a small embroidered pillow resting on her shoulder. Katherine notes how vulnerable he seems, shoulders sunk low as he contemplates his mother, his feet turned slightly inward, his bum small like a boy's. Then he sets the chair beside Lucy and sits and leans forward, fingers knit together in front of his mouth, chin resting on his thumbs. She watches him watching her and for a moment imagines Ethan as a man sitting beside an aging Katherine, tender in his longing and remembering.

She turns away and goes outside and sits on the step.

Michael contemplates the fine blue lines in his mother's face, how small she seems in this great chair in which her mother once held her. He sits back and closes his eyes to follow the sound of his breathing as he learned to do so long ago, a refuge where he could spend endless weeks and months one moment at a time. Sophie pads into the room, nails clicking on the floor, the soft grunt as she lies down nearby. And then there is only the silence and his mother's breathing and Sophie's and his own, a synchronicity of moving in and moving out.

Katherine stares at the goats lined up along the fence. She feels displaced, of no use and with no place to go, amazed at how quickly he came in and filled up the space between them as if he'd been there all along.

Which he has. No, she thinks, scolding herself, if anyone doesn't belong, it's me.

She walks across the yard and through the gate and into the barn to check water and hay, standing in the cool darkness sliced by a thin plane of sunlight coming through a crack in the wall and illuminating dust drifting in the air. She hears Michael come out of the house, the truck door open and close, his feet on the stairs, the screen door softly rapping behind. Moving in.

She runs to the rear of the barn and through a small door that opens to the fields. With the barn shielding her from the house she walks quickly through the stubble, slowing as she turns onto the path along the line of trees, giving in, letting down the tears, feeling foolish to have felt that any of this could ever be hers, that she might deserve such a thing, this place that is home to him, she thinks, and will never be to me. Or anywhere else.

She kicks a stone in the road.

What was I thinking?

She kicks the stone again, but harder, wanting to hurt, then picks it up and throws it far into the woods.

Where the path joins the road cutting through the fields she looks up at the house, the truck still parked by the porch, and feels how much she has wanted Lucy to be hers, allowed herself to feel chosen and forgiven and taken in, made the little corner room her own. But everything has come apart in little more than the time it took to dry her hands standing at the sink, and now she doesn't know what to do.

She walks up the road, imagining he watches her from the window and can see her expression even at a distance, wondering at her ungrateful mood, Lucy waking to wonder too, how long she'll stay now that he's come home.

She reaches the main road where it disappears into the woods in the direction of St. Johnsbury, and remembers the man she thought was David and the hawk and driving onto the hilltop with the hills beneath a big sky. She is startled and frightened by her anger, feeling she has no right, but too full of loss to make it go away.

She turns toward the house and sees them on the front porch swing, and then Lucy's face brightens as she waves at Katherine and calls out her name.

"Where'd you go?" Lucy says to Katherine coming up the steps.

"I thought you'd want some time."

"Come sit," says Lucy pointing to a wicker chair near the swing.

Katherine sits, glancing across the road and suddenly afraid of being asked about the grave, what made perfect sense to her and Lucy in danger of making no sense at all.

"So," says Michael, "I hear she's put you to work," smiling, "She does that, you know. That's why I stay away."

"Ouff," Lucy says, her hand on his arm.

"There's no end to it around this place," he says. "Wait'l winter," he nods, "which should be any day now."

Katherine wonders if he imagines her still here by then. "I don't mind," she says, "she's been very good to me."

"I'm sure she has," he says and then a silence. "Mom says you're up from Boston."

"Near there," she says, barely breathing now.

"What do you do when you're not up here?"

For a moment her mind is blank except for the fear of having nothing to say.

"Katherine is a teacher," says Lucy, "between jobs," picking up the pace, "we met through Ruth — you remember Ruth — and Katherine needed a place to stay and I have this big old house," looking from Katherine to Michael, "and it seemed a good idea and you know me and a good idea — "

"I do know that," he says and looks at Lucy, his head cocked a little to one side as if curious at her manner, on a bicycle she doesn't know how to stop.

"So," says Lucy, breathless, folding her hands in her lap, "we've been having a lovely time together, haven't we?"

Katherine nods. She has wondered if Lucy would tell him about her, and now feels both relieved and disappointed that she hasn't.

Lucy says it's time for lunch even though she won't have much to eat herself. "But you go ahead. Besides, if I don't eat that means I get to talk."

Katherine slices fruit and bread and tends the toaster, stealing a look at Michael at the sink, his body shaking as he laughs at something Lucy has said, the motion of his hands deliberate and unhurried, and she thinks he has a kind face, especially the softness in his eyes. They sit around the table, Sophie among their feet, and eat while the talk turns to books as Lucy says it always does when Michael comes to visit.

"So, tell me what you're reading."

"*Sophie's Choice*," he says.

"Again?"

He shrugs and Lucy sighs. "I don't read much anymore," she says. "Sometimes I feel like I've read it all." She looks at Katherine. "Isn't that a strange thing to say?"

"No."

"And you?" says Michael.

Katherine smiles and looks down and works her fork through the salad on her plate. "I've been reading my way through your mother's attic."

"Which parts?"

She breaks off a piece of toast and puts it in her mouth while she thinks of how to answer. "I guess you'd say the feminist parts."

Michael gives a little whistle, "Now there's a slippery slope."

"Would that be going up or going down?" says Lucy narrowing her eyes.

Michael looks at his mother, matching his look to hers. "Both."

"It makes a difference," says Lucy, taking a piece of apple from Katherine's plate and putting it into her mouth.

"I think," says Katherine, "it's more climbing up than sliding down."

"But there is also the descent," says Lucy. "Don't forget Persephone."

"Sometimes," says Katherine, "I feel like I'm waking up and all the furniture is nailed to the ceiling. Everything I thought was normal and sane comes out the other way around."

She looks at Michael and is surprised to see the intent expression of someone thinking about what's being said and trying to understand the person who said it, and she feels curious to know more about the man behind the face. She waits for him to speak but he is quiet, looking down at the table, taking a bite of food and slowly bringing it to his mouth.

"Would you call yourself a feminist?" she says.

"I don't know," he says with a glance at Lucy, "am I a feminist, mom?"

Lucy leans forward, her elbows on the table, "In your own way, yes. You know more than you think you do."

He looks away, his face serious, a hint of color coming in, "You think so."

"I do."

"Well, then," he says, spearing lettuce with his fork, "it must be so," and he looks up and makes an awkward smile and they eat in silence until he speaks of the cabin and preparing the house for winter.

After lunch Lucy goes upstairs to lie down and Michael gets a pair of hiking boots from his truck and sits on the back steps to put them on.

"Do you want some help?" says Katherine.

"Sure," he says, lacing a boot. "There isn't much to do, but it's easier with two."

"Give me a minute," she says and goes upstairs to change her clothes. She sits on the bed and lays a hand on her stomach to quiet the queasy agitation she has felt since he arrived. She closes her eyes and listens to him outside her window, his footsteps on the back steps and across the yard and then his voice soft and low, talking to the goats.

He turns to the sound of her coming out the door with Sophie just behind, and she is surprised to wonder if he thinks her pretty. They are quiet walking out behind the barn and along the path leading to the woods.

"How long have you been here?"

"Since July."

She waits for another question, but it doesn't come.

"How does she seem to you?" she says.

"Weaker than I thought. How long has it been?"

"A few months."

He shakes his head. "I wish she'd said something."

"I've been right here and still it's hard getting her to talk about it."

"That's my mom."

They go into the woods, the water visible through the leafless trees, Michael stepping out in front.

"She seemed to know there wasn't anything to be done," says Katherine, raising her voice to reach over his shoulder. It occurs to her that he's about to lose his mother and everyone is a child when it comes to that, and again she wonders what became of his father.

They stand on the deck looking out at the hills on the far side of the pond. "What do we need to do?"

He looks at her, his face intent, looking away then back again, "I'm sorry — what?"

"What needs doing?"

"Mostly the canoe and the dock. It's pretty easy." He goes into the cabin and comes out with two lengths of rope and they go down to the dock.

"First the canoe," he says, taking one end. She takes the other and they lift it from the water and walk it up beneath the cabin and place it on a wooden rack.

"Now we float the dock and bring it ashore."

"Why do that?"

"So it doesn't get wrecked by the ice."

He hands her the ends of the ropes and points to a place along the shore. "Stand over there with these and I'll unhitch the dock. Don't let go."

She watches him secure the ropes to cleats at either end and untie the dock from the posts sunk into the bottom of the pond, feeling a sudden tenderness for the careful and unhurried use of his hands beneath the sad slope of his shoulders.

He looks up at her and then at the foot of the dock now separated from the shore.

"Uh oh," he says putting a hand over his mouth in mock alarm at the dock beginning to float away from its moorings with him and Sophie standing in the middle. He shrugs and grins as Sophie calls out with a single croaking bark.

"What do I do?" she says.

"I'd say. . .pull!"

She strains against the ropes but the dock barely moves. "Harder!" he says, but she wants to yell back that there isn't any point, that she isn't strong enough and he shouldn't have left it to her. "Use your legs!" he says, and for a moment she doesn't understand, until it comes to her, the memory of the power in her legs that got her up off the floor, and closing her eyes she wills the center of her being downward into her thighs and knees until suddenly the ground comes in beneath her feet and she leans her weight back against the load and there is a moment when nothing seems to move but then a subtle letting go at the other end, the dock giving in to her, and she is stepping up the bank and there is the sound of small branches cracking as the dock meets the shore. Michael jumps onto solid ground and Sophie falls short and has to scramble to keep from falling in. Katherine lets go one of the ropes as he takes it in his hands and ties it to a tree. She ties the other, wondering if the knot is right.

"Good job," he says, smiling as he walks toward her up the bank, "thanks."

"Is this okay?" she says, pointing at the knot.

"I'm sure it's fine," he says walking on.

Inside he locks the windows and empties the water jugs beside the sink. "That's it."

"Do you come here in winter?"

"Sometimes," he says, silent as he takes one last look around.

2

*D*arkness comes early and fast. Katherine puts the goats in for the night while Michael cooks a stir-fry for supper. Lucy opens a bottle of wine and they eat amidst a conversation that is lean and careful. Lucy looks from one to the other and feels each surrounded by their past and the awareness of what the other doesn't know.

After supper Katherine does dishes while Michael and Lucy go out and sit in the swing.

"Who died?" he says, pointing across the road.

"No one you know," she says, staring off into the darkness, "It's a long story and not for me to tell." She looks at him. "You'll have to hold your curiosity."

He looks at her, searching her face, then shrugs, "Okay."

It's a three bath night with Lucy going first. Katherine finishes the dishes and goes up to her room to wait her turn while Michael sits on the porch and thinks about tomorrow, arranging care at home and power of attorney, like preparing for a long journey, getting necessary shots and making sure your passport is up to date, someone to collect your mail and pay the bills, deciding what to bring along.

A faucet squeaks as Lucy turns the water off and the house falls into silence. He looks across the road and wonders if she has a spot in mind. How many times she must have sat in this swing and surveyed the available space. And how many times he played among the stones, never imagining the day when his mother would be buried there, her name and dates carved in white and placed among the rest, and he, left behind to put her there and remember. He sets the swing in motion and suddenly feels alone and small.

Lucy looks down at her body and is astonished at how little of her is left. Her shoulders and hips are bony and her breasts remind her of deflated balloons. What a sad little thing it is, she thinks.

She puts on a robe and crosses the hall and knocks on Katherine's door. "It's all yours." She pauses for a moment and then opens the door enough to admit her head. Katherine is sitting on the bed, an open book in her lap.

"Are you all right?"

Katherine shakes her head. "I will be. It's a little awkward."

Lucy nods, a pause, and then, "He asked about the grave."

"Did you tell him?"

"Oh, no. Do you want me to?"

Katherine closes the book. "I don't know. I told Annie why I'm here. It just came out."

"She would understand."

"I didn't stick around long enough to ask," looking up Lucy, "maybe I should just get little cards printed up."

Lucy smiles and waits for Katherine to join her, but her faint attempt is soon gone from her face.

"The fact is," says Lucy, "he doesn't have to know. But if you decide to tell him someday, I wouldn't worry about what he'll think of you. He's got his own story, Katherine. Make no mistake. He's wondering what I've told you about him, too." She comes into the room and sits on the bed beside her.

From downstairs there is the sound of Michael coming in from the porch, the door closing behind, footsteps into the kitchen.

"I don't want you to tell him."

Michael hears Katherine's voice down the stairwell, "Bathroom's free."

"Thanks," he says. "I'll wait for the hot water to come up."

"Good night," she says.

"Good night."

He opens his bag and finds the pack of cigarettes and takes one out. He whistles softly for Sophie and hears her jump from Lucy's bed and clatter down the stairs. He follows her out the back door and sits on the step while she goes around the side of the house. He lights the cigarette and remembers the tone of Katherine's voice when she said good night, the beat of hesitation just before as if to think about it. He pictures in his mind the dark eyes and the nose that seems a little crooked, as if it had been broken and mended wrong.

Sophie mounts the porch and stands beside him, her breath fogging the air. He grabs her behind the ears, "Are you a good girl?" he says and she pants and wags her tail.

They go inside and he turns off the lights and follows her upstairs, passing by his mother's room.

"I'll be in after my bath," he says and she looks at him over her glasses and nods.

Watching the steam rising from the bath, he feels the impending emptiness of the house. He turns out the light and feels his way to the tub, stepping in and sitting down, his eyes growing accustomed to the dark as he looks out the window at the sky full of stars. He lies back and his eyes fill with tears as he wonders if the pain will take possession of his mother and become the focus of what remains of her life. He wipes his eyes and looks out at the sky, the Big Dipper just above the horizon, and remembers lying in the bottom of the canoe on graduation night three weeks before he reported for basic training. He was restless and couldn't sleep and paddled out to the middle of the pond where he lay on his back in the bottom of the canoe. He tucked the life preserver beneath his head and for almost an hour he drifted and stared, wondering if the sky looked the same from anywhere in the world or if every place had a version of its own.

He suddenly thinks of his mother waiting up for him and he sits up in the tub and hurriedly washes in the dark. When he steps into the hall the light still shines from her room, but when he looks in she is asleep, the book still open on her lap. He takes it from beneath her hands and is reaching for the light when she opens her eyes and takes in a sharp little sniff of air.

"Oh," she says, her voice sleepy and small, "sit down, Michael."

He sits beside her and she takes his hand in hers.

"I guess this is it, kiddo," she says at last.

He nods, his eyes wet.

"You let me go the way I want, okay?"

He nods.

"It's the last thing I'll ever ask of you."

"I know."

She draws his head to her chest and lets him weep, knowing that from now on it will be he who takes care of her and not the other way around.

Michael closes the door behind him and looks around his room. There is the bookcase and the writing desk, the bureau with the model ship on top, and the bed, just as he left it, with the foot against the window. And it occurs to him how remarkable it is that his mother has left his room just this way for thirty years, as if he'd died and this was all there was left of him. And then he thinks that it's not as unreasonable as it might seem to someone who didn't know.

He turns out the light and climbs into bed and stares out the window, recalling the nights when he would strain to hear the sounds from downstairs and sometimes the room next door, sounds that set his heart beating hard and made his mouth go dry with fear and, as he grew older, anger at what his father thought he had a right to do. It was in this room that he hid away and felt the shame in hiding. And it was here that he imagined killing him, with a baseball bat or a hoe or a pitchfork or a knife, anything to stop the sickening violence of bone on flesh, of furniture falling over as she fell against it, of her body landing hard on the floor and the long wait for the sound of her getting up. He remembers the smell of beer, the rough scratch of whiskers against his face, big hands grabbing him hard. And he remembers when his mother met him at the airport to take him home, trying to smile, her face stricken at the sight of his condition. His father was nowhere to be seen and they were almost home before she told him he was gone and never coming back. "Good," he said, and that was all.

There was nothing of him in the house — no jacket in the closet, no cigarettes on the table, no boots in the hall, not a trace of his existence to be found.

"Where did he go?"

"Away."

"How do you know he isn't coming back?"

"I just do," she said and he didn't ask again.

He wakes with a start. The moon is new and his room is completely dark and he can't see a thing except the faint outline of windows against the sky. It was a sound that woke him, of a kind that has shaken him out of sleep for years, and at first he thinks it must have come from him. Then there it is again and he thinks it is his mother and is halfway to the door when he hears it coming through the other wall. He turns and listens, naked in the chilly air, feet cold against the floor, to little cries and then her voice rising almost to a shout, words tumbling over one another then falling back, softer but still frantic and in pain.

He steps closer to the wall, lays a hand against the plaster and then his ear. There is the thrashing of bedclothes and the pumping of legs trying to run while lying down and then her voice rising to a word that sounds like 'ether' or 'even' and then "no." The air grows still and he can tell she is awake and staring at the dark to figure out where she is.

He steps away from the wall, from the uninvited intimacy of his listening, and sits down on the bed. Out of the silence comes a sniff and a sigh followed by creaking bedsprings and the scuffle of slippers across the floor. A door opens and then she is softly down the hall to pause at the door to Lucy's room before going down the stairs. From the kitchen comes the sound of something on the table and then silence until the front door opens and softly closes.

He lies awake to listen, but is asleep when she returns.

Katherine rides with Sophie in the back. They stop at Dewalt's for coffee and then Lucy and Michael head up the street to see Paul Howard while Katherine has a second cup and thinks of what to do. She pays the check and steps outside, going first toward the bookstore and then the other way instead. She goes into the co-op and wanders the aisles of organic produce and bins filled with nuts and grains.

She walks down to the bookstore and Annie waves at her coming through the door. She is waiting on customers and Katherine settles in a chair by the window and opens a copy of the *Hungry Mind Review*.

The store is quiet and Annie is slowly walking toward her, sitting down in the other chair, "Out on your own again."

"Lucy and Michael are up the street."

"Michael?" says Annie.

"They're seeing the doctor and lawyer."

"Oh." Annie shakes her head, "Lucy Dudley," quiet for a moment, looking away out the window, "How is he?"

"I don't know. I just met him. He seems okay."

Annie looks at her. "You don't know about him."

"No."

"Michael was a medic in Vietnam. Just before he was supposed to come home he was captured and they had him for two years. Twenty years old." She looks away. "You can do a lot to someone in two years if you have them all to yourself. Apparently they gave it their best shot."

"And then they let him go."

"In a manner of speaking. He was here for just a few weeks before he disappeared and wound up at the VA in Burlington. I think he was 30 by the time Lucy started coming in here without that tired and worried look on her face."

"Did you know him?"

"Not since high school. He was a nice kid though. Hell," she says, "they were all nice kids."

Paul Howard looks across his desk. "If you want to die at home, I don't see why not. But it's cancer, so it may get messy."

"I've been with messy," says Michael. "We'll be all right."

"You'll be, Michael, but she may not."

She holds up a hand between them. "I'll stay home," she says, "until I decide I can't."

"And there's always the hospice in Burlington if you need it," says Paul. "They're very good with pain."

"But we can do all that at home, can't we?" says Lucy.

"Oh, yes. I'll come by if you need me. You're pretty much on my way." He looks at Michael. "But you'll need some help, especially toward the end. I know a good nurse in town with hospice training. Helen Broom. I'll give you her number." He writes on a slip of paper and hands it to Michael. "Between you, me, and Helen, we should be all right. Unless things take a turn I don't foresee right now."

Lucy leans forward in her chair. "What do you foresee, exactly?"

He sighs. "The cancer's pretty much all over the place, but mostly in the liver. Probably not where it started, but with any luck it's where it stays, in which case you'll just get weaker and weaker until you go. For cancer, it's pretty good really."

"Just gobbles me up."

"Just gobbles you up."

"How long, do you think?"

They look at each other and then he lowers his head.

"Of course," he says, "the simple answer is I don't know. But if I had to say, which I guess I do, a matter of months. Several, but not many."

"Do I get another spring?"

He looks up at her. "I don't think so."

Lucy sets her lips and nods. "Okay," she says. "Anything else?"

"Not that I can think of. Michael?"

"No."

"Well. Call me anytime."

She walks to the door and Paul stands up behind the desk. "Lucy," he says, "I'm so sorry."

She turns and looks at him with a shrug, "Me, too."

In the car going home, Lucy is looking out the window and thinking that someone will have to take care of Sophie and the goats, when she notices the woods full of leaves and the sunlight playing through the grey and naked trees, the deep woods now open to a longer view. She follows the trees upward to the crisp blue sky and suddenly realizes she will never see autumn again, this season of renewal and clarity and hope, and her eyes fill with tears that flow out before a sudden and enormous grief that her living will soon come to an end. She stares out the window, determined to keep this to herself, but then there is Michael's hand on top of hers and she stifles a sob as she covers it with her own. And then there is a hand laid softly on her shoulder from behind and she thinks she cannot stand it, the awful beauty, but does not shrink from it, riding it like a wave down the road toward home.

All afternoon and evening, there is a quality of silence in the house amidst the occasional sound of voices, and Katherine feels in it a shrinking of the space around her. She imagines the two of them wanting to be alone and doesn't know where to go or where to put herself or how to be wherever she is. She goes to her room for a nap after lunch but doesn't sleep. She tends goats and takes Sophie for a walk behind the barn. She helps Michael mulch the gardens, the talk pleasant but little more.

There was no reason she can think of to include her in the visit to the doctor and the lawyer, but she realizes as she pushes a wheelbarrow full of mulch toward the garden that she wanted them to take her anyway, without reason, for some unspoken cause that would make her part of this without the need for words. She dumps the wheelbarrow and Michael smiles and says mom will be glad to have this done, and as she turns she feels how easily the word came out and settled in between them, mom, without claiming her as his.

After a bath she goes to her room and waits for the sound of the bathroom door closing behind him and water running in the tub, and then she is down the hall where she finds Lucy propped up on pillows and reading with Sophie curled into a ball by her hip. Lucy follows her with her eyes as she crosses to the far side of the bed, making a space for her to sit.

"Something on your mind."

"I can't help it. I feel so odd."

"As in 'strange'?"

"As in 'stranger.' As in 'not even.'"

"Ah."

"I've been thinking I should go." Katherine waits for Lucy to say something, some expression of assent — yes, I think you should — but the old woman's face is open and still, as if waiting to hear the rest.

"This is for family, and that isn't me," and then before she can stop herself, "I wish it were, but it's not."

Still Lucy is silent and Katherine begins to feel the panic of being caught in a mistake, but goes on, unable to stop herself, "I remember you saying you'd rather I left than take care of you. That I have things to do," the agitation growing inside of her, running fingers through her hair, wetting her lips, and then Lucy gently covers her hand, eyes intent on Katherine's face.

"Maybe," says Katherine, and then a long pause as she looks down at Lucy's hand on her own, "maybe helping you is one of those things I have to do. Maybe it's the next thing."

"Maybe it is," says Lucy.

"I want to stay," says Katherine.

"Why?"

Katherine looks up, her face pinched in disbelief. "Why?"

"Yes," says Lucy. "Tell me why."

"Because," she says, but then cannot find the words and looks at Lucy and then down as if the words had fallen in her lap. "Because I have no place to go and I feel this is what I'm supposed to do." She looks up at Lucy, everything a blur. "I love you. And I don't want to be somewhere else when you go. I couldn't stand it."

There is a shine in Lucy's eyes and the slightest trembling of her lips and then a tear breaking loose from the corner of her eye, rolling down her cheek. "I don't think I could, either," and they enfold each other in their arms and for the first time she hears Lucy Dudley cry with the sound of a woman with a broken heart, deep and mournful, born of loss and longing carried in solitude across a vast and empty place, the far side coming into view.

Michael sits in the tub surrounded by darkness and the sound of weeping from somewhere in the house, and focusing on the sound, he realizes it is two, not one. Who is this woman, he wonders, who has made her way into my mother's life so quickly and so deeply?

The house grows quiet. He hears Katherine pass by on the way to her room and then the click of the latch as she closes the door.

In the morning Michael packs his bag and carries it downstairs to the kitchen where Lucy and Katherine sit at the table, drinking coffee and tea. They are laughing and talking about Sophie falling in the pond and when he comes into the room they look up and smile. He cuts a slice of bread from the loaf and pops it in the toaster. He remembers the weeping from the night before and feels a stillness in the room as if they are all waiting for something to happen.

He butters the toast, pours a cup of coffee, and sits down at the table.

"Michael," says Lucy, "I want you to know that Katherine is going to stay."

And there it is, he thinks. "Uh huh," he says, biting off a large corner of the toast.

"She's going to help."

He nods and chews.

Katherine's mouth is going dry.

"Is that all right?" says Lucy.

"Sure," he says. "It's fine." He is looking at a spot in the middle of the table as he speaks, and it's plain to Katherine that he doesn't like the news, although she doesn't know why, and suddenly realizes she doesn't know him at all, including if he's ever hit a woman.

Lucy leans forward into the path of his gaze. "Michael," she says. "This is okay, yes?"

"Yeah," he says and looks up to see them watching him and his eyes jump from Katherine to his mother. "What."

"If you have feelings about this," says Lucy, "please say so."

He drops the toast onto his plate and pushes back his chair. "I said it was fine." They watch him wash his dishes and Katherine notices the slow sureness gone from the movement of his hands. And then it comes to her that she is between him and his dying mother and he doesn't know what to do.

He picks up his bag and puts it on the table as he leans in close, his hand on his mother's back, and kisses her. "I'll be back this week-end," he says. "Or sooner if you need me."

He zips up his jacket as he looks at Katherine. "And I'll see you again soon," he says.

She nods.

He looks at Lucy. "You call me if there's a change."

He bends down and kisses Sophie between the ears, "Goodbye, old girl," and takes his bag and lifts his hand in a wave as he goes out the door.

3

As November slides toward Thanksgiving, Lucy's focus sharpens and intensifies, ignoring what is not essential. She leaves to Michael the mail and bills, and to Katherine the care of Sophie and the goats and trips to the pharmacy for medication to soothe the worst of the rampage going on inside of her.

She feels the approach of winter but with a difference, knowing there will soon come a time when she will go inside and stay. No walks through the snow or drives into town. No liberating spring.

Like a wild animal she puts the sky above her head as long as she is able. She walks the road and into the fields, first by herself and then with Katherine to lean on, going until she needs to turn around and use what energy is left to get home. She sits on the front porch swing and looks across the road and waves at the occasional car passing by.

They walk and talk and Lucy decides about what. "I'm old and I'm dying," she says one afternoon by the cemetery gate. "I get to choose. I want you to tell me everything that happened. From the day you met him to the day you killed him. Every detail, all you can remember, exactly as it comes."

Katherine stops in the middle of the road, her hands dug deep into her pockets.

"I know you don't want to — "

"But we already have — "

"No, we have not. Not in this way." Lucy stops and faces her. "There's no time to argue. Do you understand? Just do as I say."

Katherine stares into Lucy's drawn and haggard face and nods.

She begins in the ski lodge in Vermont and tells all she can remember. It goes on throughout the day, cleaning house or making beds, folding laundry, over meals. They are sitting on the porch in the evening, having whiskey and a cigarette when Katherine nears the end. "You know the rest."

"No," says Lucy at the end of a long pause, "not really."

"You know what happened."

"Only the result."

Katherine suddenly feels sucked down into some quicksand of the mind with nothing to hang onto. "I've done everything you asked."

"Good," says Lucy. "Now, keep going."

"What do you mean, 'keep going'?"

"Tell me what happened. What's next."

"But you know what happened," says Katherine, up off the swing and walking away across the porch.

Lucy moves the swing with her foot and stares across the road until after awhile, Katherine comes and sits beside her. "Elsie pushed me, too. I didn't like it either. You don't have to, but I'm all you've got for now and I think you should, so it might be worth the chance that I'm right."

Katherine says nothing for a long time, staring in the direction of the little grave across the road and trying to find a place in her mind to begin.

"Tell me about the weather," says Lucy, "what it was like."

"It was cold."

"And what — "

"My birthday," says Katherine with the sudden smell of the kitchen filling her nose, so real it makes her look around, the charnel smell of blood, her breathing soft and shallow, Ethan asleep upstairs. The words come out of her as if spoken by someone else in another room in another time, "he forgot my birthday," and then drifting to a remote and private space inside her mind, walking in her sleep from room to room, a tingling in her lips, and then suspended in the slow motion flight across the kitchen toward the wall, taking some comfort in the silence, even the sound of breaking glass softened in her ears.

"Katherine."

no need to move or think or feel

downward floating

"Katherine," shaking her arm, "Katherine," a pause, a sudden breath of air, "where'd you go?"

surprise, not comprehending what was said

"Nowhere."

"Yes you did. You were somewhere else."

"I was here."

"No."

And then stepping on a little bridge inside her mind, remembering how this happens sometimes, thinking she is telling Lucy, but unsure until she hears her reply, "yes — "

"I didn't know — "

"I know," says Lucy, "stay with me now. You must try."

"All right."

"He forgot your birthday, and what happened then?"

A sigh flowing down into silence, nodding her head, the words starting up again before she is off the swing and walking to the railing, trying to get away, standing in the shadows, holding on.

"What else, Katherine. Tell me."

"I don't know," shaking her head against the memory of so much pain blending in her mind to a solid mass, one moment, one injury, like any other.

"You don't know."

"No."

"And Ethan?"

"You already know."

"I don't. You have never said what happened."

"I don't remember."

"You don't remember — "

"No."

"My dear Katherine, you cannot forget."

Give him to me!

away from the railing and down the steps

"Have you ever spoken of this to anyone?"

at the edge of the road, Lucy's voice coming over her shoulder

"You'll never forget, Katherine, so you might as well remember."

the sound of breaking glass, the strange sensation of flight

Lucy's footsteps coming after and then a hand on her shoulder, the small face bathed in shadow looking up with eyes searching her own, "Come on, Katherine," she says, "you've come this far — "

And then the words just coming out, "He threw me across the room."

Lucy stunned into silence. "He what?"

"He threw me. Against the wall. And then Ethan."

"He threw Ethan — "

"At me."

Katherine is breathing hard and fast through her mouth, a sob swallowed down as Lucy takes her by the arm, whispering in her ear to keep going, keep going, and then suddenly a portion of Katherine's mind stepping in, taking over, a mother's mind with a child in trouble, fear and horror pushed aside to make room for how to stanch the bleeding, lift the car, breathe life into the lifeless form on the sand, all of it so clear in front of her, the story spilling out into the night air, told to the tree she's leaning on, the road winding into the dark, the graves across the way, the small dying woman beside her now, weeping, shaking her head and weeping.

The next day they begin again, and when Katherine is done, Lucy says that's good and they'll come back to it tomorrow and the more you talk about it the smaller it gets and it will always hurt but there will come a day when it won't be able to knock you down.

Michael comes on week-ends. He shows Katherine how to rake leaves into a downward sloping pile against the stone foundation of the house so that when covered with snow it will help keep out the cold. They stack hay in the barn and she learns to split cordwood with an axe. When he shows her how, he rolls up his sleeves and she sees his arms marked from the elbow to the wrist with lines and patches of scar tissue from cuts and burns. She cannot take her eyes off them and has to ask him to show her again the proper swing because she wasn't paying attention.

At first it seems impossible, the axe too heavy to control, and she misses the mark again and again, glancing off the upturned log or over-reaching and hitting it with the handle instead of the head. When she breaks the handle, Michael says she's doing fine, and when she breaks another he shakes his head and says, "You should see *my* pile of broken handles." She doesn't break a third. Slowly she becomes acquainted with a feeling that runs down from her shoulders to her hands wrapped around the handle of the axe, the swing that arcs from above her head to the precise point that her eye has marked and never left, where the impact of the blade will split the wood just as she intends.

Lucy reaches a plateau in her descent, not worse from one week to the next except for fatigue and sleeping during the day. Her appetite is scant and she is so lost in thought that sometimes Katherine must say her name several times before she signals that she's heard. Already she is going, Katherine thinks, fading by degrees, and then she pushes the thought from her mind and goes into the kitchen and takes up the axe and goes outside to fill the air with the sound of wood coming apart and falling to the ground.

On the Sunday before Thanksgiving Michael leaves for Burlington after supper and Katherine notices the small envelope resting on the table. The front is blank except for her name in a small, uneven scrawl. She opens it and pulls out the single piece of stationary and reads.

Katherine,

    I've been thinking about the old saying that it takes a village to raise a child. It's the same with dying, I think. I'm glad you're here.

                                           Michael

After her bath, she sits on her bed and puts the note inside the book of Kenyon's poetry. She turns out the light and listens, but there is only the silence and a vacant feeling coming from the room next door.

Thanksgiving day arrives on a warm front that caps an unusually mild fall that has left Vermonters grumbling about the absence of snow. Michael brings the turkey and Lucy has Katherine pull the rocker into the kitchen so Lucy can direct the composition of the stuffing and the baking of the pumpkin pie.

"I should get you a baton," says Michael.

"A good idea," says Lucy, "why don't you? Get two in case I break one in a moment of artistic pique."

"*Pique?*"

"Yes, pique," says Lucy, lifting her nose with a sniff. "When you're my age you can have pique, too. Not too much stuffing in the bird. You'll make it mushy."

The house fills with music and the smell of roasting turkey. As the morning goes on, Katherine feels herself separating from their animated talk and puts on her coat and sits on the front porch. Leaves from the old maple are scattered across the cemetery, softening the little mound at the far corner. The door opens and then Lucy is beside her. In spite of the weather, she wears slippers and a long coat and the purple woven hat she wore to the hospital. For a long time they sit in silence, rocking back and forth.

"Are you cold?" says Katherine.

"Just the nose," says Lucy. "My heater's on the blink. But I've always had trouble with the nose. Never could figure out what to put on it either. Maybe I should wear a mask. It would go nicely with the baton."

They rock some more, looking out across the road.

"For years after he was gone," says Lucy, "Thanksgiving was so hard. And Christmas even worse." She pulls out a tissue and wipes her nose. "Mostly because it was so awful when he was here."

"This is where you lived?"

"Oh, yes."

"And you stayed."

Lucy shrugs. "It's my home. I was raised here. The bed I sleep in is where I was born."

"I don't know how you could stand it."

"It wasn't easy. Elsie and I worked our way from room to room, got rid of every trace that we could find. We repainted the walls and threw out everything that reminded me of him. I even washed the linens and we drove them to the Salvation Army in Montpelier and after that she took me out to lunch.

"That night we went into every room where he'd done me harm and she held my hands while I looked into her eyes and spoke about it, and then we lit candles and incense and said prayers. We had no idea what we were doing. We made it up as we went along. But little by little there was less of him and more of me. But he took so much from me that for a long time I thought there was nothing left and I couldn't think what to be thankful for. I couldn't imagine being whole again, because I couldn't imagine not knowing what I knew."

She looks at Katherine. "But I was wrong. He didn't get it all. They never do. You just have to know where to look."

In the middle of the afternoon they gather by the table in the kitchen. Lucy takes a small plate and places on it a piece of turkey and a daub of mashed potato and a bit of dressing and a few green beans and lays it on the floor for Sophie. Then she sits at the head of the table with Katherine on one side and Michael on the other and extends her hands which they take in their own as they reach across the table to complete the circle. And then Lucy closes her eyes and in a small and trembling voice begins to sing.

The silver rain, the shining sun,
the fields where scarlet poppies run,
and all the ripples of the wheat
are in the bread that I do eat.

So when I sit at every meal,
with thankful heart I always feel
that I am eating rain and sun
and fields where scarlet poppies run.

The last note hangs in the air as Katherine looks across the table at Michael whose eyes are fixed on his mother's face, looking through a blur of tears, his face veiled in a sadness deeper and older than Lucy's dying, visible in the lines around his eyes and a downward pull in his cheeks and jaw.

She feels a squeeze from Lucy's hand and letting go. Lucy opens her eyes and makes a smile, but for a moment it isn't clear for whom or what the smile is meant, for she is looking straight ahead into the middle distance over the table spread with food. And then she turns to them and nods and says, "Let's eat."

In the middle of the night, Michael wakes with a gasp, the dream still fresh before him in the quiet of the house. He draws up the sheet and wipes the sweat from his face. He thinks of his mother's song and feels again the sweet and awful realization that he will never hear her sing again. Each day, it seems, bears one more thing he's known all his life and will never know again except in memory.

He gets out of bed and finds a cigarette in the bottom of his suitcase and puts on his robe. He stops in the doorway to his mother's room to watch the soft rise and fall of her breathing, her face pale in the moonlight. Sophie lifts her head and looks at him, giving her tail a thump before going back down to sleep.

In the kitchen he pours a glass of whiskey and goes out to the porch and settles on the swing. He sips the whiskey and lights the cigarette and blows the smoke into the air and sees something move in the far corner of the cemetery. He stops the swing and leans forward and as his eyes grow accustomed to the dark he can see someone sitting by the little mound of earth, rocking back and forth, slowly, almost dreamily as he used to lull himself to sleep as a boy. It is Katherine, and as he watches her he wonders what she's doing there in the middle of the night and when she will turn and stand and come his way.

She looks up at the sky, her arms held loosely across her chest as she rocks and sings a lullaby, "I'll cradle you deep," the sound mostly in her mind, "and hold you while angels," drifting out into the air, "sing you to sleep." She rocks back and forth, her mind unable to hold the image of an absence, Ethan utterly gone. She feels the weight of him in her arms, her phantom limb, this ghostly aura where bone and flesh had been, a moving residue of energy that Ethan now inhabits.

She comes night after night to ask his forgiveness, the ground cold and damp beneath her as she closes her eyes and presses her hand against the earth, and night after night, hears no reply.

She stands and turns toward the house where she sees the faint glow of a cigarette and the dark outline of someone sitting on the swing. It startles her, the pinpoint of light that has figured so often in her dreams and waking visitations. She steps to the maple and pauses, her hand against the tree, waiting for him to move, to come at her as before, but the swing begins to move, the glow a small arc in the air.

"Michael?" she says, her voice breaking the stillness of the moonlit darkness. The swing stops moving.

"Yes," he says. "Did I startle you?"

She steps away from the tree. "A little."

"I'm sorry. I didn't know you were there until I was already out here."

For a moment they look at each other across the low fence and the road shining white in the moonlight, and then she walks slowly toward the house. At the top of the stairs she notices the glass in his hand.

"Would you like one?" he says.

"No." She steps toward the door, then stops, "okay, and a cigarette if you have one." She sits on the swing and listens to him moving about in the darkened house.

He seems to her a kind and gentle man, but then she thinks she's met such men before.

She hears his footsteps, the stretch of the door spring as he walks onto the porch and hands her a glass and a cigarette. He strikes a match and holds it out to her. Then he sits on the top step, leaning his back against a post.

"You can sit up here," she says.

"This is fine."

She sips the whiskey and smokes the cigarette, grateful for the distance.

"I couldn't sleep," she says.

He looks at her. "I've noticed. I'm up a lot myself." He draws on the cigarette and tamps it on the step. "I have these. . .dreams."

"Me, too."

He looks out across the road and she follows his gaze in the direction of the grave and then back to the glass in his hand, feeling the weight of having to explain and the quickening lightness of wanting to.

"Thanks for your note," she says and sees him nod and thinks he makes a smile but cannot tell through the beard and the darkness.

"Well," he says, "I think I'm gonna go up. Give it another shot." He stands amidst a soft popping and cracking of ligaments and joints. "Good night," he says.

"Good night."

The next morning Lucy notices a subtle shift in the way Katherine and Michael are with each other. Their eyes seem not quite to meet, even in conversation, as if a little shy. Their voices are quiet, even gentle, and yet held at a distance, not cold or remote or angry, but a distance nonetheless. And then it comes to her that she is seeing a mutual regard with room to move freely without the need to give an account or explain.

During the night Katherine and Michael wake as before but only lie in bed to listen in the dark for the sound of dreams spilling into the air, bed clothes thrown aside. And if only silence comes through the wall, they listen for restless sounds, doors opening, footsteps on the stairs. But there is only the creaking of the house, Sophie turning in her bed, scratching to make a nest, laying herself back down.

On Sunday afternoon he goes back to Burlington and Katherine takes Sophie across the field and through the woods to the pond. The weather is cold again and she borrows Lucy's purple hat, pulled close around her ears. Lucy watches her from the kitchen as she disappears around the barn, her hands moving in the air as if making a point to the dog who trots along at her side.

Katherine wants to tell him, tell him everything, but she doesn't know why and distrusts the urge because she also wants to leave him in the dark with no point of entry or slightest bit of leverage, and she wonders if his being a man is why she feels this way and she thinks yes, and it's enough.

In the days that follow, a sense of slowing down and turning in comes over the house, partly from the cold outside but also from the weakening of Lucy. Katherine lies awake at night and feels the house grow larger around her as Lucy grows smaller. She stares at the ceiling and thinks on death, which in her life has taken two forms, neither of which comforts her now. All her grandparents save one were dead before she entered school and she barely remembers them, much less their dying. And when her grandmother died she was a hundred miles away and it might as well have been a thousand or a million, for it would have been the same, the presence suddenly become an absence, news coming through the telephone, no time to prepare, to brace against the loss, to ask the question before it is too late.

Death was something distant and abstract until that February night when it passed by so near it covered her in blood and took her body as its instrument. Death became something that ripped and tore, emptied out, laid waste and terrified, merciless and hard.

She lies awake and floats in a darkening pall of dread and loss. She envies Michael for the ease that seems to come of being Lucy's son, the way they sit and talk, the laughter and the softly swelling voices that rise toward the point of a story. She wants to sit like that, her voice blending in and belonging with theirs. She wants to feel herself a part of this dying and the living that surrounds it. But she does not know how to do it without invoking an awful mix of loss and horror so thick and close it crowds out the air and she can scarcely breathe.

She touches Lucy less and less. She is polite and kind and dotes on her every need, but also, in a way that Lucy knows, she is not there.

On a chilly morning, the sky cloudy with no hope of sun, Lucy sits on a kitchen chair and instructs Katherine in the art of laying a fire. She watches her holding the wood and laying it in place, and recalls the ruined woman she met nearly a year ago, lost and sinking toward oblivion.

"You've changed," says Lucy.

Katherine stops and looks at her, then away.

"Open the damper," Lucy says, "and light the paper." Katherine strikes a match and sets it to yesterday's *Globe*. "Leave the door ajar for awhile to give it a good draft. It wants to get up to speed and burn hot from the git-go."

Katherine sits back on her heels and looks into the fire as it roars into life and Sophie pads in from the library and lies down on her bed by the stove. Lucy looks at Katherine and wonders where she is and what it will take to bring her back.

"You can close the door now," she says. Katherine doesn't move until she suddenly becomes aware of the silence and Lucy watching her. She closes the door and the silence grows again, Katherine on her knees before the stove, Lucy sitting just behind, the chair creaking as she clears her throat. "Talk to me, dear."

"About what?"

Lucy looks at her with soft eyes that search Katherine's face turning to her now, "Just talk to me."

"I don't know what to say."

"That's a start. What is it you don't know how to say to me?"

Katherine shrugs and her eyes fill as she feels Lucy's hand on her shoulder. "I don't know how to talk to you," she says.

"You've done all right up 'til now."

"It's different."

"Because I'm dying."

Katherine nods.

"What can't you say to me?"

Katherine wipes her nose on her sleeve. "I want to ask you things."

"About dying."

"Yes, but I don't know how."

"Nobody does, until they do."

Katherine shakes her head. "Every time I think about it, I keep seeing — " and she stops.

"Just ask," comes Lucy's gentle voice again.

But Katherine goes on as if she hasn't heard, "I can't get past it and I know it's not the same with you and dying doesn't have to be that way but it's what I keep seeing — "

"Just . . . ask," Lucy whispers.

And Katherine turns so their faces almost touch, "Are you afraid?"

"Sometimes." And then Katherine begins to cry, with her whole body, and Lucy rests her head on Katherine's and wraps an arm around her shoulders and rocks her back and forth and then begins to feel the rocking and the holding as much for herself as for her.

"I'll tell you what," says Lucy, "ever since you came I felt free to ask you anything. Well, now it's your turn. Anytime, anywhere, you ask. And I'll answer if I can. How's that?"

Katherine nods.

"Now close the damper a bit."

Katherine turns the handle and stands and goes to the window above the sink and looks out to the barn. The goats are all inside save for one who peers around the doorway and surveys the yard, a length of hay dangling from her mouth.

"What do you think will happen?" says Katherine.

"When I die?"

"Yes."

Lucy looks into the fire, the room quiet except for the heat rising in the stovepipe. "I'm aware of something," she says, "between the living on one side and the dead on the other. Like a veil, sometimes very thin, in the evening, at dusk, the way the light is. It seems that way more and more, as if I can see to the other side just by looking."

"Does it frighten you?"

"No. I like to think dying is just crossing over a distance which is really no distance at all. I expect to see my parents and grandparents and my brother and sisters. Even Philip."

"He's dead?"

They are both surprised, looking at each other, then quickly away, "I suppose," says Lucy. A long silence. "You can add more wood to the fire."

Katherine feeds the stove.

"Lucy," she says, staring into the flames.

"What, dear."

"Do you think it's possible for someone who's dead to forgive someone who's alive?"

"Yes," says Lucy. "I don't think they can help it. It's the living who have a hard time of it, not the dead."

Katherine sits in the kitchen and watches Lucy flip the wall calendar to December.

"We should talk about Christmas," says Lucy, sitting down across from Katherine. "Your first and my last." There is a pause. "Of course, you're not to worry about getting anything for me. That would be silly. Things are the last thing I need. Additions to my estate," she says, smiling to herself. "What a funny word that is," she says. "Estate. Ha."

Annie stops by one afternoon and strides into the library where Lucy sits in the rocking chair and bends low to take her in her arms, Lucy all but disappearing behind the full skirt flowing down from Annie's hips. They speak briefly but Katherine cannot make out the words absorbed by the closeness of their embrace. She puts a kettle on for tea and sets a small table in the library with cups and a plate of things to eat.

"How are you?" says Annie.

"As you see," says Lucy. "My father always complained that women pack too much when they travel." She looks at them over her glasses. "Well," she says, "not this time. Light as a feather."

They talk until the light fades into the evening sky, of books and weather and animals and things felt but unseen, but not of death or even loss. Katherine floats on an easy current of remembrance and story and occasional laughter drawing them in. When a chill comes over the house, she tends the stove to the sound of voices drifting in from the other room.

It is only when Annie stands to leave that Katherine sees something more pass between them, a subtle letting go in their faces as they look at each other and then away, holding each other for a long time as Katherine closes her eyes and feels the embrace fill up the room.

Katherine is so used to the sounds of her own nightmares that she doesn't realize at first where it's coming from, the low, keening moan and the voice, hushed, words coming in bursts and then silence before the mournful cry resumes. She goes to Lucy's room and the first thing she sees is Sophie in the corner, her tail hanging low as she looks at

Lucy sitting up in bed and staring at her hands held out in front of her face, muttering a stream of words Katherine cannot hear. She crosses the room and sits beside her. Lucy's eyes are closed and Katherine can see, even in the dark, the faint glistening of tears down her cheeks. And then there is a sharp gasp and Lucy opens her eyes wide as she drops her trembling hands into her lap.

"Lucy."

She stares straight ahead with no sign that she has heard, until suddenly she looks at Katherine and her lips begin to move without a sound except for a gasp and then she closes her eyes and Katherine leans forward, afraid that she has died.

"Lucy?"

The voice comes small from Lucy's throat, "I need you to hear my confession."

Katherine sits up straight, startled, unsure of what she's heard.

"What did you say?"

Lucy looks at her.

"I need you to hear my confession."

"What do you mean?"

Lucy stares out the window. "You remember in the hospital," she says at last, "when I said what happened to you happened to me, except not all of it."

"Yes."

"Michael is the part we don't share."

"The only part," says Katherine. She puts her hand on top of Lucy's, but Lucy draws away. "You've asked me several times why I came to get you," she says. "What I said before was true. I wanted to help you. But it was more than that."

Lucy closes her eyes, opens them again. "I killed him," she says, looking at Katherine and then away, "and I needed to tell someone who would understand."

Katherine is stunned, even though, without knowing it, she has waited for months to hear the words.

"But all those times it came up before, why didn't you tell me then?"

"Because it's a terrible thing to kill a human being. And if I said the words, what I did would be real in a way it's never been before. I couldn't."

"Did Elsie know?"

Lucy shakes her head.

"Does Michael?"

"No. Nobody does except. . ." she closes her eyes and breathes out a sigh. "No one knows but me."

"How did it happen?"

"I put poison in his whiskey. He knew what I'd done, too, after it worked on him awhile. He sat at the kitchen table and glared at me, couldn't move, just his eyes, but he knew it was me killing him. He wanted so badly to get at me one last time."

"What did you do with him?"

"I buried him. Down by the trees behind the barn."

"Will you tell Michael?"

"No. I don't know how he'd take it and I don't want that before I die. Is that so awful do you think?"

"No. But he might want to know."

"I'll write something for him. I'll leave it in the bureau. Will you give it to him when I'm gone?"

Katherine nods.

"I did something terrible," says Lucy, "but I did nothing wrong. He didn't deserve to die, but I deserved to live and there wasn't any other way. He made sure of that. What you said about paying a price for killing someone is true, and I've been paying for more than thirty years. But I've also had my life. I could easily have been dead. And Michael. But we're alive and I've done what I can to make it worth what it took."

She looks at Katherine and takes her hand.

"I know it will always be harder for you, losing Ethan, but that's why you've got to find a way to accept what you did. Think of the life it saved."

They look into each other's eyes for a long time.

"There's no one who will forgive you," says Lucy, "because they do not know what you and I know. So I will forgive you, Katherine."

"And I forgive you."

Katherine lies awake in the dark, staring at the ceiling and thinking of her father. She wipes her eyes with her sleeve and sits up in bed, turning on the light, taking paper and pen and an envelope from the table, beginning to write.

4

*K*atherine wakes in the middle of the night to the sound of a plow scraping along the road, the clatter and roar muffled by the deepening snow, the rotating amber light on the cab flashing across the walls of her room. She looks out the window at the red tail lights disappearing into the thick white air leaving the house cloaked in the deepest silence she has ever known.

In the morning the world is transformed, white as far as she can see, broken only by the grey trees spattered with wind driven snow. The air is calm, the sky blue among a few remaining clouds that scuttle to the east as if left behind and catching up.

She dresses and goes downstairs and takes Lucy's parka, purple hat, and insulated rubber boots from the closet in the front hall. Out the back door she wades to the barn while Sophie lumbers around the side of the house to the rhododendrons bent low beneath the weight. She pushes open the door and steps inside, the barn strangely silent in the stillness thick with cold. She listens to goats breathing in the gloomy light, and then a stirring as one rises to its feet and then another, fluffing out their winter coats, hooves rustling in the hay, and then they are around her, noses raised to catch her scent as she touches them and says their names.

She puts hay in the bin and carries the water buckets into the house to fill at the kitchen sink, then shovels off the porch and digs a path out to the barn. She walks down the driveway and into the road where Sophie trots along the bank thrown up by the plow, her nose close to the ground. Her eyes pass over the cemetery, the stones softly capped in white, to the little mound in the far corner, and she thinks of his small body bundled in a bright blue snowsuit, arms puffed out by the bulk, his face barely visible through the hood. She shakes her head *some things you never get over* as she shovels her way up the walk.

Inside, she feeds Sophie and goes upstairs to change her clothes turned cold with sweat. Lucy is lying on her side, looking at Katherine over hands drawn up and folded in front of her chin. Katherine sits down on the bed beside her.

"What is it?" says Katherine.

"I was just remembering the smell of my father's shoes."

"How are you?"

"All right. We had snow."

"Yes." Katherine rubs her shoulder and Lucy closes her eyes with a little moan.

"How are the goats?"

"Are you in pain?"

"A little. But don't stop."

Katherine settles into a steady rhythm of kneading what little flesh is left over bone and then makes her way down the spine, guided by Lucy's murmurs of pleasure and relief. Sunlight streams through the window and across the bed. Sophie pads up the stairs and takes to her bed in the corner.

"I'll go light the fire."

Lucy nods. "Be down in a bit."

Katherine lays a fire and puts the kettle on the stove while Sophie comes down and sits and waits for Lucy at the bottom of the stairs. Katherine looks at Sophie and wonders what she will do without the only companion she's ever known, what sort of grief that will be. She makes a soft kissing sound and bends forward, hands on her knees. Sophie hesitates, then trots into the kitchen where Katherine is squatting on the floor, and slides her face between her legs like a boat coming into a slip. Katherine lays her cheek against the fur along Sophie's spine and softly strokes her belly.

By the time the tea is brewed, Lucy is dressed and downstairs, sitting at the kitchen table and holding a steaming cup in front of her face. She looks at Katherine for a long time and then sets down the cup without moving her eyes that are moist and full of light.

"Katherine," she says, her voice small but clear, her face smooth with calm intent, and then a pause that holds them both, "I love you."

"And I love you."

"I wanted to say that while things are still okay. Before they get sticky. I wouldn't want you to wonder whether it was me or just the morphine."

Katherine begins to smile and a tear rolls down her cheek as the room grows quiet and still around them.

Two days before Christmas Michael puts a sign in the shop window and takes the highway toward Montpelier. The traffic is light and his mind wanders through the memory of his grandfather's funeral at the cemetery across from the house. Seven years old and his head full of angels, he said to his mother how 'neat' he thought it would be to die.

"And why is that?" she said.

"Because you get to fly."

"I suppose."

But when he stood in front of the long casket laid out in the living room, he wondered aloud how grandfather would get out of the box.

"It's a mystery," his mother said.

"But what's the answer?"

"There isn't one," she said. "That's what makes it a mystery."

He wrinkled up his face.

She bent down and straightened his tie and ran her hand over the cowlick at the back of his head. "Some mysteries," she said, "are like the Hardy Boys and you like the book because you find out everything in the end. But other mysteries aren't like that. Bigger ones, so big you never know the answer because it's too big for our brains to know."

He began to fidget. "So," he said, "how does he get out of the box?" and she smiled and shrugged and said she didn't know.

He can see in his mind her beautiful face as she spoke things neither of them understood. He remembers the smell of her when she bent over his bed to tuck him in at night, her skin and hair the most comforting smell he has ever known.

He leaves the highway at Montpelier and turns north. On the seat beside him are three small packages, presents for Katherine, two of which he purchased at his mother's request. He wonders about her, where she came from and what the understanding is that keeps her here. He assumes she will leave when Lucy dies, but he would like to know more about her before she goes, the grave and the dreams that shake her out of sleep.

He drives through the snowy landscape, the familiar comfort of hills and woods, slowing the truck past a dairy farm, the barn doors open wide to admit the fresh air warmed by the sun and affording a view down the long line of cows standing in their stalls, inside for the winter.

When he first sees his mother rising to greet him from her rocking chair, he instinctively looks her over as if searching for a wound from which the life seeps out of her. But when he takes her in his arms he feels the wound inside, eating her up like a black hole absorbing the available light. Her breath has a sharp and acrid edge he has smelled before as it rose from the throats of dying men.

In the afternoon he and Katherine take a saw and go out past the barn to a small patch of balsam firs. Their talk is sparse as they shake snow from branches to get a better sense of shape until they find a small one that pleases them and he holds it by the tip while she kneels in the snow and applies the saw. When she is done, he notices the cut, clean and perpendicular, and says, "Nice sawing," and she gets to her feet and says, "Nice holding," and they smile but do not look at each other as they drag the little tree back through the snow. He asks how Lucy is doing and there is little she can think to say. They prop the tree in a bucket of water on the porch and go inside, stamping snow from their feet and calling out to Lucy that they've brought her a prize, the best tree of all. She turns and smiles with an open face and for just an instant, as they stand in the doorway and look in at her, everything in the universe seems in its proper place, perfectly aligned, spinning, spiraling, coming and going as they want to believe it is meant to do.

After supper, Michael and Katherine are cleaning the kitchen while Lucy listens to music in the library.

"Have you gotten her anything for Christmas?"

"No," she says. "She said she didn't want me to."

"Right."

"I keep thinking there must be something that she'd like. I thought maybe an experience of some kind. We could take her somewhere but she must have already been everywhere close enough for her to go and not get tired out."

"An experience," he says, looking off to the side, "something we could do here." And then his face broadens in a smile.

It doesn't occur to her until she opens the door of Lucy's car and sees Michael fastening his seat belt on the other side that they will be alone together for several hours on this trip across the border into New Hampshire. In the close confining space of the car, with his attention fixed on the road, she watches him in ways she could not before. From the corner of her eye she studies his hands on the wheel, the fingers short and ringless and soft, as she'd expect on a man who sold books for a living. And then she notices the baby finger on his right hand is missing its last joint and she wonders how he came to lose it, some accident on the farm, perhaps, or in Vietnam. She remembers the scars along his arms as she listens to him going on about what he has in mind, where to set up the show to give Lucy the most spectacular view.

They pick up the highway near St. Johnsbury and pass over the Connecticut River into New Hampshire and then on to a rundown bungalow beneath a huge hand painted FIREWORKS! sign. Inside they take baskets and set off among the crowded tables and aisles of shelves. She finds herself looking at the simple handsome lines of his face which remind her of his mother, but also something underneath, especially in his eyes. He holds up a long purple stick with a large multi-colored tube at the end and smiles at her as he waggles it back and forth and suddenly she feels that everyone in the store must have watched her watching him and she quickly looks away.

They sit on a bench near the cash register and go through what they've chosen and agree that if they don't blow themselves up or set the house on fire it'll be a show that Lucy won't forget.

"Whatever that means," he says.

They are just crossing the river when he breaks the silence that has settled in between them.

"My mother hasn't told me anything about you, about why you're here."

She stiffens against the seat and looks down at the water beneath the bridge.

"I don't have to know," he says. "It's none of my business," a pause, "but that night on the porch . . . I don't know . . . it just seemed . . ." He props his elbow on the door and rests his forehead against his hand, shakes his head, "never mind, I'm sorry."

"It's all right," she says. "I know more about you than you do about me."

"From my mother?"

"No. Annie Harris."

"Annie Harris. She's still around. She told you about Vietnam."

"Some."

"That was a long time ago."

When they get home they bring the tree in from the porch and install it in a corner of the library. After lunch he tells Lucy she mustn't look out the front windows, drawing the blinds to make sure. She regards him with a skeptical squint but gives in with a shrug, retreating to the kitchen where they put the rocker in front of the stove and a pot of tea and a pile of books on the table. Then they go outside and set to work and are there until the sky begins to darken and the moon rises full and luminous in the sky.

Lucy is asleep in the chair when they come in to make their supper and wakes to the sound of dishes and silverware. After supper she puts on some Christmas music while Michael climbs the stairs to the attic and returns with a box of decorations. They string lights on the tree with Lucy giving directions from the rocker and shooing Sophie from the open box on the floor.

Katherine looks at the empty space beneath the tree and feels the weight of the depression she's been struggling to contain all day. She is, she thinks, in a strange house with people she doesn't really know, going through the motions of the season. They are not her family and she has none that she can count on, but is cut loose upon the world like an astronaut on a space walk whose tether is suddenly cut, no up or down, left or right, only a vast and empty space she cannot hope to navigate or fill.

Lucy declares the tree beautiful and says, "And now Michael if you'll read to us," looking at Katherine, "a tradition of ours."

Michael goes about the room and lights the candles Lucy has brought out — on window sills and bookshelves, in sconces along the walls — and then turns out the lights and takes a book and settles himself in a chair that he drags beside his mother. Lucy calls Sophie to lie down between them. For a moment, Katherine stands in the middle of the room not knowing what to do, until Lucy motions with her hand and says, "Come on. All for one, one for all."

Michael begins to read in a deep and mellow voice, "'Twas the night before Christmas, and all through the house, not a creature was stirring' — " he looks up over his glasses, suspensefully, as if to small children, and says in a hushed voice, " — 'not even a mouse.'" Lucy smiles and looks at Katherine who manages a little smile, and seeing the struggle in her face, Lucy reaches out and covers her hand with her own as Michael reads on. Katherine longs to feel differently, to escape the dark emptiness that coils around her heart and separates her from the rest. But whatever it takes, she cannot find it now.

He finishes the story and closes the book.

"Time for presents," says Lucy, looking at Katherine. "Is that all right with you? I'd much rather now than tomorrow."

"Now is fine," says Katherine. She goes upstairs to fetch the gift she has for Michael, a woven hat and pair of mittens she bought on Lucy's advice from a woman who lives in town and does everything from carding and dyeing the wool to the knitting. She had thought it wouldn't be enough until she stood in the shop and smelled the wool and felt the hat against her cheek, but now she isn't sure.

She hands it to him as she sits down in a chair and he smiles and pulls the yarn from around the tissue paper and reaches in and pulls out a handful of the wool. He turns to her with a look of such pleasure that she cannot help but smile.

"Thank you," he says. "Very much. This is beautiful." He smiles at her and then he reaches behind his chair to hand her a package which she can tell from its contours is a number of books. She tears back the paper to reveal a complete collection of Jane Kenyon's poetry. She takes in a little gasp to keep from crying, but it does no good as she looks down at the books and wipes her eyes.

"This is really very fine," she says, glancing up at him. "Thank you, Michael."

Then Lucy reaches beneath the blanket on her lap and hands a present to Katherine, who holds it for a moment, feeling the weight of it. It is a book, she can tell, but large and with a soft cover. And there is a curious bump along the center, like a cigar laid on top. She slowly undoes the ribbon and lets the paper fall away. It is a journal bound in leather and embossed with her name in gold. And held to its cover by a length of yarn is a fountain pen, the barrel a deep cobalt blue inside a gold cap engraved "From LD to KS." There is a card beneath the yarn and she opens it to read, "For the poetry yet to come."

She looks at Lucy whose gaze is set upon her with a fierce intensity, her lips slightly parted in a smile, her head slowly nodding in silent affirmation. She begins to feel herself come undone, but then something in the old woman's eyes draws her back and she looks at her and in a voice that is simple and full of dignity, says, "Thank you, Lucy. Thank you very much. For all of it," and Lucy's smile spreads across her face and she begins to laugh and Katherine smiles and shakes her head.

Michael doesn't see Lucy take a small package from beneath the blanket and place it on her lap beneath her hands. "I didn't know what to get you," she says, "what could possibly be right or enough at a time like this." Her eyes are wet and her lips tremble as she holds it out to him and says, "It will have to do." He sits on the floor in front of her and opens it slowly, not looking up, and takes out a framed photograph that he holds for a long time without moving.

"I don't know if you remember this," she says, "but if I had one thing to remember us by, it would be this."

Without a sound he rises to his knees and lays his head on his mother's lap and she strokes his hair as Katherine looks at the photograph of Michael just a baby in his mother's arms, their skin golden in the dim light as if they were about to take a bath. Her face is young and beautiful with a radiant smile and Michael looks out toward the camera with an expression of wonder beyond his years.

He says something into his mother's lap that Katherine cannot hear and Lucy nods and leans in close to whisper something in return, and then Michael sits back on the floor and looks at Katherine. "Her turn now, don't you think?"

"What," says Lucy.

He looks at his mother and grins.

"You look like the Cheshire cat," she says.

He wiggles his eyebrows. "Okay by me."

"I told you not to."

"And we didn't."

"What are you two up to?"

They shrug and smile in concert. "We need you to come outside," he says. "We've prepared a little something. An experience of sorts."

"Hmmm," says Lucy.

He goes into the living room and takes the cushion from a chair and carries it out the front door. He then goes upstairs and returns with an armful of blankets beneath a small pile of clothing. "Now," he says, "you will allow us to bundle you up. A sweater, your warmest coat, a hat, mittens, and boots with double socks."

"This is no way to treat an old lady who's about to kick the bucket."

"Oh yes it is," he says, beckoning her to slip a hand into the armhole of a cardigan. "Come on. No time to dawdle. You'll just get sleepy on us. Seize the moment, Mom."

She puts on the sweater and then an extra pair of socks, followed by the insulated boots. Katherine puts on her coat and hat and then helps Lucy finish dressing while Michael puts on his parka and his new hat and mittens.

"Ready?" he says.

Lucy rolls her eyes. "I can't imagine."

"Exactly," says Michael, taking her arm.

Lucy steps onto the porch to see the cushion from one of her best chairs sitting on the top step with a blanket spread over it. With Katherine on one side and Michael on the other she goes down a step and then backs up to sit down.

"And now we wrap you up," he says drawing the blanket over her legs and wrapping two more across her shoulders and around the front.

"I can't move," she says.

"You're not supposed to," says Katherine.

"Well, then," she says, her voice taking on an edge, "get on with it."

"Close your eyes, Mom. And no looking 'til we say so."

She says nothing as he bends down and looks into her face and for a moment their eyes meet and then Lucy looks down with a little shrug and lifts her head, eyes closed tight.

"Ready," she says.

There is a long silence broken only by hushed and urgent voices and footsteps crunching in the snow across the road. And then at last there is a rush of air that grows louder and faster and when Michael says "now" and Lucy opens her eyes, the trunk of the great maple is covered with whirling pinwheels of light. She smiles and shakes her head and pulls the blankets tighter as she watches the two of them dart among the tombstones, little flames in their hands, like children.

But then she loses sight of them as it begins in earnest, a sputter of light and then a rush of air and something rising from the ground and shooting into the sky where fingers of red and blue and yellow and purple light explode in all directions, filling the air. There is a pause and then another rises from the snow and another and another and soon they rise together in a great unbroken chorus that fills the sky above the maple and the horizon beyond, light and color everywhere, playing across the tombstones and snow-covered fields, washing over the house and through the windows and into the rooms where Lucy has slept and lived her entire life, even through the half-moon window in the attic where light and color flash and ripple in the darkness over the long lines of books. Lucy whoops and laughs and claps her hands beneath the blankets, unable to contain the torrent of emotion welling up inside, and Michael looks up at her, this woman he has loved for longer than he can remember, sitting beneath a sky on fire, the full moon still and pale against the brilliance of it all, the stars exploding and raining down a shower of color and light. On and on it goes and then, suddenly, something happens, something that can only be seen in the look that comes over Lucy's face, the muscles smoothed out, her mouth dropping open, eyes wide as she struggles to take in the awful and wonderful sight that appears before her, as if the sky has cracked open to reveal something more enormous and eternal than itself, more vast than even her restless and seeking mind can begin to comprehend.

The air softens and grows quiet as it settles back into the light of the moon, Michael and Katherine laughing from the cemetery, giddy as they turn and look across the road to the lone figure of Lucy on the step, motionless and silent, her face turned up toward the light of the moon. They cross the road but still she doesn't move and they are running by the time they reach the walk. She is moving her lips but they cannot hear until they draw in close and sit on the step below and look up at her.

"Oh, my," she says. "Oh, my," her face wet with tears, eyes open wide.

"Mom," he says, "are you all right?"

"Oh, my," she says again and then closes her mouth and looks down at the stones in the walk and then from side to side as if trying to remember. Her gaze passes over Katherine to Michael and then fixes on a point across the road.

"Did you like it?" says Michael.

"Oh, yes," she says. "It was . . . ." and she searches with her eyes but cannot find what she's looking for and shakes her head, letting out a sigh and taking Michael's face in her hands and kissing him on the lips, her eyes looking into his all the while, and then she turns to Katherine and does the same and they look at her, silent and still.

A small tremor passes up the length of Lucy's body and Michael gathers her into his arms, blankets and all, and lifts her, cheeks wet against his face, and carries her through the door that Katherine holds open and up the stairs to her room. They remove first the blankets and then her outer clothes. Lucy feels almost limp in their arms, like a child so tired it's all she can do to hold herself from falling asleep. Without a word they undress her and slide a nightgown over her head, guiding her arms into the sleeves and gently standing her up to let it fall around her legs. She says nothing, showing no alarm or shame at being so exposed, carried along by something larger than whatever they might do. Katherine pulls back the covers and Michael sits his mother down and lifts her legs and slides her feet between the sheets. Lucy lies back on the pillow and closes her eyes. They bend over her and kiss her face and then turn out the light and go downstairs.

She lies in the stillness of the moonlight coming through the window and feels something shift inside of her, something done, a change of course, a readiness, a sinking downward motion of her soul toward a place deeper than sleep, deeper than dream.

Katherine and Michael sit on the porch swing, cigarettes glowing in the dark. Michael is thinking about the look in his mother's eyes, a look he's seen before, in men about to die. He's always wondered what they were looking at so intently and with such a sense of awe, delivered from pain and fear by something he could not see.

"We did a good thing," he says.

"I hope she's all right. It's like she wasn't here."

"I know."

They sit and smoke and she feels again the desire to tell him everything, at war with the overwhelming need to tell him nothing at all.

"Well," he says, "at least we didn't burn the place down."

They stand and go to the door. "I'll check on the goats before I come up," she says. "In case it freaked them out."

She feels at once drawn to him and thrown back and, for a moment, suspended between the two, until, without thinking, she raises her arms, but just from the elbows out, and he looks down at her hands and steps forward and they come together in a hug that is brief and awkward and tender.

"Good night, Michael."

"Good night."

And then the door is closed behind him and she looks across the road and remembers the smell of him, unable to recall the last time she smelled the scent of a man, the simplicity of skin uncomplicated by aftershave or cologne, elemental and faintly loamy. *Skin.* And she thinks it is the skin Lucy used to bathe as she herself once bathed Ethan, in a sink when he was very small and then in a tub with boats and rubber toys.

On her way to the barn she stops and looks up at the moon and imagines Lucy asleep and dreaming in her bed.

Katherine closes the door and stands in the darkness. The goats are lying down, close in for warmth, quiet except for the soft chewing of cud and bodies shifting against the hay. She is struck by how calm they seem, and then she realizes it is for her and not for them that she has come. She kneels in the hay beside a goat that lifts its nose to catch the scent of her, and she thinks to lie down among them but cannot figure how and so she sits where she is, petting the goat in a long and gentle motion. And then it comes to her that it's Christmas Eve and presents have been opened and the fireworks are done and she feels a sinking in her heart and longs to follow it down into a sleep from which she will never wake. If only he had lived, she thinks. If only he had managed to stay asleep or stay upstairs a little while longer or hit the wall at an angle that was any less fatal. And it seems that is all that is left to her now, if only this, if only that, with nothing coming after.

She shivers in the cold but doesn't think to go inside for fear of being unable to contain the sadness welling up inside her, that she wants no one else to hear. She goes into the feed room and pulls several bales of hay from the stack to clear a little berth. Then she lays herself down and curls up tight and begins to rock and cry as if the sorrow of all the world was passing through her body and into the air.

A solitary goat, the honey white named Elsie, rises from her bed and stands vigil by the door, while up in his room Michael lies in the moonlit dark and listens to the faint but unmistakable sound coming from the direction of the barn.

5

*T*he sun does not appear on Christmas Day, the sky hung low with thick grey clouds and flurries of snow. When Katherine comes downstairs, Michael has laid a fire and is cooking breakfast.

She says good morning on her way out to the barn and he looks up and smiles. When she returns he is at the table eating eggs and toast, the kitchen warm from the stove, the fire showing orange and yellow through the glass.

"Where's Sophie?" says Katherine.

Michael gestures toward the ceiling with his fork. "Upstairs," he says. "Had breakfast and then made a beeline for mom's room. Been there ever since."

Katherine eats and then goes to the living room, closing the door and standing by the phone. She has been thinking about this for days, knowing it has to be done, dreading it nonetheless. She lifts the phone and dials the number and is surprised to hear her mother's voice.

"Oh, Katherine," she says, the words catching in her throat, "let me get your father," and Katherine waits for him to get on the line, feeling how impossible it is for just the two of them without a buffer in between. Then there is her father trying to be merry, asking how she is, her mother coming in from time to time, "oh, yes. . . me, too," making their way toward the silence that will mark the end. Katherine feels herself the same and yet changed ever since that night, no longer her parents' daughter, torn away and turned into someone else, just as they are no longer who she thought they were, and yet bound together for the rest of their lives. As she puts down the phone, it occurs to her that forgiveness can be either a beginning or an end and she has no idea of which it is between them now.

Sophie stays in Lucy's room all day long, having to be coaxed outside to pee only to go right back upstairs. Lucy wakes mid-morning and asks for tea and unbuttered toast and drinks half the one and eats even less of the other. Michael sits on the edge of the bed.

"I'm leaving you some cash," she says, "and a handful of bonds which should take the pressure off you to sell the house. I want you to let Katherine stay awhile. She needs to be here until she decides to go."

He looks at her, waiting for an explanation that does not come. "I don't have a problem with that," he says. "I'll be in Burlington most of the time."

She nods and pats his hand. "Good," she says. She hears Katherine come in the front door and calls out for her to come upstairs.

"I've just been talking with Michael," she says. "I want you to feel that you can stay here until you sort things out."

Katherine looks at her and nods. "Thank you."

"If you stay longer, that's between you and Michael." There is a silence in which everyone's gaze seems fixed on their own private portion of bedspread. Lucy dips a finger into the tea to take its temperature, then puts the cup on the bedside table. "I am concerned about the animals," she says. "Walter will take the goats, but not before spring. The winter's hard enough on them without having to cope with that." She works her fingers in her lap and then stares out the window, her eyes rimmed with tears.

"What about Sophie?" says Michael.

A tail thumps against the floor and Lucy sighs a deep and heavy sigh. "She's an old dog," she says. "With any luck she won't outlast me by much. I'd like her to be here when her time comes, but that may not be possible. You have lives of your own." She draws her sleeve across her eyes. "Walter will take her, of course, if it comes to that. She knows him. And Margaret. They'll love her up good."

Sophie lays her chin on the edge of the bed and Lucy scratches her behind the ears.

Katherine expects death to be swift and dark, but is amazed as the energy in the house rises into light and air. Lucy comes downstairs to sit in the kitchen and library. She talks about the weather and her childhood and items in the *Globe*. She wonders aloud if she made a mistake not owning a television, but then concludes she'd probably been right. She has Michael drag out boxes filled with photos and sifts through them on snowy afternoons. She sits in the kitchen with a grease pencil in her hand, making sure old photos are properly marked so he won't wonder which relation is the one in the flowered hat standing by the carriage with a baby in her arms, or who it is in the black and sepia tones who tends cows in the barn, his back to the camera.

They barely notice the coming of the New Year. As Lucy loses interest in food she becomes too weak to manage the stairs and her world shrinks to the dimensions of her room. Helen Broom stops by to see what's needed and sits with Michael and Katherine to tell them what to expect — the hastening descent of the body shutting down. Lucy shows little sign of pain that can't be managed by the lightest dose of morphine. She will grow weaker and weaker, says Helen, and eventually stop taking water, making her electrolytes go "out of whack" and bringing on hallucinations, although "she may surprise you."

They take turns in Lucy's room and reading to her from the *Globe*. At first she interrupts to comment on the news, but then she only listens, her gaze fixed on the face of the one beside her, studying the play of light on the moving lips and the expression when they look up at her and smile. And then more and more they find her asleep and lay down the paper to sit quietly looking out the window or dozing in the chair.

Michael and Katherine fall into a rhythm of stepping in and standing back and moving through Lucy's dying as dancers who anticipate the other with a singularity of purpose, taking turns at cooking and caring for animals, clearing snow and chopping wood, sitting at her bedside, reading, keeping company and keeping watch. But in their hearts they are in parallel, two lines that never intersect.

They leave open the doors to their rooms, as if the entire floor of the house has become an extension of the place where Lucy is dying. In the quiet of the night, their dreaming mingles in the hall with muted cries, covers thrown back, the anxious thump of Sophie's tail. Each lies awake and wonders if it was another or themselves that made the sound, dreamed the dream. Sleep comes fitfully and unannounced, sometimes in the middle of the afternoon.

Katherine takes long walks down the road, the fields too deep with snow. As one day flows into the next the waking hours are a continuing struggle to clear her mind of any thought of what will happen after Lucy dies, to push away the enormity of loss and emptiness.

Lucy sleeps more and more. "Going backwards," she says. "Pretty soon I'll be sucking my thumb."

Michael buys a baby monitor so they can hear her call when they're downstairs. In the middle of January, Lucy refuses water, saying it makes her queasy.

Michael has become so accustomed to being alone that he has forgotten how much he depends on the simple knowledge of his mother being somewhere in the world. He looks at her as she sleeps and remembers the presence beside his bed in the hospital, the book spread open on her lap as she waited for him to reach out from the deep, dark place where he had fallen. And now it is she who falls toward a place more dark and deep than anything he can imagine, and there is nothing he can do or she would have him do except touch her skin and comb the hair away from her face.

The world grows large around him at the thought of her not in it. And then he thinks of his father, a presence he has kept at bay since returning from Vietnam to find him gone. He had so longed to end the violence and the fear that he didn't ask for more than what she chose to tell. But now he cannot keep his father from his thoughts. He feels him in every room and every closet, hears in the wind the sound of him pitching hay in the barn, sees him in his dreams. And as he watches his mother slip away he is filled with questions he cannot bring himself to ask or to ignore — where did he go and what made him stay away, how she could be sure he wouldn't come back again.

But he thinks he already knows, has known for many years, that his father is somewhere in the fields behind the barn, near the woods where machinery is unlikely to go, where the earth is soft and free of roots and stones. She could have done it. As small as she was, she was strong enough if there was no other way, and he can imagine no other way to make it certain. He watches her sleep and imagines the bones of his father buried in the earth she scraped and lifted and threw down into the hole.

Lucy looks at Katherine in the chair, head bent over the book in her lap, and remembers when their positions were reversed. She says her name in her mind but Katherine does not look up. She wills her fingers to get her attention, but without effect. Everything is in slow motion as she closes her eyes to the sound of her own breathing and Katherine's name until a hand comes to rest on her own and she looks up into the tender eyes looking down at her.

"What was that book I read to you?" says Lucy, her voice small, almost a whisper. "In the hospital. I can't remember."

"*Pilgrim at Tinker Creek.*"

"Oh," says Lucy, closing her eyes, "Yes," silently working her lips and then opening her eyes, "that's you now, isn't it," eyelids drifting down, "Katherine," her voice soft, Katherine bending down to hear, "keep going."

Michael and Katherine wake in the middle of the night to sounds from Lucy's room. They go to her, thinking she's about to die, but discover instead the narration of trips she is taking in her mind. She talks to people they cannot see and listens for the reply, then suddenly includes them in the conversation before setting off on her own again.

"Lizzy," she says, "be careful how you push me off," her mouth hanging open as she waits, "hang on, Toby," a tremor across her face, "if I read it another time, I might have understood it better, I was probably too young," and then, "it's the best red I've ever seen" and "don't leave the chair by the window, Michael." She looks at him. "You're not running the furnace are you?"

"Yes."

"Well, turn it off. Where are we supposed to get the oil? Wood everywhere and we're burning oil from Saudi Arabia. Turn it off. Turn it off." And then she's gone again, "all right, mama," her voice becoming small.

Michael wakes to a dark and silent house and goes softly down the hall. Sophie lifts her head from Lucy's hip and lays it back again. He sits in the rocking chair and watches his mother sleep, and as his eyes adjust to the gloom he sees the moving of her lips, mouthing words without a sound. He leans forward but still can't make it out. He sits on the bed and puts his ear in close and there is a sound, but as if in code, fragments, and then he is just about to pull away when a word draws him back and then a sentence, but he cannot make it out, until the whispered words come like a ship from out of the fog, "we. . dug. . all night. . ."

"What?" he says, his lips against her ear, "what did you dig?"

". . .all night. . ." disappearing in the fog.

In the days that follow he cannot get it from his mind. He sits and watches her doze, rising like a whale to take a breath, only to return into the deep, trying to catch her attention before she disappears.

"Mom," he says, "where is dad?"

She opens her eyes and looks into this face.

"Is he here?" he says.

She makes a sigh and looks away to the window and then nods and closes her eyes and sinks beneath the waves.

In the evening they sit in the kitchen and play Scrabble, the baby monitor between them on the table. Michael is pensive and preoccupied, taking longer and longer to form each word, and when she gently prods, he seems startled from a reverie.

When the board is almost full, he's down to his last four letters which he keeps re-arranging in the tray.

"Did she tell you about my father?" he says, not looking up.

"Some."

"Did she tell you what he did?"

"Yes."

"Anything else?"

"What do you mean?"

"About what happened to him. Where he went. Why he never came back."

"No," she says, not looking at him.

He takes the tile on one end of the tray and moves it to the other and stares at the result.

"Is that why you're here?" he says, looking up.

"I don't understand."

"Is that what you have in common? What happened to her with him?"

"Yes," she says, after so much time, such a small and simple thing to say.

"Your husband beat you up?"

"Yes."

"And how did it end?"

There is a pause. "Badly."

"Would you tell me what happened?"

"If I can figure out where to begin."

"I don't care. Anywhere you want. You can always start again."

And so she begins, the hardest part first and working her way back from there. He listens, a sadness across his face, staring down at the table.

"That's why I'm here," she says.

He slowly unknits his fingers. "I'm sorry," he says, looking up at her, "especially about your boy."

"You don't want to know why I stayed?"

He shrugs, "I think I already do. You think it's how you stay alive." He slides the tiles from his tray and reaches for the box. "How old was he?"

"Who?"

"Ethan."

"Five."

He starts to speak but can only shake his head as he looks down and begins to put the pieces one by one into the little cloth bag in his hand.

Michael lays a fire in the living room and they sit on the couch and smoke.

"I wish I could have done what you did," he says. "Not that it would've worked. I couldn't kill them all. And I was in the middle of North Vietnam. I'd never have made it home. And I knew what they did to the ones who tried." He draws on the cigarette and blows the smoke into the air. "So I stayed put.

"In a way, I had it better than you. A lot of people knew I was there and were trying to get me out. And there were other guys like me just down the hall. You had none of that."

"Neither did your mother."

"I didn't know that before. She never talked about it. It was always this thing going on that you wished would stop and when it didn't you figured you hadn't wished hard enough or were fucking up or just unlucky. Something." He flicks the cigarette into the fire. "You want a drink?"

She nods.

"I'll check on Mom while I'm up."

He goes upstairs and stands beside his mother's bed, looking down at her hands and trying to imagine them killing a man and digging a big enough hole to hold him, and suddenly recalls it was 'we' who dug all night and kept the secret all these years.

He goes downstairs.

"So," he says, "my turn. What do you want to know?"

"What they did to you."

He nods at the fire. "I guess you could say whatever they could dream up and whenever they got the chance. Which was quite a lot." He looks at her. "They were good at finding excuses. We were always doing something wrong." He sips the whiskey and holds it in his mouth before swallowing.

"I remember this one guy by the name of Duc, Lieutenant Duc. 'Why you make me do this?' he'd say. 'Why you can't follow rules like the rest?' Of course the answer was there were too many rules and they kept making up new ones. He'd give me this 'poor me' look like I'd done something to him and then they'd start in on me again."

"What did you do?"

"What did I do?"

"How did you . . . cope."

"Not very well. Sometimes I could zone out a bit, a trick I learned from our dentist when I was a kid. He wasn't into novocaine." He lights another cigarette. "But he wasn't trying to hurt me, and these guys definitely were. I could only keep it up so long before the pain got through or they caught on that I was zoning out and brought me back. I remember one time this look on Duc's face when he saw I wasn't suffering enough and all of a sudden my finger got hit so hard I thought I was going to pass out and I looked at him and realized he was totally unmoved by the pain he was causing me. That's when I knew he had me. I had no defense against that look. All my little ideas about playing fair and what one person can do to another went right out the window. Didn't amount to shit. And I knew in that moment I didn't have a right in the world that mattered. Whatever happened next was all up to him."

"Is that the finger?" she says, pointing to his hand.

He holds the hand in front of him, fingers spread apart, the shortened little finger stubby and discolored beside the rest. "That's the one," he says. "It got infected and they had to cut it off."

She looks at him looking at his finger. "Do you hate them, Michael?"

"Now? I don't think so. I don't know if I hated them then. It wasn't as simple as hating them or not. Duc had all the power, which meant he could give as well as take. Sometimes he was almost nice and that felt pretty good even though I wasn't supposed to take anything from him. But it was hard not to feel grateful when he didn't beat me up or when I thought he'd really had it and was going to kill me and then he didn't. I know he hated me, or at least an idea of me, even though he knew I was just a medic. I mean, we were bombing the shit out of his people and he couldn't stop it. No matter what he did we just kept coming." He drinks the last of the whiskey in his glass. "But he sure as hell could do something about me." He looks at her. "So," he says, "how about you? Do you hate him?"

Katherine is silent for a moment, then, "yes."

He nods. "It'll pass."

"You think it will."

"I hope so."

Michael sits with his mother late into the night, a light snow falling outside the window. As he watches her, he thinks how easily everyone left her to carry the burden of his father's violence, and how she carried it until the middle of one night — which night, he will never know — when she laid it down. And yet, even then, he realizes, she had to carry the secret for the rest of her life and has never been free of his father just as he has never been free of Duc, and the simple truth is that when he returned from Vietnam and could not stay in this house, it was not only for her sake that he ran away and tried to lose himself.

He dozes in the chair and then wakes suddenly as if someone had touched him lightly on the face, and when he sees her looking at him, he makes a little smile that is mirrored in the fine skin around the corners of her eyes and then a steady gaze settles in between them. He wonders what she is thinking, what she is seeing, if it is him or someone else, and then he pulls the chair in close and rests his hands on top of hers.

"I know what you did," he says and there is a quickening in the dry rattle of her breathing and her eyes move back and forth as if trying to locate where the voice is coming from. "No," he says, "it's not what you think. It's all right," leaning down to put his face beside her cheek, his lips almost touching her ear, "thank you, Mama, for saving me," and beneath his hands he feels her chest rise from a great intake of air that she lets out on a long and trembling sigh.

6

On the morning of Lucy's fifth day without water, Helen Broom is surprised to find her still alive. When she leaves, Michael and Katherine begin a vigil at Lucy's bedside, taking naps beside her on the bed. They leave the house only to tend the goats and get the mail. Annie and Walter bring groceries. Sophie loses interest in taking walks.

That afternoon, Walter brings groceries and stands in the kitchen while Katherine puts them away. He is by the back door, hat in hand, looking at her, then the door, and then down at his hat.

"Is there something?" she says.

"No," he says, putting his hand on the knob but then taking it back as he turns to her, "yes, there is. Do you think I could see her? For just a minute?"

"I don't see why not. But let me ask Michael."

He waits in the kitchen as her footsteps fade into soft voices overhead and then Michael comes down, smiling when he sees Walter and motioning him up the stairs.

Sophie moans and wags her tail at the sight of him standing in the doorway, the hat still in his hand. He looks at Lucy for a long time. It seems to him that she's gone in all but the breath and the beating of her heart. But that's what he came for, crossing the room and bending down to look into her face as tears come into his eyes. He reaches out and touches the fine grey hair on top of her head and strokes his fingers across her face. Words form on his lips but make no sound and then he steps back from the bed and draws his sleeve across his eyes.

Downstairs, he mumbles thanks as he passes by and makes his way through the kitchen and out the door.

Lucy is turning blue as her body shuts down and the heat withdraws in the direction of her heart. She shows no outward sign of knowing anyone is there. Her eyes are closed and she doesn't speak except a murmur now and then when they touch her. Her breathing is shallow above a faint gurgling in her throat. They kneel on either side and move her to the center of the bed, then lie down beside her, Katherine on one side and Michael on the other. Sophie finds a place near the foot of the bed, her chin on Lucy's ankles. Michael speaks to his mother in tones that are soft and low, as if easing a child into sleep, and Katherine is comforted by the sound, her face smooth beneath a steady stream of tears. She strokes Lucy's hair and hums the lullaby she sang by Ethan's grave and looks at Michael and thinks how young he seems, especially in the eyes, wide and full of sadness and, on some level, in spite of all the death he has held in his arms, uncomprehending of the loss yet to come.

They lose track of time and drift in and out of sleep, the sound of Lucy's labored breath a steady presence in their dreams. Katherine wakes to see the sun just coming up in the eastern sky layered with blue grey clouds and beneath them a thin line of orange running into pink.

"Michael," she says and he opens his eyes.

Sophie presses one paw and then the other into the bedclothes, as if stamping her feet, and squeezes a low groan from her throat. Katherine lays her head on the pillow and watches the rise and fall of Lucy's chest as the sunlight angles through the window and plays across the bed. And then, with no warning, without a sound, the movement is stilled and gone. For a moment she doesn't realize what has happened, her gaze so fixed on the beauty of the light coming through the window, but then she is aware of a depth of quiet in the room that wasn't there before and with a start she looks at Lucy's open eyes and lips parted as if caught in a moment of surprise at something she no longer remembers.

There is a steady moan from Sophie who sniffs along the length of Lucy's thigh to her hip and then her hands and wrists and the little mounds of her breasts. She pulls back her ears and her tail drops low between her legs as she sits back and looks from Michael to Katherine and then at Lucy.

Michael looks at his mother. "Goodbye."

In the palpable presence of the absence that envelops the house, they pick at breakfast and then Katherine goes out to tend the goats while Michael calls the undertaker.

In the afternoon they throw themselves into cleaning the house, beginning with Lucy's room, stripping her bed and clearing away the leavings of her dying. Sophie follows them wherever they go, her agitation growing as night comes on. She stamps her feet and grunts, climbs the stairs and sniffs around Lucy's bed before going from room to room and then up and down the stairs again, the whimpers barely audible above her paws clattering on the floor.

Late in the night Katherine takes Sophie to her bed in Lucy's room and lays her down with gentle strokes before saying good night and going back down the hall. She is reading in bed when she hears a sound that makes her look up to see Sophie standing in the doorway to her room.

"Honey, it's time for bed" she says, leading her back to Lucy's room, but then she is back again, her tail moving back and forth in a fitful, hesitating wag.

"Okay," she says, and gets Sophie's bed to set beside her own, but still Sophie will not settle in, sitting and staring up at Katherine as she reads.

She puts the book aside and they look at each other until Katherine pulls back the covers and climbs out of bed and goes down the hall once again. She stands in the doorway, looking in at the bare mattress and Lucy's empty room. Then she gets fresh linens from the hall closet and makes up the bed. She returns Sophie's bed to it's place in the corner and climb's into Lucy's bed and lies back against the pillows. Sophie's head is down as if in sleep, but her eyes are open and fixed on Katherine. Katherine turns out the light and slides beneath the covers. There is a moment of silence and then a cold, wet nose appears from the darkness and inserts itself beneath her hand. Without a word, she pats the mattress and Sophie leaps onto the bed, circles twice, and lies down along Katherine's hip, and Katherine puts a hand in the soft fur behind her ears and together they sink into something resembling sleep.

On the evening before Lucy's funeral Katherine listens to Michael in the kitchen doing dishes. She reads the same paragraph over and over against the soft background of china on china muffled by water from the tap, when suddenly there is only the water and it is too soon for him to be done. She turns and looks through the doorway. His hands lean against the edge of the sink, his head bowed and his shoulders shaking gently up and down, silent above the running water. She looks at him for a moment before going in to stand behind him and lay her hands on his shoulders and rest her forehead on the tender spot at the base of his neck.

"I tried to tell her," he says.

"Tell her what?"

"That it was all right."

She steps around and looks up into his face. "What was?"

"That she killed my father. I wanted her to know she did the right thing." He looks at her, his eyes full of tears. "I don't know if she heard me."

"I think she did." She looks out the window at the goats standing about the yard in the fading light. "I'll be right back," she says and goes upstairs to Lucy's room and finds the letter in the bureau.

"She wanted you to have this."

He sits at the table and reads, tears streaming down his face.

"Right now I imagine she knows everything she needs to," she says.

"Like your boy."

She looks away.

"You think you failed him," he says, putting the letter in the envelope and looking at her darkening face. "You think there was some risk you should have taken that would've made it come out right."

She shakes her head.

"You kept him safe for five years," he says. "That's a lot."

"But not enough," she says. "It should've been me."

"Well," he says, "it wasn't. You survived and Ethan did not. And I'll tell you something, as a mother's son, if my father had managed to kill me in one of his rages, there'd be nothing more that I'd want than for my mother to be safe from him. And to live. And to remember me and how much I loved her and how much I knew she loved me."

When Katherine begins to cry, Michael leans in close, but careful not to touch her, and when she looks at him she sees the tears on his face and the nod and the little smile.

In the middle of the night Katherine is startled awake by the sound of Michael's voice softly saying her name. She is looking out a window in the living room, breathing hard as she grips the metal catch on top of the lower sash. There is pain in her fingers and she can see in the dim light that she has cut herself on the sharp edge of the mechanism. He says her name and asks if she's all right as he takes her bloody hand and wraps it in a cloth.

He leads her to the kitchen where he turns on the faucet and guides her hand into the water to wash the wound. She lets him hold the finger to the light. "Don't go away," he says, gone and back again, holding her hand over the sink while he pours over it something that stings, but she doesn't pull away, letting him do what he seems to know so well, his fingers sure and gentle as he wraps a bandage around the finger.

They sit at the kitchen table and he asks about the dream and she is surprised at how easily it comes out of her, what little she can remember, as he listens, his elbow on the arm of the chair, his cheek resting in his hand, her drawn to the softness in his eyes that gently pulls the story from her until she is done and they sit in silence before going back upstairs to sleep.

The funeral is held in a small Congregational church on the outskirts of town, the only place Michael can think of other than the house which he thinks will be too small even though he imagines it won't be much of a crowd.

Which it is, barely filling the three front rows. Katherine recognizes only Annie, Hannah, and Walter. Michael points out Lucy's doctor and lawyer and Ruth who grew up in town and came from Boston when she heard the news. There is also the librarian and a few of the curious who had heard of Lucy without knowing her.

There is little in the service that Katherine will remember, sunk too low to pay attention to anything more than Sophie lying at her feet. The minister knew Lucy only in passing and has little to say except what Michael told him on the phone the day before. A few people rise to speak of her. Annie stands beside the casket with her hand resting on the lid and makes a little speech about this giant of a woman in such a tiny body, whose ferocity of heart she hopes to never forget. She is crying before she gets to the end, her big face contorted in pain. There are others — Ruth and the librarian and then Paul Howard. Katherine doesn't hear most of what they say because her attention lingers on Ruth long after she is done speaking, wondering what she knows, being from Boston, if it was her copy of *Pilgrim at Tinker Creek*.

Katherine waits for their eyes to meet and when the moment comes, sees Ruth pause before allowing her face to fall in a sad little smile. Katherine looks away and then toward the front of the church where Annie has turned in her seat to look at her, tears still showing on her face. Katherine turns back to the gentle gaze coming from Ruth, and suddenly feels herself held at the apex of this triangle of women, seen and understood in a grief that only they and Michael can begin to know.

They do not speak on the ride home, nor does Sophie settle in for her customary nap. She is up the entire way, alert and agitated as if needing to be let out. As the car emerges from the woods they can see the dirt piled beside the freshly dug grave, a dark brown wound in the snow. A portion of the fence is laid to one side from the day before when they had to take it out to make room for the backhoe. They pull into the driveway and park by the barn and by the time they've walked around to the front of the house the rest of the cars have parked along the road and the undertakers are sliding the casket out and laying it on the heavy sled they will draw across the snow. Sophie runs ahead and sniffs the box from end to end and then turns to Katherine and Michael, whimpering, her tail hanging low, and Katherine reaches down to touch her as they pass through the little gate and cross to the hole beside the graves of Lucy's parents. The small party assembles as the undertakers slide the casket onto the belts they will use to lower it down. Michael is crying now, his face open and looking up into the bare branches of the maple as the minister intones the familiar words and Katherine reaches out to take his hand, and they are lowering the casket into the ground when Sophie begins to bark, her body angled forward and down as if aiming herself into the hole, hackles bristling along her spine, a harsh, insistent sound, a demand, protesting the loss of something she must have, receding farther and farther out of reach.

7

Wherever Katherine goes, there is Lucy. The sound of her voice, *one bath at a time*, the fierceness in her eyes, the particular creak of her weight upon the floor. Sitting at the kitchen table, Katherine sees the old face looking up at her, *just me*, hears her voice drifting in from the hall outside the bathroom, sees her among the goats from the window of her room, or working in the garden and swatting Sophie away from sniffing her hind end. Or going up into the attic to sit among the books and remember Lucy in the chair, telling the story of her life as she looks out at the driving rain.

It takes all the courage in the world to do the next thing.

It seems to Katherine that she is always crying or on the edge of it no matter what she's doing, whether sitting in Lucy's chair in the library or wheeling a carriage down the aisle of the grocery store, taking down a favorite food of Lucy's, remembering, putting it back on the shelf. It is the second full-hearted grief she has ever allowed herself to know, this sense of utter loss, final, irretrievable, inescapable. She carries it with her night and day and just when it seems unbearable — sitting in the kitchen with Michael telling about the time a goat caught Lucy unaware and sent her flying to the ground, her skirt down around her hips, her black rubber boots at the end of her skinny legs kicking the air as she tried to right herself — and as Katherine remembers the feel of Lucy's back against her own, a wave of sadness washes over her, but then she looks up and sees that Michael is laughing, bent over the table, wiping his eyes, and the sadness gives way to something like joy, that she could have known Lucy Dudley well enough to love and be loved in return. And as Michael's laughter is joined to her own, it comes to her that the agony of loss is inseparable from the joy of having, that grief is nothing more or less than the joining of the two, and then suddenly, unexpected, comes Ethan treading softly into her heart, no haunting apparition, but her little boy, and she closes her eyes and begins to cry, the feel of Michael's hand on hers, shaking her head, "I'm all right. I'm all right."

Even curled up next to Katherine on Lucy's bed, Sophie can sink into nothing deeper than a fitful, agitated sleep. She whimpers inside her dreams, paws and legs jerking and trembling, Katherine's hand against her doing no good.

Katherine comes downstairs to find Michael in the kitchen finishing his breakfast, a suitcase by the door. "I'll be back in a day or two," he says. "Are you sure you'll be all right?"

She nods and waits for him to call her on the lie, but he does not and as she listens to the truck pull out of the driveway, suddenly, for the first time in almost a year, she is alone. The house is enormous as she goes from room to room. She sits on Michael's bed and looks out the window at clouds low in the sky, as if it's about to snow.

She thinks of the women at the funeral and Ruth and the unexpected relief of seeing in her eyes that, yes, she was the one and, yes, she knew it all. Then there was Hannah Rose Parmalee and did she also know, and the unfamiliar comfort of closing her eyes to feel supported by these women, their knowledge of the truth bearing her up, like climbing a rocky cliff in the dark, her leg dangling in the air and finding the next foothold just when it seems she can reach no further and hang on no longer.

After lunch she makes a fire and falls asleep on the couch. She wakes at just past two and looks at Sophie lying before the fire and realizes it's been weeks since she's had a walk. At the sound of the word, Sophie is on her feet and in minutes they are out the door. They go down the driveway and turn left into the road, Katherine throwing snowballs out ahead and Sophie lumbering after.

They follow the road into the trees and Sophie stays with her most of the time with occasional forays into the woods or stopping to sniff the air in the direction of the house. The trees are dark, almost purple beneath a grey sky, and Katherine begins to feel a peace in the solitude of her thoughts that she hasn't known since she was a girl and still under the impression that her life was her own. She calls out to Sophie who looks at her from behind a fallen tree before coming back to the road. Katherine looks at her watch, after 3:00 and soon to be getting dark and the damp chill in the air already enough to make her parka feel thin against it.

"Come on, girl," she says, "time to go home."

She walks on with Sophie lingering behind. A bird flies across the road, too quickly for Katherine to tell what it is, hawk or owl. It lands high in a tree and she can barely make it out among the branches before it takes flight again and she walks along its path to the next tree and the next, paralleling the road. And then it rises above her and she can see it is a hawk and imagines Lucy looking down to where she stands and waves.

She looks about for Sophie, but she is nowhere in sight. She calls her name and waits for the sound of paws on crusty snow, but the air is silent and still. She goes back down the road, calling out her name, stopping to listen, then walking on, her pace quickened by the panic slowly coming in as she struggles to focus her mind.

She stops in the middle of the road and turns slowly to look in every direction, scanning the darkening woods for the slightest sign. "Where the hell are you?"

Then it occurs to her that she may have come out of the woods behind her and be waiting for her return. She turns and goes toward home, quickening her pace to a jog with her breath fogging the air in front of her. A drop of moisture touches her cheek and she realizes it is starting to rain.

By the time the house comes into view it is dark and a fine rain comes steadily down and she can tell by the slippery footing that it's freezing as it hits the cold ground. She goes to the barn, calling out her name, but she is not there. She puts the goats in and goes to the house, leaving the barn door ajar. She lights a fire in the stove and then takes a flashlight and goes out to the car.

She retraces their route along the icy road, the front windows down so she can call out as she goes. Ice is dripping from utility wires and the trees, but the dirt and gravel in the road still provide some traction. She drives a short distance and stops, then another and stops again, listening and shining the light into the woods on either side of the road. When the blacktop comes into view she turns around and repeats the process all the way back to the house and then continues on toward Walter Finch's farm.

"What's the matter?" he says, staring at the purple woven hat on her head.

"I can't find Sophie. Have you seen her?"

"No," he says, "I haven't," taking a step away from the door. "You want to come in and get warm?"

"No. Thanks. I have to keep looking."

"I'll call if I see her," he says, but Katherine is already halfway to the car.

She checks the barn but there are only goats. She sits on a bale of hay and begins to cry, imagining Sophie lying in the woods, injured and slowly freezing to death, her black fur absorbed by the night. It is the worst thing she can imagine to happen now, for Lucy's Sophie to die in the cold, invisible, unheard, and alone.

She goes into the house and checks the front porch before calling Michael.

"How long has she been gone?"

"A couple of hours."

"Labs are pretty tough," he says. "They like the cold and the wet. I've seen them go swimming in winter."

"But she's old."

There is a long pause. "I don't know what to tell you, Katherine."

"Do you think she can find her way home?"

"I'm sure of it," he says.

"Unless she can't walk."

"Right."

"She's got arthritis."

"I know."

She leans against the kitchen wall.

"You must feel terrible," he says. "You want me to come down?"

"No. There's nothing to do but wait. It's pitch black outside and freezing rain."

"I could come in the morning."

"If she's not home by then."

He sighs. "I'm trying to think if there's anything else you could do. Is the barn door open?"

"Yes."

"You could leave the front and back doors ajar."

"Okay."

She pulls a chair from the table and sits down.

"Call me anytime," he says, "even just to talk. And when she gets home."

She hangs up the phone and goes out to the barn and then back to the house to set the doors ajar. Her head aches from hunger and she makes a sandwich but eats only a few bites before pushing it away. It is just past 7:00 and she figures Sophie's been out in the freezing rain for more than four hours, unless she's found some kind of shelter, an abandoned shed, perhaps, or the space beneath a fallen tree. A chill passes through her and she realizes her clothes are wet and goes upstairs and changes and then goes back out to the car. She scrapes the ice from the windshield and lets the motor run before setting off again as far as the highway and then back again to Walter's farm. It is, she realizes, an exercise in futility, driving through the rainy night in search of a black dog somewhere in dark woods extending for miles on either side of the road, all on the off chance that she'll appear in the headlights, tail wagging, glad to be found at last.

Katherine is sitting in the rocking chair where she has been since she got home shortly before 8:00, going out to check the barn every half hour or so. She drifts in and out of a half-sleep that skirts the near edge of a dream until around midnight, when a presence gently pushes her beyond the edge like a soft wind filling a sail. She is walking in the fields behind the barn, the sun low and new in the sky, the air already warm as she follows the path through the woods to the pond. Cool air rises up from the water below and she is half-way there when something moves behind her. She stops and looks to see a fawn among the trees, looking right at her, backlit by sunlight streaming through the woods, making the thin membrane of its ears seem to glow on either side of its head erect and flitting back and forth as if her view of Katherine is obstructed by something moving in-between. Katherine turns to go on but the deer snorts in alarm and bounds upward along the path, its white tail waving like a pennant in the air.

She watches it disappear, wondering why it would run for safety toward an open field and the barn and house beyond.

Then she is sitting on the dock, looking out over the water as a kingfisher flies along the shore, its chirp high and urgent as it passes by. She closes her eyes to the sound of water lapping against the dock, and doesn't notice it at first, the small hand resting lightly on her shoulder. She sits, eyes closed, reaching back and startled to find mostly bone wrapped in a thin sheath of flesh and skin. She turns to see Lucy standing behind her looking down with such a look of concentration as she has never seen, as if she were trying to penetrate through Katherine's eyes to something on the other side, "so beautiful," she says, "and right under your nose," shaking her head, her gaze still fixed on Katherine, "isn't that the way, the most important things, right under your nose," and then suddenly Katherine is awake, her heart beating hard and breath coming fast and shallow, her eyes growing wide, "Oh my God," on her feet and making for the door, pushing her arms into the sleeves of her coat.

She looks from the porch out across the road through the rain. "No," she says, "not all this time." She takes the icy steps one at a time, then down the walk and across the road, her feet breaking through the crust, running and stumbling past the gate into the cemetery.

There are signs of digging all around the mound of dirt that rises from Lucy's grave, paw-sized holes, big enough to admit a nose. Sophie is lying against the far side, out of sight from the road. Katherine kneels and touches the fur soaked with rain, the body hard and dense beneath her hands, showing no sign of life, eyes closed and motionless as Katherine calls out her name in a voice full of protest and mounting rage.

"No!" she screams, rubbing her hands hard across the cold icy body, "Sophie, no! No! NO!"

She is wild, deep inside a billowing fury in her mind. She looks up at the house and then at Sophie and at the house again and then she is on her feet and running through the snow and across the road and around the side of the house to the barn. She feels along the back wall until she finds the toboggan. She drags it out and across the road, tripping and falling as it lurches forward and comes down on her heels. She rolls Sophie onto the toboggan and pulls it toward the house, leaning her whole body against the weight to make it move. At the steps she stops to look at Sophie lying at her feet. She knows she cannot lift her. She has tried it before. But the more she looks at the front door and the light coming through the window and then down at Sophie's lifeless form, the more frantic she becomes, until she runs again to the barn and emerges with a length of rope. Kneeling down, she ties Sophie to the toboggan and then begins to pull her up the stairs. Her feet slip on the ice and she falls and gets up only to fall again. She is screaming now, screaming at the ice and the rain and the weakness in her body and then her feet find a place where the ice has given way and she feels the toboggan follow her up the stairs and onto the porch.

She slams open the door and drags the toboggan into the hall, kicking the door closed and kneeling on the floor. There is no movement, no flicker of the soft skin along the jaw, no faint twitching in the nose. Katherine lays her ear on Sophie's chest where she imagines the heart to be, but there is nothing but the sound of her own panting breath. "Sophie," she says, her face near the old grey muzzle, "come on, girl," closing her eyes, "don't be dead, no, no, no, not dead, not now, no, no," her mind reeling from panic colliding with despair and then she opens her eyes and suddenly throws herself back against the wall, horrified by the sight of Ethan lying in front of her, lifeless and blue. She squirms, frantic to push herself away, to make it go away, blinking her eyes in disbelief, crying out "NO!" again and again, until slowly a force long ago given up for dead and buried deep, rises up inside of her to coalesce into a desperate fury, that propels her to her feet, dragging the toboggan into the kitchen and shoving it in close to the stove. She runs upstairs and draws warm water into the tub, goes to the hall closet and takes down all the towels and lays them on the bathroom floor before running back down to the kitchen. She drags the toboggan to the stairs, lifting and heaving it around the newel post, grunting and screaming to push the strength she needs into the burning muscles of her back and legs and arms. Outside the bathroom she unties the rope and drags the body across the floor to the tub, wrapping her arms around to lift her over the edge and then with all the strength she has left heaving her the rest of the way into the water, knowing now it is Sophie and not Ethan in her hands, but the thought not registering on her mind, the two of them now one, the boy and the dog, a single life slipping away. Sophie's head goes under and Katherine quickly scoops it into the air, leaning forward against the tub. She moves her fingers across the fur but Sophie doesn't move and even in the water feels cold in Katherine's hands. But she does not relent as the wildness inside her settles into something deeper, a slow rhythm of moving water and the sound of her voice speaking Sophie's name, alternately soothing and gently coaxing, "Sweet baby, my girl, what'd you do that for? Did you miss her so much? Were you trying to find your mother, girl?"

She closes her eyes around the tears running down her face, slowly losing track of time, the words and water and Sophie's body beneath her hands blending into a seamless flow of touch and sound, lowering her down into the reality of loss, the bottomless depth of a mother's failure to save her own child. And then something registers in her mind, faint and far away, a movement so slight she barely notices, but enough to make her open her eyes and look down at Sophie lying in the water just as before, and yet still showing no sign of life. She stares at her for a moment and then holds a wet finger in front of Sophie's nose and closes her eyes to focus all her attention on the front and back sides of the finger and as a tiny puff of breeze cools the front side faster than the back, Katherine takes in a sudden gasp and her eyes grow wide in amazement as her cry comes out in a single wracking sob.

She reaches down and pulls Sophie from the water and over the edge and sets her on the towels laid on the floor. Quickly she rubs her up and down and then rolls her onto fresh towels and drags her into the hall and through the door to Lucy's room. She looks for a moment at the round bed in the corner before pulling back the covers and with one final heave lifting Sophie from the floor onto the mattress. She lays her head on the pillow and climbs in beside her, drawing the covers over them both.

Katherine turns out the light and lies in the darkness, the tears and sobs pouring out of her again, her hand against the fur along Sophie's chest and belly, the skin beginning to warm, and by the time exhaustion overtakes her grief and drops her into sleep, they are breathing together in a soft synchronicity that will appear in Katherine's dreams as a sound as comforting and deep as the beating of a mother's heart.

Michael calls the state police at just past 4:00a.m. and when they tell him most roads are sanded and safe, in a few minutes he's on his way.

When he steps onto the back porch he notices the door slightly ajar. The house is cold and a long puddle of water stands in the front hall. He turns on the furnace and goes upstairs.

On the landing he notices wet towels strewn about and the toboggan just outside the bathroom door. Through the doorway to Lucy's room he sees Katherine beneath the covers, lying on her side with her back facing him. Seeing no sign of Sophie, he goes quietly down the hall, looking into the bathroom where more wet towels are draped on the tub still half-full of water. Something fine and black floats on the surface. He steps in closer and sees that it's fur.

"Michael?"

He steps into the hall. "Yes."

"We're in here."

Around the corner of the bed he sees Sophie's head on the pillow, like an old lady, he thinks, grey whiskered and lacking only a sleeping cap. Her eyes are open and move toward the sound of his voice but her body remains still beneath the covers. Katherine gently rubs her face. Taking a chair from the corner, Michael sits down beside the bed.

"She was on the grave," says Katherine. "She was frozen. I was sure she was dead."

"But not entirely sure," he says, smiling.

"No."

"You brought her back."

She shakes her head. "It was the least I could do after being so stupid to not think of it before."

"I didn't either. I wouldn't figure a dog for suicide. Or whatever it was."

He passes his hand down the length of Sophie's body. "She's a tough old girl."

"Like her mother."

"I didn't know her mother," he says and then looks up at Katherine and realizes who she meant.

"You think she was tough?" he says.

"Among other things."

"Well," he says, "it looks like you're the mother now."

Sophie is slow and lethargic all day long. She stands at the edge of the bed, legs trembling and tail hung low, until they lift her to the floor, and at the top of the stairs she waits again until they grab hold and carry her down.

In the afternoon Michael waits for Walter to deliver a load of hay while Katherine drives Sophie into town for a visit to the vet who takes a blood sample to check for liver and kidney damage.

"She looks okay to me," he says. "It takes a lot of cold to kill a dog. Labs especially. It's a good thing she wasn't out there all night, though."

He looks at Katherine, taking in the measure of her small stature. "The bath was a good idea. How'd you ever get her up there?"

"A toboggan," she says, shaking her head. "I tied her to a toboggan."

"No kidding," he says. "Well, whatever works."

Michael and Walter bring the hay into the barn, Michael deferring to Walter's habit of working in silence. When they're done they stand in the side doorway and look out across the field to the line of trees beyond.

"How are you holding up?" says Walter.

"All right, I guess," he says, pauses, and then, "I miss my mother."

"Yes," says Walter, "I'll bet you do. I miss her, too." He sighs. "She had a hard life. Up to a point."

"I know about my father."

Walter puts his hands in his pockets and shifts from one foot to the other.

"It was unforgivable, what he did to her," says Walter, his voice measured and slow. "There's others like him around here, beat their wives. I never understood it. They deserve whatever they get."

Michael looks at him until Walter turns his head and their eyes meet.

"I know what he got, Walter."

The muscles in the old man's face, already sagging with age, seem suddenly to let go.

"It's all right, Walter. She told me. He was my father and he deserved what he got."

"She told you about me?"

"No. That was a guess. I knew she'd need some help."

"I'd've killed him myself if she'd asked," says Walter, his voice trembling, "but she didn't. So, I just helped clean up. I guess that makes me. . . what do you call it?"

"A friend," says Michael, "who loved her."

Walter shakes his head. "A man'd be a fool not to. But she was never that way about me, and I've always had Margaret, which was enough. Besides, I was never smart enough for your mother."

"Who was?"

Walter smiles and looks down. "You won't tell anyone."

Michael turns and holds out his hand which Walter takes in his own.

"Thank you, Walter," he says, looking into his eyes, "for being such a good friend to my mother. I will always be grateful for that."

The old man looks at him through eyes brimming with tears. "You're very welcome, Michael. It was the least a man could do."

Michael stands in the kitchen, a small duffle in his hand. "You going to be okay?" he says.

"I think so," she says, believing herself for the first time she can remember.

He draws her into his arms and then, stepping back, says, "bye" and "I'll see you soon" and turns and is out the door.

Katherine takes Sophie wherever she goes. She pulls her bed in close to Lucy's, which has now become her own, and they sleep together, their breath mingling in the night.

In the morning Katherine lies in bed to look out the east window and consider what she'll do with the next day in the expanse of time stretching out before her. She contemplates breakfast and walking among the goats, going into town or exploring back country roads. Sophie stands beside the bed and stamps her feet until Katherine beckons her up.

On some mornings she imagines Lucy sitting beside her, the talk gentle and low until the presence fades and with a sigh Katherine throws back the covers and swings herself out of bed.

Her sleep is dreamless for weeks at a time, until one night she finds herself running along a familiar street, her body heavy with dread and panic, the sound of footsteps close behind and then silence as they fade only to emerge again from the shadows all around. Still she runs, not daring to call out or even think his name, the sweat on her face and her lungs aching as she feels him gain on her with every step. And then suddenly at the far end of the road is the figure of a woman watching her approach, holding up a hand that slows Katherine to a walk as behind her she feels him narrowing the gap, the palpable nearness of his rage as still she walks on, her breathing slowed by the calm and steady look in the woman's eyes. Then the woman nods and Katherine turns to meet the onslaught bearing down on her, the murderous firestorm of rage that seems to suck the air from her lungs as she closes her eyes to brace for the annihilating blow, but instead her mind coming clear with the recognition of a great wind moving through her, finding no resistance in the empty space of the smallest particles of her being letting go their bonds to one another for the instant it takes for the awful specter to pass through and out the other side. She rocks slowly back and forth like a tall tree in a fading wind, the only sound her breathing in and breathing out, opening her eyes to see she is once again alone, the night still and quiet as she sets off down the road toward home.

8

*A*s the snow deepens in the middle of the Vermont winter, Katherine's life takes on a steady and unremarkable rhythm. She wakes early and after breakfast she sits in the library and reads. She writes in her journal, long paragraphs at first that gradually give way to the ragged edge of verse. In the afternoon she splits wood for the stove, cleans out the barn, or when the sky hangs thick and grey over the hills, settles in for a nap. Michael comes on week-ends to stack hay or shovel snow or mend the occasional shutter that comes loose in the wind. He teaches her the use of snowshoes which allow her to go out across the fields.

Sophie becomes stronger and joins Katherine for trips into town. She stays in the car outside the grocery store — standing on the back seat, nose against the glass — but comes along for visits to the bookstore, camping out in the corner by the window. When customers come in and disturb the little bell above the door, Sophie raises her head and murmurs in alarm, but Katherine gently takes hold of her and speaks to her in soothing tones. Soon they are a familiar sight among the locals and people she doesn't know nod and smile and say hello.

"You getting lonely?" says Annie.

"Sometimes. Michael comes to visit. I have Sophie."

"Not much of a talker."

"You'd be surprised."

"I bet not. Winter up here can be hard on a person, dog or no. You start talking to yourself."

"I do that anyway," says Katherine. "I'm okay."

"Maybe so. But if you ever want company, let me know. I can pack my little overnight bag and we can have a slumber party."

Katherine looks down and feels her face grow warm.

"Just a thought," says Annie, looking out the window.

Katherine turns and looks to see Hannah Rose Parmalee coming up the sidewalk.

"You might give her a try sometime," Annie says.

Katherine looks away. "Does she know about me?"

"She does."

"You told her."

"I did." Annie is still looking out the window as Hannah pauses outside Dewalt's. "Town's too small and life's too short," she says with a sigh. "I told her because I believe she's someone you could stand to know what happened."

"Lucy wouldn't have told her," say Katherine, looking away.

"Oh, yes she would. She asked me to. The last day I came to see her."

The bell over the door rings and Katherine lifts her head to the sight of Hannah stepping into the shop and looking in their direction.

"Good morning," she says, red hair flaring out from beneath her hat. Sophie thumps her tail against the floor as Katherine watches Hannah walk toward them, stopping several feet away and dropping to her haunches with a marriage of strength and ease, her voice gentle and high in her throat as she extends a hand to Sophie, palm turned up as if to reveal an offering, leaving it to Sophie to decide the terms of their meeting. And Katherine cannot help but notice the hand — long-fingered and steady in the air as if floating without effort — and wonder what are the tides these hands know how to move.

Sophie rolls onto her back, front legs in the air, paws flopped over like limp wrists, and sweeps her tail across the floor.

Kneeling over Sophie's upturned belly, Hannah looks up into Katherine's face and asks her how she is and Katherine says she's fine and the gaze between them reveals both the plainness of the lie and the willingness to let it be.

The talk turns to weather and the novel in Katherine's lap and the declining quality of coffee at Dewalt's and then Hannah gets up to leave with a parting rub on Sophie's belly and a wave as she steps out the door.

Katherine draws a bath and sits on the edge of the tub to watch the water rise. She thinks of Hannah, the smell of her, a light scent of oil rising from her hands. She turns off the water and drops her robe around her feet to step into the tub. She lies back and looks down the length of her body, closing her eyes to imagine something like a tide moving through her. But there is only a dense stillness, a lack of feeling going back so far she can hardly remember it being any other way. She has no idea of the last time her hand wandered to the soft opening between her legs, her fingers bearing her aloft on wave after wave of pleasure. Now it is only to wash herself that she goes there and without considering anything else.

Michael's face appears in her mind and she remembers his body held loosely in her arms and tries to recall a feeling that went with it, some sensation in her hands or breasts or belly or hips or thighs or where her feet met the floor. But his body, it seems, shows little affinity for hers. There was the hug on the front porch, she thinks, so tender and yet tentative with no pull in her direction. She wonders if he's gay or if he simply finds nothing about her attractive, seeing only a damaged, ruined woman when he looks at her, to be pitied and helped but nothing more. And then she thinks of Hannah kneeling down in front of Sophie and wonders if Michael has been just this way almost from the beginning, his hand held out to offer something she cannot see.

A week past Valentine's Day Katherine steps into Annie's shop and notices a display of greeting cards splashed with red hearts and thinks Annie should weed them out since the day has passed. It isn't until she's sitting in the corner and scanning the same paragraph over and over without a clue of what she's reading, that she remembers that the day her world exploded and collapsed around her was her birthday, February 24th, beneath the sign of Pisces, the fish who swims in the sea.

She looks at Annie sitting in her glassed-in office in the corner, who suddenly looks up at her.

"What?" she calls out.

"Nothing."

"Bullshit," says Annie, her mouth stretching in a smile that seems to go from one side of her face to the other.

Their eyes meet for a moment and then Annie shrugs and looks back down at her desk.

Katherine gets out of the chair and walks across the store to where Annie looks up and makes a self-satisfied little smile, knowing she was right and content to wait it out.

"I'm coming up on an anniversary," says Katherine.

Annie leans back in the chair.

"It'll be a year on the 24th."

Annie nods. "Then we should do something."

"I have no idea."

"Me neither. But you shouldn't be alone. I'll pack my little bag."

"That's okay," says Katherine, backing away, shaking her head.

"I will."

"No, it's all right, really," and Katherine stands there for a moment, trying to think of what to say, how to avoid Annie looking at her and waiting for her to change her mind, which Katherine knows she will, because it is the next thing.

"You wouldn't mind?"

"Hell no."

Katherine blinks away the tears.

"But will I be enough?" says Annie. "You need to be surrounded and there's not enough of me for that."

"I could ask Michael."

"And Hannah."

Katherine looks away, then slowly back. "Okay."

Michael comes in the night before and Hannah and Annie just after breakfast. Katherine worries there won't be anything to do and dreads the focus turning on her. She jumps at the sound of the car turning into the driveway, but settles down when the two women stride through the door and smile at her and set to making coffee as Michael joins them and the kitchen fills with talk about everything but her and the day. There are awkward moments when looks pass among them that Katherine doesn't see, glances in her direction, smiles out of place in the conversation. But nothing more, until Annie wades in as they all sit around the kitchen table over lunch.

"So what were you doing this time a year ago?"

Katherine stares at a point in the air just above the table, then turns to glance at the clock on the wall. "Recess," she says. "I was out at recess with the children."

"You're a teacher."

"I was."

They go for a walk and the questions come gentle and slow with long stretches of silence in between, or idle talk — what's for supper or how to tell a particular tree in winter. But she knows from the way they measure their pace and lean in that they're hearing every word. She has told the story so many times to Lucy and then to Michael, but this is something new, not a secret passed from one hiding place to another, but emerging into the open above the road and among the trees and breathing the air in the fading light, no longer held inside of her but finding something larger to contain and bear it along.

They cook supper making creative use of what they've assembled — an odd lot of vegetables and fruit, chicken, a loaf of bread from Dewalt's, bottles of wine. Katherine pauses in her slicing of carrots, closing her eyes to listen to the friendly talk sprinkled with bits of laughter, so normal and unremarkable she finds it astonishing that such a thing would find its way into this of all nights. As they sit around the table she looks from one to the other and then holds out her hands to Annie on her left and Michael on her right and tears come into her eyes as the circle is complete.

She is sitting at the table and watching them clean up when she notices the light in the kitchen, the evening glow against the darkened windows, and knows she only need close her eyes to be there again, that to enter the past it takes nothing more than a veil drawn across the present. She gets up and takes her glass of wine to the front porch and sits in the swing, voices drifting out from the kitchen, and then a pair of headlights comes out of the woods and down the road toward the house, and when the car draws abreast and passes by, she lifts the glass in the gesture of a toast and feels Lucy on the swing beside her and her eyes fill with tears. Then the door opens and closes and Annie leans over her shoulder, asking how she's doing, and Katherine's soft reply, "all right," and Michael at the door, "how about a fire in the living room," and Annie taking her by the hand, "come on."

Katherine is on the couch with Annie on one side and Hannah on the other. Sticks of kindling pop and snap as Michael slides a cushion from an easy chair onto the floor and sits beside Katherine's legs, his back leaning into the couch. Sophie stands in front, tail wagging, a little moan in her throat until Michael pats the floor and she lies down on Katherine's feet.

"I'd say you're properly surrounded," says Annie. "Whatever it is will have to get through all of us to get to you."

"I wish it were as simple as that."

"Maybe it is," says Michael.

She feels the closeness of the women's bodies and wishes Lucy were still alive, beside her and looking into the fire.

She waits for questions that do not come. The flames climb over the split oak, reaching toward a round of birch on top. As silence deepens into a presence of its own, she waits for restlessness, but this, too, does not appear. Slowly, by degrees, she loses track of time as if they might sit here together all through the night, safe and held by one another and the warmth of the fire. She closes her eyes and feels herself let down in a gentle descent into her heart, but then her mind begins to wander to the past and she opens her eyes to stare into the fire.

Michael rearranges the logs and then stands with his back to the flames stirring up behind him. He looks at her and she at him, her face smooth in the soft light cast by the fire. It seems remarkable to him, how calm she is, nothing like what he'd imagined. He tries to picture her in the kitchen, covered in blood, the moment she realized Ethan was gone, and feels a depth of sadness he thought he'd left behind a long time ago.

Katherine sees something in his eyes she hasn't seen before, a steady and gentle look, patient and unadorned like a father watching over a feverish child. It is then that he sees a small line appear in her smooth facade, like a hairline crazing in a ceramic glaze yielding to the pressure of a shifting underneath, a small tremor curling her lips and spreading across her face, loosening her cheeks and drawing her eyes downward. He kneels in front of her and looks into her face and she wants to look away but cannot, feeling the question in his eyes, open and waiting.

"I miss him so much," she says and he nods and reaches up and wipes away a tear. "I still can't believe he's really gone. Sometimes it seems so far away, like it never happened at all. And other times it's all there is, the only thing that ever was." She is rocking slowly forward and back to comfort herself when she feels the women draw closer in, holding her in a way that seems so long ago and strange and yet so elemental that it finally releases the tears down her face. She lets it come, unable to resist, until finally she sits among them, held by a stillness that fills the room.

She lays her head on Annie's shoulder and as she feels her arms come around her, lays her head in the broad expanse of Annie's lap. Hannah picks up Katherine's legs and lays them on the couch. Michael shakes out a blanket and settles it over her and then goes back to his place on the floor. They sit in silence before the fire, Annie stroking Katherine's hair.

At just past midnight Hannah kneels on the floor beside her. "I have to go," she says in a hushed voice. "I wish I didn't. But it's late and I have clients in the morning."

Katherine nods, her eyes sleepy.

"I'd like to give you something," says Hannah.

"You already have."

"I know. But something else. Come in for a session sometime. On me."

They look at each other, their faces close, and then Hannah touches her lips between Katherine's eyes. "Good night."

"Good night," says Katherine. "Thank you."

She hears the back door close and looks up into Annie's face. "Don't you have to go?"

"Not tonight," says Annie. "I have little elves who take care of the store when I have to be away. I'm not going anywhere." Her face becomes serious. "You will not be alone tonight. Not for a minute. Unless that's what you want."

Katherine looks at Michael who smiles and shrugs. "You're stuck with us."

They sit and talk in the firelight and Annie wonders aloud what Katherine will do now. "You could always teach."

"I don't know."

"You've forgotten how?"

Katherine shakes her head.

"Sounds like a teacher to me," says Michael.

"I don't know if I could be around children so much."

"Maybe not," says Annie, "and maybe you could."

"And live up here," says Katherine.

Michael shrugs, "You have to live somewhere."

Katherine opens her eyes and looks up into Annie's face. "You were asleep," says Annie.

"I was?"

Annie smiles and nods.

As the sky begins to lighten behind the eastern hills they are in the kitchen eating breakfast. Then they climb the stairs to sleep the morning away.

Katherine wakes at just past noon and lies in bed looking out the window at the air thick with snow. The house is still. Sophie stays in bed as Katherine steps quietly from the room and down the stairs. She puts a kettle on and sits at the long table and looks through the doorway to the library and the chair in front of the east window.

I forgive you.

The afternoon passes quietly except for the plow passing once or twice before the snow stops around 3:00. Katherine sits in the rocking chair and reads while Michael's and Annie's voices drift in from the kitchen. They all go out for a walk before dark. The snow is just wet enough for packing and a snowball fight ensues from an accident, a glop of snow that falls from an overhanging branch, which Annie takes to have been deliberate and of human origin. It begins as a free for all, but after scoring a few direct hits Michael finds himself besieged by a fury of women who chase him all the way home.

Annie leaves after supper, dropping her bag by the back door to take Katherine in her arms. "You keep going," she says and Katherine nods and follows her onto the porch and watches her drive away.

"Do you want me to stay the night?" he says. "Or would you like the house to yourself?"

"What about you?"

"Either way is fine with me. Tell me what you need."

"You can go."

When they say goodbye the hug is neither awkward nor brief. "If you want some company," he says, "give me a call. Or write. I prefer letters." He leans down and picks up his bag. "I'd like to hear from you, actually. Or see you. And of course if the furnace blows up or something, just let me know." He opens the door. "But it's up to you."

She listens to the truck going down the driveway and onto the road and then the silence closing in behind. She adds a log to the fire and puts a kettle on for tea before going out to settle the goats in for the night.

9

*K*atherine waits more than a week before going into town. Annie, Michael, and Hannah call to see how she's doing, but she has little to say. She enjoys the quiet of lying in bed in the morning and snowshoeing out behind the barn and along the line of trees, stopping to look up at the sky. She sits among the goats as Lucy used to do, her eyes closed as they huddle in around her. She writes poetry in her journal, first phrases and single lines, then stringing them together to form something larger and closer to being whole.

Often the house feels large and strange and empty, and when the sun goes down and the March wind throws itself against the window, she imagines Annie packing her little bag.

She parks up the street from the bookstore and climbs the stairs to Hannah's office with Sophie close behind. There is sunlight through a skylight in the hall and the office door is open. When Katherine leans her head into the room, Hannah is looking down at an appointment book on a high writing desk. She's wearing loose cotton pants and a t-shirt and her feet are bare against the floor. She looks up and smiles and says hello and there is an awkward silence as Katherine stands just outside the room.

"How are you?"

"Okay," says Katherine. "Thank you again for coming last week."

"You're welcome."

A silence longer than before.

"You all right?"

Katherine tries to take a deep breath, but cannot.

"God," she says, shaking her head, "I had all kinds of courage coming up the stairs."

"Why don't you come in and look around. I don't have anyone for awhile."

She follows Hannah into a large and airy room with a high padded table and a view of sky and trees through windows along the length of the wall. Plants hang from the ceiling and on a wall there are colored charts showing the structure of the human body. From a far corner comes soft music, cello and piano, and there is a faint smell of scented oil.

"It's nice," says Katherine.

"It's a good place to work."

"What do you do, exactly?"

Hannah looks at her for a moment and Katherine wonders if she said something wrong until Hannah makes a little smile. "I suppose you could say I try to help people get their bodies back." She goes to the window and sits on the sill. "When bad things happen, the body stores it up and, in a way, you become what was done to you. And then you get like the Tin Man in *The Wizard of Oz*."

"All rusted up."

"Right. And not much life getting through."

"And you think that's me."

There is a look of carefully measured tenderness in Hannah's face. "Well, it's all of us to some degree, but, yes, you more than most. Much more."

Katherine passes her hand over the sheet that covers the table. "What would you do. . . with someone like me?"

"Very little at first. I'd want you to feel safe and comfortable more than anything."

"I wouldn't have to take off my clothes."

"No. Or do anything else you didn't want."

Katherine is staring at a patch of sunlight on the floor. "This takes a long time," she says, not looking up.

"Yes. It does."

She nods. "I've got to go."

"Okay."

In the evening she dials Hannah's number and a machine answers. She hangs up before the beep. An hour later she calls again.

"Hi," she says, "it's Katherine," picturing her voice in the darkened office with no one there to hear. "I thought I'd come see you. When you have time. You could call and tell me when." Her words drop into the silence like pebbles in a well, and suddenly she feels foolish and wishes she could take it back but then there is another beep and she hangs up the phone.

She feels the heavy burden of the mistake she thinks she's made. She takes a bath and avoids looking at her body, like a nun dressing beneath a sheet. In bed she cannot sleep. Just before dawn she dreams of walking beneath a sky full of large black birds and wakes with a start, bathed in sweat.

Late in the morning Hannah calls to tell her she can come this afternoon, around 4:00, and Katherine stands by the phone, going back and forth between longing and fear. "Okay," she says, and is hanging up the phone when she suddenly pulls it back to say "thank you," but Hannah is no longer there.

With the exception of an occasional hug, no one has touched Katherine since she left the hospital almost a year ago. Only Lucy has seen what was done to her and even she did not reach out to touch what she saw. Katherine can think of nothing else as she drives to town, that someone will know the true extent of her ruination, feel it beneath her hands, seeking out the tides that are no longer there.

"Just put your coat anywhere," says Hannah, "and take off your shoes and socks before you get on the table. You can lie on your back or your stomach. It's up to you. There's a sheet you can get under if you like. I'll be back in a few minutes. Take your time."

The door closes and Katherine stands beside the table, feeling the stillness in the room settling in around her, and then takes off her coat and lays it on the back of a chair. The rug is soft against her feet as she steps to the table and lies down, first on her back and then her stomach and then her back again. There is a soft rap on the door and when it opens she is careful not to move, like a child pretending sleep, closing her eyes and listening to Hannah move about. There is music, a piano wandering through a melody, and then Hannah sitting down and laying a hand on Katherine's shoulder as she sits behind her head.

"Are you comfortable?"

"I'm okay."

Katherine feels her head gently raised as Hannah makes a cradle of her hands. Katherine waits for her to move, but the hands are still as she continues to wait, wondering what this is, lying there and being held, until unable to bear the suspense she opens her eyes and looks up into Hannah's face. Her head is slightly forward as if listening and her eyes are closed. Katherine looks at her, the muscles in her face smooth and calm, and then feels her eyes closing again as if heavy with sleep and slowly, irresistibly drawn down, the muscles in her head and neck giving in one by one to the warm embrace. She feels fingertips against the soft spot at the base of her skull, the place where her hand would always come to rest when she felt most tender toward Ethan as he bowed his head in sadness or regret for something he had done, vulnerable and laid low. And tears come into her eyes, the tenderness all but unbearable, wanting to get off the table but unable to move for the weight of her own need bearing down upon her, tears flowing from the corners of her eyes and into Hannah's hands.

Hannah slowly withdraws her hands and lays Katherine's head on a pillow. "Take your time. Get up when you're ready. I'll be outside."

The door closes and Katherine is alone except for Sophie sleeping in the corner. She looks up at the ceiling, the room bathed in the half light of dusk. She glances at her watch. She has been here for more than an hour.

She is startled by the light when she steps into the waiting room. Hannah looks at her and smiles.

"How do you feel?"

"I don't know."

"That's okay."

Katherine stands for a moment and looks at the floor, then up at Hannah. "Can I come back?"

"Of course."

"It means touching me, doesn't it. More than today."

"Yes."

Katherine has to work to make the breaths go in and out.

"That bothers you," says Hannah.

"Yes."

"We can go slow."

"And I don't have much money."

"We'll work it out. I have clients with less money than you. We're a long ways from Boston."

A week later Katherine comes to Hannah for a second time. They begin as before, and then she hears the stool moved to the side of the table and Hannah lifts Katherine's hand from where it rests on her belly and slowly begins to massage the fingers, working down each knuckle and joint to the palm and then from the wrist to the elbow.

"If you can, try letting go of this arm," says Hannah, her voice soft. "Keep the other one, but see if you can give this one up for just a little while. When you breathe, imagine the air going into your lungs and then down your arm. Imagine it full of air."

Katherine tries but cannot let go of the arm, wanting to pull it away.

After awhile, Hannah moves the stool to the other side and takes up the other arm. There is a moment when Katherine enjoys the touch along her fingers and the milking motion toward the elbow, but soon she wants the arm back and Hannah can feel the stiffening against her.

In the waiting room Katherine sits in a chair by the door. "Am I as pathetic as I feel?"

"No," says Hannah, "I'm sure you're not. I won't kid you, though, your body is a train wreck right now. You're very frozen, but if you weren't, you'd probably be dead. Or out of your mind." Hannah pulls a chair in close and sits down. "It's like freezing to death," she says, "and the body survives by shutting down and withdrawing deep into itself. When I sit with you, I can feel how you did something like that, buried your life under all this fear and grief and pain, so deep inside you don't even know it's there anymore. So, in a way, it's true, it's a real train wreck in there. But the miracle is that it's also a very clever way to survive when all else fails. Which you did."

Michael and Katherine linger at the table after lunch. "I've been wanting to ask you," she says, "about when you came back from Vietnam, how you dealt with it."

"Badly."

"But you seem okay now."

"I'm a long way from that," he says, shaking his head and slowly moving the salt shaker back and forth between his fingers. "Do you know last week I was in the grocery store and I swear to God there was lieutenant Duc holding a quart of blood in his hand. It wasn't him and the jar was spaghetti sauce, but for a second I was right there with him."

He sprinkles a little salt onto the table and tries to balance the shaker on its edge among the grains. "There's no way I can be a man this didn't happen to. The best I can do is live with it."

"But how?"

"I don't know," he says, "but I'll tell you one thing. You're way ahead of where I was when I got back. I didn't know how to ask for help and nobody seemed to mind it much when I went away. And it didn't help that people didn't want to know what really happened."

"Not even Lucy?"

"She did the best she could. But she knew me as this boy who was always okay, and now I wasn't. Depressed all the time, crawling out of my skin, not feeling anything at all. Always off balance, up all night, sleeping all day. She didn't know what to do, and I could tell how much it hurt her to see me that way, which is why I left."

"You disappeared."

"I tried."

"Sometimes that's all I want to do."

"I know. But it's not all it's cracked up to be."

Evening comes, but neither seems to notice in the glow cast by the fire in the stove.

Michael leans back in his chair as he talks, hands behind his head. She looks into his eyes, that seem old and sad.

"I tried to find out what was left of my life," he says, "and get it back. After detox, it was all I could do to focus on simple things — sleep, eat, take a bath, go for a walk, get a haircut. Be with people, be alone. Feel something in my body again. Not be scared all the time."

He turns his attention to the salt shaker, holds it still over the grains of salt, lets it go, watches it fall, shrugs.

"I fucked up a lot. But every once in a while there'd be this little bit of beauty," he says, holding up a tiny space between his fingers, "or feeling good, almost alive. I found this apartment in Burlington with a window facing west and I started making a point of being there to watch the sun go down. The thing is that what they take from you is really huge and you only get it back a little at time, so it seems impossible. But it's not."

He sits back and opens his fingers, leaving the saltshaker balancing on a few grains of salt.

"Taadaaaa."

10

*H*annah Rose Parmalee sits in her office, a mug of coffee in her hand. It is the middle of April and she is waiting for Katherine and for spring. She stares out the window at the sky, grey with a line of blue running along the ridge of western hills. Hovering in her mind is the feel of Katherine's body beneath her hands. She has been coming twice a week for more than a month, some weeks more. The trauma that she brings into the room is palpable, hardening and cooling the body as if to mimic death.

Hannah has worked her way in slowly from Katherine's arms and legs and only last week touched her back, and even then without touching skin. Katherine lay on her stomach, hands at her sides, rhythmically tapping her thumb against the tip of each finger until Hannah cupped her hand to still the motion.

Through the window she watches Katherine cross the street, Sophie at her side. She notices the slump in her shoulders, still anticipating the blow, and feels suddenly angry and tries to remember his name, but cannot.

She begins as before but then asks Katherine to roll on her stomach and slowly inserts her hand beneath her sweater and lays it against her skin that is barely warm, almost cool.

"I want you to focus on the place where your skin touches mine.

"Feel the weight of my hand. And the warmth.

"Feel how your body pushes back, supporting the weight.

"Feel the rise and fall with every breath, how we move together as you breathe."

Katherine listens to the voice and feels her body rising into the hand that seems enormous now, as if spanning her entire back, and her eyes fill with tears.

Katherine returns three days later and it goes as before. Afterward they are sitting in the waiting room. "I need to try something different next time," says Hannah.

Katherine looks away.

"I have to touch your skin, Katherine, if I'm going to help you. It's essential."

"You want me to take off my clothes."

"Some. Not all. And there'll be a sheet everywhere except where I'm working."

"You can't do it some other way."

Hannah shakes her head. "I know this is hard. And you probably think I have no idea how hard it is, but you have to trust that I do." Hannah pulls her chair in front of Katherine and cradles her hands in her own. "Your body's been carrying you for so long, storing up so much fear and pain and all that was taken from you. It has protected you well. It got you here. But now it's like a prison and you can't get out unless you let it go so that it can let go of all that horror and give you back your life."

Katherine stares down at Hannah's hands.

"You have so much courage," says Hannah, "don't let go of it now."

There is a long silence and then Katherine takes her hand and wipes her eyes and nods.

"Bring Lucy with you," says Hannah. "Put her in your pocket." Then she leans down and looks up into Katherine's face. "We can do this, Katherine. You can do this."

The next day Katherine makes a call to Christine Bartlett, the principal of her old school. It's the first time they've spoken since her last day at school.

She tells her where she's calling from and Christine seems surprised. "Way up there?"

"I might stay here for awhile. There may be an opening. I'll need a recommendation. One good enough to get me the job."

In the silence Katherine tries to picture her standing in her office, her voice competing with the steady din of children in the hall.

"Give me the name and address," she says. "I'll be happy to."

Going to Montpelier is Annie's idea. "It's a funky town," she says. "I mean, it's the state capitol and it's got a college or two, but it's *Vermont*, you know? Like *Northern Exposure* without the dog sleds and mukluks. You'll have a terrific time. And besides, they have a great used book store."

Katherine gives Annie a disbelieving look.

Annie shrugs. "On your budget, you need used. Just be my friend. I don't need more customers."

Katherine drives down on a Thursday morning, the sky dotted with white clouds and the air warming as she goes farther south. She parks on the main street and walks from one end to the other, noting the banner across the steps leading into the community theater, a Ben and Jerry's ice cream shop, and just across the street a display of used books beneath a weathered awning. Inside the shop there is the smell of old bindings and pages scented with the oil of countless fingers. She stands between the rows of bookcases, the wide pine boards beneath her feet, and scans the titles, occasionally opening one to read a paragraph or two. From the corner of her eye she notices the figure of a woman standing by the far wall, small and grey haired, and watches the long thin fingers turn the pages, the head slowly nodding up and down.

She buys three novels and a book of poems by an unfamiliar poet and then walks up the street to a restaurant that Annie recommended. There are small tables along the sidewalk and she sits and feels the sun on her face. She watches people going by and tries to imagine their lives, and if they could possibly imagine hers as they glance down at this woman with her small shopping bag of books.

She stands beside the table and waits for the sound of Hannah closing the door behind her, wondering what she has in mind, if there's a way to stretch minutes into days or weeks or something longer. She puts her hand in her pocket where she tried to imagine putting Lucy that morning as she stood in the barn, closing her eyes, the smell of hay, Lucy in the palm of her hand, looking up at into her face, *the next thing*.

She removes her shoes and socks and then sits on the table and looks out the window at the sky. Slowly she unbuttons her shirt and follows with her eyes the line along her belly, then slides off the table and unbuttons her pants and lets them drop to the floor. She moves as in a dream, watching herself go through the motions of doing what needs to be done. Stepping out of the pants, she slips the shirt off her shoulders, letting it fall as she climbs onto the table and pulls up the sheet. She turns on her side and looks out the window and remembers the night Lucy saw her and the breathless hush in her voice when she said, "Oh, my," and wonders what Hannah will say now.

The door opens and closes, the hand on her shoulder, the gentle voice, "over on your tummy," and then, settling in, "tell me if you need me to stop. . .if anything's not okay."

Hannah stands at Katherine's head and rests her hands across her back before working slowly along the spine and the muscles fanning out to either side, seeking out the hardness, pressing sinew against bone until Katherine cries out in pain. But Hannah does not relent until she feels some crack in the frozen stiffness as it begins to give way. Katherine holds her breath to steel herself against the pain, but then there is Hannah's voice telling her to breathe, to fill her lungs and imagine the air flowing to the pain. With each breath she swells upward into Hannah's hands and suddenly she is expanding into the pain, crying out and barely noticing when Hannah pulls the sheet away to reveal the gentle rise of buttock below the waist and lays her hands along the scars and the touch feels hot as Katherine realizes what has happened and where the heat is coming from. Soft and strong, the hands work along her waist and down across the broad muscles that girdle her hips as Katherine floats inside herself, borne along by the pulsing of her life flowing in and out across the membranes of the smallest cell, crying out as something wanting to be born.

They sit in the waiting room. Katherine closes her eyes and breathes quietly, trying to focus her mind as in remembering a dream.

Hannah looks at her and decides not to tell her this is only the beginning, that she has found the grief and loss where she thought they'd be, wrapped in vestiges of horror lodged deep inside the pelvis where the sacrum lies frozen at the base of the spine, the chill beneath her hands reminding her of an abandoned house in winter. But today something happened, an awakening now settling in the silence between them.

Katherine opens her eyes. "Is there a name for what happened in there?"

Hannah fixes a look on her and nods. "Katherine."

At the end of April the snow pulls away from the house and retreats from the fields into the partial shade of the woods. Katherine is sitting on the front porch, drinking coffee in the early morning sun when she notices a host of crocuses scattered across the lawn. Her eye drifts above the blossoms and over the road to the cemetery and she considers what to plant around Lucy's grave and wonders when the first flowers will appear on Ethan's and then thinks of the grave she has never seen.

They decide to make a day of it, the four of them driving down on a Sunday morning in early May. For the first twenty miles they are quiet until Annie makes a big sigh and noisily clears her throat and wants to know what they're going to talk about. "I'm as serious as the next person," she says, "but if I have to sit in silence for the next three hours I'm gonna go out of my tree. Who's read a good book lately?"

Michael pipes up from the back seat and from there the conversation grows book by book, with even Katherine joining in just north of White River Junction, and Annie sits back and smiles in self-satisfaction, content to feel herself once again among her species doing what they do best.

Katherine's heart sinks when she sees the cemetery, plain and exposed on a broad hillside dotted with a half dozen trees that are old and scraggly, providing little shade. They inquire at the gatehouse and are directed to a little granite stone set in the grass. "Ethan Weston," it reads, and beneath it the two years so close together, startling, how easy it is to subtract one from the other. Katherine stands in front of the stone with Annie on one side and Michael on the other and Hannah just behind, her hands on Katherine's shoulders.

"They got the name wrong," she says at last, her voice so low that Hannah has to ask what she said. She says it again, louder than before, "They gave him his father's name. I can't believe they did that."

"You can change the stone," says Michael.

Katherine nods as a tear rolls down her face. "I can't believe it," she says, her jaw moving stiffly around the words. She turns and walks away, then stops and looks up the slope of the hill, then down at the ground, and then toward them as she walks briskly back.

"Do I have to leave him here?" she says.

The three of them look at one another and then at her. "You mean," says Michael, "can you bury him someplace else?"

"Yes. Can I?"

"I don't know why the hell not," says Annie. "You're his mother."

Katherine drives to town for sessions with Hannah twice a week. She can't afford it, even at the low end of Hannah's sliding scale, but she also cannot stay away, so drawn is she to whatever it is that has begun to stir inside her. Toward the end of May she calls the regional elementary school and speaks to the principal, who startles her by saying, "Oh, yes," when she tells him her name, only to note later his mention of his old friend, the woman who runs the local bookstore. She makes an appointment for an interview the next day.

When she arrives at the school, children are out at recess in the yard and she watches them from the car, unsure if she could stand to move among them every day, the scent of childhood, voices so full of life, knowing that some will inevitably love her and want her love in return.

She walks across the yard and through a high wooden door. The building is old, the floors creaking as she walks past drinking fountains at knee level and bulletin boards covered with brightly colored construction paper and crayon drawings.

She hands the principal the letter and he sits behind the desk ands reads, a finger along his lips and one foot up on the edge of the desk.

"She thinks very highly of you," he says. "Why did you leave?"

She does not look away. "Family troubles," she says.

"What brought you here?"

"Lucy Dudley."

"Ahh," he says, nodding. "She taught here for awhile, you know."

"No. I didn't."

"Oh, yes," he says. "Before my time, though. How did you know her?"

Katherine looks out the window. A bell rings in a distant hallway and she can feel the tide of children's voices moving toward the building.

"It's a long story."

As the weather warms she plants impatiens around Lucy's grave. Off in the corner, the first shoots of iris appear over Ethan's little plot, to be followed by columbine and bleeding heart.

In the evening she draws a bath and opens the window at the foot of the tub and sits back to listen to the liquid song of thrush and smell the earth still soggy from the melted snow. She closes her eyes and her legs fall open against the cool sides of the tub and her fingers grace the skin along her thighs, and a faint sweet impulse travels higher and a little moan issues from her throat as her fingers follow after.

On the first week-end in June, Michael and Katherine and Sophie go down to the pond to free the dock from its tether and then open up the cabin for the summer. A pair of loons comes by to find the source of the commotion and Katherine and Sophie stand at the end of the dock and watch them dive and swim beneath the water.

On Monday morning, Katherine wakes early, the air sweet through the open window. She dresses quickly and goes downstairs and outside to rouse the goats. She eats breakfast over yesterday's *Globe* and then she and Sophie drive into town.

The room is warm but bathed in shadow. Katherine stands by the table, so familiar now, and slowly takes off her clothes and lies down, naked beneath the sheet, and waits.

When it comes, it is by surprise. She is lying on her back, eyes closed, Hannah working on her legs, and it seems to go just as before, one muscle at a time, when suddenly she feels her leg lifted into the air, hands sliding beneath her hip and buttock and the small of her back to move her in one continuous motion that raises her up and sets her down as if a wave were passing beneath her, gently opening her pelvis, muscle and bone letting go with a great sigh that is bigger than her, bigger than the room, opening her lungs to receive a gulp of air that flows out again, a wave pulling back from the shore, pushing before it a deep, long "Ohhhh" that makes Hannah lift her eyes and smile as she repeats the motion again and again, feeling this body in her hands, this woman's body that for so many years was the relentless object of such brutality and near destruction, now begin to ebb and flow, drawn to its own life like an ocean embracing the pulling moon.

In the afternoon she walks through the woods to the water and sits on the edge of the dock while Sophie sniffs along the shore. The breeze is from the west and she closes her eyes and feels it wash across her face. The water is chilly around her feet that she swirls in little circles, wetting the rolled up cuffs of her jeans. She is remembering the morning and trying to recreate in her mind that sense of her body moving, or rather of something moving through her body, or rather still, of her body dissolving in the air and becoming part of whatever it was that moved.

From across the pond a loon calls out to another, the cry fluttering in the air, the sound pure like an open throated soprano sax. And then there is the far-off rhythmic beating of the water as a loon labors to overcome its own inertia. She watches its progress across the water, the tips of its wings raising small white splashes into the air, and then the beating of the air replaces the beating of the water and its flight becomes soundless save for the squeaking grunt of its exertion, its neck stretched forward as if to pull itself along.

So intent is she upon the bird that she doesn't see the clouds coming over the western hills like a dark wave rising from the ocean floor and hurling itself headlong against the shore. There is a distant roll of thunder and Sophie lets out a little grunt of alarm as she seeks shelter beneath the cabin. Katherine watches the squall advance, fascinated by how the clouds roll over the ridge and rise up into the air. She thinks to go inside and lifts her feet out of the water and stands, but something keeps her where she is. The air turns suddenly cool as the rain moves toward her like a juggernaut shrouded in mist. Again she thinks to go inside, but stands her ground until suddenly the rain is upon her, heavy and thunderous as if poured from a great container in the sky. She is shocked by the cold, closing her eyes as she gasps for breath and leans back her head, water pelting against her face, and feels again the movement in the center of her being, the rise and fall as she moves and dissolves.

As quickly as it came, the rain is gone. Before the far shore, a parade of ghosts rises in misty plumes floating across the water to settle in hollows along the hillsides like loosely spun angora. She steps backward toward the shore, water dripping from her clothes, her feet light against the dock. The clouds move quickly over, churning and swirling around patches of blue. And then, without a thought, she is in motion down the dock, her footsteps sounding off the boards and echoing from the far shore until the silence closes in behind and she leaves the edge of the dock, like a girl released from her father's arms, leaping into the air, arching her back, arms and legs flung outward from her body, and turning her face toward the wild sky, she imagines, for just an instant, that it's almost like flying.

With Gratitude

Over a period of almost seven years, *The First Thing and the Last* was rejected more than fifty times by commercial publishers, many of whom openly acknowledged their unwillingness to publish a novel that tells the truth about domestic violence, no matter how compelling the story or how well it is told. I will be forever grateful to Susan Bright, my editor and publisher at Plain View Press, for having the courage to take on what so many others would not.

I offer my thanks to Richard Abraham, M.D., for helping me to grasp what violence can do to the body of a human being; to Judith Lewis Herman, M.D., for *Trauma and Recovery* and Ann Jones for *Next Time She'll Be Dead*, two books that taught me much of what I know about the psychic and emotional damage caused by severe trauma; to a generation of feminist writers and activists who shaped my understanding of men's violence, especially Susan Brownmiller, Andrea Dworkin, and Marilyn French; to Jane Kenyon, whose poetry I visited each day before I sat down to write; to Tina Borders, Donna Landerman, Nancy Tripp, Roseanne Bilodeau and the other brave and brilliant women who founded and ran the Sexual Assault Crisis Service in Hartford, Connecticut in the 1970s, and who allowed a handful of men to take part in the work to end men's violence against women; to Liz Davis for her thoughtful reading of an early draft and to Susan Ostoff for helping me understand how the legal system responds to women who protect themselves from men who batter. I take full responsibility for my artistic use of the knowledge they have all so generously shared.

To my teachers — Dudley Fitts who saw the poet in the boy and Leonard Wallace Robinson who saw the novelist in the young man long before I could imagine either for myself — goes my most profound gratitude.

My deepest thanks go to Jeanne Robertson Bonaca for her friendship, patience, and editorial wisdom during the writing of this book. And to my artists' 'pod' — Annie Barrett, Kristin Flyntz, and

Cat Proper — who sustained both me and the work in more ways than they or I will ever know. I am also thankful to Victoria Sanders for all the ways in which she supported this novel.

There are no words to do justice to the depth of my gratitude to Nora Jamieson, my soul companion and partner in life for thirty years, who planted the seed for this novel more than ten years ago when she wished aloud for a book that would tell a story of what domestic violence really is. And then she was with me every step of the way, not only through the writing and countless revisions, but through the long and arduous process of finding a publisher, bringing her fierce love to those dark nights of the soul when she believed in me more than I was able to believe in myself. This is not the first time I have said this, nor will it be the last — I could not have done this, could not have gone so deep into the mystery, could not have come this far, without you.

About the Author

Allan G. Johnson is a writer and public speaker who has worked on issues of gender and social justice since receiving his Ph.D. in sociology from the University of Michigan in 1972. He first became involved in the issue of men's violence against women in 1977 as a volunteer at the Rape Crisis Service in Hartford, Connecticut. He has authored research on sexual violence, testified before legislative committees, consulted with the National Center for the Prevention of Rape and the Connecticut Commissioner of Public Health, and served on the board of the Connecticut Coalition against Domestic Violence. During thirty years of college teaching, he regularly taught courses on gender, race, and social class. His books have been translated into several languages and excerpted in numerous anthologies. For more on his work, visit his website at www.agjohnson.us. *The First Thing and the Last* is his first published novel. He is married to Nora L. Jamieson, a writer, healer, and gatherer of women. They live in the hills of northwestern Connecticut.

Photo by Mark Bennington.